To
I hope you
the read.
Thank you for
Chats & help.
Your
friend
Tania
Monn

Darkness Embraced

Darkness Embraced

SARRI MORIN

iUniverse

DARKNESS EMBRACED

Copyright © 2012, 2015 Sarri Morin.

All rights reserved. No part of this book may be used or reproduced by any means, graphic, electronic, or mechanical, including photocopying, recording, taping or by any information storage retrieval system without the written permission of the author except in the case of brief quotations embodied in critical articles and reviews.

iUniverse books may be ordered through booksellers or by contacting:

iUniverse
1663 Liberty Drive
Bloomington, IN 47403
www.iuniverse.com
1-800-Authors (1-800-288-4677)

Because of the dynamic nature of the Internet, any web addresses or links contained in this book may have changed since publication and may no longer be valid. The views expressed in this work are solely those of the author and do not necessarily reflect the views of the publisher, and the publisher hereby disclaims any responsibility for them.

Any people depicted in stock imagery provided by Thinkstock are models, and such images are being used for illustrative purposes only. Certain stock imagery © Thinkstock.

Cover background photo taken by Sarri Morin

ISBN: 978-1-4917-7191-4 (sc)
ISBN: 978-1-4917-7192-1 (e)

Library of Congress Control Number: 2015912644

Print information available on the last page.

iUniverse rev. date: 8/24/2015

This is dedicated to my husband Chris for all his love, support and I.T. expertise, without which this dream would not be possible.

For my two awesome boys Sebastian and Connor, thanks for your suggestions. I would also like to thank my sister Barb and my girlfriends Dina and Victoria, without their support and feedback my dream wouldn't be a reality. For my friend Riz, who let me borrow his name.

For my parents; thank you for your continued support and unending motivation to keep going through all the good and difficult times

I love you all.

For my fans, I hope you enjoy the read. Without you, I would have no one to share with.

Thank you, from the bottom of my heart

chapter 1

A sultry seductress. A pleasure goddess. That's what I will be tonight. Josephine thought, as she chuckled to herself while she stared back at the full-length mirror. "The boys are being looked after, dinner is in the oven and I can't forget the main course, he's on his way home." Josephine said, out loud to her reflection as if she were talking to another person. One by one she pulled out every single sexy piece of clothing she owned. She was very excited about this evening and very frustrated that she couldn't seem to find what she was looking for. After hours of rummaging through her closet, she finally settled on the slinky black dress. It made her look thin—well thinner. It hugged her shapely curves just right. Josephine quickly slipped out of her bathrobe into the slinky black dress. She looked at the cascade of auburn hair that came down to the middle of her back. *Rick loves long hair* she thought to herself as she fiddled with it; pulling it this way and that. Making the decision to finally pull it back, she left some loose hanging tendrils in front and back. *It will all come down anyways.* Laughing she made the final adjustments to her hair and wardrobe.

Quickly she gave herself a once over and then hastily ran down the stairs. Surveying the room, she wanted to make sure that she had the right atmosphere in the house. The table was set for two, with candlelight, several candles in fact. In the ice bucket was contained a nice bottle of Rosé wine and the crystal wine glasses were just waiting to be used. Everything was perfect. Heading upstairs, she stopped and poked her head into the bathroom, ensuring that everything was ready. The bath foam was sitting on the edge of the Jacuzzi, the bubble jets set, and the candles. They had been strategically placed, *tonight is going to be heaven,* and Josephine smiled to herself as she continued upstairs.

Satisfied, Josephine walked into her room, she quickly took another glance at herself in the mirror to make sure she was looking her best and then she sat down on the window ledge, one leg dangling. Patiently, she waited. Looking down at the street to see if Rick had arrived home yet, when she didn't see him she turned her emerald eyes skywards. Making herself more comfortable she watched as the day sky, slowly start to fade. The once blinding yellow sun had turned to a great big ball of orange and the bright blue sky was now turning to darker shades of blue with a touch of light mauve breaking through. As the sky faded, and the darkness of the night chased the day away, Josephine contemplated her life. Actually, no she was *celebrating* her life. She had two beautiful children, Charlie being the oldest and full of child innocence, which continued to be reflected in his enormous brown eyes, and yes although he was mischievous, it was hidden behind his angelic face. Josephine smiled as she thought him and his beautiful contagious laugh. He was a happy child and anyone looking into those big brown eyes could see that. His younger brother Alex was only four months old. With his chubby little legs and his chubby little toes, he was adorable and he was the child that when you looked at him you thought *'I want to eat him up'*. Laughing at her own thoughts, she wandered back to Alex. He had a head full of dark brown hair like his older brother and the same huge brown eyes. *'A spitting image of his brother'* is what people called him, she thought to herself.

Josephine was happy with her life; she was a remarkable private eye for an elite security company. A lot of hard work and dedication got her to her position. All the training courses both classroom and defensive. As well, she was a black belt in Kung Fu and she had a license to carry a firearm. Her career was extremely fulfilling. Now, she had her family, something she had dreamed of from when she was a little girl. Her childhood was difficult and as a little girl, she had made one vow; she would be different from those in her family. Josephine was. She did what she had always dreamed of doing. She had her family and a great career. She had Rick Macloud, her husband and her family. Nothing could come between them, how could she not be content with that?

Rick was on his way home; she had called him earlier to confirm that he wasn't working late and she also let him know that she needed whip cream. *There are so many uses for whip cream. Yummy.* So for now or at least until Rick arrived she figured she would read. Still settled on the ledge of the window Josephine was already getting into the book when she was startled by the loud "DING DONG!" She all but fell off the ledge. Immediately regaining her balance, she headed for the door. "DING DONG!" "Okay. Okay. I'm coming. Hang on!" She said out loud knowing full well that no one could hear her. Josephine had already reached the door as another DING DONG sounded off in her ear. Nanook and Timber were barking up a storm. It was as if chaos had erupted all at once. After stumbling over both mammoth dogs, she managed to turn the lock, and open the door. Without looking up, "Couldn't wait to see me huh? Fumbled around with your keys thinking of me all sexied up for you? Eh?" Josephine said laughing.

"Hum, hum." The husky voice of a male said. Josephine's smile faded and color ran into her cheeks.

"Oh my god, I am so sorry. I was expecting my husband." She rushed out in a slur of words as she held on to both dogs by their choker chains, both dogs were pulling and growling at the intruders

"Are you Mrs. Josephine Macloud?" The man asked.

"Who wants to know?" She asked as her security training kicked in. She had no time to censor her words.

"I'm homicide detective Easterbrook and this is my partner Detective Davis. May we come in?"

"Where is your identification, I want to see it." She said once again as her security instincts remained in full force. The detectives took out their badges and showed them to her. She looked carefully at both badges and both men. There was a pause.

"*Now* may we come in?" He said as his agitation started to rear its ugly head.

"Sure." She held her dogs close to her and motioned with a nod of head to come in. When they were in, she released her dogs but maintained voice control over them. "What can I do for you detectives?" *Kind of a lame question* she thought. *I should be panicking right now. Homicide detectives don't show up on front doors every day.* As the words that

Josephine thought to herself sunk into her thick, stubborn, brain panic actually did start to form inside her gut. The pit of her stomach started doing funny things. Her body started to convulse as if she were going to puke. Leaning her hands on the table to brace herself. *It's Rick. Something has happened to Rick.* The words shimmered in her mind. No sooner did she think the words, did detective Easterbrook confirm them.

"There has been an accident. I am sorry we have to tell you this but there has been an accident and your husband has died. We need you come down and I.D the body." Josephine's body went limp. If the second detective wasn't standing behind her she would have fallen to the ground and landed on her ass taking her table cloth with her.

"What? How? Oh God! Not Rick! Not Rick! There must be some mistake." She sobbed with her hand covering her mouth with fresh tears streaming from her eyes. "This can't be, I spoke to him not two hours ago, he was picking up some groceries for me before he came home," she fumbled out through hallowed breaths.

"Ma'am, we're terribly sorry for your loss, but we really need you to come identify the body." Detective Easterbrook said gently. Josephine needed time to assimilate the information.

"Do I have to come now?" She asked, her voice was pleading.

"I'm afraid so, we'll take you down to the where the body is." Easterbrook said as he chose he words carefully. "An officer will drive you back afterwards." Josephine wiped her face and tried to control her shorts breaths.

"No. I'll call my mother, she'll get me." Josephine wanted someone to comfort her she didn't want to be around a police man who couldn't offer his support. Josephine tried to get her breathing under control as she fought hard to keep back the tears, but the battle was useless. The tears came anyways. Josephine dragged herself to the phone and was about to pick up the receiver when the phone rang. "Hello." Josephine said. "Who's this? Mallory? Thank god. I was just going to call my mom. Since I have you though." The sobs were getting harder to control. "I need a favor. Something terrible has happened. It's Rick. He's… He's." She couldn't get the words out, the phone fell from her hand and she slid down the kitchen wall to the floor. Detective Easterbrook picked up the receiver. While Detective Davis attended to Josephine.

"This is Detective Easterbrook, I can't get into specifics, but I can tell you that we need Josephine to come with us, can you please come pick her up." He muttered out an address. He hung up the receiver. "How is she?" He asked his partner grimly.

"She'll be fine. It's the shock." Davis said casually as he shrugged his shoulders. Josephine was sitting at the table with her cheek down. Davis took it upon himself to find a glass and get some water. When she came to Davis shoved the glass towards her. "Here drink some of this, it should help." He said gruffly. He hadn't intended for it to come out that way it just did. Embarrassed he shrugged. Josephine smiled warily accepting his unspoken and pathetic attempt at an apology.

"When she's up, let's get going." Easterbrook said gently. It was a command though and Josephine heard it.

At the morgue, the detectives escorted her to where Rick was. Detective Easterbrook tapped on the window, the curtain opened and Josephine found a young man in a white lab coat waiting on the other side. Detective Easterbrook nodded his head and the young man pulled back the blanket. All the way. Josephine nodded her head but not before a horrified gasp escaped from her throat. Immediately the man in the white coat pulled the cover back over Rick's body.

Somewhere in that moment of insanity, she heard the detective cursing the stupidity of the "new guy" on staff. She also picked up part of a conversation that she was not supposed to be privy to. "The blood loss is unexplainable." Josephine's conscious self-ignored the comment, but her sub conscious stored it away for further examination.

Detective Easterbrook apologized to Josephine for the brutality of what she saw as he escorted to the reception area, where she found Mallory waiting with the same puffy eyes she herself was donning. Mallory ran up to her friend pulled her close and hugged her tightly.

"I'm so sorry." Mallory offered.

"Please just take me home." Josephine whispered. Both women left and the ride home was silent except for the sobs that escaped Josephine.

It was late when Josephine and Mallory returned home. Marcia and Rachel were already there, Mallory had called them on her way to get Josephine. All Josephine wanted to do was crawl in bed and go to sleep. Rachel, Josephine's mom offered to stay and help her out for the next couple of days. She wasn't old but the stress of the night looked as if it aged her, her short strawberry blond hair was ruffled, she had bags under her eyes. She looked as if she had new stress lines etched into her gentle caring face.

Marcia offered the same as well, and she looked bad compared to her usual self. Her usual sky blue eyes looked darker and puffy from obvious crying bouts. She had bags under her eyes as well. Her flowing sunshine blond hair was pulled back in what looked like an old lady bun. Mallory looked rather composed. She stood tall and her hair was in a ponytail, her amber eyes were darker and puffy along with bags. All in all everyone looked as good as could be considering.

"Is there anything we can do for you?" Marcia offered with her smooth soft voice.

"No. Thanks anyways. I am going to bed," Josephine answered quietly. She didn't ask about the boys because she knew the answer, everything was done. She heard Mallory yell as she headed upstairs.

"If you need anything, let us know," Mallory called out after her.

"Thanks." Josephine called back in a barely audible voice.

Mallory locked and closed the front door and let the dogs out into the backyard. She fed the fish brought the dogs back in. She locked the patio door, and finally turned out the lights.

※※※

For Josephine this had been the longest day of her life. She found both boys in her room. They were out like lights and oblivious to how their life had without warning changed. Josephine put Alex to bed first since he was still in his cradle, which was in her room and then she picked up Charlie and brought him to his bed. As she tucked him in she realized that she would be going to bed by herself for the first time in ten years, as the thoughts came flooding back the tears welled in her eyes and finally spilled once again. She quickly went to the washroom and put on her p-jays. She didn't bother to put up the gate because someone was downstairs and since Charlie could walk and Alex could barely turn over she had nothing to worry about. She had leaned over the stair railing and called out to Nanook and Timber, "upstairs." She said as she pulled away from the railing and turned to walk into her room when she caught a glimpse of her wedding picture on the wall. She leaned back against the railing for balance, for just a brief moment. She turned and went to her room and silently cried herself to sleep.

Josephine tossed and turned the whole night; she woke up from nightmares twice; this last time it was Ricks' body she saw. Motionless. Gray. He was on a gurney in the morgue. There were marks on what was left of his neck, his throat had been ravaged. In hindsight, she had figured the coroner was new or something because she got the distinct feeling, she was not supposed to see Ricks' entire body. When she finally sank back into a deep slumber Alex woke up. Sighing in frustration he pushed the cradle over got her nursing pillow and picked up Alex. She fed him and he went back to sleep right away. She put him back down and got out of bed to check on Charlie. She peeked in his room and saw that he was sound asleep; she went in anyways and pulled his covers over him. She looked at the clock and it read five o'clock on the dot. She tried to get back to sleep but it was a futile attempt. Since she couldn't get back to sleep Josephine decided to let the dogs out, when they were done she went back upstairs to her room and they followed. She crawled back into bed and grabbed the remote. She turned on the television. The news was still talking about her husbands' brutal death. She didn't even listen to what was being said, she just quickly changed the channel and ended up watching Buffy the Vampire Slayer.

Both kids were up at seven thirty, and so the first day of her new life had begun.

"Where's daddy?" Charlie asked. He quickly answered his own question "Daddy went to work." Charlie shrugged his shoulders in his new spider man pajamas and laughed.

Josephine gulped hard. *So it begins.* She thought to herself. She didn't answer Charlie, she wasn't ready to face the reality yet and besides that she needed time to try and figure out exactly how she would explain death to a three year old. Josephine was visibly distressed and her heart was breaking. Again she felt the tears begin to fill her eyes.

"Are you sad? Are you ok mommy?" Charlie asked innocently. When Josephine didn't answer he proudly handed her a tissue. As she looked into Charlie's big brown eyes and saw the concerned look on his face, it brought a warm feeling to her and she put on a brave smile.

"I am ok baby," she said weakly. "Mommy is tired that is all."

Josephine had taken a shower and gave both Alex and Charlie a bath. She told both of them that they would be staying with grandma and Aunt Mallory and even Aunt Marcia today because mommy had some errands to run. Charlie was excited and couldn't wait to go downstairs.

"Hurry up mommy, hurry up." Charlie bellowed as he slid down the stairs on his bum. Josephine finished dressing Alex and dragged her butt downstairs. She found her mom and friends already waiting for her and they had a fresh pot of coffee waiting. Everyone looked better this morning, her mom didn't look old anymore and her friends well they looked refreshed. The bags under the eyes were still present, but the wonders of makeup are a miracle. Josephine did her best to put on a smile, but everyone present knew it was a front.

"I have to do stuff today, like the funeral arrangements. I am going to need some help. I don't think I can do this on my own." Josephine said as she tried to swallow back the sob that forming in her throat.

"I'll help you," Mallory said. Marcia didn't protest because although she was one of Josephine's best friends she wasn't quite as strong as Mallory and she knew instinctively that Josephine needed someone much stronger than her to aid her in the tasks that lie ahead.

"I think it's better if I stay and help your mom. By the way Rick's parents are coming to town they won't be here for a couple of days they have to arrange for some stuff. Mallory made sure to call them last night." Marcia added. Josephine looked at her friend and silently thanked her. Josephine knew that was her task but last night she handled about as much as she could take.

Josephine and Mallory headed out. While Mallory drove Josephine called her insurance broker and her lawyer she advised both people of last night's events. Mallory noted that she didn't go into details she just gave the short version. Josephine set up her meetings and then she got off the phone.

"Something is very wrong with how Rick died." Josephine blurted out. Mallory was more than a little taken aback by the comment.

"You think?" Mallory said with a somewhat puzzled look on her face.

"No. There was something about the way he died. I mean the police said something about an animal, Mallory he had a goddamned frigging wound, that what from what I saw looked like tooth marks on his neck. His throat was non-existent. What kind of animal do you know that does that? I also heard someone say that they couldn't explain the 'loss of blood' go figure that." Josephine was all but shouting at Mallory.

"Is it possible you misunderstood?" Mallory asked. "You had an extremely rough night Josephine. Maybe you should give Manny a call? After all, he's a cop and you are friends. It's not like you haven't teamed up on cases before," Mallory added. He might be able to clear some of the questions up. I mean it, you should give him a call." Mallory suggested in the hopes that it might calm Josephine down.

"You know what, you're right." Josephine said as she hit the button that was programmed to dial Manny's direct line. "Manny? Hi it's Josephine. Thank you. I need a big favor. Can you please pull all the reports including the forensic ones on Rick? I know. Pause. I'm asking a lot and you'd be risking your job, but I gotta tell you, something's not right. I saw Rick last night, *all of him*. I think the coroner was new. I saw the marks. I saw everything on Ricks' body. I know I shouldn't have seen those. Something's not right and that's the reason I'm asking for help. I know I am not a P.I. anymore, but every instinct in me is screaming to me that something is off. Please Manny, I wouldn't ask otherwise." There was pleading in Josephine's voice. "I need to do this Manny." There was a pause. "Thank you, I owe you big time." Josephine said with conviction and emotion. She meant every word.

"Well what did Manny say?" Mallory asked.

"Manny is going to get me the files I need." Josephine said as she let out a small sigh of relief.

"Really?" Mallory asked surprised. "He is going to get them for you, just like that?" Mallory asked a little shocked.

"Why?" Josephine asked. "I can just picture Manny now my *little* six-foot mafia friend." She laughed. "The cigarette hanging out the corner of his mouth, his mop of brown hair slicked back and his clean-cut baby face with those ever-dark piercing eyes." She said laughing. Can't you just imagine him barking out orders with his suave Italian accent?" Josephine asked, laughing so hard that it hurt. It felt good to laugh even though it was at her friends' expense. Mallory joined Josephine's laughter as she pictured the image. *Manny is a true friend, both professionally and personally. You know what they say it's not what you know but whom you know that counts.* Josephine thought to herself.

※※※

Mallory drove up to the curb and parked directly across from the funeral home. Josephine said nothing. The car was eerily silent. If it was possible to hear a person wince then Mallory heard Josephine loud and clear. Both women exited the vehicle and while crossing the street Mallory wrapped her arm across Josephine's shoulder. They walked into the quite, parlor of death. "Have you ever noticed how serene it is in these places?" Mallory stated in a low voice trying to ease the tension.

Josephine gave Mallory an exasperated look as new tears formed in her already puffy eyes, while the old ones dried and streaked her face. Stepping through the door Josephine's heart began to race, the sorrow that overwhelmed her made her nauseous, she couldn't help but feel like her soul was being ripped out. All that remained was the void in her chest and it was as black as a starless night. Mallory sighed at her own stupidity and hung her head when she saw the pain in her friends' misty eyes.

"I'm so sorry, I was just… just trying to ease the tension is all." Josephine looked at her and feigned a smiled.

"I know. I know you were. It's okay," Josephine said reassuringly to her friend. Just then, a short, slightly pudgy man appeared in a dark suit. Looking at both women he chose his words-- carefully.

"My name is Kevin Belmont. Please accept my sincere condolences on your loss." He said as he handed a box of tissue to Josephine. He waited a moment. Two, before he spoke again. "I would like to start by showing you the caskets. I find that most people are uncomfortable around them and it only adds discomfort. Pause. . Please follow me." He said with a smile and extended his arm in a leading gesture. Josephine and Mallory followed the man in complete silence. Pointing out the caskets he advised the women of the prices. Josephine chose what she wanted. Next were the details of the service and the cards that would be handed out. Josephine wasted no time. This was an extremely painful ordeal and all she wanted to do was get out of that place. When everything was finished, she stood up and shook hands with the man. Mallory and her left, and headed home. Josephine knew she needed to make adjustments and amendments to her will; however, this would all be dealt with after the funeral. Right now she was overwhelmed. *How will I deal with all of this?* Josephine thought to herself. She wanted to scream.

"Mallory, I 'm changing my will and insurance policy. I'm adding you and Marcia as beneficiaries in trust for my policy, in case anything happens to me. You should also know that both you and Marcia will be named as guardians for the boys." Josephine announced. "All of this is going to happen after Rick's funeral. I just wanted you to know." Josephine added.

"What? Why? What are you thinking about doing?" Mallory asked in a concerned voice.

"Nothing. This situation just put things into perspective for me. Anything could happen at any time to me and in the event that something does happen, I need to know that the kids and pooches will be provided for. I need to make sure that I have taken care of my loved ones. That's all. The boys are my main concern." Josephine said matter of factly. Mallory was about to protest, but Josephine eyes shone with that determined look, the one that said, *'don't bother to question my motives'*. Mallory backed off for now. That wasn't to say she wouldn't figure out what Missy was up to and why.

As Mallory drove home Josephine closed her eyes and went over all the events of the night before, it was a painful process but her gut said she was missing something. *Homicide Detectives, ravaged throat, pin pricks or tooth marks. What am I missing?* Josephine's eyes flew open. "What's wrong Josephine? What are you thinking?" Mallory questioned. Josephine looked at her friend and seeing the concern in her eyes she immediately sought to remove her friends concern.

"Nothing Mallory, I was...er...just thinking of last night, that's all." Josephine tried to sound causal and calm, when she saw the tension leave Mallory's face she forced herself to relax for her friend's sake.

That night was a difficult night. Although Josephine had her mom and friends there for support, it was still difficult. Everywhere Josephine turned or looked there was something reminding her of Rick. The most difficult part was that she had to pick out a suit for him to be buried in. She would also have to eventually go through his clothes and pack them away. *How do other people get through this?* Josephine asked herself. *I don't know if I can do this, if I can be strong enough for my children. God, little Alex would never know his father and Charlie; he'll only have vague memories. Why God, why did you take him?* Josephine was screamed inside her mind. She found her emotions in conflict; sadness against anger, hate against anguish. The battle was constant her emotions were in turmoil and she was struggling to be strong. Eventually she knew though, the inevitable would come. She would breakdown. She tried to close her eyes so that she could get some sleep. Tomorrow was another day. It would be a long day.

chapter 2

Manny's day wasn't going to get any easier. He had just finished lunch with Josephine, assessed her emotional state and tried to figure out just how much she knew about Rick's death. He reluctantly provided her with the reports like she had requested.

"Josephine, you know I'm very sorry for what happened to Rick. You have my deepest sympathies," he said as he walked with her to her car.

"Thank you Manny, she said as she pulled him in for a hug. "You've been a good friend and you have given me everything I need to solve this. She said as she kissed him on the cheek and stepped into her car. Manny reached for his cell phone as he watched his friend drive away. He called his silent partner.

"Yeah, it's me. We have to meet as soon as possible. I have just handed off all the paperwork concerning Rick's death to Josephine. Let's meet at the coffee shop up on Lexington in, say, a half hour." Putting his phone away Manny walked to his car, he got in and put the car first gear. He left to meet his colleague. *Josephine, what are you getting yourself into? You should have just left things alone and move on. What triggered you?* The ringing phone interrupted Manny's thoughts. *Great, it is the chief.* Manny answered the phone, "Hello Chief, what's up? Yeah I know that this investigation is classified. Well, she's my friend and she's a colleague. Bottom line, Sir, I feel responsible for this mess. We owe it to her; she doesn't even know what is coming for her. Maybe we should..." Manny was cut off in mid-sentence, by the Chief's protest. "No, nothing will be divulged. I understand. Well, from what Josephine and I talked about, I could not really assess the situation and determine what she remembers. Already done. I have already called him. He is going to play ex-cop for now and monitor the situation. I am on my way to meet him now. I'll keep you posted." Click. *If anything happens to you, Josephine... God forbid I run into the bastard.*

Meanwhile, Donovan O'Hara was heading out the door when his phone rang. He ignored the call, but he stayed and listened to the message. "Mr. O'Hara, my name is Josephine Macloud. Manny recommended that I give you a call." The message ended with Josephine rambling out her phone number. Donovan quickly grabbed a pen and paper and jotted down the phone number. With the number in his hand, he headed out for his rendezvous. Donovan arrived at the coffee shop shortly after Manny did. Walking inside he looked around and found Manny sitting at a table in the corner. Manny had his back to the door, yet when the rays of the sun were suddenly blocked, he knew instinctively that his massive friend was there. Manny, turned and smiled and motioned for him to come and join him at the table instead of getting up to greet him. Manny sat watched as his friend casually walked over, he noted that Donovan's face, which was normally solid as stone, was donning a smile, the smile didn't quite hide the truth of what he did for a living; his face said with no uncertainty that he was an experienced man, and that he was a warrior just like Manny. When Donovan reached the table, his friend was already standing to greet him with a strong handshake. Donovan reciprocated the gesture and then pulled out a chair and sat down.

"Make yourself comfortable Donovan. We are going to be here for a while." Donovan looked a little perplexed, as he pulled the chair toward the table. The waitress came by and dropped off a menu, full of dessert and pastries.

"I'll give you gentlemen a few minutes. Can I get you any drinks in the meantime?" she asked.

"I'll have a café au lait," Manny said. "I'm trying to lay off the hard stuff," he glanced in Donovan's direction. The waitress nodded and looked over at Donovan.

"I'll have a double espresso, with a little cream on the side, please." Donovan said with a small hint of a smile on his face.

Both men watched as the petite waitress walked away. They noted how her ass swayed side to side as she walked, and how her ponytail followed the same movement. Donovan and Manny both shook their heads, "Ah to be young again," Donovan sighed.

"Yeah, yeah, I know what you mean," Manny added.

"Manny, you going to order some grub?" Donovan asked, as he waved the dessert menu in front of him.

"Maybe, let me see the menu." Manny took it from Donovan's hand. When the waitress returned with the coffees, she bent over the table and placed them down gently, exposing her cleavage to both men. "Can I take your orders now?" she asked.

"I will have the lemon meringue pie, please, with a scoop of vanilla ice cream on the side," Donovan said. She jotted it down on her pad. She looked at Manny.

"I'll have the apple crumble pie, with a scoop of butterscotch ice cream on the side," Manny said.

"Thank you, I'll be back shortly," she said, as she took the menus, turned, and walked away.

"Now, let's get down to business." Manny was already reaching for his black leather case that held a laptop and some folders.

Donovan reached over and put his hand on the case. "Can we eat first, and then talk?"

"Fine, food first," Manny said, with a hint of annoyance in his eyes.

"Well, let me tell you what happened before I got here." Donovan started to say. "I got a call from Josephine Macloud just before I left the house to come and meet you. She said you had recommended me for a job. I took her number before calling her back I wanted to wait and see what's up before calling her. Is this what our little meeting is about?" Donovan asked.

"Yeah! I'm sorry I didn't tell you when I called, but I didn't want to explain things over the phone. I also got a call from the chief," Manny said.

"Well what's the skinny and why did you recommended me for a job?" Donovan asked.

"It's actually because of Josephine. I think she's going to start digging into Rick's death, actually I know she will. She seems to think that there is more to his death than meets the eye, if you catch my meaning. I'm not exactly sure what she's thinking, I can only guess that it's not good." Manny shook his head.

"Did something go wrong with the memory suppression?" Donovan tilted his head sideways, waiting for an answer.

"The conversation I had with her today indicates no. She doesn't seem to remember anything. If she had she would have remembered you, don't you think?" Manny said. It was a statement.

"Then what's the problem, and what exactly do you want me to do?" Donovan asked as he sipped some espresso. Just as Manny was about to expose his little operation to Donovan, the waitress came over with their food.

"The apple crumble is yours," she placed the plate down in front of Manny. "The lemon meringue is for you," and she placed the plate down in front of Donovan.

"Thanks." Both of them said at the same time. The waitress smiled sweetly, turned and walked away.

"So, where were we?" Donovan said, as he picked up his fork and dug into the pie.

"I was about to tell you what has to be done," Manny said, as he lifted the piece of pie to his mouth. "Basically, in a nutshell, you're to monitor the situation with Josephine."

"Why are you putting me on this? Why not just have some cops monitor her and tap the lines?" Donovan asked.

"For one we have to figure out if any of the memories were triggered. Josephine, you and I are the only ones that were privy to the operation. Maybe the memories weren't triggered, and she is just guessing and pulling at strings. The Chief said he wants you there, besides this is your area of expertise, if anything goes down you're all that stands between Josephine and what's coming for her. As for Josephine and line taps, I know her, she will not talk about this on the phone. Second, I think and I *stress* the "I think part", she is going to start her own little investigation. I really do not want to see her hurt. I already feel responsible as it is," Manny said, playing with the remainder of his pie like a kid. "Listen, this situation doesn't sit right with me. My gut tells me she is up to something. It's also saying…" He trailed off.

"Well, spill it. What's on your mind?" Donovan asked, although he already knew the answer.

"C'mon, tell me you don't think the same thing is happening all over again except with different players?" Manny answered without looking up at Donovan. "I know. It's guilt about what happened. What proof do we have? The guy was a pile of ash along with a wooden stake. We don't know who knew, we don't even know if his buddies knew. I have already been over this a thousand times in my mind," Manny said, now looking directly at Donovan. "Don't you think it is a bit coincidental that Rick died two years later…to the very day. I feel responsible for this. Josephine is suffering because we called her in." Manny said, as he slammed his fists into the table, making the pie plates rattle and the coffee spill over.

"She is a great P.I. with a unique ability. She's also trustworthy. You know this couldn't have gone down any other way," Donovan stated.

"Well, if she is so trustworthy, why did we have her hypnotized?" Manny asked accusingly.

"We didn't have a choice; rather I didn't have a choice. The division I work with is very secretive. We can't have people running around with information that could wreak havoc if it ever got out. Besides, it was for her protection as much as it was for ours. Trust me Manny, I feel terrible about what has happened," Donovan stated. There was no blame just truth.

"We could have trusted her with this. I doubt that she would've told anyone that she tracked down a vampire that brutally murdered some innocent fifty years ago. People would have thought she was a crackpot. This whole thing doesn't feel right and it didn't sit with me from the beginning and now, because of what we did, look at the consequences. She may have consented willingly but in the end, we had no right. Right now, all I know is, I'm feeling guilty as hell about Rick's death," Manny said with guilt in his eyes. He didn't try to hide his shame.

Donovan looked at Manny and saw the torment in his face. "You can't do this to yourself. Josephine knew what she was getting into she wasn't blind. For all you and I know..." he trailed off.

"Don't. Even. Go. There. We have been investigating the paranormal for too long now for you to even consider that this was a regular death or random act. Someone is gunning for her, I am sure of it, and I think…no, I know we both know what's coming after her. It's a vampire and we both know it. It's Nawzir, it's Jonah, or it's both? That is the real question, though, isn't it?" Manny said, with his brows furrowed and his jaw tight.

Donovan couldn't hide his agreement. He knew that a vampire had killed Rick. The reports that the police put out were just a cover up. Something to say, you know, to keep attention away from what had actually happened. Donovan knew, most vampires kept to themselves, except for the few rogue ones. However, in all his years of service he never knew, of any vampire that had targeted people. *Moreover, what is with the two-year delay? Why not go after Josephine and her family right away?* Donovan sat in silence, as if pondering what Manny had said and like Manny he plucked away at his pie in silence.

"Let me see the files on Rick and what our surveillance picked up on Josephine," Donovan managed to say through a mouthful of food.

Manny bent down and picked up the black bag he had been carrying and placed it on the table. He opened the bag and pulled out two files. The first file contained everything that pertained to Rick's death. The second contained information from the case two years ago. "Did you bring the case file from fifty years ago?" Donovan asked. When Manny looked up at his friend, Donovan clearly saw and interpreted what Manny's eyes were saying, *do you think I am stupid or something?*

"No. I don't think you're stupid, it was a simple question, that's all I had to ask, and it's in my nature;" Donovan smiled knowing that he was irritating his friend. Manny grimaced and pulled out another file.

Donovan took the remaining files, and started rifling through them. He was paying special attention to the details of the very first murder and comparing them to Rick's death. Manny watched as Donovan nodded his head several times and managed to make an "hmm" sound. Manny was fidgeting and becoming more impatient as he continued watching Donovan. "Well? What are you thinking?" Manny finally asked.

"There's no question, Manny. The two incidences are identical. The only thing that appears to be different is the actual wound. Don't get me wrong, they both had their throats ripped out, but the actual bite marks look slightly different. I guess that would be expected, since two different vampires committed the acts. Tell me again, what Josephine knows and why do you think she has this urge to find out more?" Donovan asked as he tapped his fingers against the table.

"Personally I think it's just her instincts as a private investigator. You can also thank the flimsy coroner down at the morgue; he certainly didn't help our situation. Actually, he's the reason this started. He pulled the blanket further back than he should have. Josephine saw the bite marks, the ravaged throat, everything. That's when I guess she started thinking. I don't think it is more than that, unless the trauma of losing Rick set off some sort of defense mechanism in her sub-conscious. On a conscious level, I don't think she has any clue, and what scares me the most right now is that we know that a vamp is here. I'm certain that Rick's death was no random attack; I think she's next. She's vulnerable right now. Josephine will not recall anything or realize why this is happening to her. That's why I recommended you. I need you to go in and keep an eye on things. Actually, to be frank, when she called and asked for the files, I agreed to give her the copies. When we met up for lunch I gave her the files, and your name." Manny sighed and took a deep breath. "It occurred to me to get you involved as quickly as possible. When she picked up the files, I told her to call you. I told her you were retired and just looking for some extra bucks. Since she has called you, it means she's definitely up to something. In any case, I'm glad that your name's on the table."

"Is that it?" Donovan asked, with a raised eyebrow.

"What she thinks is that you're a reliable and trustworthy friend that I'd give my life for," Manny smiled teasingly.

"So she thinks that I have worked with you before and I'm a dead beat out of work looking for some extra money." Donovan corrected and let out a laugh that sounded like a grunt.

"Huhum," Manny cleared his throat. "I made it seem like I had no clue what she was up to," Manny continued.

"Well, at least we can rule out that her memories resurfaced. Now, we just have to figure why the visit to the morgue got her wheels turning. We also have to figure out why she called me, besides the fact that you told her too. Looking through your notes, I notice that she is planning to see her lawyer and insurance broker. Is she amending her will? She certainly is going to great lengths to ensure that business is taken care of, in case something does happen to her. And by the way what does the chief have to say about all this?" Donovan asked as he chugged down the last of his espresso.

"Well, he wants to make damn sure our butts our covered. We have been given a go-ahead to investigate and monitor the situation. Obviously this is deemed as classified and no one is to know," Manny added.

"What about unseen complications such as other persons becoming involved? We don't have control over that. More importantly, what if the need arises that we have to invoke Josephine's memories…," Donovan trailed off.

"Listen; just do what has to be done. We cannot have people knowing that vampires, ghouls and goblins exist. We are the twenty-first century. We have to use our common sense and ensure that none of this gets out. We'll be the laughing stock of the media and branded as lunatics." Manny stated matter-of-factly.

"Got it. But I don't like charades. It's dangerous. What about the vamp or person that took care of business two years ago? What if the person or *it* should rear its ugly face? Then what? I don't like this one bit," Donovan slammed his hand palm down on the table. "We know for certain someone or something is out there that is every bit as dangerous as the person targeting Josephine," Donovan said, showing some concern.

"Well, let's hope he is one of the good guys," Manny said, with a forced smile. Just then, the petite waitress as if on cue came back.

"Would you gentlemen like anything else? Perhaps a refill on your coffees?"

"No, thanks, just the bill, please," Manny said, smiling at her.

"Separate or together?" The waitress asked.

"One bill will be fine, thanks." Donovan said, looking up at her.

"I won't be a moment." The waitress turned herself around and headed to the cash. She came back within a minute. She slid the black booklet onto the centre of the table. "Here you go." She said carefully, so as not to assume who would be paying. "Thanks for coming and have a great day," she said, and then she walked away.

Donovan slid his hand across the table and snatched the booklet before Manny could get it. He looked at the tiny white paper inside and then reached in his back pocket and pulled out his wallet. He put some cash in the booklet along with the bill and closed it shut.

"Thanks!" Manny said.

"Anytime. Besides, we haven't done this in a while. It

brings back memories of the good old days, when things were less complicated." Donovan smiled as he gathered up all the files and placed them in a neat pile. Manny closed his leather case and got up. Putting the leather case strap over his shoulder, he pushed in the chair and held out his hand. Donovan got up and pushed his chair aside and shook Manny's hand.

"I guess I'll be seeing you around," he said, as his hand dropped.

"No, not really, but you will be able to contact me twenty-four seven. I can't get involved; otherwise Josephine will think something is up," Manny said.

"Ah, I see. No problem. Anyways, I've got a lady to call." Donovan said, with a wink. Both men walked out of the coffee shop. "I'll be in touch Manny. Take care," Donovan said, as he walked toward his car.

"Take care, buddy, and *be* careful." Manny said, as he sat his car with one foot still out.

Donovan pulled out before Manny did. He pulled out the paper with Josephine's number and dialed her number. "Hello Josephine, its Donovan. I'm returning your call. What can I do for you? Well, we would have to talk about it first. I was not really looking for work, but since Manny recommended me, I'm willing to explore the opportunity. Did you want to meet somewhere? Well, I'm in my car: I can meet you wherever is most convenient. Okay then, I'll see you shortly. What's the address?" Donovan made a mental note. "Bye for now." Donovan hung up the phone.

※※※

Meanwhile, Manny had called in to report what had happened. "Let me speak to the chief," he told the receptionist.

"Hey, Chief, it's me, Josephine has left and already made contact with Donovan. He is going to make contact with her. Yeah, he's been briefed on the situation and the package has been delivered. When he makes contact with her the first time, we will have more of an idea what is going down and we'll set up a schedule at that point. That's all I have to report for now. Will do, sir, bye." Manny hung up the phone. *God Josephine, I hope you have not bitten off more than you can chew. God help us if you did.*

chapter 3

After Josephine obtained what she had asked Manny, she said goodbye to Manny, as she had to get back to the house. She had an appointment to keep, Donovan O'Hara had called her and was on his way. *Gawd this has to be the dumbest thing I have ever thought of doing; asking a complete stranger to come into my house. What are you thinking Josephine? On the other hand, Manny did recommend him. In fact, the recommendation was a glowing one.* Josephine justified to herself. She called home just to check in and let everyone know what was up. She really did want to have some-one-on one time with Donovan. She wanted to confirm for herself who he was and then when she figured out what she really wanted then and only then would she announce her plans to everyone. *Tomorrow I have to meet with the lawyer and insurance person, to make the changes and the amendments. Better to get the hard things dealt with; at least I can have peace of mind knowing that my children will be taken care of if anything happens to me.* Josephine's thoughts were interrupted when "Could I have this kiss forever" by Whitney Houston and Enrique Iglesias came on. This was *their* song. The tears were automatic, and Josephine sang along out loud, off key and her voice cracked; she didn't care. She found that this was actually helping her. It didn't bother her that passers-by looked at her as if she were crazy. This was a release. Her release.

Pulling into the driveway, she grabbed the file, which contained information that she would no doubt find disturbing, she knew that when she looked at the information it would be like losing Rick all over again. Shaking off the chill that ran down her spine, she hurried into the house. Entering the kitchen she threw the files on table, she quickly cleaned up; picking up the toys and doing a quick sweep of all the dog hair. She put some fresh coffee on. Josephine put out the fresh fruits and a coffee cake that she managed to get before she came home. She had just about finished getting things in order when the doorbell rang. *Donovan is here.* The dogs started going crazy and barking up a storm. She called the dogs over and let them outside. Calmly, she went to door, peeked through the peephole. She found the frame of a very large man. His jaw was tight and his hair was long. *Weird for an ex-cop,* she thought. Josephine opened the door.

"Josephine?" Donovan said, in a smooth, velvet voice.

"Donovan?" Josephine answered back with a cautious smile. Donovan acknowledged with a nod of his head. "Come in, please." Josephine stepped to the side and pulled the door back to accommodate his large frame. Donovan obliged her and followed her into the kitchen.

"Have a seat." Josephine gestured to the chairs. "Coffee?"

"Sure, just black." Donovan replied. Josephine pulled out two mugs, poured the coffee and sat down at the table. She moved the files out of the way.

"Important papers?" Donovan asked, knowing what was inside.

"Some personal documentation, that's all," she responded. Josephine was suddenly all too aware of her uneasiness around Donovan. He was a big man and trained. In her present state of mind, if he decides to attack her, then she is done for. Josephine kept her face serene; she was adept at hiding her feelings. *There it is, that awkward silence*, Josephine thought as the two of them drank their coffee. Donovan watched her, trying to figure out what was going on in her head. Briefly his mind flashed back; he remembered how confident she was, how strong willed she could be. Now he was seeing her in a very different light. She was vulnerable and hurt. He could literally feel her pain, it was radiating from her. In that brief realization, one other very important detail stood out. He wanted to protect her now more than ever from that thing that was out there, hunting her.

Manny had been right the relationship that they all once shared suddenly became clear, she may not be able to remember him, but they had worked side by side before and there was a bond that had formed. It was loyalty. Although she could not possibly remember the friendship that they had, he knew it had existed and like any cop, you protect one of your own. The feeling took him by surprise; this was not what he was expecting. Old habits die-hard, he guessed. His decision was made, regardless if she asked him to work for her or not.

"This is my situation," Josephine startled Donovan from his deep thoughts. She put all her cards on the table, leaving nothing out. She explained what she expected, she explained the boundaries. "In a nutshell I have some loose ends to deal with." As the words came out of her mouth, something made her stop and think. *Why would you want to baby sit children, I'm sure you have better things to do with your time?* "Are you sure you want to baby sit children?" Josephine tried to laugh away her doubt. Before Donovan could answer, she continued. "I don't have closure: where it concerns my husband. I need closure. I need someone who has experience in protection and security. Manny said you are the man for the job. I want the best for my kids and I'm hoping and praying that it's not needed. Personally, I really didn't want to get a bodyguard and I wanted someone that I could trust. As it is, I am having difficulty accepting that an ex-cop has nothing better to do than take up *babysitting*. However, Manny did recommend you, and if I can't trust Manny, then who can I trust?" Josephine said while she drummed her fingers nervously on the table. "The only question is are you willing to use my basement apartment?" There was a long silence before Donovan spoke.

Donovan cursed inwardly at himself for what he was about to do; he hated acting like an arrogant ass. However, if he didn't he knew she would suspect something. *She should have been a cop.* "This is the deal. Since Manny recommended me, I figured I would come out and have a serious discussion about this job. I can already feel your hesitance to me and your resolve to protect your children. Manny really didn't get into details about what happened with your husband," he lied. "As a former cop, my instincts are red flagging what you're up to, but I won't tell what to do; it's not my place. However, I would be a bad cop, person or *babysitter* if I didn't suggest that you be careful. Oh and for the record, I'm not a babysitter, I *really* do have better things to do. That being said and against my better judgment I'll take the job," Donovan responded confidently, arrogantly and just a hint of a smug smirk on his face.

"So as previously mentioned, I would need you to live here. My basement apartment is currently vacant. It is self-contained and has a separate entrance. As part of the job, you can live here rent-free and I will pay you a salary. I can't afford more than that," she said casually, even though inside her stomach was doing somersaults. "I would also need you start right away, like tomorrow right away."

Donovan just looked at her for a moment before answering. Although she had a cool exterior, he could see anxiety in those enormous emerald green eyes of hers. Donovan answered her. "I'll take the job and if it's alright with you, I will stay at my place until I can rent it out, then I will come and stay here. At the risk of sounding like a jackass I just want to let you know, this is a business relationship, nothing more."

Josephine was appalled at the suggestion; her eyes said it all. Rather than get into a debate she bit her tongue and kept her comments to herself. "I understand. That's how I expect it to be," she said calmly. *Asshole. Wait until I talk to Manny. As if, I would ever. Talk about presumptuous. Arrogant.* The doorbell rang again and it startled Josephine out of her ranting thoughts. She got up to answer the door, explaining who was at the door. Charlie ran into his mother's arms.

"Mommy! Mommy!" He cried out. Mallory walked in after him with Alex, who was sleeping. Marcia followed, holding some groceries.

"We picked up some stuff; we knew you were running low on groceries," The voice said behind the paper bags.

Marcia walked past everyone and into the kitchen, dropping the bags on the table in front of Donovan. Marcia jumped back with a feminine retreat. "Oh, I'm sorry," she said as she glanced at her friend. Donovan's mouth was ajar and he couldn't stop staring at the blond beauty. Her eyes captured his. Josephine stood there horrified at what she was watching. *Ok not horrified, shocked.* Gently she tapped Donovan on the shoulder.

"This is Marcia Winters; she is one of my very best friends, and this is Mallory Malone. She is my other partner in crime. To be honest, we all consider ourselves sisters since we are all only children. Mallory here is a journalist and Marcia works at the same company I do. She works in the office though; she works in our accounting department. Most people who know us hate us because we are, well, to put it mildly, assertive. I think that's why we all get along," Josephine laughed.

Donovan extended his hand to each of the women. *Mallory Malone, she is trouble. She almost broke our cover. Note to self: watch her.* Donovan thought to himself.

"Ladies, meet Donovan O'Hara. He's a friend of Manny's and he's agreed to help me out around the house until I get things in order," she announced, before anyone could drill her or protest. "By the way, where's Mom?" she asked, ensuring that the subject was changed to a safer topic of discussion.

"She went home. She said for you to call her if you want her to come back. We told her that we would be staying with you for a while," Mallory offered.

Charlie came into the kitchen and asked for something to drink. While she got his juice, Josephine said, "Charlie, I would like you to meet Mr. Donovan O'Hara. He is a friend of Mommies and he will be helping Mommy look after you and Alex."

"Hi, Mr. O'Fara," Charlie said.

"No, it is Mr. O'Hara," Josephine repeated. "Repeat after me O' Ha-ra."

"O' Ha-ra." Charlie said.

"Good work, baby," Josephine said. Donovan just smiled gently down at Charlie."

"Well, I hate to cut this short but I really should be going. You look as if you have your hands full. It was a pleasure meeting you ladies and it was nice meeting you, Charlie." Donovan ruffled his hand through Charlie's hair. "I guess I'll be seeing you tomorrow at seven," Donovan said as he walked over and put the glass in the sink. Josephine walked Donovan to the door.

"Seven it is." She held out her hand and Donovan reached out and shook hers. Donovan looked over at Charlie and smiled; he said, "I'll see you tomorrow, Charlie."

"Ok," Charlie said.

Josephine watched while Donovan got into his car. She closed the door and locked it behind her. Josephine ushered Charlie back into the living room and sat him down in front of the television while she went back to the kitchen to help unload the groceries.

"Go ahead. Say it. Get your concerns and opinions out of the way," Josephine said as she busily unpacked the grocery bags.

"What's he talking about?" Mallory asked calmly.

"This is the friend that Manny recommended. He is going to baby sit the boys for me while I figure out some stuff and put closure to this whole situation." She answered.

"There will never be closure, Josephine. Rick is dead," Marcia said as gently as she could. She tried not to raise her voice.

Josephine held back her tears as Marcia's words ripped through her. "Well, that's point isn't it?" Josephine said calmly.

"What?" Mallory said. "You're not making any sense Josephine."

"Listen, I have the paper work on Rick. I haven't looked at it yet, but I don't expect it will be much different from what I saw at the morgue. Something is wrong, something the police are not telling me. I know you will not understand, but I consider myself to be on the up and up as a private investigator. My gut is telling me something is off. Something is not right. I can't accept what the police are saying. There's more and I'm gonna find out, if it's the last thing I do." Josephine said. Her temper was rising but she fought for control. "You are practically my sisters you know me better than anyone else. Has my gut feeling ever been wrong?" Mallory and Marcia shook their heads in silence. "My gut is always right. It's what has kept me safe. I need to do this, and I need your support, not your permission," Josephine stated. It was clear to both Mallory and Marcia that she was determined and they both knew when Josephine set her mind to something there was no force on earth that could stop her.

"Fine. Where does Donovan fit into all this?" Mallory asked.

"I feel like I'm in danger. I feel like whatever happened to Rick was only the beginning. When I had lunch with Manny today, I asked him if he knew anyone good with security. I didn't go into details; he would've thought that I was a lunatic. He recommended Donovan. He's a 'former' cop." Josephine raised her hands to show the quotations. Mallory and Marcia laughed. "He'll move in downstairs and watch the boys for me and make sure that the house is secure," she added.

Josephine got up and let her friends absorb the information. She started to prepare supper. Her friends pulled the manila envelope over to them and pulled out the files and photos. Without looking up Marcia asked, "Josephine, where did you get these?" Marcia and Mallory were holding their mouths, to stop themselves from throwing up.

"I told you already; Manny got them for me," Josephine said.

"Why? Why would you want them?" asked Mallory.

"As I already mentioned, I didn't buy what the cops had to say from the get-go. I needed to see for myself. Now I'm certain that I'm right. Again, as I said, right now I just need you guys to support me. I don't intend to get myself killed, I have too much too live for," Josephine said. She looked at her friends, silently pleading with her eyes for their understanding. Both women lowered their heads.

"I understand. I'm here for you Josephine, just please be careful," Mallory said as she looked straight into Josephine's face, letting her know that she would support her.

"I've got your back too, and don't think for a second that because I understand why you are doing this, that you have my OK to go off half cocked and get yourself killed. Got it?" Marcia said as she looked up from the folder of papers at her friend.

Josephine sighed with relief. She knew that without her friends' support it would be more difficult to do this. Besides, she didn't relish the thought of lying to them. With all her news out of the way, supper cooking, she walked over to where Charlie was sitting. She sat down beside him, pulled him onto her lap and gave him a big hug and a big kiss on the cheek.

"Guys, I need a favor," Josephine blurted out.

"You're asking a lot there, Josephine. It's a good thing we're friends." Mallory said laughing. "What's up?" She asked.

"I need to go out for a bit. Can you guys watch the boys for me?" Josephine asked.

"Sure! Anything to get quality time with our boys!" Marcia said. She was the worrywart of the trio. *Be safe.* The words shimmered through Marcia's mind and echoed into Josephine's head.

"Charlie, Mommy is going out for bit. Aunt Mallory and Aunt Marcia are going to stay with you and Alex. You be good, Okay."

Mallory and Marcia walked into the room. Marcia was holding Alex, when Josephine walked up to him and gave him a kiss on the cheek. Grabbing she picked up the phone and called a cab. "I am leaving the van in case you guys need it, the car seats and all," Josephine said before they could question her motives. "I won't be long," she called out as she stepped outside and closed the door.

The cab was just pulling up to the curb. Josephine got in and the driver asked, "Where to?"

"Lexington Street, please," she replied. Josephine glanced back at the house then lowered her head. Tonight she would visit the place where they said her husband died. She wasn't sure why she was going. She knew that the crime scene was still being preserved. *Why are you doing this to yourself*

Josephine? Aren't you in enough pain? The voice in head asked.
"I need to do this," she said out loud.

"Pardon me, miss?" asked the cab driver, a little confused.

"Nothing. Nothing. I'm just talking to myself. I do that occasionally," Josephine supplied. The driver, now looking at her through the rear-view mirror, was shaking his head. *Probably wondering what kind of lunatic he has in the car,* Josephine chuckled to herself. The cab pulled up to the curb; the driver reiterated the price for her. Josephine pulled out her wallet and handed the driver some bills. "Thanks", she said as she stepped out and closed the door behind her.

Josephine sat on the curb just looking across the street for a moment. Then she got up and forced herself to walk across. Before entering the alleyway, she stopped short. The hairs on the back of her neck stood up. Something was wrong. She knew it instinctively. She always knew when danger was lurking around: even as a young girl, she knew. *Don't go in*, the voice in her head warned. Ignoring the voice and summoning all her strength she started to walk. One foot in front of the other she ignored her 'danger! danger!' alarm, which always went off, when something was wrong. Josephine stepped confidently in the alleyway and made her way up to where the yellow crime scene tape was. Intuitively, she was on high alert, scanning the area with her mini-maglite, making sure no one was lurking in the dark shadows to confront her. Satisfied, she continued to enter and found no one, which was rather strange because she had the distinct feeling that someone was watching her. Brushing off her feeling and chalking it up to paranoia, she continued on what she had set out to do. All though truthfully she wasn't sure what she was there to do.

Josephine searched the alleyway for some sort of break and all she ended up finding was nothing. Zilch. Exhausted and extremely frustrated, she hunkered down beside the spot where she *felt* Rick had died. "What happened to you, Rick? Who did this? Why? Talk to me, Rick. Please talk to me." Bringing her knees up close she rested her head and softly cried in anger. In pain and in frustration. She was alone for the first time with her all her emotions surrounded by the darkness. . From deep within the dark shadows, something rustled. The noise, made Josephine spring to her feet. "Hello?" There was silence. Josephine fumbled to grab her mini-maglite. Quickly she turned it on. "Who's there?" She asked. "I'm a private investigator. My name is Josephine Macloud." She identified herself. "I have some questions for you."

"I know who you are," the menacing voice replied.

Josephine was in 'fight or flight' mode now and the stubborn Scottish in her stayed, to fight. "Come out, so I can see you," she ordered in her most authoritarian voice.

"All in due time," was the response. "Let's talk for a while." The taunting voice responded.

chapter 4

Walsenburg, Colorado

The key turned the lock and clicked open. Corin entered the room throwing his key down on the table. Corin was just returning from his nightly patrol. Although the night had been uneventful, he found himself feeling rather drained. He had not felt like this once, in all the years since his people demanded that he hunt their enemies, the enemies that *he* had created. It was his duty to bring them to justice for their crimes against humanity and crimes against their kind. First, justice has to be dispatched. It was demanded by their law; his law. Once his task was complete, he would return to his solitary way life. *It is the dreams. It has to be,* Corin had thought to himself.

Corin's dreams of late had been causing his regeneration sleep to be somewhat restless. This in itself is unusual for his kind, but more disturbing was that he was dreaming of a female, and not just any female. She was the one who led Corin to Rowen. Corin had seen her only once and that was two years ago. Since then she had been in his mind, calling to him, talking to him. *This has to be the explanation for the overwhelming feeling of being tired,* Corin decided, but it also left many unanswered questions.

Corin tried to focus on the problem at hand, *Nawzir and Jonah had apparently moved on, but to where? He has been here for some time now and there has been no trace of them. How am I going to find them now? Now there is a young woman that is haunting my sleep.* The thoughts slowly crept back to the surface. Corin shook his head to clear his thoughts. The attempt was futile, so he planted himself in the chair, letting new thoughts take over. It was a disturbing feeling; Corin had been able to sense her for some time now. He knew that there was a connection but he never put any real thought into it. *Now is as good a time as any, I suppose, and since my brain seems to have a mind of its own these days, I see no point in fighting a losing battle,* Corin thought as he laughed out loud. *There has been no blood exchange;* he knew that could only mean only one thing. She was a psychic. *That has to be it; there is no other possible reason.* The connection between them wasn't the problem; for the last two years, he had always been able to sense her during his waking hours. The concern was that she was connecting to him while he slept. This was disrupting his regeneration sleep.

He knew she was mortal and with a family, yet there was sadness, he felt her weep. Her pain pierced his heart. Corin had allowed the connection to him, each time knowing that a future with her was impossible. The connection brought a small comfort to him. He felt as if she were calling him to her, to come and help her. It felt as if she were broadcasting her feelings for only him. Corin had come to know this woman over the past two years; he knew that she would talk to herself when she was upset; he knew that she could dwell in her emotions. These last connections though seemed much more intense. Something was terribly wrong; *maybe this new intensity is the cause for my sleep disturbance,* Corin mused. Corin had picked up odd feelings from her; it was as if she did not even know that she was connecting to him. This was perplexing and he wanted to be sure, he would have examine her mind for that. Deciding to follow the mental link Corin learned to his surprise, that she did not know about her ability, curious, he wanted to find out how and why but he refrained from invading her mind further.

Corin shook his head, clearing the distraction from his mind. Right now, he needed to find his enemies. Nawzir was out there. So was Jonah. Every kill was becoming more brutal and reckless than the last.

Standing up he started to pace, after a short while he turned his attention to the window, it was still a night sky, but his body knew; it would be dawn soon. He pulled the heavy dark colored drapes closed and helped himself to his favorite drink, AB RH Positive; it had nice flavor when chilled correctly. He sat back in the chair and extended the footrest. He grabbed the remote from the table and turned on the television. Only the news was playing nothing of interest. Flipping through the channels, he stopped when he came across the international news.

The newscaster had said, "There has been a violent and vicious attack on Rick Macloud, in Hagensborg, B.C." *This* caught Corin's attention putting his drink down his attention was on the report. "The police are on the lookout for a wild animal. There has been no significant evidence to pinpoint the breed of the animal. Right now authorities are only speculating. They warn that you should be on the lookout for one of the following: feline, canine, or ursine. If you should see such an animal in close proximity you should contact Wildlife Control immediately at this number: 1-888-953-5433 (WLD-LIFE)". The newscaster continued with the story as a family picture displayed in the background.

Corin's flame blue eyes wandered to the picture as the newscaster spoke. The woman in the picture was the same woman he had seen two years ago, the woman that continued to plague his sleep. He didn't wait to hear anything else. He turned off the television. Corin finished off the last few sips of his drink as he walked over to the door and ensured that the "do not disturb" sign was on the outside of his door. He closed the door then turned the deadbolt, making sure the room was secure. He secured the draped and turned out the lights, he really didn't need them to see. Corin removed his clothes and placed them carefully back in his duffel bag. Settling into bed he pulled the covers over him. As the regeneration sleep started to take over, he thought about his next move. Tonight he would head for Hagensbourg. Corin was going to make a reservation at the Holiday Inn as soon as he woke.

※※※

Corin woke refreshed and strong. His hunger was beating at him so he walked over to the kitchenette and took a glass from the tray. Taking a pint of blood, he fixed his meal. He took a few sips, walking over to his cell phone he retrieved the number for the Holiday Inn. When the young woman on the other end of the line answered, he said, "I would like to make a reservation for tonight." He gave the details and made one additional request; he informed the receptionist that his duration was unknown; he asked if some sort of arrangement could be made so he could rent the suite for the duration of his stay. He reached for his wallet on the table, and provided his credit card number.

Corin walked over to the bathroom he pulled the shower curtain open. He ran the water adjusting the temperature until it was nice and hot. Getting into the shower the water cascaded down his very muscular, very toned body. He washed his thick, long dark hair. He rinsed himself and took a few minutes to enjoy the water beating down on his back. He grabbed the towel from the vanity and dried himself. Corin couldn't help but wonder how he looked after all these years. He knew he was very muscular and well defined; he also knew that his hair was as black as a panther's fur. He knew he was very tall, since he towered over most people. His eyes were blue; blue as fire, so he had been told. He was also told that his eyes held *mystery*. *Yes, I believe that's the word of choice that was used,* he mused. Corin assumed that he was easy on the eyes. As for how he truly came across to those he encountered, he didn't know; one day, when his duty has been fulfilled he would have to let an artist paint him or let someone describe him in every detail. Given the choice, though, he would prefer a painting so he could actually see himself. Corin shook his head and smiled. He dismissed the though; there was more urgent things that needed attending. Once dried, he hung up his towel and walked over to where his clothes were.

Corin slipped on a pair of black jeans that complimented his exceptional form. He got his shirt on rummaged through the closet for his black leather jacket. He found it; he pulled out and put it on. He grabbed his black biker boots, to which he was accustomed. They made him look rugged, and allowed him to blend in with the humans. Corin reached for his stash of money and stuffed it into his inner pocket.

Packing his belongings into his the duffel bag and doing a quick once over of the room to make sure he had left nothing behind. Corin was satisfied. He left the room, making his way to the elevator; he quickened his pace as the doors slid open. He put his arm in between the closing doors and stepped in; the button to the ground level was already lit up. Corin waited patiently. When the doors opened again he walked out and over to the front desk. Once there, a young man greeted him.

"Can I help you, Sir?"

"I would like to pay my bill and check out."

The young man started typing on the computer busily and when all the information appeared on the screen, he asked, "Will that be all, Mr. O'Leary?"

Corin nodded his head, "Yes, thank you."

"Will you be paying by credit or cash?"

"Cash," Corin replied. The young man reiterated the price. Corin nodded his head in acknowledgement and handed over the cash. The clerk took the money and began to once again type busily on the computer to finish the transaction. The clerk handed Corin the receipt."Thank you," Corin said as he turned to leave.

"You're welcome." the clerk replied as he watched Corin leave. The clerk quickly added, "Please come again."

Corin exited the building. The valet motioned for a cab and Corin just shook his head and started to walk. He would not be traveling by conventional means: tonight he would be flying. His own flight plans. He walked until he came to an area that wasn't busy with people; he glanced around, opened his mind and scanned the area. When he was sure that he was alone, he thought about his destination. As the vortex of air engulfed him, Corin embraced it, reveled in the feeling of freedom that accompanied this method of travel: all the while maintaining his focus. Within a short time, he found himself in the general vicinity; he scanned the area below looking for a secluded area, hidden deep within the shadows, when he emerged it was as if he belonged there.

The cards have dealt. My enemies will soon be dealt with; quickly. Quietly, Corin mused. Corin named them his enemies, but once they had been friends, once they were *his* fledglings, he had created them. That night soon became a nightmare for Corin. Something had gone wrong or maybe it was *them,* they were wrong, whatever the reason they should not have been allowed to live. *I should never have fought on their behalf; it was a mistake that bought time for them to get strong followed by a wake of innocent human blood shed. Now these vampires, no these rogue vampires, were being ruthless and reckless. Predators. It was one thing to go after humans that would not be missed; it was another thing to go after humans that were of importance to someone.* Corin thought as he remembered the travesties. Shortly after Corin's fight for their lives, he made the decision; he decided that his fledglings were leaving a trail that which was no doubt being documented by persons that with a vested interest. This was unacceptable. The laws of his people demanded that the rogues die by his hand. Corin knew this was his burden to bear, the consequences were dire if he failed; the exposure of his people. People were already paying attention. His people could not afford this kind of attention. This time, Nawzir and Jonah had would be stopped, no matter what the consequences were to him. He vowed that he would stop them before any more damage to his people or the humans could be done.

Corin got his bearings then headed south to the Holiday Inn. He entered the hotel and went to the front desk, where an attractive, young woman greeted him. "Can I help you sir?" she asked?

"Yes, my name is Corin O'Leary and I have reservations."

"Sure, let me just pull up the information and I'll get you checked in," she said with a smile. Corin waited patiently while she retrieved the information. When it finally came up, she said, "You will be staying in room five-oh-five. Give me a moment while I get your key." Running the card through a machine, she handed over the key. "Here you go, Mr. O'Leary. Is there anything else that I can get for you? Would you like something from the house restaurant brought to your room?"

"No thank you." Corin replied. He took his card from the young woman smiled and headed for the elevator. The young woman watched longingly as Corin walked towards the elevators and the doors opened. There was a rather simple looking bellhop waiting as Corin walked in.

"What floor?" The young man asked.

"Five." Corin replied. The bellhop pushed the button and the doors closed. When the elevator doors opened again, Corin smiled and stepped out. He looked at the numbers and started to walk in the direction of his room. When he got to the door marked five-oh-five, he put the card against the flat black box that was there. A green light appeared and he opened the door. Dropping his bag, he took a quick glance around the room. The night was still young and he was feeling hungry. He grabbed his bag and brought it to the table, opening it he pulled out a stack of bags that were full of blood. He looked around the room for the fridge; spotting it, he walked over to it and placed all but one bag inside. He took the bag over to the table that had the glasses and the coffee maker. With his hunger beating at him and his fangs sliding out of their sheaths, Corin turned up the glass and punctured the bag of blood with the tip of his fang. He emptied the bag into the glass. Corin walked over to the chair and table that was meant represent a living room. He hunkered down into the chair, grabbed the remote and turned on the television; Corin was looking for the local news as he drank his food. Nothing on the news interested Corin. He was actually hoping to hear something more about the death of Rick Macloud; it was still recent enough to be announced, yet nothing was mentioned. After he finished his meal, he decided he would into the city to see if he could pick up his foes' trail. *Maybe my luck would change and I could happen on someone still talking about the murder. Yeah right, as if,* he thought to himself as he closed the door behind him.

Corin used the stairs; he did not want to see the bellhop again. He didn't much like bellhops; they were too *nosey* for his liking. Corin made his way down the stairwell. He entered the lobby, silently and unnoticed, just the way he liked it. He moved stealthily to the front entrance and left the building. Once outside he hailed a cab and got in.

"Where to, mate?" the cabbie asked, as Corin settled into the back seat.

"Downtown, please," Corin answered.

"Any place in particular?" he asked with his down-under accent.

"No, I will tell you where to let me off." The driver nodded his head and drove away from the curb. It wasn't long before the driver announced that they had reached the downtown vicinity. Corin nodded and motioned to keep going. When the driver started driving along the heart of the downtown streets, Corin watched as the crowds became busier and larger. "Please pull over here." The driver pulled over to the curb. Putting the car in park, he stopped the meter and turned the overhead light on; he mumbled out the total with his heavy accent. Corin paid the cabbie and thanked him. "Keep the change." Corin said as he closed the door behind him.

"Thanks." The cabbie said and he pulled away. Corin quickly scanned the area, ensuring that no danger was present. He also scanned the people as they passed him to see if he could pick up anything. Corin sensed nothing; he continued walking for a short time. During his walk he passed prostitutes, homeless people, and still nothing. He made quick scans of the clubs he passed, without results. Corin had been wandering the streets for a couple of hours now and he was starting to get frustrated. He had no leads and only conclusions from the news broadcast to draw on. Corin had nothing. Nothing about his enemies, and nothing about what had happened to Rick Macloud.

Surely, the papers should have some information. Magazines or perhaps some news papers; I have nothing to lose by looking? . Corin thought. He started looking around the area for a newsstand or convenience store. *Finally,* he thought to himself. *A news stand.* Corin crossed the road and started glancing carefully over the papers and magazines, ensuring that he wouldn't miss anything. They were neatly stacked so he could to see all of the papers that were available. Corin stopped when he came across a gossip paper. The headline, "Was it Animal or Vampire that attacked Rick Macloud?" caught his attention. Corin laughed out loud and shook his head. *Leave it to a paper that is nothing but gossip to have something on it that is the truth.* Corin picked up the paper and inquired about the price.

"How much?"

"That will be a buck and a quarter," he said with a rough voice. Corin reached into his pocket and pulled out the money. Corin paid the man and bowed his slightly. He took his paper and left.

Corin decided to back track to the park that he noticed a few blocks back. Finding a secluded park bench, he sat down and started to flip through the paper. He stopped when he reached the section about Rick Macloud. He quickly committed details of the incident to memory. As he read on, new details surfaced. Corin now knew where the victim had been found. Even though no pictures were in the paper, the words were graphic and detailed enough to paint the gruesome event. The journalist who reported this was very thorough. *Perhaps to detailed.* Corin thought. According this news article, *the victim was on his way home from work when he stopped at the convenience store. He never made it to the store*; according to the papers; *the victim apparently heard something in the alley just beside the store and went to investigate, that is where he was attacked. His throat was apparently had bite marks and there was almost nothing left.* Corin continued to read; *allegedly there was a lack of blood at the scene, considering what had happened. Since the attack was so brutal and because of the damage caused by the attack the authorities had claimed that it was some sort of animal.* Corin finished reading and threw the paper in the garbage. He decided to go to back where the cab let him off, this time he used his preternatural speed to get where he was going. He thought about he wanted to be and in the blink of an eye he was there. He made sure to stay shielded as he did not want people to see him 'appear' out of thin air. So he ducked into a lowly lit area and emerged as if he were casually walking along.

Corin surveyed his surroundings and spotted the store. Crossing the street as if he were heading in that direction, he scanned the area. He walked towards the darkened alleyway and using his vampiric eyes, he looked into the dark alley. Into the black shadows, he looked for any signs of humans while he listened with heightened senses before entering. Sensing no immediate danger, he kept walking. The deeper he went into the shadows he began to feel and recognize a presence. Reaching out with his mind, he touched the person's essence. Corin's was not prepared for the deep sadness, and uncontrollable anger that emanated from this person. He also felt the need for resolution and justice. Instantly, he recognized the mental pathway. It was her. Josephine. This woman invaded his regeneration sleep. The woman he saw two years ago. Rather than intrude on her, he let her have her time and space. Corin watched her from the shadows. He would wait until she was finished before he would continue with his search. Dissolving into mist, he swirled over the cold concrete staying close and not seen and always connected to her in the shadow of her mind.

※※

As a shadow in her mind, Corin's senses were dulled since the connection was purely physic, had there been a blood connection this would not be this would not be as draining. Corin was expending a lot of power and would have to feed later. Normally this manner of connection difficult to accomplish, not many of his kind could do this, an advantage of being a pure blood vampire. Corin continued to listen.

Suddenly the conversation that Josephine was having became odd. It was causing her distress, at first, he thought it was her imagination running amok yet he sensed her uneasiness. *This is not right.* The feeling was so disturbing that Corin removed slipped out of her mind to see what was going on; he needed to assure himself that she was okay because his normal senses were somewhat hindered by this type of connection. Once the connection was broken he automatically scanned the area. He noticed another presence. *Nawzir. My enemy is here and he is with her.* Putting the pieces together, his anger burned deep within him and his beast rose to the surface; roaring to life and wanting to protect her. *Nawzir is here for her.* Corin thoughts raced as knew this to be true. Wasting no time; he remained in the form of mist and ensured that he masked himself carefully. He didn't want Nawzir to know he was here. *Am I too late? Corin questioned himself* as he floated deeper into the alleyway. Corin once again quickly scanned Josephine's mind to see her memories of what just happened.

chapter 5

Corin stopped short when he saw the scene that was unfolding in the alleyway. He was enraged that Josephine was fighting for her life. Reigning in his temper Corin hid in the shadows and shielded himself from Nawzir, staying alert he kept a watchful eye. He would protect Josephine from this monster and destroy his enemy. Corin found Josephine and being mindful of his enemy he stayed in the form of mist. Corin, in his mist form rolled along slowly, always watching the scene that his enemy and Josephine as the events unfolded. Already locked into a fight, Nawzir had Josephine. She could not win. There was *no way* for a *mortal* to win. Nawzir was toying with his intended victim. He was savoring the moment. He had her pinned to the wall in a dark corner; Josephine's hands were guarding her throat, she was trying to stop him from choking her.

"Who are you and what do you want?" Josephine said through her gasps of air.

"You killed my brother and for that you are going to die," Nawzir sneered through clenched teeth.

"I don't know what you are talking about! I haven't killed

anyone!" She cried there was anger and defiance in her voice. Tears were forming in her eyes, threatening to spill. Nawzir smiled as he bared his fangs at her. His eerie yellow eyes which had an outline of red. They glowed dimly as stare bored into her. Giving into fear, she screamed, hoping that someone, anyone would hear her. She was sure that all she needed was a distraction and she would be able to get away from him. Instead, Nawzir struck her hard across the face, knocking her head back into the brick wall and causing blood to flow freely. Nawzir bent his head and sticking his tongue between his fangs, he licked the blood that dripped down the side of Josephine's face. It was a gesture of fear, intimidation. Josephine watched in hatred and disgust. The fear that she felt was fading, and a new emotion surfaced. Anger. Anger was quickly becoming a friend and she hoped it would aid her as her struggles against Nawzir seemed to be futile.

Josephine was furious at being trapped. She felt helpless. Anger fueled her to keep kicking; managing to break free from his grasp, she tried to run. Nawzir released her only to grab her by the hair, then he maliciously slammed her head repeatedly against the concrete wall repeating the words

"I am Nawzir, brother to Rowen, whom you killed. Now the hunter becomes the hunted accept your fate, let nature take its course and accept that you are going to die. Your fate is my revenge."

Within the shadows Corin felt for her. Her essence was fading. *She is a fighter, hanging on to life,* he thought to himself. Nawzir threw the unconscious Josephine down on the ground as if she was mere garbage, as a last indignity. Bending over her, he lowered his head to sink his fangs into her throat.

Josephine was lying on the ground in a pool of her own blood, continuing to rapidly lose blood. Corin needed to act quickly, if he did not Josephine would die this night. Corin attacked from the depths of shadows. Taking Nawzir by surprise. From behind. Nawzir felt the strong, hands, grab him and forcibly remove him from his victim. Nawzir struggled to turn and face his enemy, hissing oaths in his native language, he realized who his enemy was. Corin. Corin had thrown Nawzir further into the darkness of the alley to keep the battle hidden from passers-by.

Corin smiled knowing that he threw his enemy off balance. He had actually been counting on the fact that Nawzir would not be expecting him. Nawzir had kept his mind closed and focused on the kill. With Nawzir clear of Josephine, Corin focused on the battle. His predatory nature already in complete control, baring his fangs, his nails already unsheathing and exposed he leaped into the air covering the distanced between them. Both vampires stood facing each other, waiting for the attack. Nawzir could not resist the urge to break the silence.

"Old friend, it's been a while, I'd say at least two years." Nawzir stated. His smile was evil and menacing. "I shall enjoy killing you both, but first you suffer. I will take the woman first; I will enjoy tasting her hot, sweet, adrenaline filled blood then I will enjoy the feel of her body beneath me as I take her over and over while you watch." Nawzir shuddered as he made a hideous sucking sound.

Corin's anger took over. His once-blue eyes became black and lifeless; there was a hint of fire burning in the dark depths of his eyes. There was no warning when he attacked. The sounds of tearing flesh and breaking bones echoed through the alley as the resonance of bricks smashed into pieces when a body hit them. Each vampire taking punches that sent them flying through the air, there were low rumbling growls that were emanating from the darkness. If someone overheard the battle they would think they were listening to wild animals. Corin had the sense to shield the battle. If anyone was watching or looking for the commotion, all they would be able to see is an area that was blurred and fogged over. The battle raged on and with another powerful blow, Corin sent Nawzir sailing further into the alley. Corin followed, as he towered over Nawzir, Corin spoke.

"I will finish this Nawzir," Corin declared. As fate would have it, at that very same moment, Corin, with his vampire hearing heard Josephine moaning and starting to come around. Corin muttered some oaths as he brought his beast under control, concerned infuriated he went to her. Knowing he could not finish this now without possibly causing Josephine her life or drawing any undue attention the shield was meant to act for outside viewers not those confined within it. Corin neared Josephine, only steps away from her he sent out his final thoughts to Nawzir with his mind. *Nawzir, this is not over. I will find you and I will destroy you and Jonah.* When Corin reached Josephine, he could hear Nawzir's words shimmer in his mind.

I can't wait Corin. I will enjoy holding you captive while you watch as I kill the woman, the one who lead you to my brother Rowen. Then I will kill you. Until then, my old friend. The connection ended.

Corin approached Josephine; she was dazed and bewildered. Corin lowered himself and picked her up. "You must get to a hospital," he said. Josephine looked up into

Corin's eyes, she went to say something but she passed out again, in his arms. Corin managed to obtain a cab; he had to resort to using mind control since his hands were otherwise engaged. Gently he placed Josephine inside. He instructed the driver to go to the nearest hospital. When they got there Corin gave the cab driver some bills. "This should cover the fare." Without waiting for his change, he stepped out of the car and picked up Josephine. Corin went to the desk, supplied a fake story to the nurse and demanded that someone examine Josephine right away. The nurse pursed her lips, pushed her hands on the desk, pushing her chair away, stood up, and hastily walked to the examination area and summoned a doctor.

While waiting for the young woman, he realized that time was not on his side. It was still several hours from dawn, but it still had him slightly worried. He got up, walked over to the nurses' desk.

"When will Josephine Macloud be released or will she have to stay in the hospital?" Corin asked.

"She will be another few minutes. The doctor had to take some x-rays to make sure that she is not suffering from any concussions. The results just came back a few minutes ago and he is going over them now. Your friend has also had stitches," the nurse added.

"Thank you," Corin said. Ultimately Corin knew that he would wait for Josephine, not only to make sure that she was safe but he also wanted the information that he knew she had. Corin's next concern was how to befriend her. He needed to gain her trust. *The one thing we have in common is Nawzir.*

Even though Corin had made the decision to see her safely home regardless of what he would feel he was still concerned, it certainly was not going to be a comfortable time, either way the consequences that he would suffer were irrelevant. He needed to make sure she arrived at her home safely. Corin was fairly certain she would not object; after all, he did save her life. If she did give him trouble, it would be an easy fix, not that he enjoyed doing that sort of thing, especially to someone he had come to know in the last two years and someone he learned to care about. Nevertheless, if push came to shove, then he would compel her. The decision was made. Again, Corin found himself in thought about the situation, no matter the outcome Josephine's safety was priority. Everything else including his situation were secondary.

Being a pure blood vampire as old as time had its advantages like being able to withstand at least the morning sunlight, albeit his great strength would diminish, and he would be virtually powerless and be vulnerable to anything. On the upside of things, Josephine would be safe, and that is really all that mattered.

Corin turned around when he caught Josephine's scent. Her blood was still damp on her blouse and the sweet smell was teasing the taste buds on his tongue. He could not help but lick his lips as he walked towards her. The closer he got, the stronger the smell became. He fought to keep control and his hunger at bay. Corin's mind was whirling with images of erotic pleasure, a sated hunger. A draw back to being immortal, he was a sexual creature with feral needs and wants. *What am I thinking? She is a recent widow, with a family. She is alluring. Sensuous... she is human.* Not liking the thoughts that were plaguing his mind Corin had to re-focus his mind. He was not sure what to do with these thoughts, normally he would have acted on them, taken what he wanted, sated his hunger and wiped the mind of the woman he used. With this one, Josephine he could not. These thoughts consumed him; the answer was simple, he was going to have to maintain control. Now he was only a few feet from her. When he reached an arm's length distance from her, he held out his hand and introduced himself.

"I am Corin O'Leary".

"Mine is Josephine Macloud. The doctors advised me that you brought me in. So… thank you for your help back in the alleyway".

"I was passing by, that's all. I heard the struggle and saw what was happening; I couldn't just leave you there". Corin smiled gently at her as they walked toward the exit, "Forgive my boldness but do you have a car? I hailed a cab to get you here…" he trailed off. "I would like to accompany you home, that is, if you don't mind. I do not feel right just leaving you to fend for yourself right at this moment. I think you have been through enough for one night." Corin said genuinely concerned.

"Uh… no, I don't have my car." Josephine answered. *I don't even have any cash on me to pay for a cab.* Josephine thought to herself, as her uneasiness threatened to rear its ugly face. Trying to keep her feelings hidden she lowered her eyes and smiled shyly.

Corin let out a little laugh, "That's okay, I have no problem picking up the fare, and I am concerned for you." He smiled gently as he held her gaze.

Josephine uneasily accepted the proposal. "I'll pay you back for the cab, I promise. For now why don't we do this, we'll share a cab to get me home where I can get money, thus you'll be escorting me home, which, by the way, is appreciated. Thank you. This way we will kill two birds with one stone. You will get your money and me home safely. As a bonus, you will have the cab to get you home as well." Josephine said as she smiled and kept a cool exterior, but deep in her mind, she was terrified. She was remembering the fangs and those horrible, glowing eyes. The red flags in her brain should have been flashing on and off in warning against Corin, but that wasn't going to stop her; she wanted to feel safe and right now Corin was her only guarantee, besides he couldn't be that bad he did, after all, bring her to the hospital. *It is only a ride home.* She told herself.

"Only if you're sure," Corin interrupted her trance-like state; he had answered her almost as if he were reading her mind. Corin smiled gently, reassuringly hoping to ease her mind. Josephine and Corin walked out through the emergency doors. Corin beckoned to a cab that was already coming forward. He opened the door and helped Josephine get into the car. Once he was inside, he told the driver what the plans were, Josephine interrupted, reciting her address. The driver pulled out and turned on the meter.

"Well," Josephine said, "I would just like to thank you once again for saving my life." She was trying to avoid the awkward silence. She already felt uncomfortable as it was, but somehow she knew that he was not a threat to her. It eased her mind somewhat.

"It was my pleasure," Corin said. "You put up quite a fight," he added casually. "Although I can't help but wonder what you were doing in a dark alleyway alone at that time of night." Corin said casually.

Without even thinking about what she said, Josephine

found herself telling her life story to a complete stranger. "My husband died recently and I'm trying to get some closure. I don't really believe what I've been told, so I came here, in the hopes of finding something. Anything, to lead me to the truth. The police said some sort of animal killed him…they ruled his death accidental. It's…it's just not sitting right with my gut. Something is off. I want to know the truth, actually let me rephrase, I need to know the truth." Josephine's voice was barely audible and it was shaky. Corin heard her every word, though. "What were you doing in the alleyway?" she asked casually.

"Actually, I am here, looking for some people myself. They have been doing some horrible things, I am afraid they have been leaving a trail of dead people in their wake. I have been tracking them for some time now. One of them or possibly both…" He trailed off. "The truth is, I am not sure how they are doing what they are doing, that is whether they are working together or separately. Either way, I have to stop them both. While I was in the States, I got wind of what happened out here and, well, it looked like their signature. So here I am." Corin said.

"Are you a cop?" Josephine asked.

"No. Not exactly. However, it is my responsibility to go after these men and…" He was searching for an appropriate word, "capture them."

"That still doesn't explain why you were in the alleyway," Josephine stated.

"I was following a lead," Corin said, trying not to disclose any more information than he needed to. "The lead I was following brought me to the vicinity of where you were. As it happens, I was passing by when I heard the commotion."

Yeah, right, I was not screaming you couldn't have heard anything. What were you really doing there? What's really going on and why are you really here? Josephine was not convinced that he was telling the whole truth. Nevertheless, she would have to accept his explanation for now. She remained silent for a few moments as if she was thinking up a plan. Corin easily tuned into her thoughts. "I can't get into the specifics of what I am working on but rest assured, there are some monsters out there that need to be stopped."

He studied her face for a few moments and he could see the wheels turning. Corin could not risk any mistrust, reluctantly he crept into her mind and placed the subtle suggestion that they work together. Within moments of Corin's suggestion. Josephine could hardly believe what came out of her mouth.

"Maybe we can collaborate. My husband died in that alleyway and well, maybe your perp will go back there." Josephine had no idea why she had thought that there was a connection between Corin's perp and her husband's death. She shrugged off the thought, stored it away for later evaluation. "I think I can help you find your guy and just maybe you can help me find mine. Are you up for it?"

What I think, is you have some problems with your memories; you seem to have no recollection of the case you worked on two years ago and the results. Corin thought to himself, yet he acted as if he was shocked by her invitation. He waited before he answered, pretending to weigh the pros and cons of them teaming up. He hated knowing that he had used his power to compel her; he would have preferred that she come to her decision on her own, but there was too much at risk. *His need was too great* and he wanted to selfish. *Forgive me, Josephine, for using mind control but this is the only way to ensure that we work together. This is the only way I can protect you. This is my chance, to finally get Nawzir and Jonah and finish this.* He thought to himself, keeping his face neutral, Corin responded.

"I think that it is a great idea. That being said, we are going to have to compare notes at some point. When do you think would be a good time?" Corin asked.

"Well, tonight is definitely out of the question," Josephine said smiling. "What about tomorrow around noon?" Corin turned away from her stare. "Well?" Josephine asked.

"I prefer to work at night if that is not going to be a problem. I guess it is force of habit, working night shifts does that you," Corin said.

"I can relate. I used to work nights myself; that all changed when my children arrived. What time then, and where?"

"How about just after sunset. I am usually up by then, as I said I am more accustomed to working nights. You can choose the location, I am not from here, you know the area better and you are the one with children. I think that we should make this as easy as possible," Corin said.

"My place, I'll write my address down for you when I go and get the money I owe you," Josephine said after weighing her options carefully.

"Are you sure? You do not even know me. You know, I could be some maniac," Corin said, trying not to smile.

"Well, a maniac wouldn't have saved my life for one thing, and second, you have had the opportunity to kill me and you didn't. Therefore, I am willing to gamble that you are not a homicidal maniac. Besides, I have friends that are staying with me and if that were to fail, I have had enough training to know how to protect myself," Josephine said, with complete confidence.

"Well, what about..."Corin was interrupted.

"Tonight, I was caught off guard that will not happen again, I can promise you that!" she snapped.

"I am sorry, I was out of line." Corin said. "I didn't mean to..." He lowered his eyes, wishing he could take back what he said.

"That's fine. It was a fair question, I shouldn't have snapped. Just a little defensive, I guess," Josephine said with a gentler, apologetic voice. Looking out the window Josephine established that they were almost at her house. "We'll be at my place soon, can I expect you tomorrow night?" She said as she turned to face Corin with those emerald green eyes.

"I will come by tomorrow night. "Corin said as he faced Josephine. For a brief moment their eyes locked. Then Corin held out his hand like he was waiting to shake hands on a deal that had been made. Reluctantly, Josephine stuck out her hand, Corin turned her hand so that the back of was facing him. He bent his head and brushed a kiss against her hand. Neither Josephine nor Corin were prepared for the jolt that went through their bodies, when they touched. Pulling her hand away quickly, Josephine tried to occupy herself for the few minutes that it would take to arrive at her house. *That was too weird, now would have been a good time to fumble through my purse. Note to self always bring your purse,* she thought to herself. Corin and Josephine sat in silence for the remaining time. When the cab finally stopped, she had to stop herself from jumping out the door. The cab driver told Josephine what the fare was. Josephine opened the door and stepped out.

"One minute, I have to go inside and get the money," she said. Josephine jogged back to the house, went in and grabbed some money. She came back, tapped at the driver's window, and handed the driver the money. Josephine moved towards the back door, Corin had rolled down the window. She handed Corin money for the cab that he had paid earlier, she also handed a paper with her address written on it.

"It was my pleasure Take it easy and have a good night, well what's left of it and I will see you tomorrow," Corin said, he extended his hand but instead of taking the money, he just closed Josephine's hand around the money.

Josephine smiled. "Thanks," she said. "Until tomorrow, then." Corin closed the window and watched Josephine walk back to the house. At her door, Josephine turned around to see the cab turning around and leaving. Josephine walked into the house to find Mallory and Marcia waiting for her with curious faces.

"What in the hell happened to you?" Mallory asked, with a hint of concern and lot anger in her voice.

As nonchalantly as Josephine could muster, she answered. "I went to where Rick died and I was attacked by someone."

"Oh. My. God." Marcia stated angrily. "I knew you shouldn't have gone out," she remarked as she began to pace back and forth.

"Why, in the world would you go back to where Rick died? Are you insane?" Mallory asked in a calm, aggressive tone.

"If you'd both would let me finish, I'd have a chance to tell you what happened," Josephine said as she tried to remain calm. "As I said I went to where Rick died to look around and get a feel for the place. When I got there, I had a really strange conversation with someone who was hiding in the shadows, then, out of nowhere the bastard attacked me." Josephine paused for a moment as she recalled the incident. *Those hideous eyes, those fangs. They were definitely fangs.* Her thoughts were interrupted when Mallory smacked her on the shoulder, urging her to continue her tale. "Anyways, I was knocked unconscious because my head had the unfortunate pleasure of meeting the brick wall and the concrete floor several times. What I can say for sure about my admirer is that he is extremely strong, and from my conversation with him, I can conclude with certainty, that he has some marbles loose, and that's putting things mildly. He was rambling on about how I killed his brother. He muttered something about revenge after knocking me around. After that, I remember nothing. I woke up in the hospital, and was told who brought me in." Josephine stopped there. Josephine boiled some water for tea, waiting for her friends to give her grief and tell her how foolish she was. "Well?!" Josephine asked.

"Corin?" Mallory said, with a weary look.

"Corin O'Leary," replied Josephine. "He is the man who saved my life. He took me to the hospital and fought off whoever attacked me."

"And you believe him, why?" Marcia asked gently. Josephine thought about her answer and actually thought it was a great question. She was not exactly sure herself why she believed this man. For all she knew, he was the one who had attacked her. Josephine quickly dismissed the thought.

"The man brought me to the hospital. If he wanted to kill me, he would have. Besides, the man who attacked me was different. He was very different."

Marcia did not press her anymore. Both Mallory and

Marcia figured Josephine had enough on her mind after having such a rough night. "Well, at least you're in one piece. There that's a silver lining for you," Mallory laughed, trying to lighten the tension that was still lingering.

"Actually, I'm fine. A bruised ego, bruises, and some stitches, and hey, nothing broken, thank god. I know for sure that this incident could have been much worse. Right now though, I'm going to count my lucky stars that Corin happened to be in the right place at the right time," Josephine stated with confidence as she nodded her head. Mallory and Marcia knew she was hiding her true feelings. They didn't push her though. "Well, ladies, it's almost morning, I have Donovan O'Hara coming here first thing and quite honestly, I could use some rest. Can you guys sleep over? I would really like your input on him, just in case my instincts and Manny's are wrong." Josephine asked. It was her way of feeling safe and they both knew it.

"Sure I'll stay," Mallory said.

"Same goes for me. I'm looking forward to getting to know Mr. Donovan O'Hara better," Marcia said, with a glint of mischief in her eyes.

"One of you can sleep in Charlie's room and someone can sleep downstairs on the sofa bed. I'll be up in a few hours and so will the kids," Josephine added. Josephine finished her last bit of tea and put the mug in the sink. "Good night," she said to Mallory and Marcia, and headed upstairs. Mallory followed.

Josephine went into Charlie's room to get him. Mallory watched as Josephine was about to leave the room, Mallory touched her lightly.

"Please be careful with your venture, Josephine; I couldn't

stand it if anything were to happen to you." Mallory said with a concerned, sincere voice."

"Everything is going to be all right. I'm taking all the necessary precautions," Josephine whispered in a low voice. "Mallory, you should know something that I didn't mention earlier, I was planning to tell everyone tomorrow... Corin is some sort of cop or something; he is here looking for someone. We have decided to team up. I'm going to help him find his perp and he will help me. I think... it is the same guy. Don't ask how; I just have a suspicion." Mallory was about to protest and Josephine shook her head. "Just listen, I've got a good feeling about this Mallory. He is coming over tomorrow night, so we can go over each other's files. I'm hoping and praying to God, that something good comes from this tragedy. I promise you that I will be very careful. I made a promise to myself; I need to be here for my babies. I have a lot to live for, you know." Josephine said.

Mallory lowered her head in defeat; she knew that she couldn't protest, it would be a lost cause. Josephine needed closure, if this was how she was going to get it, then so be it. Josephine walked out of Charlie's room. "Good night Mallory. We'll see you in the morning and please, don't worry." Josephine said.

Mallory just sighed. "Good night Josephine."

Josephine took Charlie into her room, laid him down on Rick's side of the bed, and put a pillow there to block him from falling. She got into her nightclothes and checked on Alex; she crawled into bed and pulled the covers over her. She hugged a pillow close to her and wept.

"Goodnight Rick, I miss you," silently she cried herself to sleep.

chapter 6

Finally a good night's sleep well, a couple of hours at least, of undisturbed sleep. Josephine thought as she woke up to Alex's gurgling noises. Turning over with a heavy sigh, she looked at Alex and smiled. He lay there on his back, arms and legs moving in all directions. *Thank you God for sending Corin my way, without his help, I would probably be dead in a dumpster somewhere.* Tears formed in her eyes; quickly she wiped them away before they fell. Kicking the covers off and picking Alex up from his cradle, Josephine cleaned the drool at the corner of his mouth. Changing his diaper quickly she took Alex into the washroom while she freshened up. Josephine heard Charlie's morning wail. She finished quickly so she could get to her screaming son but when she poked her face around the doorframe making funny faces, she was surprised. Mallory was already there; she turned to see Josephine making funny faces, sitting back Mallory laughed out loud. Josephine stepped into the room and gave her best motherly look to Mallory, and then she just broke out in laughter that resounded throughout the house.

"Morning, Mommy," Charlie said.

"Good morning, baby. What are you and Aunt Mallory up to?" Josephine asked still smiling. "Did you say good morning to your Aunt yet?"

"Yes, Mommy," Mallory answered with a teasing note in her voice.

"Charlie, Aunt Marcia is downstairs. Go jump on her and wake her up for Mommy okay?" Charlie excitedly jumped out of bed and ran for the door. He stopped suddenly, turned around and grabbed his sippy-cup then continued on his way. Josephine and Mallory listened as Charlie slid down the stairs on his bum. They both laughed when the heard the sound of little feet running through the house. Josephine looked at the clock then over to Mallory. "Can you take Alex, I have to grab a shower; Donovan is on his way." Josephine asked.

"Yeah I got this," Mallory said as she winked." Just remember you owe me. I expect to get the favor returned," she said with a laugh.

Josephine walked hastily through her room grabbing a pair of black jeans and a tank top along with everything else. Quickening her pace, she padded over to the washroom, and got the shower going. The water temperature was perfect; grabbing her toothbrush and toothpaste, she hopped into the shower. Josephine took all of ten minutes to get showered and dried. Quickly toweling drying her long hair she pulled it back into a half bun, half ponytail. She slapped on some deodorant and lipstick and rushed downstairs. The coffee was already brewed and Alex was being fed. Marcia walked up to Josephine and smacked her in the shoulder.

"That was for sending Charlie down to jump on me," Marcia grumbled with a smile, she really wasn't a morning person. Josephine just laughed. Charlie continued to eat as Mallory continued to feed Alex.

"Thanks, Mallory. Why don't you and Marcia go and get ready?" Josephine said as she shooed Mallory out of the way with her hands so that she could take over feeding Alex.

"So when is Mr. Bodyguard getting here?" asked Marcia with a glint of curiosity in her eyes.

"Any minute now, I would think." Josephine glanced down at her watch.

"So soon? I guess I better get my ass in gear then," Marcia said, still grinning.

"Oh. Really? Is there something I should know?" Josephine asked mockingly. "Both showers are working so you can both take one." She didn't give time for Marcia to respond.

"Sounds good to me," Mallory said, already heading up the stairs. Josephine was just about to sit down next to Alex when she heard the doorbell. She glanced at her watch *wow, he is punctual, I'll give him that,* she thought to herself as she pushed in her chair and walked over to the door. Turning the deadbolt she opened the door.

"Morning, Donovan," she said as she walked back to the kitchen. She pulled out her chair and waited for him to come in. Before she took her seat, she grabbed an empty mug from the table. "Would you like a coffee?" she asked.

"That would be great, thanks. Two sugars, please, and milk," Donovan replied. She made a mental note that yesterday the coffee was black. Josephine got Donovan his coffee, and she brought it to him. She looked surprised when she saw him staring at her; he had a look of shock and disbelief on his face.

"Is there a problem?" Josephine asked.

"Your face?" He placed his hand against his forehead to show Josephine what he was looking at.

"Oh." She had almost forgotten about that. Either the bruises were not hurting as much, or she just had too much on her mind to think about them. "It happened last night." Josephine answered as nonchalantly as she could, not wanting the discussion to start.

"Did you go to the police? Did you make a report?" Donovan asked, as his police instincts took over.

"No. It was late. I was brought to the hospital and patched up, and then I left the hospital, got in a cab and came home," Josephine replied.

It was clear to Donovan that Josephine did not want to carry on this conversation. He decided to let it go for the moment. However, this would be brought up again. For now, though, he settled back, enjoyed his cup of coffee, and was joking around with Charlie when Mallory came downstairs and Marcia came upstairs from the basement. They both entered the kitchen at the same time. Sitting around the table, everyone was engaging in small talk, drinking their coffee. Josephine smiled to herself, *Marcia seems to enjoy watching Donovan,* Josephine thought to herself as she chuckled out loud. Everyone looked at Josephine to see what she was laughing at. Josephine just shrugged. "What?" She said with a childlike innocence. As she sneaked a glance at Mallory, wondering if her friend was seeing the same thing as she was. When the two women locked eyes, they shared a silent laugh and little nod of the head.

Josephine could see what Marcia found attractive about Donovan. He was tall and his skin was a golden tone. He was built to play football; his body was lean, hard and his shoulders were broad. His eyes were…unique. They were amber colored eyes; Josephine had never seen a man with eyes quite like his. *Actually, Corin has amazing eyes.* Josephine shook her head to clear her thoughts. *Where had that thought come from?* Still not focused, Josephine forced her thoughts back to reality; back to seeing what Marcia saw could see in Donovan. His hair was a mix of blond and light brown, his face was hard, chiseled and etched with stress lines. Looking at this man, you could see that he knew and has seen too much of a distasteful world. His hands were rough and powerful, yet there was gentleness there. She saw this as she watched him hold Alex and play with Charlie. *He was certainly a catch and if Marcia could make a go of it, all the power to her,* Josephine thought to herself. *Why shouldn't my friend be happy?*

"Can I get anything to eat for anyone;" Josephine asked as the women finished their coffee and Donovan downed his last few sips.

"We ate while you were in the shower, hon," Mallory replied.

"No, I'm good," Donovan answered.

"Well then, Donovan, shall we get down to business. A lot has happened since we last met as you pointed out earlier. To make last night's adventure a short story, I was attacked." Donovan went to speak but Josephine stopped him. "A man by the name of Corin O'Leary happened to be passing by, apparently he heard the struggle and he intervened. He fought off my attacker, at least that's what he told me and that is what I think happened. I think, he was the one that brought me to the hospital."

"How in the hell?" Donovan started to say.

"Wait there's more." Josephine said nervously. She already knew Mallory did not like her idea so she was more than a little anxious about telling Marcia and Donovan. "Corin is here on..." Josephine found herself searching for the right word. "Official business, he's looking for some people. When he escorted me home in the cab we decided that maybe working together would be to our advantage. Being that I was a private eye and I know the city, you know all that fun stuff."

"Working? Together?" Marcia asked shaking her head. "Josephine, what are you doing? I, er, scratch that, we know you need closure, but don't you think this is a little much? Allow me to be the voice of reason here; you have two young boys that need their mother. Just because you were a private eye does not mean you can go off half-cocked. It's great that you have amazing instincts and know when things are wrong, but you are not invincible. Would it not be in your best interest to rethink this?" Marcia tried to ask gently.

Donovan wasn't shocked in the least. He knew Josephine, her stubborn ways. What he didn't expect is how soon this would come. He was also concerned with this mystery person in Josephine's life. *Could it be him?* Donovan sat back and watched the show, taking in as much information as he could. He was definitely going to have to report this back to Manny. Mallory did not get into the conversation; she already knew where Josephine stood. She just watched. Once Josephine set her mind on something, nothing was going to stop her. She had already planned things. She took precautions to ensure things were in place in case anything did happen to her. Mallory was angry; she was angry with herself for not seeing it sooner. Josephine had told her the day they went to the funeral home. It was subtle but Josephine had told her., Mallory did not bother to question her, now she was wasn't sure who she was angrier with, herself or with Josephine. Marcia looked over at Mallory expecting back up from her, but Mallory had that defeated look on her face.

"Listen, Marcia, I know you're worried, but don't be, you'll meet Corin tonight. He's coming over."

"I can't believe you're doing this. You have not even buried Rick. You're going out there and placing yourself in danger." Marcia snapped. Marcia watched as a strange look came across Josephine's face, in that moment she wished she could take back her words, Marcia swallowed hard.

"Marcia!" Mallory jumped to Josephine's defense. "You know, for someone who is timid your aggressive side is showing its ugly face," Mallory snapped. "What the hell is your problem anyway? Josephine is a grown woman; she has issues that she needs to resolve. You and I have no business telling her how she has to live her life. We do not know what is going on inside her mind and we will not until God forbid we get into her position. More than that, we are her friends and right now, she needs our support. End of story." Mallory said, a little calmer now. Josephine sat on her chair in shock. First, they were talking about her as if she were not even in the room with them; second, Marcia had never been that outspoken before. Marcia occasionally said her piece, but never as if she were reprimanding someone.

"Look, Marcia, I'm sorry if you don't agree with what I'm doing, but I need to do this. You have my word that I won't be going in guns-a-blazing, I'll be very careful and you'll know what I'm up to every step of the way." Josephine said as she tried to reassure her friend. Donovan was still there, sitting, at the table just watching as the episode unfolded.

"Hum, hum, if I could interject here, I agree with Marcia. I'm sorry, Josephine, but you have things to focus on right now, and if your attention is divided, something is bound to happen." Marcia raised her chin in triumph. "At least someone is siding with me," Marcia said in a triumphant voice. *Even if he is a stranger, a good looking rugged stranger,* Marcia was careful to keep her thoughts to herself.

At this point in the conversation both Mallory and Marcia decided that it was their queue to exit the stage. Donovan would have to deal with Josephine on his own.

"Josephine I have to go for a bit, I need to check in with work. They did give me the time but I need to make sure no hot stories are running around. I'll be back later on." Mallory said casually.

"I have to go too. Even though, I have the time off, I would feel better knowing that the department is running smoothly, I don't need any unforeseen problems, if you catch my drift," Marcia said smoothly. Both Mallory and Marcia said bye to the boys, grabbed their things and took off.

"Sorry. I had to tell you what I thought, besides, I was feeling a little left out." Donovan said shrugging his shoulders. Josephine glared at Donovan. "What, I did," he said. Josephine's emerald eyes softened. Donovan smiled. "Do you know anything solid about Corin? Other than he might be a cop?" Donovan asked.

"Not really, but we can discuss Corin in the car. I have some errands to do, if you don't mind tagging along." Josephine said, as she started clearing the table. "By the way, what were you thinking about living arrangements? I know we discussed it; I can't remember where we left it," Josephine commented as she cleared the last of the dishes.

"Honestly, it's easier for me to be here, so I put an ad in the paper and I will sublet my condo," Donovan answered.

"Great! I think I mentioned that the basement is fully self-contained with a separate entrance," Josephine replied.

"You did. That's one of the reasons I decided that living here is a better option," Donovan answered.

"One of the reasons?"

"Yup, the second is that I have a better chance of helping if the need should arise." Donovan said with a smile. "By the way, if it's not too in appropriate would you kindly explain me what happened to you last night? If I am to be your bodyguard I need to know what is going, I cannot do my job if I don't the whole story. It's a fault of mine, I know, but being a cop for most of my adult life drills certain things in, it makes you question everything, even though I'm retired… I guess you can say old habits die hard," Donovan said as if this were just another conversation.

Josephine gave a long sigh, then she told Donovan what happened as she got the boys ready to go out. She collected the supplies that she needed for them, while she told him about Corin, the hospital and how they ended becoming partners so-to-speak. When she finished telling her tale, she looked over at Donovan, fully expecting him to say that she was an idiot for going out last night and for teaming up with someone she did not even know. Donovan surprised her though.

"I'm not going to tell you how to go about your business, however just because you were attacked doesn't mean that it is related to Rick's death. As a matter of fact this was probably just a random attack," he lied. "As for your new partner, what do you know about him? Can you be sure he is not the one who attacked you? You may not like hearing this, yet this needs to be heard otherwise I would not be a very good bodyguard. I strongly recommend that you be wary of new people coming into your life Josephine, especially at this particular crossroad. You're still vulnerable and you are going through a difficult time," Donovan said gently. There was no reprimand in his voice, only truth and sincerity.

"Thanks for not lecturing me, I appreciate it. Josephine looked at him and smiled You are right about one thing; I know I shouldn't be as trusting with newcomers into my life and just so you know, I don't exactly trust Corin but realistically if he was truly trying to kill me, he had his opportunity. He saved my life." Josephine said. Her answer was short and she didn't bother with the rest of the details. There were things about this whole situation that she was determined to figure out. After all, this is what she did. She was a private eye and a damned good one at that. She always trusted her instincts and right now, her instincts trusted in Corin, and that was enough for her. "Maybe you could get some back ground information on Corin. Do you have any contacts that you've stayed in touch with?" She asked Donovan.

"I'll see what I can dig up for you. What do you know about him so far?" Donovan questioned.

"Not a whole hell of a lot. He saved my life. He said he was some sort of cop or something; and that he was looking for some people. Tracking them. He wasn't very specific about the people only that they were bad news and that they were and have been leaving trails of dead people behind them. He also mentioned that he prefers working at night," Josephine said as she remembered her conversation with Corin. "I can describe him to you if you want. She waited for Donovan to respond.

"Sure," he answered.

"He's got long black hair, very muscular. Very defined. He is tall, I'd peg him at six foot one at the very least and he's got deep blue eyes," she supplied. *He is a looker,* was the unspoken thought that shimmered through her mind. Josephine felt the color rushing to her face as she blushed at her own thoughts, turning away quickly, Josephine hoped that Donovan wouldn't catch her betraying mind.

"I'll see what information I can get and let you know. A word to the wise if you're starting to feel weird about this guy then maybe you should rethink your strategy." Donovan pointed out.

"No, I think I will stick to my plan, I think he knows more than what he's letting on. I have a feeling he's going to be very useful to me, and I think he'll be able to help. It's only a gut feeling, but it's persistent. Besides, I have you here during the day and with any luck, you will be living here shortly. I'm not that worried," Josephine said with confidence. "Before we start any investigating, I think I should get you familiar with Alex and his feeding habits," Josephine laughed out loud.

"What?" Donovan looked at her, his eyes questioning her laughter.

"It's is hard to picture you feeding and taking care of a baby that is only four months old," Josephine said, trying to hold back more laughter.

Donovan looked at her and just laughed out loud himself.

He assured her that he has nieces and nephews and that they considered him 'The God of Play'. "I have also been around babies before," he added for an extra measure of comfort.

"We should head out for some groceries for you and anything else that you need. I also have to pick some stuff for the baby. We will take my van since I have the car seats."

"Sure, but I'm driving. I need to feel like I'm doing something and not being a lap dog, excuse the expression," Donovan, said with a smirk on his face.

Josephine went and got Charlie, got him dressed. Then she got Alex and got him ready. Donovan just stood there and watched. She grabbed her purse and cell phone. She motioned to Donovan that she was ready. Josephine locked the door, and pressed the key remote to unlock the doors to the van. She handed the keys to Donovan so that she could get Alex and Charlie settled. She hopped in the front and off they went.

Donovan pulled out his cell phone called his connection. He was calling in a favor. He was owed a favor so this would be dealt with. He stayed on the phone for several minutes catching up with his so-called friend and playing nice. Josephine listened as he played the game. When he was done, he hung up the phone.

"I should know something by this evening," Donovan finally said.

"Corin and I will probably be going out tonight, do mind staying a little late?" Josephine asked casually.

"That's what you're paying me for, it is my job," Donovan said with a smile. Donovan and Josephine continued talking. Donovan was going to extract as much information from her as he could. "So, tell me a little about yourself, Manny didn't say much other than you are a very good friend," he lied. He was trying to act as if they didn't know each other. He hated the charade but he had a job to do.

"Well there is not much to tell. I was a private investigator before I decided to have a family. I've got a license to carry a firearm and I'm a black belt student in Kung Fu. I met Rick at work and, well, we hit it off. Mallory and Marcia are my best friends. They know everything about me and I love them like sisters. We have been through everything together, and we all have each other's backs. There is one thing I can think of that I have not shared with them… actually, I'm going to tell you. I think, no I need to get it off my chest and since I don't know you all that well, it just seems easier to tell you. For the last two years, on and off, I've had this...dream," Josephine said.

"What's it about?" Donovan asked.

"Well, it was about someone dying. Someone that is close to me. I was never able to see the face of the person; but every single time I woke up I felt sad and a sense of loss. I also felt a need for revenge. The person that died…died because of a need for revenge." Josephine's voice was coarse and dry as she said the words. Funny thing is I haven't had the dream since Rick died. The dream, although it was on and off, came two or three times a week, and now…now, there's nothing," Josephine said. Pause." I feel responsible for Rick's death," she blurted out. "I'm not sure why but somehow I know I'm responsible. I can't help but wonder maybe if I had just said something, to someone, or to Rick, maybe he'd be alive now," Josephine said through a cracked voice.

Donovan looked at her, surprise in his eyes; he hoped that guilt was not showing on his face. The guilt that he was desperately trying to block, it quickly began to rise within him. *Revenge? You can't know. Your memory was suppressed. Something's has gone wrong.* "You can't blame yourself, you couldn't have known what was going to happen," he said, as tried to get a grip of everything that she had said.

"I can tell you this; I'll do whatever needs to be done. I need to find out the truth. I'm missing something. I intend to figure it out. Whatever it takes except of course my life," Josephine said determinedly.

"Josephine, that's fine and I hope for your sake you can get to the bottom of this. I just want you to remember that you have two young children that need their mother. You're going to have to think things out logically. You need to plan carefully. I'll help you as much as I can and I'll use every available resource that I can get my hands onto, but at the end of the day, you really need to be careful," Donovan said with serious tone. The ride became silent.

Donovan pulled into the grocery store. Josephine got Charlie and Alex ready to go while Donovan brought a cart over. They went into the store picked up some groceries making sure to pick up anything that Donovan needed. They paid for the groceries and they shoved everything into the van along with kids and headed back to the house. Josephine was tending to Alex most of the way home so there wasn't conversation, which gave Donovan time to think of a game plan. Donovan pulled into the driveway. They unloaded the van, when Josephine and the boys were inside, Donovan slipped out to go to his car, and he retrieved his laptop. When he came back in, he put the computer down on the kitchen table.

"Where should I set up?"

"Well, downstairs is yours, unless you want to put the computer up here," Josephine replied.

"I think I'll put it downstairs for now; if we need it upstairs, I'll just move it."

"That's fine," Josephine said, as she continued putting groceries away and pulling out what she wanted for dinner. "I'm going to make supper is there anything you don't like?" She stopped what she was doing and looked over at him.

"No, I eat just about anything and I have no allergies that I know of," he said.

"Great! Steak and salad then?" she asked.

"Haven't had steak in a while sounds great. I like it medium," he said laughing.

"10-4," she said with a smile, as she continued to prepare the meat. Once dinner had been prepared and put in the oven to cook, she went into the living room to check on Alex and Charlie. Alex was still sleeping and Charlie was watching his favorite movie, "The Lion King." Mallory loaned them the movie, unfortunately, Josephine was positive that it would be worn by the time she gave it back from overuse. Shaking her head, she smiled to herself while leaning against the wall she watched Charlie sit happily and ever so engrossed in his movie. *At least he is not looking for Daddy* she thought to herself. The thought actually saddened her a little because she wanted Charlie to remember his daddy but at the same time she didn't want him suffer the way she was with the loss. Josephine snapped herself out of her trance. *This is not the time to be emotional or confused. I have to stay focused long enough to figure out what happened.* Josephine's thoughts drifted to Corin. *He's too good to be true. Focus Josephine. Focus. Something's off with this guy. Nights?* Then she thought of her attacker. *Fangs. Brute strength. How did Corin fight him off?* Something was nagging at her; gut feeling, intuition.

Vampire. The word shimmered through her mind. *Yeah right. We're in the twenty first century. Besides, vampires don't exist. Nope, no such thing as a vampire. Note to self: stop watching Buffy and reading vampire novels.* Josephine shook her head, dismissing the troubling thoughts and walked back into the kitchen. Donovan was in there searching for a glass when he saw Josephine.

"Are you okay? You looked a little troubled," he commented.

"I'm fine. I'm just thinking about Corin and the man who attacked me. Have you heard back from your contact, anything about Corin?" Josephine asked, quickly changing the subject.

"Actually, yeah, he did and he found nothing. It's as if the guy is invisible, except for some property out in Ireland. I suggest you watch your back, and I do mean that literally," Donovan said.

"Oh, I have every intention of watching my back," Josephine said. "In the meantime, dinner is just about done. Let me get the table ready and then we'll eat," Josephine said as she put plates and cutlery down on the table. Walking into the living room she got Charlie and Alex. When the boys were settled, she served dinner. When everyone was finished, Charlie went back to the television to finish his movie and Alex remained in the kitchen, Donovan seemed to be enjoying the company. Josephine was about to brew some coffee, when the doorbell rang, Donovan got up to answer; he found Mallory and Marcia with donuts and coffee.

"Come in, ladies," he said as he stepped out of the way. "Josephine is in the kitchen just about to start some coffee, better tell her to stop," he said casually and feeling completely at home. Mallory and Marcia walked into the kitchen and made themselves at home. Marcia was all giddy and in a better mood. Josephine assumed it was because of Donovan and she just smiled to herself. Donovan excused himself. "Call me when Corin arrives," he said as he headed downstairs.

Josephine looked at Marcia. "Marcia? What's up with you? You seem…giddy. Is something wrong?" Josephine asked teasingly.

"He is so hot. I mean for an ex-cop and all." Marcia said with a mischievous smile.

Mallory and Josephine just rolled their eyes and laughed. "He is all yours," Josephine said laughing out loud. "Although you might have competition," she added as she looked in Mallory's direction.

"Nope! I have my eyes set on no one right now. You can have him, Marcia," she said with a chuckle.

"Good! I would be worried if you tried to get him Mallory," Marcia said in a teasing way.

"Should I tell him you are interested, Marcia?" Josephine asked trying to control her laughter.

"Nope, don't need your help, I will do it in my own sweet time," she said with a confident smile.

"It's great to see you laugh, Josephine," Mallory said as she sipped her coffee. "Ooh, that hit the spot." Mallory sighed.

"It feels good to laugh, however I find the hardest part at night, that's when I'm alone with my thoughts, you know? I know that time heals all wounds, but putting closure to this, will definitely help with the healing process," Josephine said in a low voice and with tears brimming in her eyes. The doorbell rang startling Josephine; she called out to Donovan as she opened the door. "Hey Corin, please come in," she said as she stepped out of the way. Corin and Josephine walked into the kitchen; the look on Corin's face suggested that he was shocked to see all these people. Josephine noticed his surprise. "Corin, I would like you to meet Mallory and Marcia, these are my closest friends, actually they're pretty much family to me. The person over here is Donovan O'Hara and he works for me. Donovan has invaluable resources at his disposal that can help us, and just so we're on the same page, I told everyone what happened last night. I think it will be beneficial to use all and any resources available to us," Josephine said quickly as she assured him that there was nothing to worry about while she enforced the idea that they could be trusted.

"I have to agree," Corin said, trying to sound sincere. *Although, not what I had in mind, considering the stakes.* His thoughts remained his own. Josephine pulled up a chair, as did Donovan. Mallory and Marcia were already seated.

"Shall we get started?" Josephine began.

chapter 7

The sun had finally set and Nawzir felt his heart begin to beat. His lungs filled with air, before he opened his eyes he let his senses flare out to scan the surrounding area ensuring it was safe to rise. Nawzir sensed another of his kind around, the other was close; smiling he pulled himself from his shallow grave.

"Jonah, I know you are here come where I can see you," Nawzir commanded.

Jonah was a tall, broad shouldered man; his eyes were dark as was his long hair. When he was human, his attributes were average. Now that he was converted the change amplified his attributes, as it did for the women, the change enhanced their curves, and made the body softer, their natural beauty more enhanced.

"Brother, how dare you decide to play without me? I'm hurt," Jonah said with an unbecoming pout on his face. Jonah, who was usually quite the looker, was looking quite pathetic. "No time for arguments. I found the woman called Josephine, the one who lead Corin to our lost brother Rowen. I had it all planned so well, I killed her husband sucked him dry, left him in an alleyway to be found. She was notified, and as expected, she came out looking for truth about what had happened. She was right there in the alleyway, I toyed with her and finally when I was but mere inches away from her neck…" Nawzir trailed off. He was pacing and looking as though he wanted to rip the heart out of someone.

"What?" Jonah asked, as he licked his lips and rubbed his hands together, like a child waiting for a candy.

"Corin," he spat out." He engaged me in battle. Not only did he stop my kill, the bastard took my prey and left instead of finishing the fight. He took her took to the damned hospital and saved her pathetic life." Nawzir said between clenched teeth.

"The woman lives then." Jonah stated, annoyed, yet satisfied that she still lived for him to exact his revenge.

"Yes, she lives," Nawzir hissed. "Since we know that Corin is here, we must be careful. I suggest that we dine on the homeless and less important people. They make much easier prey; we will be harder to track. More to the point, their deaths will go unnoticed. Corin will no doubt be watching for us, waiting for us to make our move. We must keep low and off Corin's radar if we are going to succeed. Now that you are here my brother, we shall succeed; we will rid ourselves of Corin and Josephine." Nawzir said as a wicked smile formed on his chiseled hard face.

Hungry from his sleep and battle with Corin, Nawzir and Jonah went out and fed., they took care to eliminate the bodies. Jonah finished feeding on his last victim; and waited in the shadows as Nawzir approached his victim. Nawzir had found a young man, a drug dealer no less. He watched as the man finished his transaction and then he motioned for the young man to come to him in the alleyway. As the young man approached Nawzir, he pulled out his stash and was ready to offer it to Nawzir. "What can I do you for tonight my man?" The dealer asked.

"Nothing that you are selling, however you may have something that I may yet want," Nawzir said with a menacing smile. The dealer sensing that something was not quite right with his next customer stepped back, he turned to run but Nawzir grabbed him by the coat and slammed him into the wall. Nawzir was holding the drug dealer by his neck cutting off his vocal chords; the young man struggled but found that it was no use. Nawzir's eyes had changed, they became an eerie yellow with a rim of red; lowering the dealer to his feet and forced his head to one side. The dealers' eyes were moving side to side frantically, trying to see what was happening, then, finally, he caught a glimpse of Nawzir. Fear gripped the dealer as he saw the fangs slide from their sheaths in Nawzir's mouth. The man kicked and punched to no avail. With flailing arms, he tried desperately to get away. Nawzir simply laughed, his grip tightened. Bringing his head down slowly, ensuring that the dealers fear permeated the air around his kill, Nawzir was satisfied. He bit down on the pulsating vein in the dealers' throat. Nawzir has loosened his grip allowing his victim one last attempt at a scream, to the dealers dismay he tried and found that there was nothing, no sound was escaped his mouth. The dealer realized then that his fate was upon him. Nawzir ravaged his throat and when he was done with this victim, he collected the body. The two vampires used their preternatural speed to get to the city limits, they were using the river there as a dumping ground.

As the two vampires walked in silence, Jonah heard the whisper that escaped Nawzir's mind. *Corin will suffer for this.*

Easy brother, all in due time. Jonah directed the thought towards Nawzir.

"We must find shelter, something more accommodating than where you found me." Nawzir said. As they, both continued scoping out the area, Nawzir saw a building. As they got nearer, they realized it was an old, abandoned church. Both vampires scanned the church ensuring no one was in there. Jonah opened the door and both he and Nawzir walked inside. Their senses still open. They scanned the ruin. There was no electricity in the building, not that it was needed. Both Jonah and Nawzir saw perfectly in the dark, but they would need light eventually, after all they would be *entertaining* guests. Nawzir saw some old candles sitting on the altar. Focusing his mind the candles sprang to life. A soft, orangey glow filled the room. "This will do," Nawzir said, with a twisted evil smile.

"Yes, I do believe it will do nicely for our purposes," Jonah replied.

"We will have to get some supplies to make it just right for our soon-to-be guests." Nawzir said. Both Nawzir and Jonah finished looking around the abandoned church. They found a confession room, a storage room and they found a basement, which would be good for sleeping arrangements. They noted that all the windows had boards to keep out light. They were satisfied that no light would be getting in. Satisfied with their new accommodation, they decided to head out to and get what they needed and maybe have some more fun; there were still several hours before dawn.

Meanwhile Josephine, Corin, Donovan, Mallory and Marcia had finished going through all the documentation about Rick's death and Corin's cases. They had the opportunity to express views and go through all the details bit by bit. At the end of a very lengthy discussion, Corin had made the decision to go back to the crime scene.

"I'm coming with you," Josephine said. Everyone in the room was dumbfounded and the facial expressions could not have made it any clearer. Josephine saw the protest that was about to come. "Listen, before anyone says anything, I'll be fine. Corin is with me. My cell phone is with me and if anything happens. Pause. You can believe me when I say I'm really not looking for any trouble. Besides, the sooner and faster I get this over with the faster I...we can go back to our normal lives," she said as reassuringly as possible. She glanced over in Corin's direction, he was about to speak. Silently with her eyes, she told him to stay quiet. Corin remained there saying nothing, his large frame filling the doorway.

"Corin, you'll watch her back or you will be answering to me, got it." Donovan said. It was a command and a warning. Corin understood it well and he acknowledged Donovan by bowing his head. Mallory and Marcia said nothing, knowing that Donovan intended to keep his word.

Josephine said goodbye to her children and kissed them on the cheek. Then as Corin and Josephine were heading, out Mallory grabbed Josephine by the arm, "You, watch your back." Mallory said. It was a demand. Nodding Josephine headed towards the car where Corin was waiting.

Josephine and Corin pulled out of the driveway. "So, where are we heading?" she asked jokingly.

"I think we should start where I found you. In the alleyway," Corin started to answer.

"Ah...sure." Josephine shook her head in disbelief. *Maybe the police missed something. Maybe I missed something.* She thought to herself. "That was sarcasm. I know where we are going," she supplied with a little grin on her face.

"There's not much else to go on and you were attacked while trying to investigate on your own. Maybe there is something there that the police missed." Corin said as he dismissed her sarcasm.

"That is just too freaking weird. It is like you were reading my mind." Josephine commented.

"That's not quite what you were thinking," Corin said smugly, realizing then what he had just done. *What the hell was that? How could I have been so...absent minded? Maybe it is better this way, maybe I should tell her the truth.*

Josephine looked at him wide eyed and she looked like she was on the brink of making a run for it. Gathering her nerves she looked as if she were about to light into him for. Corin watched her reaction... *What exactly can I say to him? Chew him out, because he knew what I was thinking. Or even better, ream him because he caught you in a lie. Caught me in a lie? How the hell...?* Josephine gave herself a mental nod. "Listen," Josephine said. "I'm not one for small talk and nonsense. I think you know something. Actually, I think you know a whole lot more then you're letting on. In fact, I'm pretty damn sure you're hiding something, she said curtly. Your files are useless. Wait, I take that back maybe they contain some details about the 'deaths' you're investigating, like his alleged name, and you 'claim' to know that there is a second person involved. I don't have a name or a picture, so how exactly do you think the cases are related?" She asked haughtily.

"I am going out on a limb here, but Rick's death has remarkable similarities to all of the murders that I have been following; the lack of blood, the facts that the killer or killers are striking the throats and the murders have all taken place in alleyways. I think it is more than just coincidence. I believe that you are onto something and the police are just giving you the run around. Any seasoned police officer would be able to make a link between my murders and Rick's death. It is unfortunate but I think we are looking for the same killer, sorry killers. I believe Rick was killed...intentionally."

Processing Corin's words Josephine digested what he said. "I don't know what to believe anymore," she held back her grief. "The police tell me one thing, you tell me something else. I don't even know what you do for a living. Why should I believe what you say?" Josephine asked. Her knuckles were turning white from holding the steering wheel so hard. "You're holding information back from me. I feel it in my gut. If you aren't going to be honest and upfront with me, then we can't work together," Josephine said as she tried to calm herself down.

Corin looked stunned as the words flew from Josephine's mouth. But instead of answering her, he snuck into her mind. *Remember. Try to remember what you uncovered two years ago. Vampires. You found out about the existence of vampires. You saw the truth for yourself, when you found the ashes and a wooden stake. Open your mind, Josephine. Remember me. Remember seeing me.* As Corin continued to stay in the shadows of her mind, he found that she was more open to the possibility that something paranormal could exist. *How... intriguing.* He pushed into the deepest recesses of her mind. What he found was sadness and blame. She was blaming herself for Rick's death. She still believed that she was responsible because she somehow had dreams of what was to come. Again, he saw the dreams that haunted her at night. Her mind was filled with feelings of mistrust and confusion regarding him. Her thoughts were puzzling, yet they intrigued him. Corin retreated from her mind feeling helplessness, something that he did not understand. Her anger and sadness burned like a fire inside him. *You are right my sweet, you need the truth. There is no sense in you finding out my secrets on your own, that would just put a barrier between us. You shall know the truth.*

"You're right; there is much to discuss Josephine. Can you head to my place?"

"Why? Can't we talk in the car?" She asked, skeptically. *Something had happened when we touched that night. Something I'm not sure I can face.* Josephine kept her thoughts guarded; working with him and being in close proximity would make these feelings surface. She wasn't comfortable with these new feelings; *this is wrong, where are these feelings coming from?* Josephine was in her own world, while she tried to dissuade Corin from going to his place.

"I prefer to discuss things at my place. You want me to make things clear. If you want the truth, my place is where I will tell you," Corin answered curtly.

Arrogant ass. Frustrated, annoyed and realizing that Corin would say nothing more, she turned off at the nearest exit. She turned the car around and started heading back to where Corin was staying. Slamming on the brakes, the van screeched to a stop. Josephine and Corin jerked forward with the sudden stop.

"He came out of nowhere!" she screamed, as they both stared at the man in the middle of the road. *Nawzir.* Corin felt his presence. In his mind he could hear the echo of Nawzir's menacing laugh.

"Keep. Driving." Corin said. "Keep driving." Corin demanded. Josephine could hear the urgency in his voice but she also heard her inner voice. *If you keep driving, you'll hit the man, if you swerve to avoid him, we'll hit the guardrail and crash.* Decision made. She released the brake and was about to hit the gas when the man jumped onto the hood of the car. His eyes burned an eerie yellow with an outline of red. His smile was pure evil and malice poured from him. *Omigod, it's him.* The thoughts raced through her mind, she recognized this man. Nawzir opened his mouth displaying the gleaming, white, sharp, long, canines. Fangs.

"What the hell?" Josephine said while she slammed the brakes. The car swerved until it came to a stop after colliding with the guardrail. The man or whatever was thrown from the car. Undoing her belt, she exited the car, along with Corin, who was muttering some curse words in some foreign language. Making her way towards the man that she had hit she slammed into what felt like a stone wall. She tried to push through and couldn't. *Corin.* She thought to herself as her blood heated in anger. Corin walked to her pushed her backwards, when he got her where he wanted her, he opened the car door and pushed her into the car.

"Stay here." It was a command; he locked his gaze to hers. The seriousness of his voice emphasized that he expected obedience. Josephine gritted her teeth as her body did exactly as it was told, when she wanted to do the exact opposite. *What in the hell is going on?* Josephine sat in the passenger seat, pondering the situation over in her head. Without warning, the sensation of heat from where Corin touched her bombarded her body. Her head was swirling, emotions were tumbling over each other. Trying desperately to get control, she took deep calming breaths. *In, out, in, out. That's better.* Looking at Corin she saw hunger. Worry. Their gazes locked. Electricity filled her body, warming her blood and places that were best left alone. The feeling was familiar now; it is how she felt when he touched her hand in the cab. Corin was in the drivers' seat, now her nervousness became living breathing anger. Corin took complete control, issuing commands.

"Just who in the hell do you think you are?" She snapped between clenched teeth. Corin put the car in reverse and peeled out. "Damn you. Answer. Me. Pause. Another pause. "Corin!?" Josephine snapped. "That man could be hurt. Stop the car. Stop the damn car, Corin." Josephine demanded.

Corin ran the man over and continued to put distance between them and the situation before he finally stopped. He turned his head and looked at Josephine. She was unable to hold back her gasp. It was like looking into a blue flame in the depths of darkness.

"Josephine, you have to trust me. There are things that you do not know, but when you do, you will understand. I assure you, you will see this whole thing differently. I promise I will tell you everything. For now until we are in the safety of my place, you have to trust in me. Josephine glared at Corin.

"You better have a damn good reason for all this insanity, Corin." Josephine uttered angrily.

"I do," Corin said flatly. They continued driving until they reached his place. Reaching into his pocket, he pulled out his card and pressed it against the pad opening the garage door. He pulled into his parking spot and killed the engine. Corin got out, went to Josephine's side and opened the door. Josephine stepped out; facing Corin, she realized that his eyes were now the same blue flame color they normally are. Shaking her head, she muttered under her breath. Corin just watched and smiled. He locked the doors with the remote as they walked towards the elevators. Josephine followed behind. The elevator was empty when it arrived; Corin and Josephine stepped inside. Corin hit the penthouse button. When they reached their destination Corin stepped out followed closely by Josephine. He opened his front door and stepped inside, opening the lights so that Josephine could see.

Josephine stopped short the moment when she stepped inside. She was in awe; the décor of place was simply magnificent. From the Persian rugs, to the crystal chandelier. Everything complemented each other. The sofas and chairs were deep mahogany wood. Everything looked...well just right.

"Well, I must say, you have impeccable taste, Corin. Your place is gorgeous. I thought...I remember you saying you didn't live here." Josephine said, with her head cocked to the side and her brow raised.

"I do not live here. This place was vacant and up for sale. I was unsure how long I would be in town. Rather than continuing to rent a hotel, I purchased this. Rather I had my lawyer purchase it, on my behalf. At least, now I will have a place to stay when I come into town, should the need arise again," Corin said.

"I see," Josephine said with skepticism written across her face. "How does one go about acquiring a piece of real estate in a day? Never mind, it's none of my business." Josephine shook off the feeling of awe and shock. Josephine focused on the reason she was here, with that her anger consumed her. Summoning her courage, she blasted Corin again for his earlier actions. "What in the hell did you think you were doing back there? You ran over that man. Then we bloody well took off?"

"It was for your own good, you have no idea what this is about." Corin replied as he absorbed her anger calmly.

"Why not start from the beginning?" Josephine said calmly.

"I am not the person you think I am. I am…different. The person you are after is not your typical villain either. I have some rather spectacular stuff to tell you, which you will undoubtedly find difficult to believe, but you have to trust that what I say is true. Can you promise me that, Josephine? Can you promise that you will not overreact and run?" Corin said with a long restless sigh. Josephine noted that he was pacing like a trapped tiger.

"I feel like I am signing a contract with the devil," she said. Josephine plopped herself down in the comfy loveseat and stared at Corin for a long while. With a long sigh, she agreed to stay and listen, she promised not to run.

"I am a… centuries old vampire. I need blood to live. The person that we are tracking is Nawzir he has a partner his name is Jonah. I sired both of them. I also sired Rowen, whom you had the pleasure of tracking, you met what was left of him." Corin said. *Not bad she is still here*, he thought to himself as he watched her.

Josephine was shocked, her eyes wild. Instead of speaking she only stared, she let Corin continue. "Two years ago I tracked all three of them here, I found Rowen thanks to you and I dispatched justice in the way of my people for his crimes. Now, Nawzir is back. He is here for revenge. He is here for *you*." Josephine was sitting upright in her comfy chair, mouth wide opened. "You and I, I suspect are his primary targets. Jonah has not made his presence known yet but I am sure he will. I never expected to run into you again, but when I saw your picture on the news, I knew I had to get to you." Corin finished saying.

"Yeah right. You're a vamp...vampire and I helped you track one? I really don't think so. I'm a P.I. not a vampire hunter," she said mockingly. "There's no way I could have helped you, I think I would've remembered that tid bit about my job." Josephine said with sarcasm. . Sitting there, numb. Her mouth was closed; not sure if she should laugh or cry. *Great I have partnered up with a delusional person who is a real hotty. Great! Just what I need in my messed- up life.* She thought to herself.

"Do you want me to go on?" Corin asked. Josephine only nodded. "The night that you were in the alley I was there. Watching you. I recognized you the minute I saw you. I knew what you were doing, what I could not figure out is why you were there by yourself. Instead of leaving you alone, I stayed close by; I read your mind and stayed connected to you so I could determine what you were doing, and to know if you were in danger." Corin said not ashamed by his actions.

"Inside my mind? What?" Josephine asked anger rising.

"Let me finish. While I was a shadow in your mind, I found out about the forensic file on Rick. I needed to get the information from you somehow, so I was going to try to befriend you. Instead, Nawzir attacked. Although the attack on you was not what I had in mind, it was the opportunity I needed," Corin said, as he lowered his head in regret. "While you were unconscious I fought Nawzir off and would have ended it then and there but you started coming around so I left taking you with me."

"You said revenge. Revenge? For what? I haven't done anything and you can rest assured that Rick didn't do anything. As for that whole blurb about *me* helping you two years ago... really? I think I would remember that tidbit about my job, don't you? I would also think that I would remember you? This..." Josephine shook her head. "This is just not possible. There has to be some logical explanation for all this." Josephine kept rambling and spurting out questions. Shaking her head while muttering to herself she started pacing.

Walking up to her Corin grabbed her by her shoulders. She tried to avoid his touch knowing what was going to happen. Her body was in close proximity to his, her heart was beating a mile a minute. Feeling hot and irritated she wanted to move but she was feeling weak in the knees. His touch was sending fire through her body, along with sensations she was unaccustomed too. She tried to break free but couldn't. Corin walked her over to the couch and sat her down.

Josephine looked at Corin and saw his eyes had changed color again. They were the most amazing blue color. Sapphire. She shut her eyes and shook her head. *This is not possible. The man's eyes change with his emotions. This is not real. You're imagining things.* Josephine looked again at Corin and his eyes. Still sapphire.

"Josephine, I am for real. I am a vampire, I have been for centuries. I was born in the sixteen hundreds. Both my parents were vampires, which makes me a pure blood. I have strengths and weaknesses *and* I can be killed. I can tolerate the sun with protection and not for very long. Only fire can destroys me when my heart has been destroyed. I need blood to survive; however, I rarely take from humans. I take blood from the blood banks and from humans, however I never kill them. I take only what I need, nothing more," Corin said with a sigh. He looked at Josephine and tried to assess her state of mind. "I can prove to you that I am a vampire," he said. Slipping inside her mind, Corin planted the thought; *Josephine, go over to the fridge and open it.*

Feeling an urge to go over to the fridge Josephine got up. Puzzled by her actions she stopped short and opened it. A loud gasp escaped her as she turned and faced Corin who was already there behind her, towering over her. Slamming the fridge, she glared up at him.

"That could be fake blood, planted there for this sick demonstration. You know what…you need help. Serious help." She pushed by him and went over by the window, keeping her back to him. "You know I don't see any fangs, where are those? Oh…wait you have to go put them on. Where do you sleep? I don't see any coffins." Josephine said. Her emerald eyes were blazing with fury.

"You know, I have always considered myself patient even understanding, but you…you are treading on thin ice. Ask yourself why you went to the fridge?" When she turned to face him, he was right there, pressing close to her body, with his fangs bared. His eyes had gone from sapphire, to what resembled black onyx with a blue flame burning in the darkness of his eyes. Josephine stepped back in fear. Corin's anger softened when he saw her retreat. His anger dissipated as quickly as it came.

Corin reached out to her, bringing her back to sit. Sitting down she faced Corin and listened. "I am four centuries old and you mock me. No one has dared, in all my centuries to talk to me that way," Corin said with a curve to his rigid face. "Let me ask you something, does my coming to your house at night only, not shock you? Does the lack of food in my fridge, cupboards not send up a warning flag? You have no idea how much power I wield. It would be wise if you don't push me again," Corin said calmly. It wasn't a threat but a warning. "I am what I am. Believe it or not. The choice is yours. However, know this; without me, you cannot find Nawzir, you can be assured he will surely find you."

Josephine was still sitting in the chair, fear radiating from her pores. Her hands were now steadily shaking and fear holding her tightly in its grip, but she remained poised and defiant. Although her emerald green eyes told a different story, Corin looked at her and lowered his eyes in shame. Moving closer to her, he found that she was trying to stay out of his reach, shrinking herself into the chair as much as she could. He reached for her regardless; he brushed his hand against her cheek he pulled a lock of her auburn hair from her face. "I am sorry Josephine. I did not…I did not mean to…," he turned away from her giving her space. Corin walked to the window.

Mustering up her courage, she walked over to him. Placing her unsteady hand on his shoulder, she ignited a fire within him, his body tensed. The urge to pull her into his body and kiss her was overwhelming. He wanted to pull away, tried to pull away, but he couldn't. Turning he pulled her close that was the only warning she had. Corin bent his head and kissed her, before she could stop herself she found herself embraced in his arms and kissing him back. When Josephine finally had control of senses, she pulled away.

"I am sorry, Josephine," Corin said. "I am truly sorry about everything. I should never have allowed my anger to consume me, and I should never have kissed you." The sincerity in his voice tugged at Josephine's heart.

"It's okay." Josephine said in a soft voice. "It's okay." Although Josephine was still a little frightened and overwhelmed, something in her gut told her she would be alright and that Corin wouldn't hurt her. She couldn't very well get angry at the kiss because she had been feeling this odd sort of attraction to him ever since they first met. *This can't happen, get control Josephine, get control.*

Corin remained silent, admiring her courage, her strength, and her beauty. Josephine had auburn hair and the most beautiful green eyes. Her body was a medium build and her stomach was flat. The shirt she wore confined her breasts snuggly and her bottom was something to admire. Her skin was pale against her hair and eyes. Her full lips were moist with tears; they looked delicious. He wanted to taste her lips again. Hell, he wanted her more than anything he had ever wanted in his eternal life. *Could she be my salvation? Could she be one who will make me whole? Can she save me from my lonely existence? No you cannot have her, she is a widow. She is a human.* Corin shook off the thought. "I am pleased that you have not run from me yet, Josephine," was all Corin could bring himself to say.

"Corin, this is a lot to absorb, I always imagined that vampires could exist and now I know they do. Still, I have so many questions. For example, I don't understand why you think I helped you two years ago and I really don't understand why this Nawzir character wants revenge on me. Is my family safe? And how does a vampire have a baby? I always thought vampires were soulless creatures. Then again I thought they were also myths told to scare young children," Josephine said thoughtfully.

"My real parents were human. My human father died before I was born and a vampire claimed my mother. When the vampire turned her, she died, as did the fetus she carried. When the essence of life is provided, all that has died regains life. Thus, I was born a vampire. Then the one who sired my human mother took me as his own. As for your aid to me two years ago, I do not know why you cannot recall the circumstances. Although I do have my own theories; I suggest you speak with Donovan: I believe he can help you." Josephine had a puzzled look on her face. Before she could ask more, Corin went into more details. "Last but not least… Nawzir. Nawzir wants to avenge the death of his brother. Rowen. The vampire I dispatched two years ago. The reason he fancies you, is because you lead me to Rowen. I suspect he has been watching you for some time. Now he is out for blood. Rick's passing was no accident. It was intentional, it was meant as an attack at you."

Josephine tried putting the information together in her mind. There were still gaps. "At least we don't have to go hunting for useless clues. Now that I know the details we can officially start hunting him right?" She said trying to put a lighthearted spin on things. "I would like to start fresh tomorrow. Right now I think I'd like to go home and get some rest." Josephine said tiredly.

"I will take you home; however, I must insist that you don't tell the others about me," Corin said. It was command.

"I will keep your secret, I promise." Josephine crossed her heart and smiled. Corin and Josephine left. The elevator ride was silent, just like the ride home. *Have I pushed her too far? Did I cross line?* Corin thought as they drove.

"Josephine you are the bravest woman I know. You have not fled from me, even knowing the truth. Events have been blocked from you. Yet you continue to trust in me. You are truly remarkable. I will protect you, your family and I will see to it that Nawzir and Jonah are brought to justice even if it costs me my life. You will return to your life as you once knew it." His last words struck at his heart. *I will be saddened to lose your company but I* will *happy knowing that you are safe.*

Turning her head Josephine faced him; really looking at him, she saw the heavy weight of sadness and loneliness. His eyes had also changed color: *almost gray,* she thought. She mentally noted that she felt some awkwardness at not having him around. *Chalk it up to a comfort zone, missy. You're not ready for anything else.* As they approached Josephine's home, she said, "I'll see you tomorrow. Same bat time. Same bat channel," she said, holding back her laugh.

Corin let out a laugh as he pulled into her driveway and parked the car. "Come inside, I'll call a cab," she said.

"There is no need. 'Till tomorrow." Josephine went to argue with him but when she turned to face him, he was gone. Walking to her front door, she was startled when Donovan opened it for her.

"Any luck?" Marcia asked.

"Nope. However, things are much clearer. Where's Mallory? The kids, are they sleeping?" Josephine asked.

"Mallory is gone and the kids are tucked in bed,"

Donovan said. "I'll be escorting young Marcia home, if you don't need me for anything else."

"No, that's fine. I'll see you tomorrow," Josephine said. They said their good-byes and good-nights. Josephine saw Donovan and Marcia to the door and watched them leave. Locking up for the night, she went upstairs. Checking on the Charlie, she kissed him on the cheek, closing the door as she left. She put on her p-jays and fell into bed, literally.

"Rick, I promise to fix this; your killer will be brought to justice. I promise, and Rick please forgive me for the kiss, I didn't mean to kiss back, it…it just happened," Josephine sighed. She closed her eyes that were filling with fresh tears, from guilt. From pain.

chapter 8

Donovan let himself in. He went upstairs, there was absolute silence, not liking the scenario; he began going upstairs Nanook and Timber immediately started barking. Josephine jumped up out of bed scared half to death; reaching for her PR-24 she rushed downstairs to face the intruder. Arm raised and ready to strike, Josephine was poised to strike.

"It's me, Donovan," he said collectedly. "I was worried when I didn't see anyone, he added for extra measure."

"Everyone is fine. I'll be down in a minute with the boys. Can you get some coffee going?" Josephine asked, half yawning and her heart beating a mile a minute.

"Sure, see you in a bit," Donovan said.

Josephine walked downstairs in her bedclothes, which wasn't more than a tee shirt and some fleece pajama pants. She had put on a sweater to cover up, as she wasn't fully clothed. "Morning," she said to Donovan.

"Morning," he replied. "Sorry for scaring you."

"That's okay, I guess I overslept," Josephine managed to say through her yawn.

"What are your plans for the day?" Donovan asked.

"Today I'm just going to spend time with the kids, me and Mallory actually. I'm just going to get ready and go out with them, I'm going to Island; Charlie is excited, he's never been on the ferryboat. Apparently, it has a small amusement park; I was thinking maybe we'd have a picnic there or something. You don't have to stay if you don't want to. I'll be coming back later this evening to meet up with Corin. Then we'll be going back out. I'll need you then, is that okay?" Josephine asked.

"I guess I could stick around, not much for me to do these days," Donovan said, grinning. "The movers will be bringing some of my stuff over and besides, when I dropped Marcia off last night I mentioned the movers to her and she offered to drop bye and help. I guess I'll hang with her." Donovan said, with a sly grin.

Josephine didn't miss the grin, quietly she smiled to herself. "That's a great idea. Can I get you some coffee? I know I need to wake up." Josephine said as she poured a cup for herself and boiled water to get food for Alex. "Did you eat?" she asked.

"Yeah, I picked up breakfast," Donovan replied. Just then, Charlie came bumping down the stairs on his bum, he ran into the kitchen and asked for some breakfast. Making himself useful Donovan went to the cupboard sorted through some cereal while Josephine fed Alex. He poured corn pop cereal into a bowl for Charlie with some milk. He placed the bowl down for Charlie. "Here you go buddy, enjoy," Donovan said, with a warm friendly smile.

Josephine finished feeding Alex and then prepared breakfast for both her and Donovan. As they both sat down and ate, Josephine rambled about what her plans for the day, she couldn't stand the awkward silence. Josephine and Donovan finished breakfast. Quickly clearing the dishes and loaded the dishwasher. She decided to run the dishwasher after her shower. Turning to Donovan she asked, "Would you mind watching the boys?"

"No problem," he gently picked up Alex from his seat and grabbed his blankets, taking Charlie by the hand they walked over to the living room. Charlie put on his movies while Donovan placed himself in the comfortable sofa cradling Alex. Josephine watched the whole scene and smiled to herself. *At least Charlie is living his life*, she thought to herself. She was glad both boys were too young to really understand what happened. *Alex will never know his father and Charlie has at least three years' worth of memories, soon to be forgotten, they were just getting to know one another. Stop it Josephine! She yelled at herself,* as she was reminded that she that she has started to cry. She wiped her tears away. She wasn't going to let sad thoughts get the best of her today. *Today I'm spending time with my kids; I'm going to enjoy my day.*

Josephine marched herself upstairs like a woman on a mission. She went to her dresser, quickly pulling out her undergarments and tank top. Then she walked over to her armoire and pulled out some faded jeans along with a button-up sweater. She went into the bathroom, ran the water, so that her shower would be a little hotter than normal. When it was just right, sliding off her p-jays and hopped in. She was out in fifteen minutes; washed, dried and dressed. She brushed her teeth and then she pulled her back into a ponytail. She put on her running shoes and rushed downstairs.

Walking into the kitchen, she busied herself preparing bottles for Alex and two juice sippy cups for Charlie. She checked the diaper bag over once, ensuring that she had extra clothing for both boys and lots of diapers and at least three blankets for Alex. When she was satisfied that she had everything, she made sure to put her cell phone in her purse. She put both her purse, diaper bag by the front door, and then grabbed the stroller. She loaded the car first knowing that she had too much stuff to lug back and forth. Plopping herself down in the kitchen chair she took a breather. Charlie was waiting excitedly by the door, jumping excitedly. Donovan was standing close to the door with Alex. "Okay now I'm ready," Josephine said, with a little laugh. "Charlie go pee," she said taking Alex from Donovan. "We're going to leave," she said.

Charlie shrugged his shoulders and went upstairs. When he was done, he came sliding down the stairs on his bum with his pants and underwear wrapped around one leg. Josephine laughed out loud when she saw him. Handing Alex to Donovan, She kneeled down and dressed Charlie. "Gimme your feet Charlie," she said, as she put on his running shoes. With Charlie all ready to go, she took Alex once again. "I'm gone Donovan, if you need anything call the cell." Donovan watched as Josephine got both boys in the car then got in. Donovan heard the engine start and was about to close the door, when he heard Josephine call out to him.

"Thanks for the help Donovan, and have a good one."

"No problem. You guys go out and enjoy the beautiful weather. You all need a nice break. I'll see you when you get home," Donovan said, as he waved to her.

"Thanks again," she pulled out of drive way and reached

into her purse grabbing her cell. She dialed Mallory's number. When she heard Mallory's voice she said, "I'm on my way to get you. We're still on for the Island right?"

"Yes, of course, I wouldn't miss it," Mallory said.

"See you soon," she hung up the phone. "Charlie, close your eyes baby, and try to get some sleep, it's going to be a long day."

"Close my eyes? I go sleep okay," Charlie said.

Josephine glanced in the rear view mirror and smiled. Charlie was sleeping within five minutes. She could tell that without even looking at him by the way he was breathing. While driving, Josephine mulled over the events that had recently occurred. She was deciding whether she should tell Mallory about Corin. She had to tell someone. She trusted both her friends with her life; she just wasn't sure who would be able to handle the weirdness of the situation right now. *Marcia is occupied with someone else right now. Donovan. If I tell Marcia that would open up another opportunity for Corin's secret to get out. I can't risk that happening right now. Mallory on the other hand is single and has no immediate complications in her life.* After considering these things, she decided that telling Marcia would have to wait. *The remaining question is, do I betray Corin and tell Mallory? Yes. Someone has to know, just in case something happens to Corin and me. Corin, I hope you can forgive me, I have a family to worry about and...*Josephine's thoughts were cut off. Corin was inside her mind.

It is okay Josephine. Tell Mallory but no one else.

"How are you doing this, and how are you in my mind?" Josephine asked, puzzled.

My kind has telepathic powers; normally we cannot

communicate when we are in regeneration sleep, but you have managed to awaken my senses by talking to me and directing your thoughts to me. Your ability is strong.

"Ability?"

Never mind, we will talk about that at a better time.

"Well, now that I have your attention, I'm going with Mallory to the Island, I will be a little late getting back to my place, so don't worry if you arrive before I do." Josephine said out loud as if she were speaking to him right there.

That will be fine. Do you trust Mallory; I mean trust her with my life?

"I trust her with mine. Your secret is safe, I promise. I'm going to tell her everything. The dream. Nawzir. Everything. If I were to die today, she would be taking care of my children. You'll see, everything will be fine," Josephine said, she sounded as if she was justifying her decision.

I trust your judgment Josephine; remember Mallory can be the only one that knows. Corin's communication was sounding weak to Josephine, her heart sunk.

"Corin?" Pause. "Corin." Pause. Josephine's heart rate sped up.

I must sleep, do not worry.

Josephine continued driving, when it hit her, she forgot to drill Donovan. *Damn, it'll have to wait, now I have more questions to add to the list.* Charlie and Alex were sound asleep as she pulled into the Tim Horton's drive thru, she ordered two large double double coffees with the big box of Timbits. She pulled up to the cash window and gave the cashier what was owed. Taking the change Josephine put it her coat pocket. She pulled out and headed for Mallory's place. Josephine pulled into Mallory's driveway, she spotted Mallory locking her door and making her way to van. Josephine rolled down her window.

"Hurry up," Josephine said with a loud heartfelt laugh.

"Thanks for thinking of me," she said with a grin. As Mallory settled in and saw the coffees. Mallory moved Josephine's purse and pulled her cell out, she placed it in the basket that was located between the two seats. "Lets' get going missy," Mallory said as she pulled the belt across her.

"Off we go," Josephine said as she pulled the van into gear and backed out. Josephine glanced back at the boys, making sure they were still sleeping. Then she turned to Mallory. "I have to tell you something...something that you will find very hard to believe. You're going to have to trust what I say," she said.

"Ah...okay," Mallory replied.

"One more thing, you have to promise to keep this to yourself. If you can promise that then I'll tell you, if you can't then this conversation has to end. I really mean it, what is said here and now, has to go to your grave with you," Josephine said.

"First of all you know you can tell me anything. Anything at all. I swear that whatever you have to say will remain between the two of us until I die. I promise you," Mallory stated with complete honesty in her voice. Mallory looked at Josephine her amber eyes expressing concern.

"Are you sure?" Josephine asked her one more time. "This is big, really big. It's a big burden and under no circumstance you can't say anything. Someone's life depends on this." Josephine added.

"I promise you, Josephine, nothing that you say to me

today will leave this car," Mallory re-affirmed. Mallory looked at her, concern increasing in her eyes.

"Okay, here goes nothing. The man that killed Rick, his name is Nawzir and Corin has been hunting him for several months now." Josephine began; she stopped because Mallory had interrupted her.

"That is it? That's your big secret?" Mallory said teasingly.

"No, let me finish. Nawzir is a vampire. He has been on a killing spree all over the world. Corin's been tracking him. That is the reason he's here, he saw Rick's story on the international news while he was in Colorado. He recognized his 'foes' handy work," Josephine said as she made the quotation signs with her hands. Sighing, Josephine continued, "Brace yourself, there's more, Corin's also a vampire. When I was attacked the other night, Corin rescued me from this Nawzir person," she said as she gave Mallory sideways glance to gauge her reaction. Mallory looked like she was about to burst out in laughter. "Yup, I felt the same way, believe me." Josephine said.

"Vampires, eh? That's a new one," Mallory said in an almost ridiculing way.

"I'm very serious. Last night when Corin and I left, I told Corin that I knew he was holding something back from me. Long story short we hit Nawzir on the way back to his place," Josephine was interrupted. Again.

"Oh my god, you hit a man and kept driving?" Mallory said stunned.

"Let. Me. Finish. Please. I know this is a lot to take in but just listen. As I said I hit the guy, I got out of the car and was going to see if he was okay and was forced by Corin back into the car and he drove back to his place. When we got to

Corin's place, he told me everything. How he found me, why he befriended me, even why he saved my life. When I still didn't believe him, he *made* me go to his fridge and open it. Sure enough I saw bags and bags of blood. When I still didn't believe him he turned into his vampire self in front of my eyes," Josephine said calmly.

"Were you scared? What did you do?" Mallory asked, sounding as if she were buying into what she was hearing.

"I was. Pause. Angry to say the least. When I finally calmed down, he explained the situation; why Nawzir is here. In a nutshell, Corin really is a vampire and so is Nawzir. Nawzir is coming after me Mallory, and for Corin. He wants revenge for the death of his brother, which I apparently caused," Josephine stated as she looked at her friend with fear in her eyes. "I'm telling you this, because you need to know the situation in case anything happens to me. Corin can't protect me during the day. Nawzir is strong, there's no way that I could defend myself if he should attack me. Should something happen to me, you will have to get in touch with Corin and tell him what the situation is. Are you up for that?" Josephine asked.

Mallory was stunned and not sure what to say or believe. Still absorbing all that Josephine had said, Mallory looked at Josephine. She had reached a decision. Josephine was more than her friend, she was family. No matter how bizarre this sounded, she would take her word. "I'll let Corin know if anything happens, and I'll keep your secret, if I were to say anything, people are going to think I have gone off the deep end. I'm not sure if I believe the whole thing, but you are my friend and I have to trust that what you say is true," Mallory said with a hint of uncertainty in her voice.

Josephine pulled into the parking lot for the ferry tour to the Island, just as the boys woke up. "Were here," Josephine said. "Mallory thank you for believing in me and listening to what I had to say. Thanks for not having me committed," Josephine said laughing.

Josephine parked the car and then she and Mallory got both boys and the diaper bag out of the car. Josephine lifted the hatch to the trunk of the van and pulled out the stroller. She opened her purse and pulled out her wallet, and then she put the purse along with the diaper bag in the bottom of the stroller. She made sure to have a bottle and a sippy cup handy, the cup holder on the stroller. She put the cell phone on her belt clip and off they went.

They stood in line and waited until they reached the booth. Josephine paid for the round trip on the ferry. They entered the waiting area and waited for the ferry to arrive. As the ferry approached Charlie's excitement grew, his laughter echoed as he jumped up and down. Josephine saw such happiness and such innocence, all at once. It made her smile, to see her son so happy. Then the sad thoughts intruded once again, as her mind wandered. *Is he thinking about his daddy? Does he want his father to be here with him?* The thought weighed heavy on her mind, shaking off the intrusive thought she refocused her mind. She was determined to have a good day. Putting on her bravest smile she buried her thoughts deep inside; she didn't want Charlie to notice her sadness. With a deep sigh, she knew she succeeded Charlie didn't pick up on her distress. Mallory on the other hand was another storey. Mallory couldn't help but pull Josephine close and give her a hug.

"It'll be alright. Remember time heals all wounds,"

Mallory whispered in Josephine's ear and squeezed her once more.

The ferry finally docked and all the people shuffled on in an orderly fashion. Josephine and Mallory headed for the front of the boat where they could get a good view across the lake. Charlie stood on the bars with Josephine behind him, holding him. He watched the water as the ferry started its engines and he laughed out with glee when the boat started to move. The ride was short, about fifteen minutes. They all got off the ferry and headed for the amusement park. Josephine paid for tickets and Charlie ran to the first ride he saw. Josephine and Mallory followed, both women enjoying all of Charlie's happiness.

Lunchtime came and went, as did the rest of the day. Charlie was exhausted and, by the looks of both women, so were they. The sun was starting to set; Josephine decided that now would be a good time to start heading home. Josephine the boys, along with Mallory, started heading towards the dock where the ferry was waiting. Once they boarded, they found some seats and just waited patiently for everyone to get on. When the ferry was at full capacity, the engines started to rumble beneath their feet. The ferry started heading for the main Island. The ride was short, but it seemed like an eternity, only because everyone was exhausted. Josephine and Mallory were beat and Charlie looked as though he was going to pass out right there on the ferry. Josephine couldn't wait to get home, then she remembered that she would be going back out. *Oh well at least the boys will be safe at home.*

The ferry docked and they all got off and headed towards the exit gates. At the van Josephine loaded the kids in. Charlie was asleep as soon as he hit the pillow on his chair: Alex had been asleep since the ferry ride. Josephine opened the hatch to the trunk and put in the stroller, Mallory put in the diaper bag. Josephine closed the trunk door and caught her breath. She felt a clenching of her stomach. *Odd, I only feel like this when something is going to go wrong.* Poking her head around the van to speak to Mallory she saw fear staring back at her.

"Mallory?" Josephine asked, trying to keep her panic in check. Her friends look wasn't helping.

"Behind you," was her only warning.

"What?" Josephine said as she spun around. Josephine's blood went ice cold through her veins when she heard a man's' voice.

"I believe she is referring to me," the man said. Josephine immediately recognized the voice.

"You!" Josephine tried to sound calm. "You're him!" Josephine tried to side step. It was too late, Nawzir raised the bat and swung at her head. As darkness started to claim her, the thought of not seeing her children took over. The tears filled her eyes; they were already falling when she succumbed to the dark depths. Nawzir caught Josephine's limp body and flung her over his shoulder. He traced over to Mallory, baring his sharp fangs.

"Be sure to tell Corin I have his woman. Make sure to tell him that Nawzir has her and I am waiting for him. Tell him not to waste too much time; Josephine does not have very much." With no further words, Nawzir disappeared before her eyes taking Josephine with him.

Mallory, still stunned ran to the driver's side. Thanking God that Josephine had a spare set of keys in the glove box she rummaged around in the glove box until she found them. Putting the keys into the ignition she started the car and pulled out. Mallory picked up Josephine's cell phone and searched for Corin's number. She dialed the number as quick as her hands could move. The phone rang several times with no answer. Banging her hands on the steering wheel she cursed...*Think Mallory! Think! That's it.* She dialed the number to Josephine's house. Donovan picked up.

"Donovan, hi it's Mallory," she said trying to sound calm. Is Corin there by any chance? She asked remaining as calm as her voice would allow.

"As a matter fact, he is," Donovan replied.

"Can you put him on please? Thanks." The next voice Mallory heard was Corin's.

"Hello," Corin answered, sounding a little confused.

"Corin? It's Mallory. Something has happened. I was told to tell only you. Josephine was taken by a guy calling himself Nawzir. He said to tell you he has your woman and that he's waiting for you. He also said Josephine does not have much time. One more thing, he hit her over the head with a bat. She's hurt, not sure how bad.

"Get here as quickly as you can." Corin hung up the phone.

Josephine, please forgive me for thinking that you were crazy. I believe you now. I only hope you'll be around for me to tell you. I'm so sorry. Mallory scolded herself. She looked in the rearview mirror to check on the boys. Both were asleep and doing fine. *What am I going to tell Donovan and Marcia?* Mallory wondered to herself as she continued driving. She began to pick up speed as the fear for her friend kicked in. Before she knew it, she was turning into Josephine's driveway. Corin was there waiting for her. Corin walked over to the van, opened the trunk and gathered the stroller. He said nothing. Mallory reached in and grabbed the boys, along with everything else. Once inside Mallory and Marcia brought the boys upstairs and put them to bed. As the women came downstairs, they heard the men talking.

"Mallory and I are going after Josephine. Donovan, Marcia, you will have to stay here and watch the boys. Do not call the police. They can't help," Corin stated. It was a command and Donovan knew it. Donovan nodded. He also knew that he had to contact Manny and let him know what was going down; he also had to let him know about Corin. *At least the guy is on our side.* Donovan thought to himself.

"Shouldn't we tell Rachel, Josephine's mother?" Marcia asked.

"No. There is no reason to alarm her, we will get her back, I promise." Corin added. "Mallory, get your stuff together, we need to leave. Do you have a cell phone?" Corin asked.

"Yes. I've also got Josephine's," Mallory replied.

"Good. Keep them both, in case one dies," Corin said. Without anything further, he grabbed Mallory and the keys to the van. Donovan and Marcia followed to the door. Donovan was about to ask a question, he heard Corin say, "We will call if we need any help. Rest assured I will bring her back to her family." A vow that Corin intended to keep.

Donovan looked at Marcia with confusion written all over his face. They watched the van peel out of the driveway and closed the door. Marcia buried her head in Donovan's shoulder and cried until she couldn't cry anymore. "Charlie and Alex can't lose their mom and I can't lose another friend," she sobbed.

"It'll be alright. Something tells me that Corin knows what and whom he's up against. He'll bring her back I'm sure of it," Donovan said, trying to be as soothing and comforting as he could. They walked into the living room and sat on the couch. Donovan held her close, as he prayed in silence for Josephine's safe return.

chapter 9

Corin and Mallory sped away, Corin was deep in thought; the one thought that weighed heaviest on his mind was how he was going to find her. He had no way of communicating with her, and from what he understood of the situation, she was badly hurt. *I should have taken her blood, and then I could have found her, no matter where she was being held;* silently he cursed himself. His second concern was getting Josephine out; as long as Jonah was not in the picture, it would not be too hard. Mallory could get Josephine while he dealt with Nawzir. Mallory sat there in silence; feeling numb and overwhelmed. She was trying to get a handle on everything that just happened. The tears were filling her eyes so rapidly that she had to wipe her eyes in order to see. She was confused, angry and she wanted answers. Demanded answers.

"Corin, Josephine told me about you and this Nawzir character, so I know what you and Nawzir are. What I don't know and what Josephine didn't know is why he is after her?" Mallory said through angry sobs. "I want answers. I want them now. I want to know how in the hell did he pull that disappearing act? What I need to hear from you is how we are going to get Josephine back. Answer me dammit! Tell me why this is happening? I don't understand." Mallory pleaded as she slammed her hands against the steering wheel, tears steadily flowing. Pause. "Help me understand."

Corin stayed focused on the road, he didn't want to see Mallory's pain, and it was emanating from her so much that he was becoming enveloped in it. "Nawzir is after Josephine for revenge. He believes Josephine helped me find his brother; this is true, what he does not know... is that I was *following* Josephine, *without* her knowledge. There are things, which are not my place to tell you. There are factors here that are unknown and the only person who can truly shed any light is Donovan. I am truly sorry, I cannot explain anymore. As for Nawzir's disappearing act, it is one of the gifts of being a vampire. Nawzir simply used his speed, we move too quickly for the human eye, we can and do appear as a blur, we call it tracing," Corin supplied. He watched Mallory looking for her reaction to the information he provided. "As for why this is happening...Well, the night that Josephine was attacked, I saved her from him. He would have killed her then and there but I intervened." Corin sighed. "Right now he is holding her and probably torturing her. He will undoubtedly keep her alive; she is bait. He has other plans, I am afraid. His ultimate goal is to take happiness from my suffering, while I watch helplessly as he kills Josephine." Corin lowered his head as if in defeat. "This is nothing more than a game to him. You have to understand that I have been hunting Nawzir for some time now. He has shamelessly killed humans for the sheer joy of it; he has tortured and fed off their fear and in doing so, he has called attention to my kind. This is unacceptable. My people want me to dispatch justice. When this is over, I will leave. Then Josephine and her children can live normal lives," he said, careful not to show his emotions.

Mallory absorbed what he said and then anger took her over. "So my best friend's life is just a game. What is it to you to Corin? What do you get out of this?" She snapped.

The words cut through Corin and stung him. "Listen very carefully to me, Mallory, if this was nothing more than a game, I would have let Josephine die the night Nawzir first attacked. I came here to stop him and that is what I intend to do, with or without you. As for Josephine, I care very much for and her well-being. Josephine must live. Pause. The night I saved Josephine, she came under my protection. By my peoples' standards that responsibility is taken most seriously. It's unfortunate that you have had the misfortune of encountering one bad vampire do not judge us all and do not make the mistake of passing judgment on me. I am nothing like Nawzir and *unlike* him, I care about all life. I will save Josephine; even if it costs me mine. When that time does come you won't be able to stop me," Corin spat back at Mallory through gritted teeth.

Mallory lowered her head in shame for her misjudgment. When she looked at him all she saw was raw anger, there was worry in his eyes, and a sadness that she couldn't quite place. In spite of herself, she found that she was relieved. "I'm sorry," she said in a low voice. "By the way how will we find her?" She asked.

"From the blood of her head wound," Corin answered. "That is the only way I can track her. I just hope that we can find her in time," he said in a low voice.

"Yeah her head was bleeding a lot," Mallory confirmed. Are you sure you can track her?" she asked curiously.

"The first night we met, she was injured in the attack with Nawzir, she was bleeding as well. I have committed her scent to memory, everyone smells different," Corin said. "When we get close to her, I will be able to pick up the scent. That is all I can do for the time being until I can connect to her telepathically. However, time is not our friend as you can see the sky is starting to lighten. I must sleep during day to maintain my strength, I will take cover in the back, but I must have a heavy blanket, one that is impenetrable. We will stop by my place before leaving," Corin said, it was a statement.

"Fine, let's do this" She was frustrated and anxious; Corin could hear it in her voice. "Here's a stupid question; how do we know which way to go, when we leave?" Mallory asked.

While Corin directed Mallory to his place, he thought about the question she had just asked. *Where are we going to start looking?* He thought to himself. He was in deep thought when she looked over at him. She left him alone.

"Um hum, this is your place right?" Mallory asked. Luckily, it was not too far away from Josephine's because they certainly had a fair share of driving to do and not a whole lot of time to waste.

"I believe Nawzir took her somewhere on the outskirts of the town," Corin announced.

"Why would you think that?" She asked, surprised by the comment.

"It makes the most sense. He knows I can pick her scent up, he also is aware that within the city, he would be limited to what he could do, because I can track him.

I believe the best place to head is towards the city limits; there are mountains and caves there. It is where I would go," Corin said, his face was expressionless and he looked like the predator that he was.

"It's my best friends life I'm trusting you with, you better be right for all our sakes," Mallory said calmly, underneath it was a warning.

"Do not worry, Nawzir wants me as much as he does Josephine, when I am close he will let me find him," Corin stated. Corin's building looked inviting from outside. She drove into the underground parking and parked. "I will be but a few moments, do you want to come up or stay in the car?" He asked.

"I'll wait in the car, if you don't mind," she replied.

Corin left, once inside he headed right to the fridge, grabbed a surplus of blood and put them in a cooler. Then he grabbed one, pierced it with his fang and drank from the bag. Finishing the pouch, he discarded the empty one. He went to his room and took the drapes off the windows. These would block any sunlight that would penetrate the car windows. After he was done with the drapes, he went back to the kitchen with his duffel bag; he crammed everything in. He looked around once, turned out the lights and locked the door behind him.

Mallory was in the car fidgeting with the radio, trying to find some music that would calm her nerves. She didn't even realize that Corin had come back. When the door opened, he frightened her so much that she practically jumped out of her seat. Corin let out a hearty laugh and then excused himself. "I am sorry," he said, "I didn't mean to frighten you."

Mallory just laughed and tried to hide her embarrassment. "That is okay, I wasn't paying attention, that's all."

"Mallory, I will drive, you need some sleep because once I can no longer drive it will be up to you," Corin said. Mallory got out from the driver's side and Corin got in, when Mallory was in her seat, he pulled out. Heading north, and driving nonstop Corin felt the pull of dawn, he was starting to feel lethargic; the regeneration sleep cycle was starting. He drove into the morning until just after sunrise for as long as he could before pulling over. Touching Mallory lightly on her shoulder he jostled her awake. Mallory lifted her eyelids and the blinding beams of the sun hit her. She jumped up in her seat. "Corin?! Corin?!" She said in panicked voice. Concern was etched in her voice... "What are you doing? Are you okay? The sun? It's out, you're...you're," she trailed off.

Mallory, calm down, I am okay. I am able to tolerate the early morning sun, I woke you because now, I need to sleep. You need to drive," Corin said. Mallory could hear the sleepiness in his voice. Since there is no actual trunk, I am going to put myself on the floor between the seats. I am going to cover myself to shield me from the sun light that gets through the windows. I am not sure if we will reach the city limits before dusk. If you do, pull over in a secluded place and get some sleep. I have to be awake in order to sense Josephine. If she summons me in my sleep I won't be able to do anything for her or you, so please don't proceed until I wake," Corin said gently, but it was a command and she heard it.

"Sure, fine. If we reach the city limits before you wake up, I'll pull over and wait for you," Mallory replied. "Now get in the back will you, your no use to me or Josephine if you're baked," she tried to sound as if she just teasing, but underneath the humor, she was dead serious.

Corin traced from the front of the van to the back, rather than risk the sun by getting out. A little startled by the move Mallory kept her cool, she waited in the drivers' side until Corin was comfortable. He placed himself on the floor between the front and middle seats. He pushed the chairs back as far they would go. Once in place, he pulled the heavy drapes over him, concealing every inch of his body. Mallory glanced at him on the floor and all she saw was a black drape, it reminded her of a tarp. "Are you ready to go?" She asked.

"Yes. Mallory please be careful," Corin said in a barely audible voice as he succumbed to his regeneration sleep.

Mallory pulled back out onto the highway and continued driving. She was tired and she was hungry. She had not eaten since the lunchtime the day before; when this nightmare started. She kept driving until she saw a Tim Horton's; going through the drive-thru, she ordered the breakfast meal and a large coffee. She pulled back out onto the road and continued to drive. Once she was finished eating, she pulled out her cell phone and called Marcia and Donovan to let them know what was going on.

※※※

Meanwhile, back on the home front, Donovan was preparing breakfast for the kids with a nice pot of fresh, brewed coffee for both himself and Marcia. Neither of them had slept well last night, between watching the kids and being worried about their friends. Donovan had managed to comfort Marcia and keep her calm and prevented her from doing anything rash. Charlie was up early, he came bombarding down the stairs. He poked his head into the kitchen, only to find that his mommy wasn't around.

"Where's mommy?" Charlie asked.

Marcia and Donovan looked at each other, unsure of what to say. "Charlie, honey mommy had to do something important so she asked Donovan and I stay with you," Marcia replied, it was the only thing she could think of.

"Okay, Auntie Marcia. I watch a dvdv okay," Charlie blurted out as he ran to the television.

"Did you go to the bathroom?" Marcia asked.

"No, I don't. I'm fine!" Charlie yelled back.

"Well before you watch the dvdv you have to go pee," Marcia said more authorative like.

"Okay, you have to hep me, I go upstais," Charlie called as he ran from the living room and started climbing the stairs.

Donovan stood there laughing at the conversation that the three-year-old was having with a grown woman. Marcia made a sour face at Donovan, as she got up from the table and followed Charlie upstairs. When she reached the top, Alex started to cry.

"Donovan, I need a hand up here?" She called down to him. Donovan was more than happy to oblige, he marched himself upstairs, went into Josephine's room and picked Alex up. He felt a little awkward going into Josephine's room, after all this room was his employer's personal place. Donovan dismissed the thought, he knew Josephine very well, and after all, they had worked together on many occasions, hell she was like family, his little sister. *Okay so Josephine couldn't remember, minor problem. In any case, he would or should be considered family after all that has happened.* Donovan shrugged off the awkwardness and picked up little crying

Alex, he held him close, comforting him. Marcia stood in the doorway, watching from behind. She couldn't help but notice how gentle and nurturing he could be. She smiled, then guilt crept in, *my best friend is missing, this is not the time or the place.*

Marcia, Donovan, Charlie and Alex all went downstairs. Charlie returned to the television, Donovan, along with Alex and Marcia, returned to the kitchen. Marcia quickly made Alex a bottle mixed with some pablum. Breakfast was dealt with. Marcia tidied up while Donovan took care of the kids. After she was finished Marcia came through to where Donovan was, she sat down.

"What are we going to do; the day is half over, Charlie will be expecting his mommy. The rest of the day is going to be a different ballgame," she said worriedly. Donovan could not only hear the worry in her voice he could see the worry in her eyes. Right now, Marcia was wishing she could be Alex, being three months old was a blessing in disguise, he didn't understand much. *What were they going to do if Josephine didn't get home? What's going to happen if Josephine does die?* Marcia thought. She was scared. Really, really scared. Silently, she prayed, hoping that someone would hear.

※※※

Mallory had been driving most of the day. She had been stopping every now and then to catch a catnap. Her eyes were heavy, not to mention burning from crying. *We're going to get you back Josephine,* Mallory kept the thought at the front of her mind. She needed to keep herself focused. She made brief stops so she wouldn't pass the city limits; remembering what Corin's words were. Her eyelids were half closed; she was so tired. *Maybe now is a good time for food,* she mused. Pulling over at the next exit, she got out of the van and she stretched. She walked into the restaurant, keeping a very close eye on the van. Mallory ordered food, and went back to the van. She leaned against the door instead of getting in. Stretching her arms above her head, she bowed her back. "Ah, that felt good," she said out loud." The breeze felt cool against her face, it was refreshing. Nice. Mallory noticed the sky darkening. Soon, Corin would be up. *Soon, I can sleep,* she thought. Getting back into the van, she heard the cell phone ring. Grabbing the phone, she looked at the number to see who was calling.

"Hello, we are close to the city limits. Everything's good. Yes, I have eaten and yes, we've taken turns driving. Listen, I have to go, but I'll call when we find Josephine, or if we need backup. Before I go though, how are the boys doing? Has Charlie realized that mum is not there? Well, smart thinking, keep up the good work, we'll be in touch soon." Mallory hung up the phone.

Starting the van, Mallory pulled out and headed back towards the road. Shortly after she left the stop, Mallory heard rustling noises coming from behind her. She glanced quickly at the drape that covered Corin and saw it come off. "Sleep well?" she asked.

Corin traced to the front seat, he looked out the window, then at her. "I thought we agreed to stop when we were at the city limits," he said calmly, trying not letting his agitation show.

"We're barely past the city limits; besides you were sleeping and I couldn't pull over on the shoulder," Mallory said defiantly.

Corin disregarded her tone; under normal circumstances, this would have angered him, right now there were more pressing issues to deal with at the moment. Josephine. Corin reached for the conveniently placed duffel bag, in the front seat. He ripped open the pouch with his fang and drank. Discarding his garbage when he finished. "I can drive now if you want. You need to get some sleep." He said. Shrugging her shoulders Mallory pulled over; happy to relinquish the chore. She was exhausted, she wanted to crash. She pulled to the side and got out of the car, Corin slid over to the driver seat and she settled into the passenger seat.

"Let me know when we're there," then sleep claimed her.

Nawzir awoke from his regeneration sleep and went to look in on his guest. Before he opened the door, he scanned the room to see if there had been any change, not that she could have done much. He sensed nothing but he still used caution when opening the door.

Josephine was lying down on the bed with hands and feet in shackles. The blood had dried on her face and started to scab over the cut. She was still unconscious, she couldn't remain like that. He needed her to be awake so that she could call to Corin and bring him here. Nawzir stalked over to his little stash of supplies, pulling out a bottle of water he brought it back to where she was. He walked over to Josephine and he took a moment to gawk at her body, he admired it. He liked the way she looked, the way she cared for others, so much so that he would have taken her for himself, had he not wanted to kill Corin and her. As he watched her motionless body, he imagined what it would be like to have her thighs wrapped around him. He imagined what it would be like to taste her, what it would be like to hold her down, and forcibly, take her. His lips curved at the thought. His fantasies were enticing him so much, that his eyes were starting to change; he could feel the blood rushing to his shaft, awakening him. He hadn't taken a woman in long while, the taste of fear on his tongue, it enticed him more. His mind brought him back to reality; he knew he had to get away from her. He threw the cold bottled water on her face.

Josephine's body jumped from the shock, she quickly realized that her legs and arms were strapped down. "You. Bastard. What do want?" she said through gritted teeth.

Her anger, her strength brought a pleasure to him that was unexpected. Her eyes flashed with such emotion, it made him tingle all over. "It is good that he wants you," Nawzir said. "It will make my taking you so much sweeter, and I will take you over and over, while he watches. Perhaps I will take before he comes just for kicks," he said with a vicious smile. "Now, be a good little girl, and summon him for me."

"Go to hell you son of a bitch! I'll do no such thing." Josephine spat out.

"It will be interesting to see how long you will hold out," Nawzir said as he walked towards her. With one quick slash, he tore at Josephine's shirt and the material fell to her sides. Nawzir ripped off the remainder of the shirt. Twisting, and turning, Josephine was yelling obscenities at him. Nawzir laughed. He moved his hands over her partially exposed breasts, making Josephine's body cringe; then his hand slid down her stomach past her waist. He undid the button to her jeans, which lead to the undoing of the zipper. Nawzir's hand moved over her lace panties. He took enjoyment in her revulsion.

"Are you going to summon my pet or shall I continue," he asked with an evil grin. *I can do this all day, until you are completely exposed, I don't mind in the least.*

"Go. To. Hell." Was all Josephine said.

"With pleasure, my dear," Nawzir said as he continued to pull down her pants, leaving her lower body partially exposed. Nawzir bulldozed into her mind to see what her fear was. He was mildly surprised to find that she had a block up, as pitiful as it was. Bypassing her block, he found what he was looking for. Josephine knew the instant he did, as a slow maniacal, evil smile came across his face. His smile told her that there was a retribution coming. Without a word, he exited the room.

When he came back, there were two items in his hands. A knife and something, that looked like a broomstick handle. Josephine forced her throbbing head off the pillow, looking defiantly at Nawzir. Challenging him. Her eyes moved to his hands and the items they harbored; she turned a shade whiter, as she realized her worst fear was about to come true.

※※※

Slamming on the brakes, Corin brought the screeching van to a dead stop.

"What's wrong?" Mallory tried to say calmly.

"She's around here, I can smell her," Corin said. He opened his mind to trying to sense her; it proved difficult, her mental path was closed nevertheless he was able to find the connection. Although he was happy to sense her, his concern grew. *She is in danger. We have to find her.* Corin kept his thoughts to himself. Corin secured the van and ushered Mallory out. "We have to hurry, Mallory," Corin said, concern weighing heavily on his voice. With his senses and mind opened, they headed out. He hoped Josephine would reach out to him; as of now he was tracking her by scent alone.

"Can't you just fly us there or run really fast with me in tow? We'll never find her like this," Mallory said in frustration.

"It is not that simple, I cannot just simply locate her. Her mental path is very weak and I suspect she is holding off on calling me, because it is a trap. Her scent is all I have to work with; it is really weak. We have to do this the hard way. Had I taken blood from her I could have easily tracked her, that however is not the case. I am sorry," Corin explained. Mallory and Corin kept going, plowing through the bushes; the forest seemed endless.

"Corin, I'm getting tired I can't keep up this pace," she said. She was about to give up, Corin sensed her defeat.

"No, we must continue, Mallory," it was a command, not a request. Frustrated, Mallory followed. It seemed like they had been walking for hours, when they finally reached the river. Corin was able to pick up Josephine's scent. It was stronger. "Josephine is close by," he said. Mallory looked at him and rolled her eyes.

"You've already said that," Mallory stated. Corin heard the frustration in her voice.

"I know you are having difficulty trusting me and I know you are tired; you just have to trust me a little longer. I can assure you that Josephine is very close," Corin stated confidently. They were walking along the shoreline when an abandoned building in the distance caught his attention. Corin switched directions; heading towards the building. Josephine's scent filled his lungs as they closed the gap. "She is in there." Corin pointed at the building. Mallory quickened her pace to try to catch up to him.

Corin realized that the building was in fact a church, as they approached it. He used caution as they neared the old looking abandoned structure. Searching and scanning the area with his mind completely, Corin wanted to ensure Nawzir was not hiding. He wanted to locate Josephine, her blood trail was strong. When he sensed that they were alone, Corin slowed down, there was a trap waiting. Corin knew his enemy, Corin could be sharp and alert however, they would be useless if Nawzir was masking his presence. There was also Jonah to consider, *had he grown as competent as Nawzir?* Corin thought to himself. Mallory looked up to see where Corin was, she was trying to keep up, and keep a sharp eye but she was tired and had slowed down. A mistake she would soon regret.

From out of the recesses of the dark woods came a hand, not from the front but the back, it was against Mallory's mouth and the other around her waist. She was lifted from the ground, silently. Flailing her arms and kicking, she struggled, but the hands that held were very strong and felt like steel around her body. Managing to shift positions Mallory was now facing her captor. Fear settled in, when she realized that she was no longer on the ground. Mallory stopped struggling for concern of being dropped. Mallory tried to scream, but the last thing she felt was the sting of a fist made of steel connecting with her face and blood pooling in her mouth. Darkness was claiming her; *I failed you Josephine.* That was the last thought she had before darkness claimed her. Then there was nothing.

Corin was focused and was assessing the situation that he didn't realize that Mallory was no longer there. When he no longer felt her grabbing his clothing for support he turned to see where she was. He saw nothing. Corin muttered an oath, as his blood filled with fire. *Now I have two women to save.*

Corin, it would seem that you have trouble keeping your women by your side. You should really work on that. Nawzir said as his laugh echoed in Corin's mind. *If it is any solace to you, Josephine lives—for now. I prefer to have my fun with her first, she has such spirit— your Josephine. I will truly enjoy her suffering, the thought of it excites me, even now. Then when I am done, I will end her life, slowly, painfully.*

She is quite lovely you know—she has full, ripe, breasts. Strong thighs. A perfectly flat, smooth, stomach. Her skin is like satin, soft to the touch. The second female, although she is not my type, she will be dessert, after all Josephine is the main course. I can hardly wait to see you. Better come quick, your Josephine is barely hanging on to her life. To her credit though, I was completely entertained, watching her squirm, trying to fight me off, I got off on watching her, helpless and fearful of me. Secretly praying for a quick death.

Nawzir's words burned in Corin's mind. Anger overwhelmed him, causing his beast to roar to life, demanding control. Demanding retribution. He lifted his head to the heavens and roared, all the animals near and far scurried, running for cover from the predator that was among them. There would be no mercy. Justice would dispatched; *you had better hope you can best me 'old friend' because if you do not you will truly know my wrath.* Corin's words were sent back on the same mental pathway.

chapter 10

arcia and Donovan had tried to contact Mallory and Corin, since they hadn't heard from them. They had no luck. Donovan read Marcia's mannerisms, he could see that she was growing tenser. "Marcia, you need to calm down. If the boys see you stressed, it will add to the tension in here," Donovan said calmly, but underneath the cool facade, it was a demand.

"I know, I know. I can't help it. Something is gnawing at me, telling me that something has gone terribly wrong. Maybe we should call the police." Marcia said fidgeting with her hands.

"Marcia, let's be realistic here; we don't even know where they are. Let's give them some time to get in touch with us. If we don't hear from them in a couple of hours, we'll see what we can do," Donovan said in an even tone.

"What do we do in the meantime? Sit here and wait for something or nothing to happen?" Marcia retorted.

Donovan was getting a little agitated. He was not used to this sort of thing, dealing with antsy, worried people. He could remain calm, it was a discipline well learned. Marcia, on the other hand couldn't, she certainly didn't have the ability to, or the discipline needed to stay calm. With both boys entertained in the living room, Donovan grabbed Marcia by the hand. "I have something to show you," he said as they walked down to his apartment, she sat on the edge of his bed. . Donovan walked over to his computer and started plugging away. He stopped suddenly; grabbing his cell phone, he dialed a number, walking out of the room to make the call. Marcia tried to listen but only heard muffled sounds, frustrated she grumbled to herself and waited patiently. Donovan came back into the room and sat back down at the computer, he started to plug away at the keyboard. "I'm going to use some old security clearance to get access to a program that might be able to help pinpoint Mallory," he said, as if he were reading her mind. Marcia stretched her hands back behind her as she watched Donovan *Wow, he really is yummy.* She thought to herself. Marcia continued watching him and she found herself thinking about him in more than just a friendship way. *Hell, he's gorgeous. Great, what am I doing? Thinking about romance while my best friend is trapped somewhere. Smooth. Very smooth.* Angry with herself she got up, walked over to Donovan and looked at the screen, nothing she understood.

"I'm going up; I don't want to leave the kids to long. Call me if you find anything." She squeezed his shoulders and walked away. Stunned by her touch, Donovan stopped working. He watched as she walked away; his eyes followed the sway of her hips. He ground his teeth and let out a low moan. Marcia went upstairs to check on the boys. Charlie was watching a movie and Alex was sleeping. Marcia paced back and forth. *I should call Rachel, she should know.* Marcia picked up the phone and dialed Rachel's number. Rethinking what she was about to do she quickly hung up and flushed when she saw Donovan coming towards her.

He was holding a laptop. "I'm using the using the computer to try and triangulate on Mallory's location. I figured you needed some comforting, so I came up. It's great having these gizmos and gadgets. Don't you think?" He asked, donning a boyish smile. Marcia just stared at him. Relief flowing over her. All she could do was smile. "I don't think I can pin point her exact location but I can narrow it down. If we haven't heard anything by dawn, you and I will head out after them," he said, satisfied that he at least had some control. "We're going to have to drop the boys off. Do you know where her Mom lives? More importantly, do you have her number? We should probably give her a call now and make sure that she can baby-sit if we need her to."

"I'll call her." Marcia took the phone out from behind her back, trying not to look guilty; she pressed the speed dial button to Josephine's mom. "Rachel, hi, it's Marcia. I was wondering would you mind looking after the boys, overnight." Marcia was trying to choose her words carefully; she didn't want to accidentally divulge any information. If Rachel asked her about Josephine and her whereabouts, she was going to have to lie. "That's great," Marcia said. As an afterthought, Marcia added, "We may not need you to baby-sit, so I will call ahead if it turns out that we do. Thanks a bunch." Marcia put the phone down. "There, that's problem number one tackled. Now what?" she asked.

"We can only wait. On the bright side, I was able to get a location that should put us right around Mallory. I have some more stuff to check, so hang tight. Why don't you sit back and watch a movie with the boys, they should be heading off to bed shortly, right?" Donovan asked. "I promise, if anything happens, or something develops I'll let you know," Donovan added, as he stalked across the room to the door leading downstairs. "Hovering doesn't work for me when I'm working that is," he called back. *Feel free though to hover over me when I am not working and preferably, when I am lying on my back.* Donovan mused as he walked downstairs.

Marcia's mind wondered as she fed Alex; it wandered right to Donovan. He was much taller than she was; *and she pictured his face as it came closer to her, she could imagine his breath as he leaned for a kiss. Forget about him Marcia. Now is not the time,* she thought to herself. Alex's crying brought her out of her dream like trance; she was feeding the bottle to his nose. It obviously didn't do anything for Alex. She laughed when she realized what she had done. *Focus Marcia, focus.* Marcia had given Alex a bottle and a half by the time he had fallen to sleep. "Poor little guy, you were hungry, weren't you," she cooed. Charlie had crashed beside her on the couch. Carefully, Marcia put Alex in the playpen, making sure to cover him. She covered Charlie with a blanket, and then pushed the playpen up against the couch making a barrier so Charlie wouldn't fall off. Once they were secure she headed back downstairs.

Donovan finished his investigative work and was more than disappointed that he had found nothing of use. Shutting down the computer, he got up and headed upstairs. Whack! Marcia and Donovan collided Donovan turned out of his apartment and Marcia was already heading into his apartment with her face down.

"Shit. That frigging hurt!" Marcia complained.

"You think." His response was curt and sarcastic and was out of his mouth before he could censor his words. Glowering at him Marcia grabbed her nose in her hands; she couldn't stop the tears that were an automatic response from sliding down her face. Donovan looked at her, "Let. Me. See." He demanded. Marcia moved her hands from her face, meeting his gaze; she let him check her injuries, like a broken nose. Donovan, gently felt around her nose making sure there was no break. He looked down into her eyes, as he let his right hand caress her cheek to remove the tears. His hand ruthlessly made its way to her perfect, moist lips. Marcia closed her eyes; her heart was beating a mile a minute, his touch was exhilarating, and making her feel like a wanton prostitute. Donovan was fighting the urge to pull her into him and kiss the hell out of her. *Control. Control Donovan. Screw it.* He pulled Marcia closer and leaned in. He kissed her. Alex's cry separated them.

"I...er...have to go," Marcia said as she retreated backwards, still stunned by what happened. Donovan slid his fingers through his hair.

"Marcia. Marcia, I'm sorry...I shouldn't have done that."

"Shhh. Yes, you should've, it's was amazing." Like a shy teenage girl, she took off up the stairs, yet she wasn't a teenage girl, she was all woman. Marcia felt amazing; she had never, in her whole life, been kissed like that, ever. Hurrying up the stairs, she ran to Alex. Picking him up and cradling him, she grabbed his bottle off the side table and fed him. When Alex calmed down, she changed his diaper and then burped him. Alex went back to sleep, after what felt like an hour.

Embarrassed by his actions Donovan decided get back to work. Donovan started looking through the files that he had on Rick's death, he also had the case from two years ago, and they original fifty-year-old case. Donovan placed the files side by side wanting to compare them. The more he looked at the details, the more he started to feel a familiarity. The connection was there he just had to find it. His gut was telling him something. *Corin! God damn, it's Corin! He's the unknown factor.* He was hoping and praying that he was right, because if he was, then he knew Josephine had a fighting chance. As he sorted through the files, the lack of blood at each scene caught his attention; the ripped out-throat also grabbed his attention. Pouring through all the details over and over the same nagging fact came to light; Rick had no blood left in his body, and neither did the victim fifty years ago. Both victims had their throats ravaged. The little blood that remained at the each scene was from the neck wounds. There was no doubt in his mind that a vampire attacked Rick. Slamming his hands on the desk in frustration Donovan pushed his chair away from the desk. *There were no leads, no information as to who the attacker was. The question that remained was, if Corin was a good vamp or a bad one. Nawzir is here and no doubt with Jonah, so where does Corin fit into the puzzle? Is it possible he was the one who destroyed Rowen? If that's the case then Corin is as much a target as Josephine.*

Donovan ran the sequence of events over in his head, *how did Josephine put the pieces together? The hypnotism wiped her mind clean. There was no trigger placed in her mind to enable the memories to re- surface. This is a coincidence. It has to be.* Donovan sat back down at his computer, frustrated wiped his face taking the invisible sweat away. He started typing quickly; accessing all his old cases. As he whipped through them, one caught his attention. It was one that he solved. He looked at the details and it was like a smack in the face, a witness mentioned that a man had been lingering around. They description of the lingering person matched someone. Corin. Corin didn't look a day older. When he compared the composite sketch to the mental picture he had of Corin, he put one and one together. *Well I'll be damned,* he thought to himself. Donovan was now dealing with not two but three vampires.

Upstairs, Marcia was slowly drifting off, she was trying to watch a movie for some distraction. Repeatedly her head would snap up and startle her when she nodded off. She was still holding Alex, even though he was asleep. She needed to comfort him—she needed to comfort herself. When she finally snapped out of her dozing fit, she snuggled closer to Alex, murmuring in his ear, reassuring him.

Looking down at his sleeping face, she leaned in and lightly kissed his cheek. "Everything will be okay Alex; your mommy will be safe at home again soon. I promise." She looked him over once more, and then she got up and placed him gently in the playpen. Curling back up on the couch, she actually fell asleep, when Charlie's scream woke her. "Holy shit" she said scrambling to a sitting position. "Charlie? Charlie? It's okay baby, what's wrong? Come here." She patted the seat next to her. "Come sit here and tell Auntie Marcia what's wrong."

"I want my Mommy. I want my Mommy," Charlie cried.

Marcia reached out to Charlie, making him get up and come to her. She pulled him into the shelter of her arm and hugged him tight. She got comfortable on the couch and placed Charlie in the crook of her shoulder. "Its okay, Charlie, mommy will be back soon. It's okay." She rocked him until his sobs were calmed down and his body stopped convulsing.

She stayed with Charlie rubbing his back until he was sound asleep. Getting up she found a blanket and covered Charlie. She moved the playpen to the couch that he occupied and she checked on Alex once more before going downstairs. *Josephine I hope you are okay. No, I take that back, I know you are okay. You're too stubborn a woman to die, and you are one of the toughest people I know. Please be okay, please be okay. Your children need you. I need you. Please God, please let Josephine be safe.* Marcia silently prayed.

Marcia saw that the entrance to Donovan's place was open so she walked right in and confronted him.

"I don't understand Donovan, you kissed me. You seemed to like enjoy it, then you hide down here for hours. What's up with that?" Marcia said annoyed. "I want an answer." Waiting. Still waiting. When he didn't answer, she stalked over to the computer where he was sitting and put her hand on his shoulder. Surprised, he looked up at her.

"What are you doing here?" He said feigning ignorance.

"Looking for answers," she said with more attitude. "I also came down to see if you needed something." She said with a subtle, yet seductive smile.

Still ashamed of his earlier actions he avoided eye contact with Marcia. Although she managed to see him squirm a little, that made her smile. She also noticed that he was avoiding eye contact with her. That satisfied her on a completely new level; *at least I am not the only one who enjoyed that.*

"Food. I meant, do you want any food," she said, smiling back at him.

"I knew what you meant, I'm good for now. I'll finish up and be up in a bit. Why don't you go and get some rest, you should be resting," he said.

"I was, Charlie was scared and he woke up, scaring the crap outta me," she replied.

"Ah. From the looks of things it seems we will be taking a trip tomorrow, or should I say today," he corrected as he looked at his watch.

"Okay, so why do I have to leave, why can't I stay down here? And why did you minimize your screen? Something going on?

"No not really, just looking over some old case files, confidential, you know what I mean," he said lowering his eyes. *I hate lying. She'll never understand and if she does find out she'll think I'm nuttier then peanut butter.* "I'll be up in a bit. I just have to finish looking over some details," he said once again avoiding her eyes.

"Fine, I will just go and amuse myself 'somehow'," she said winking her eye.

"Now that is something I would like to see," Donovan muttered in a low voice. "You know what; if it's not too much trouble can you make me something, anything to eat. I'm going to log out and come upstairs."

"What do you want?"

"Surprise me," Donovan replied.

"Oh, you can bet your ass off I'll surprise you." Marcia had that mischievous look in her eyes. Donovan was in trouble now.

"I'll hold you to that," he said as he reciprocated her look.

Marcia walked out of the room smiling. *I could enjoy having that man around*, she thought to herself. She went upstairs and straight to the kitchen where she rummaged through the fridge and freezer to see what she could make. *Nothing extravagant* she thought to herself. *Just a little something to hold us over.* While Marcia made herself busy cooking, Donovan logged out. Before he had done that though he printed out the file that he didn't let Marcia see. When the printer spit out the last page, Donovan picked up the printed sheets and briefly skimmed over them ensuring that everything was there. Stapling everything together he folded them neatly so that he could stuff them into his jean pocket. *Poor Marcia, the woman is going to have a nervous breakdown when she finally sees what we are dealing with. Hopefully Corin will not have to do anything to instigate any questions. I should be so lucky.* Without even thinking, Donovan pulled out his duffel bag filled with weapons; he inspected the stakes that were made of wood and then he pulled out a sword. He wiped his index finger against the blade, ensuring that it was still sharp. The blade shimmered in the light. He put the stakes and the sword back into the bag and covered the weapons with a blanket. Taking a quick glance around room, he placed the bag by the door making sure he left nothing behind I *hope that I don't have to use these weapons on Corin.*

"Donovan," he heard Marcia calling. "Dinner slash breakfast is served," she said.

"I'll be right up," Donovan called out. Marcia set the table for two and then walked over to the fridge. She pulled out some milk and beer just in case Donovan wanted one. She also pulled out a couple of salad dressings. When Donovan came into the kitchen, she was just putting the dressing on the table.

"Have a seat," she said. She put corning ware dishes on the table, one was filled with cauliflower and the other one had white sauce. Then came another dish, it had scrambled eggs. Last and not least was a serving plate with pieces of steak on it. She had prepared food for two but she wasn't sure how hungry she was or how hungry Donovan was. She had decided to cut the steaks into chunks. Donovan looked at the plate of steak chunks. He cocked his head to side, and had a confused look on his face.

"What's this? He asked."

"Shut your mouth and just eat." She answered, but then she humored him and explained. .Marcia laughed as he rolled his eyes at her explanation. Donovan savored the moment, he enjoyed seeing her smile; it seemed like an eternity since he had seen a genuine smile from anyone, and not just a facade. It had been a long hard couple of days and he knew she was worried for her friends. *It'll be over soon, Marcia, I promise you,* he prayed he was right.

"This is really good! Do you do breakfast in bed as well?" Donovan asked as he continued to dig into his food.

"Wouldn't you like to know? Maybe I will tell you someday, if you play your cards right," Marcia said with a teasing laugh. Marcia and Donovan finished eating their supper slash breakfast and Donovan finished his beer, typical male. Marcia finished her milk. "That most definitely hit the spot," she said. "Are you full?" she asked, looking directly at Donovan.

"I am." He answered.

Marcia started to clear the dishes, she was just about done, when she glanced up at the time, she didn't have to say a word. Donovan saw everything she was thinking when he looked into her eyes.

"It'll be all right, I promise. Give it a couple of hours, that's all. We'll bring the kids to Rachel's at first light then head out. We'll get 'em back." He said confidently. Marcia nodded her head and padded quietly over to the living room, sitting on the couch she curled into a ball and hugged herself for comfort. Donovan took a quick glimpse of her and the boys and started to head downstairs. He reached the bottom of stairs, and stopped in mid step. Turning he looked up and he saw Marcia at the top of the landing.

"Stay with me please." Knowing he shouldn't stay he swallowed hard at the idea, he had to remain professional. He didn't want a more involved relationship, but looking at her he knew it might be too late. Taking a deep breath, he forced himself to calm down. Donovan went back upstairs. Marcia snuggled in as close as she could and fell asleep in his arms.

chapter 11

Frustrated at his own failings, Corin considered that he now had the lives of two women on his hands. Although, Josephine is, without a shred of doubt, an unacceptable loss, he also found himself concerned with Mallory's life. He could not let her die at the hands of Nawzir. Josephine would never forgive him or herself. He needed a plan, one that included the safe extraction of both women.

For the briefest of moments, he was unsure of himself and the abilities at his disposal. Josephine was injured, he was not even sure of the extent of the damage. He knew what atrocities Nawzir had committed, what he was capable of doing. His beast roared to life demanding retribution for both women. The more he thought things over the more he was convinced that Jonah was in the mix. He was convinced that this is how Mallory was stolen, he was sure of it.

Corin's mind screamed for Josephine to wake up, he needed information, needed to get an idea of what he was up against. Knowledge is how he would win; one thing he knew for certain, Nawzir and Jonah had indeed become more powerful. *I hope you can pull through this Josephine. If not, by yourself, then with my help. I will not let you die. I will do what I must in order for you to survive. God, forgive me. I need you.* Corin prayed as he quickened his pace towards the building.

Corin breathed deep, inhaling the night air. He was trying to steady himself. There was a battle going on, only it wasn't with Nawzir, it was within him. He was struggling, trying desperately to get a grip on his feelings. He could not afford to lose control, he needed control right now, if he was to save his friends. As his emotions tore through him, his beast fighting for control, demanding retaliation, Corin fought to reign in his beast. Eventually the beast succumbed, hiding beneath the surface.

Without thinking about his actions he called to Josephine again, he focused hard on her mental path that was so clearly ingrained in his mind, he used every ounce of strength he had. *JOSEPHINE WAKE UP! Please open your mind; I need to know if you are all right. Please. Dawn is approaching; it will be upon us in a few hours. I need to get you out tonight.*

Nawzir walked into the room where Josephine was laying barely clothed. Her body was tattered, covered with lacerations and bruises of multiple colors. All that remained of her clothing was her torn white bra which was now covered in scarlet streaks. Her panties had been torn, were now exposing some of her vulnerability. Her legs were still strapped and spread eagle, allowing him to take her at his leisure if he so desired. Her face was covered with dirt, and stained with blood and dried tears. The blood on her head was dried and the actual wound had scabbed over.

Across from her on the floor, Mallory was in chains; she was secured to a metal pole. The chains he had placed on her were fashioned so that they would expose her, making her vulnerable. Each hand in its own shackle, the chains were then linked in the middle by a padlock. A third chain then joined them, which was then attached to the pole. Mallory could see her friend, she was even able to come within an inch of her but she couldn't touch her. Nawzir smiled at his cleverness. Color flushed her face when she realized that she was useless and the evil that permeated the air sent shivers up her spine.

Nawzir was basking in the scent of fear and disgust that filled his senses. He stood in between both women and watched intently as Mallory struggled with all her might against the chains, he paid particular attention to her breasts, as they stuck out, inviting him to touch and perhaps taste them. Taking pleasure in Mallory's struggles, his sex instantly hardened.

"You bastard!" Mallory spit out as she fell backwards after charging at him. The chains reached their limit and yanked her forcibly back. When she regained her posture, she took a new tone on, realizing that he was turned on by her weakness and vulnerability. . "You filthy piece of shit, you are going to die a slow painful death for this," she said the words with such a coolness, that if he weren't a vampire, he might have actually been scared.

Nawzir decided to make use of this opportunity; the urge to feel her anger was just too tempting for him. With a gleam of malice in his eyes, he sauntered over to Josephine, who lay defenseless. He manhandled her breasts, inflicting pain where he could. Touching her body all over, while Mallory stood by helplessly and watched. Mallory struggled with her chains as she relentlessly tried to free herself.

"Leave her alone you vile excuse for a being! Get the hell

away from her!" Mallory shouted as she continued a losing battle to get free. Nawzir's enjoyment was evident. Mallory's vulnerability and Josephine's helplessness encouraged him. Nawzir, rubbed his crotch against the still Josephine, picking up the billy stick, he took it and started to rub it in between Josephine's thighs, getting ever closer to the juncture between her thighs. He rammed part of the stick in between the folds of bruised skin. Mallory's scream was deafening, she was like a raging bull, the chains pulled at her wrists, as she ripped into her own skin trying to get closer to him.

"Leave her alone, you bastard! You wanna play? Come and get some!" she shouted, her voice was raw and filled with hatred. Nawzir watched as her chest heaved in and out.

"I don't need Corin here, I can have all the fun I want with the two of you," Nawzir said as he let out a menacing laugh.

"What is your fuckin' problem? Don't get enough from willing women, so you have to take it forcefully from women who are helpless? You're pathetic." Mallory said in her haughtiest voice. Changing tactics.

Nawzir dropped the billy stick on Josephine's belly, stalked up to Mallory and threw her into the wall; he pressed his hard body against her pinning her. He wanted her to feel how hard he was. With Mallory pinned to the wall, he took his free hand and he ripped the front of her shirt open, obliterating her bra as well. Then he took it upon himself to sample her. Roughly, he grabbed her breasts, pinching her nipples until she wailed in pain. Releasing her breast, he licked the side of her face.

"You taste good," he remarked. "I think I will enjoy you, as well." He sneered.

He released Mallory and returned his attention on Josephine. He walked away from Mallory and attended his prize possession. Josephine. He undid his pants and got on top of Josephine, who was now semiconscious from all the commotion. Striking Josephine in the face, he made her mouth open, then with one smooth motion he stuck his fully erected shaft into her mouth, holding her mouth closed Nawzir thrust in and out, in and out as Mallory watched helplessly. His moans increased as he came in Josephine's mouth, and over her face. Satisfied he looked over at Mallory, and smiled maliciously. Mallory was stunned, numbed by what she had just seen.

"Mallory, please, keep up your retaliation. It turns me on, makes me feel alive, I enjoyed pleasuring myself with your friend, I can do it over and over," Nawzir climbed off Josephine and pulled his pants up. He walked over Mallory who now sitting on the floor, he yanked her up by her throat, then he took her mouth forcing her mouth to open to his as he fondled her bare breast until she winced in pain. He dropped her as if she was just a piece of garbage, and left the room. *Bastard! You are going to fucking die for this.* She kept her thoughts to herself afraid that any more outbursts would cause him to do more harm to Josephine who couldn't defend herself.

Josephine came out of her semiconscious state. She tasted a foreign substance in her mouth, when she realized what it was, she cried silently. Her body ached, the very core of her hurt. She licked her lips and the same substance that was in her mouth was on her face, she cried, letting sob escape her. Nawzir entered the room, he had two other people, some guy, and someone who looked like he was a vampire.

"You are awake," Nawzir said to Josephine. The man that Nawzir was holding in a tight grip looked scared to death. Everyone heard the whimpers that came from the man. In front of Mallory and Josephine Nawzir forced the man's head to the side.

"Let him go! You don't need him!" Mallory and Josephine cried simultaneously. Baring his fangs at the women, he bit the man. The man tried to struggle free but, Jonah came in from the other side. It was useless the stranger had no chance. When Nawzir and Jonah finished, they dropped the man to the ground. Nawzir, turned and looked at Josephine, whose eyes were wide with a combination of rage and fear.

"Not quite as good as Rick, but he did nicely."

Josephine turned her head, trying to shut out his words, she closed her eyes; tears sliding down her face, she managed to mutter "You son of a bitch." Mallory dropped to the floor, defeated, sick to the stomach. Her heart was aching for her best friend, as Nawzir spat out those horrible words. She wanted desperately not to look as terrified as she felt.

Corin, where are you? Please help us. He's crazy. I don't know what he will do to us next. Please Corin, I'm begging you. Josephine kept her thoughts to herself, praying, that Nawzir could not hear her pleas to Corin. Corin almost lost his footing when he heard Josephine's voice.

Josephine I am almost there. What has he done to you? Are you ok? Is Mallory ok?

Hearing the heartfelt concern in Corin's voice, Josephine chose her words and tone of voice carefully. *I think we've seen better days, overall though I guess we're ok. I don't know for how long. Please hurry.* Josephine focused on trying to guard her thoughts as she spoke with Corin. Bound and helpless,

Josephine closed her eyes in the hope that her unconscious state would save her from any more depraved sex acts. She focused her thoughts on her children. On Corin. Her anchors.

"Since you are going to kill us anyway, why not share what you're going to do." Mallory didn't know why she asked, she just did.

"I will tell about my plans for Corin. Our kind reacts badly to anything holy. I have obtained a special pair of shackles, they were made especially for him, and one could say they have been blessed," Nawzir laughed. "Once I get him in them, they will start searing his skin, and then I will have the pleasure of watching him writhe in pain and burn with anger as I have my way with his helpless Josephine, over and over again until she dies. Corin will be powerless to do anything." Nawzir licked his lips in anticipation. He reached over to Mallory and brushed his cold, clammy hand down the side of her cheek. "None of you will survive this, I promise you. Your suffering will end when you die, and your death, will not be a quick one," he said with an evil smile curving his mouth. Mallory tilted her head upwards, and glared at him, she held his gaze until she was able to muster all the phlegm that she could possibly summon, and then she spat at him, hitting him squarely in the face.

Nawzir wiped his face clean of the vile substance; with the flick of his wrist, he flung the gross discharge from Mallory's mouth to the floor. Then with one powerful movement, he backhanded Mallory's jawbone, knocking her to the ground, exposing her back to him. Mallory's face contorted as she tried to readjust her jaw. With her face still stinging from the backhand, pain racked her body, the sensation, reverberated through her. She managed to steady herself, knowing that her jaw was broken, she turned, looked up, and managed to say.

"Is that all you got?" Nawzir could hardly contain his rage, he was already lashing out at her, when he stopped short; Nawzir heard a rustling sound. He turned to look over at his helpless victim, Josephine was moving around.

Corin was almost at the church when he was stopped dead in his tracks. The pain in his stomach was unreal; his body was aching all over. *What in the hell is this?* When he was able to control the sensations, he refocused on his task; he knew what had happened to him. Josephine. He somehow connected to her, and all her pain was spilling out into him. Corin scanned her mind; a flood of emotions took over, threatening to overwhelm him. Corin broke the connection. Forcing back the emotions, he re-established the connection. He could feel her life force fading; she was close to death. *Hang on Josephine, for your family, hang on. I am here. I am sorry I did not get here sooner. Are you all right?* Corin tried to keep her conscious and aware of her surroundings. Frantically searching her mind he needed to see her memories; he needed to determine what happened to her, needed to see if Nawzir took her blood. Josephine had erected a barrier; evidently, she suffered badly enough to bury it deep enough that he could not find what he was looking for.

He was at the church; he put a shield up and scanned the interior. His only advantage was that Nawzir did not know about Josephine's physic ability, and that he and Josephine could communicate telepathically. Corin had attempted to keep the lines of communication open, but Josephine was not much help. She was falling in and out of consciousness.

Corin called for backup before arriving at the church. Donovan and Marcia were already enroute.

"I need your help to get them out. Both you and Marcia have to come at once. We are at the riverfront just outside the city limits. Look for an abandoned church along the shoreline. Josephine has been severely hurt and Mallory has been captured. I can't wait for you, I can't wait for you, I have to go in now and do what I can. If I fail, then you are Josephine's and Mallory's last hope." Corin remembered the conversation and how unimpressed Donovan sounded. *JOSEPHINE, WAKE UP! I am here, I need you awake!*

Corin was just about to burst in, when he stopped himself. *It is almost dawn; I can wait until the very last moment to go in. The place is boarded up tight. If I wait, no harm will come to Josephine or Mallory; the others will have time to arrive.*

"Josephine! Josephine! Josephine!" Corin called her name as if she were in front of him.

"Wh---what?" she asked out loud.

Nawzir turned and glared at Josephine. "What are you muttering over there?" he said.

Corin noticed the question that was asked of Josephine. *Say nothing, just listen. I have a plan. Listen carefully. I have called Donovan and Marcia. They are on their way. I will wait until the sun rises to come in. Since Nawzir and Jonah are both vampires, they will both succumb to the regeneration sleep. You and Mallory will be safe during the day. I hope that by the time the sunsets reinforcements will here. You will have to hang on just a little longer.*

I...We will do our best. Corin, I'll do my best to hang on, but I'm very weak, I'm tired, very tired. I don't know if I can make it. Josephine's voice was weak, Corin heard it. He bowed his head.

You have to Josephine, for your children and….and for me.

Corin's stomach tightened. *You have to pull through Josephine. I can save you. I can make you strong. I will heal your wounds and then we will finish this. Hear my words Josephine. You will hang on, I will accept nothing else.* Corin waited in the shadows and kept talking to Josephine. He continued talking to her and he would keep talking until he could talk no more.

※※※

Donovan hung up the phone, told the impatient Marcia what was happening.

"We can't wait until dawn to go," Donovan said. "We have to get the boys and go to Rachel's now. It will take us a couple of hours, if not longer, to get up to the city limits." Marcia nodded her head, she walked over to the phone and dialed Rachel's house.

A sleepy voice answered. "Rachel? This is Marcia, there's been a change of plans, Donovan and I have to bring the boys to you now. Something has happened, we can't wait until morning. I'm not going to lie to you Rachel, someone has taken Josephine." Donovan could hear the scream that came from the phone. Marcia continued. "Mallory and a friend went after her, but something happened to complicate the situation; Mallory." Harsh words were coming through the phone now, along with the sounds of hysteric crying. Marcia pushed forward, tears filling her own eyes. "No we can't call the cops. The police can't help." Anger was seeping through the phone receiver, Rachel was furious, ranting about how stupid all of us were being, throwing out accusations that indicated Marcia and Donovan didn't care about her daughter. Donovan grabbed the phone from Marcia.

"Rachel, its Donovan, just so you know, I'm a retired police officer, I happen to know that involving the police would only serve to damage the chances we have of getting both Josephine and Mallory back safely. Rest assured that *we*, Marcia and I will get your daughter and Mallory back. We'll be careful Rachel and we'll get your daughter back." Donovan handed the phone back to Marcia. "Can we bring the boys by? Thanks. We'll be leaving here in about ten minutes. Bye. We'll see you soon." Marcia hung up the phone. Donovan was looking at her, concern in his eyes.

"What?" Marcia snapped. "The woman has a right to know what has happened to her daughter."

"If she tells the cops, it will hurt our chances of getting Josephine and Mallory back. You shouldn't have said anything," Donovan said with a calmness that made Marcia shudder.

"Listen, Mr. Ex-cop or whatever you are. When we have Josephine and Mallory back safe and sound, you can argue tactics with me; until then, I'll divulge what I deem necessary to Rachel," Marcia's voice was heartfelt but firm.

Donovan shook his head. *You wouldn't be saying that if you knew what we're dealing with.* Donovan watched as Marcia gathered up all the things that the boys would need. "Diapers, baby food, milk, clothes etc. Can I get anything?" he asked.

"No but you can warm up the car. I don't suppose you have extra car seats?"

Donovan's eyebrows raised in confusion. "No, should I?"

"Well, for starters, we don't have any spare car seats,

which means, I have to hold Alex. Charlie will be sitting by himself without a seat. It's illegal, if you get stopped."

"Don't worry," he said, throwing on his jacket. "Go get the kids, I'll pack the car." Marcia complied. She brought up Charlie and Alex's jacket, she got Charlie dressed then Alex. She was careful so she wouldn't wake either of them. Donovan came upstairs as she picked up Charlie. "Here, give me Charlie," Donovan demanded. She handed Charlie over and went to fetch Alex. Donovan had already placed Charlie in the car; she squeezed into the backseat with Alex in her arms. She opened the back seat and put Charlie down. Marcia got comfortable and covered Alex with a blanket and then she struggled to cover Charlie with a blanket. *How does Josephine manage?*

Donovan locked up and then got in the car. "Please, tell me you let the dogs out." Marcia said.

"Yes I did, don't worry." Donovan said. Donovan put the car in gear and pulled out. With one hand, Marcia held Alex, she placed her free hand on Charlie, needing the contact. Finally, Marcia sat back and closed her eyes. *It'll be okay, everything will be okay*, she thought to herself

Marcia slept the whole way to Rachel's house. When the vehicle came to a stop, Marcia opened her eyes. Marcia opened the door and headed up the walkway with Alex. Rachel was already standing at the door, nervously awaiting their arrival. Rachel took Alex and brought him upstairs to the crib, while Marcia and Donovan brought in Charlie and the kids' stuff. Rachel was at the door again, waiting for either Charlie or the diaper bag, Donovan walked up with Charlie, Rachel pointed upstairs and whispered where to put Charlie. Donovan disappeared upstairs. Marcia who was trailing behind Donovan walked in with the diaper bag and bottles.

"Everything is there Rachel; food, milk, diapers, cream and clothes." Marcia said, as she put the bag down.

"Can you tell me anything more, Marcia?" Tears filled Rachel's eyes. Donovan was coming down the stairs and Marcia looked up at him. Her eyes asking for help.

"We can't say more than we've already told you, Rachel," Donovan said gently, but firmly.

"I'm her mother, dammit! I need to know if she's alive, if she's hurt. Tell me something! Anything!" Rachel said.

"She's alive, Rachel, but she's hurt. We've got to get there quickly. I'm sorry but we've got to get going," Donovan said, trying to avoid more conversation.

"Bring her back, alive, please!" It was a demand and a plea.

Marcia hugged Rachel hard and whispered in her ear. "We will." It was a confirmation. Rachel reluctantly released Marcia and showed them out. "Josephine is a tough cookie she'll be all right." Marcia called back, as they got into the SUV.

"Let's go," Marcia said impatiently.

Donovan didn't speak he just put the SUV in reverse and pulled out. Marcia watched Rachel wipe her face and then wave them off.

***

Nawzir was getting impatient. "Why has your knight in shining armor not come yet? I know he is here, he has chosen not to mask himself from me. Why?" Nawzir directed his question to Josephine. *What are you waiting for Corin? I know you are here. Do come in and join our little gathering.*

"Why do you care?" Josephine managed to slur out.

"You are the bait as well as my prize; I am becoming impatient. You see, until our guest arrives, I can't claim my prize. I find myself wondering where Corin could be. According to my brother he was not far, when he retrieved our newest guest," Nawzir said.

Josephine's anger flared, her eyes betraying her. Adrenaline surged through her body. She may be in a weakened state, but her brain was fully functional. "Maybe Corin will choose not show," she lied. "Then what?" She hissed.

"My well thought out plan needs Corin. I know he will show, in case you have not heard, Corin created me, I know him as well as you know your friend over there," Nawzir smiled.

"Out of curiosity; why my husband? Why my friends? Why me?" Josephine asked, hoping to get some answers. She followed Nawzir with her eyes, as he paced back and forth, waiting for an answer. She noticed then that something was happening his movements looked clumsy, lazy even, he was no longer moving with fluid grace, as he was before. *Regeneration sleep.* The words shimmered in her mind.

"It is funny you asked that question," he said. "Let me tell you a story," he began. "I had a family once, two brothers and myself. We did not follow the rules of our people very well, and as it happened, my younger brother got into trouble."

"I thought you weren't a 'pure blood'," Josephine stated.

"I am not. As I mentioned earlier, Corin sired all three of us."

Josephine gasped, and her eyes widened. *Why didn't*

he tell me? Why didn't you tell me, Corin? "Is that why he's after you?"

"Yes. That pathetic thing he calls a conscience. Corin turned all three us and he when we did not conform to the rules put before us; we were exiled from Ireland, never to return." The lethargic feeling was starting to take over; Nawzir was starting to feel weighted down, his movements demonstrated the effects. *I must go.* Jonah brought some water over to Josephine and poured down her throat.

"We cannot allow you to die before the fun starts, he said with a twisted smile on his face. Jonah left a glass of water beside Mallory. This will end tomorrow, if you are lucky," He said so both women could hear. Nawzir and Jonah stalked out of the room and went down into the basement.

Josephine looked over at her astonished friend. "Mallory, we'll get out of here. Corin is here, he's called Marcia and Donovan."

"Josephine, how are you feeling?" Mallory said her voice wavering, concern, showing in her eyes.

"Not good. Corin has been telling me to hold on, but I have no strength left in me," Josephine said weakly. *Corin, I think Nawzir has gone to sleep. Please hurry.*

"Try, Josephine. Damn you! You will try to live through this." Fear had taken hold of Mallory. "Damn you, Corin where in the hell are you? CORIN, WHERE ARE YOU?" Mallory screamed out loud.

Just then, the door flew open. Mallory looked up, across the room, it was Corin. Mallory blinked her eyes and said a quick prayer hoping that what she was seeing was real, and not something out of her imagination. Corin entered the area where both women were. He looked around finding

Josephine, examining her from a distance. He turned to Mallory, fury burning in the depths of his eyes, replacing the worry. He leapt to Mallory's side, destroying the chains that bound her. Then he attended Josephine, gently he removed her chains.

Corin examined Josephine more thoroughly; the bruising, the lacerations on her body, and the crimson colored streaks that covered her body. His stomach tightened as he moved the blood soaked tendrils of hair from her face. His rage finally broke free and was untamed, his need to avenge Josephine finally knew no bounds. He lifted Josephine and hugged her close to his chest. "I'm sorry," he whispered as he tried to wipe away the dried blood from her face. Reluctantly he placed Josephine down and removed his shirt and covered Josephine. He placed her lightly on the bed, when he was satisfied; he went over to Mallory and made sure that she was all right.

"We cannot leave. It is daylight outside, I could normally withstand sunlight for a short time, but I need to get Josephine to safety, I cannot do it without inflicting more pain. Donovan and Marcia are on their way. When they arrive, hopefully it will be during daylight hours, you must take Josephine and go. Should they arrive when it is dark, you and the others must get out while you can and do what it takes to get free of here, take my phone and call them, find out where they are. If night falls and you are still here, you will have to hide until Marcia and Donovan are here. Nawzir will be coming and I am the only one who can fight him."

"We won't leave you, Corin. He has a trap for you; he said something about shackles that can burn your skin. Besides, Josephine would never forgive me if we left you behind and something happened." Mallory was shaking her head side to side, as she continued to speak. "No, we won't leave you."

"I have no time to argue; the regeneration sleep is calling to me. Go to her and keep her safe until I am awake. I promised you that she would not die, I intend to keep that promise." Corin fell back against the wall and slept.

Mallory got up, grabbing the phone from Corin. Mallory went to her friend. She bent over Josephine, her hands shaking, as she touched her friend's face, her eyes going over her lacerated body. "Look what he has he done to you?" Anger rising in her blood and new tears forming, Mallory searched the room for some water and a cloth, anything that would help her clean Josephine's wounds. She saw the billy stick that Nawzir used. "Oh God," she gasped, holding her stomach. "That bastard will pay for what he has done to you! I swear to you Josephine. He's going pay." Tears were falling now, blinding her. When she finally found what she was looking for, bottled water, Mallory ripped off a piece of her shirt. Dousing the fabric with water, she began dabbing at Josephine's wounds.

Josephine was barely conscious but she knew that Corin had been there and she knew that Mallory was taking care of her. The room was spinning, she wasn't sure if they had left or were still trapped in the house, she had no idea where she was. Mallory kept vigil, cleaning Josephine's wounds and watching over her. The wounds would heel, provided Josephine didn't die. Mallory was unsure, though, how Josephine would handle the trauma of what had happened to her.

For the remainder of the day, Mallory kept tending to Josephine's wounds. She also made sure to get rid of all the shackles, handcuffs, and blunt objects that she could see. Making sure that Josephine couldn't be upset by any visual aids. Mallory didn't think that help would be there before sunset, but she called Marcia and Donovan anyway. Mallory put the phone down, her fears confirmed. It shouldn't have shocked her though, after all it took some time for her and Corin to get here. Donovan and Marcia would get here by sunset, or close to it. The silver lining was that all of them would take down Nawzir and Jonah.

chapter 12

The sun was almost setting by the time Marcia and Donovan reached the city limits. Donovan followed his instincts, as well as Corin's directions for the rest of the way. He parked the car so that it wouldn't be seen.

"Marcia we will have to walk the rest of the way. Corin said they were by the river front and according to my directions we have to cross through this forest."

Marcia gathered their things and made sure to grab the phone. Opening the door, she found Donovan waiting for her. "What are you waiting for? Let's go." She didn't wait for a response before she closed the door. She hastily walked around to Donovan's door, she stopped, crossing her arms over her chest, and tapping her right foot against the ground impatiently.

"Well?" She looked back at Donovan. Donovan looked at her shaking his head, gathering his belongings, including the duffel bag, he closed the hatch of the SUV. He walked up beside her, put out his hands to the side saying

"After you," he gestured with his hands. Rather than

admit that she had no clue as to where she was going she started heading in the direction of what she hoped was the river. Donovan followed, quietly, laughing to himself. *Women. So, stubborn. I could get used to her though. Now where did that thought come from?* Donovan and his thoughts were interrupted when Marcia asked.

"Did we bring a flashlight?"

"Yeah, I have one in my bag. Would you like me to get it out now?" Although Donovan responded to Marcia, he hadn't the faintest clue as to what she had said. He was immersed, for the moment in his own thoughts. Donovan was weighing the consequences, of his soon-to-be actions. He was considering telling Marcia. Everything. The two inevitable possibilities that could result as the outcome of this rescue put things into perspective for him. *She deserves to know, screw the job, and screw the mission.*

"If you don't mind," Marcia said." I don't feel like walking in the woods in the dark." There was a long pause before Marcia spoke up again. "Donovan? Are you still here with me?" The biting sarcasm in Marcia's voice, snapped him out of thoughts.

"Er...ah..."

"The flashlights!"

"I'll get it out," Donovan said as he pulled his bag around so that the zipper was in front of him; opening the bag, he shoved his hand in pulling out two mag lights. *Hope I have extra batteries.* He tapped Marcia on the shoulder with one of them and she grabbed it from him." Marcia, I've got to tell you something. This isn't easy for me and there's no real easy way to say what needs to be said. Therefore, I'm just going to say it. You don't know everything that is going on;

and with the cards that we've been dealt, I feel that you need to know." Marcia stopped walking, turned and looked deep into Donovan's amber eyes. Her stare was deadly, but more than that, it held disappointment. Donovan could feel his stomach clench, but he continued. "A warning; this is going to be difficult to accept."

"You can tell me anything, Donovan," she said trying to keep the bite out of her voice. *Where do I begin?*

"First of all, you know that Josephine was a private investigator, and that she occasionally helped out the police." Donovan didn't wait for a response; he just kept going. "Well about two years ago, her friend Manny, called Josephine for a job that required her unique skills; Manny and I, were investigating an unsolved murder case," he said, trying to keep the details to a minimum. "The murder itself had suspicious circumstances; which is where I come in, it's the field I work in," Donovan said, as he looked at Marcia watching her expression, trying to gauge her state of mind. "Shit, this isn't going the way I want it to. Long story short, Josephine helped locate a killer, the day we were going to bring him in, we found him dead, and actually the perpetrator was a pile of ashes. With a wooden stake resting in the pile. The original crime that I was working on is identical to that of Rick's." Marcia's facial expression changed; the look of disappointment mixed in with confusion, anger and hurt was evident in her eyes. The display of her emotions ate at Donovan, yet he went on. "We started an investigation to find out what happened, the only thing we were able to come up with was a composite sketch of a man found lingering in the vicinity. The man is Corin. There was a second man but there wasn't enough information to get a second sketch. The only thing that was found to be of interest was that both Corin and the other person were keeping their distance, as if they were watching." Donovan paused looking at Marcia. She was standing there; the shock was evident in her face. Donovan knew from the look on her face that she was trying to assimilate the information. Marcia said nothing.

"Josephine found our killer, that's the bottom line, but she also uncovered vast amounts of information that was not pertinent at that time, it seems that there were unseen consequences. The killer that she eventually tracked went by the name of Rowen and he had two very close friends or relatives we're not sure which. One goes by the name of Nawzir and the other goes by Jonah. Again long story short, our killer was a pile of ashes. What I believe happened was Josephine led Corin to this guy and Corin took care of business the only way he knew how. I believe that Josephine is the target of revenge. I think Rowen's brothers or friends are here to avenge their friend or brother. I think Corin is here to stop them, actually, I know he's the only one that can stop them. I know this probably doesn't make sense, but I figured you needed to know the details, considering..." Donovan stopped to get gauge her reaction.

"You know what I think; I think you've lost your mind. Stress… maybe? Josephine doesn't even know you, remember? Second, I think she would have remembered working on a case with you, and I know for certain that Mallory and I would've known. Explain that one, please." Marcia said with a hint of sarcasm in her voice.

"Josephine was hypnotized; her memories of me and the job were suppressed. She doesn't remember me and that's exactly what is putting her at risk," Donovan said. "Don't you think it's strange that Rick dies, two bad guys are in town, Josephine is attacked twice and Corin is here? That's an awful lot of coincidence," Donovan said. "The cases I work are classified; Josephine knew that coming in, she accepted the condition, which is the only reason she was allowed to working with us. She knew exactly what we were going to do after the job was complete," Donovan added. Marcia's legs buckled, Donovan caught her in his arms. Without having, enough strength to control her emotions Marcia cried. Then her anger took over she started punching at Donovan's chest.

"You lied! You bastard, you lied, I trusted you, she trusted you! How could you do this to her? To me?" Marcia tried to pull away, but Donovan held her close and tight. "You said fifty years ago," she cried into his chest. "Corin doesn't look a day over thirty five," she said through gasping breaths.

"Yes I said fifty years ago." Marcia pulled away enough to look up into Donovan's hard chiseled face.

"Are you telling me what I think you're telling me; that he is a *vampire?*"

"Yes." Donovan said quietly.

"That's impossible vampires don't exist, they're myths, fables, legends, dark lore, whatever you want to call them. They don't exist," Marcia argued.

"Listen to me Marcia, this is for real. I know how this sounds, I'm not crazy and you need to be prepared. The guy was a pile of ash, we have the photos, and we have irrefutable proof. I can show them to you, if that's what it's going to take to make you believe," Donovan said. "This is not a joke, Donovan said with all the seriousness he could muster. Josephine and Mallory are in danger, Josephine has pieced together some bits and pieces of what is going on, I don't know how much. What I do know for sure is that she probably has no idea why this is happening to her. She is grave danger because she is not supposed to remember anything, which means she has no way of knowing what she is up against. . . The reason buddy came after her and her family is because she helped to catch one of them. The only real mystery here is Corin, but you already know what I think, it makes sense, this is the only thing that is can explain the why's about everything that is happening.. Marcia, this is confidential, and by telling you, I'm blowing my cover." Donovan said thoughtfully. I'm pretty sure it's gonna cost me my job." he said rubbing his chin. I don't care about my job, right now your life could be on the line that makes this information a need to know," Donovan added.

"Okay, okay, I get it," Marcia said irritated with the situation but pleads that he gave the secret up to protect her.

"Since you know that I'm not a retired cop, here's the deal; I work for a special division in the police force. I'm involved in solving and investigating unsolved murders that are considered to have 'mysterious circumstances' surrounding them. In many cases, I work side by side with the CIA. Manny, Josephine's friend knows me because we have worked several cases together. Manny's a detective in Homicide, occasionally he gets special assignments. When this whole thing with Rick happened, Manny took it very personally and wanted to help. The only way he could do that was to utilize me. Eventually the 'big bosses' made the decision to have the situation monitored and investigated. Manny jumped through hoops to make it appear as if I was retired. Josephine thought that Manny and I were friends. Josephine has no memory of me, or our past at all. I was brought in to ensure her safety, and to establish what she knew." Donovan said.

Marcia pulled away completely; pacing back and forth and speaking out loud.

"I see how well you kept her safe—okay, say I believe you. Why did Josephine start digging around then? She obviously wasn't supposed to have any memory of what had happened in the case you were working on. So what happened?" Marcia asked. Before Donovan could answer, Marcia lit into him again. "I'll tell you, you guys screwed up. That's what." She answered, as frustration rolled off her.

"That's the other question; we don't know why she decided to start poking around. We were careful not to give her any triggers; you know something that would enable her to access the repressed memories. We truly don't know." Donovan defended.

Marcia wanted to run from him, from the deadly situation, from everything. *Where could I go? Nowhere,* she thought to herself, as she quickened her pace to put distance between them. Donovan followed her.

"Marcia." Donovan called out after her.

Marcia turned around and continued walking backwards; she took careful steps so she wouldn't lose her footing. Marcia couldn't contain her anger any more.

"You know, you guys are jerks, my best friends' lives are in mortal danger; hell, if they aren't already dead, and you… you frigging knew the whole damn time! You knew what they were up against, and still you kept your silence. You saw how worried I was. How in the hell do you expect me to trust you again? This goes way beyond just my friends; it's about you and me. You know what forget what I just said. All

I care about, all I know is that Josephine and Mallory better be alive and nothing I mean nothing better have happened to them, or I will never forgive you," Marcia snapped. "Don't just stand there. Get moving. We have to get to them, we've been traveling since this morning, it seems like we've gotten nowhere. Now it's almost evening, it's going to be dark soon, and if what you are saying is true well, I sure as hell don't want to be around this blood-sucking vampire and I certainly don't want my friends around him." Marcia said angrily. She turned herself around and picked up the pace. Donovan was still in shock from the outburst; he did a little jog and caught up with her.

When he reached Marcia, he put his hand on her shoulder and stopped her. He turned her around and looked straight into those sky blue eyes, "I'm very sorry for lying to you Marcia, you've got to know that this wasn't my intention. I was under orders not to tell anyone. This is considered confidential and unfortunately, I'm not at liberty to discuss these things. I'm truly sorry and I hope that you can forgive me although I don't expect your forgiveness you need to know that I can go on without you in my life, what will be difficult is knowing that you can't and won't forgive me. ." Donovan let her go and took the lead. *Those were the hardest words I have ever said in my life. Did I mean them?* He thought to himself as he trudged forward.

Marcia followed muttering to herself. *Go figure. Why is it that, that man can screw up so royally, and leave me feeling as if I've just killed his best friend? Get over it, Marcia. You know you want him. Just forgive him and tell him he can make it up to you after this whole ugly mess is over and done with.* "Donovan, it's dark. How much longer till we reach them?" she asked, there was a softness in her voice that Donovan noticed. He smiled to himself.

That's a good sign, her tone has softened up. There's hope for you yet, Donovan. "We're at the water front, now we just have to find the building. I'm not sure but I think I see it, a few hundred yards or so from us." Donovan waved his flashlight in the direction of the church. "You think you can run it?" he asked.

"Not sure but I'm willing to try, I don't want to risk their lives on me not being able to run," Marcia said as she passed him. Donovan was following closely behind. When they reached the building they tried to look inside to determine the odds, they couldn't; the windows were boarded. Donovan and Marcia leaned up against what was once a window and listened for anything out of the ordinary. They heard some loud banging and crashing. Reaching for his weapon they entered.

Kicking the old wooden door in, they saw Corin fighting another man ferociously. Quickly taking a survey of the room they found Mallory covering Josephine. Corin sensed their presence right away.

"Get the women out of here now!" he yelled.

"I can help you!" Donovan yelled back.

"No! Josephine is badly hurt! Get her and Mallory out of here! I will hold off Nawzir as long as I can. Trust me, just get them and go. I will catch up and explain." Corin ordered.

Donovan and Marcia rushed over to the bed where Mallory and Josephine were.

"Come on, sweetie we've got to go," Marcia said, as she leaned over to pull Mallory off Josephine. When she did, Marcia stepped back and gasped at the sight of her friend's naked, bruised, beaten and lacerated body. Marcia took a step closer, this time with more urgency in her voice she called to Mallory, "Get up, Mallory, we have to go!" Mallory was still protecting Josephine. "Listen, we have to get Josephine out of here." Marcia said, this time it was a command. Mallory recognized her friends' voice and moved out of the way. Donovan moved towards Josephine and he leaned in to pick up her frail body and anger filled his body when he saw Josephine. The adrenaline rush and the need to join Corin and wreak havoc on the bastards that did this to his friend was almost uncontrollable. He lifted Josephine gently off the so-called bed. Mallory was now leaning against Marcia for support, and Josephine was in Donovan's arms, they maneuvered passed the dueling Corin and Nawzir on the way out and they left the church as quickly as they could.

Even once they were out of the church, they could still hear the loud, crashing, thundering noises from the continuous fighting. They made their way back through the forest, trying desperately to reach the car. Mallory was hungry, tired and sore but she managed to find the strength to keep going; Donovan was a strong man, but Josephine was not petite, her weight was slowing him down. The odds were against them, but they still kept going.

Meanwhile, Corin was able to keep both Nawzir and Jonah occupied long enough so that the others could make a safe get away. Corin knew that there was no way for him to safely eliminate both Nawzir and Jonah and escape unscathed, so he opted to distract them. That's what this had been right up until he saw Josephine. Now his plan was changed. Josephine would die if he didn't get to her. It had been a mistake on his part to wait until dawn to get to her. That mistake could very well cost Josephine her life. His battle would have to wait. Right now, his focus was Josephine. He needed to get to her.

"This is not finished." Corin said as he dealt several severe blows at Nawzir and Jonah. Both vampires were on the floor, he didn't give them time to recover and engage once more in battle. They were trying to stall him; they needed to keep him otherwise engaged so that Josephine would have no hope in surviving her ordeal. Corin left.

You are right my friend we will finish this. The words shimmered in Corin's mind as he changed forms. *Josephine.* Corin ran through the forest, his sense of smell much more accurate, led him right to Donovan. He changed from a wolf back into the man. Donovan and the others were just up a head, busy trying to get out of the forest that they hadn't heard the rustling of the trees and the breaking of the branches on the forest floor.

"Donovan." Corin called out to him. Donovan who was trailing behind the women, stopped dead in his tracks. He turned to see Corin coming up behind him. Stunned.

"I will take her. I am much faster than you, your questions will have to wait. I need to go if I am to save Josephine." That was the only warning Donovan got. Corin had taken Josephine and vanished. Donovan caught up with Marcia and Mallory.

"Where's Josephine?" Marcia asked, trying to remain calm.

"Corin's got her, don't ask let's just get a move on. Do you want me to take Mallory?" Donovan asked.

"No, let's both help her walk, it will be much faster that way," Marcia stated. They were almost running, but not quite, the strain on Mallory was too much. Finally, they reached the car. They got Mallory in and placing her so that she was comfortable.

※※※

Corin kept up his pace, knowing full well that he was hurting Josephine. She winced from pain a couple of times, but he couldn't afford to stop. He didn't stop until he reached Josephine's home. When Corin reached her house, he traced inside and then headed upstairs. Both dogs were agitated by the presence of someone unnatural and tried to attack as he made his way upstairs with Josephine. Laying Josephine gently down on her bed, Corin shook her, lightly, rousing her from her sleep.

"Josephine, you have to listen to me, the damage and blood loss to your body is too severe. The doctors, will not be able to help you, even if there were the slightest possibility that they could help, there is no time. I can help you," Corin said smoothly. Josephine looked up at him her eyes barely open and her mind hardly registering what he was saying. She held onto his hand, her grip tightening. "In order to save you, Josephine, I have to change you into a vampire. You must suffer a mortal death in order to live. You will not be human. Do you understand this? I will not change you if I do not have your permission, you must decide either way, there is not much time left. You are dying. I know you have children and this is a concern, but we can deal with all the issues when you are well. Do you want to live?" Corin asked.

Josephine tightened her grip on his hand; nodding her head up and down with her last bit of strength. The tears in her eyes rolled sideways down her cheeks. "This is going to feel strange. You will feel intense pain, I will do my best to buffer it, then you will sleep and when you wake, I will be here by your side. Do you understand?" Josephine couldn't answer she just blinked, she didn't have enough energy to answer. Josephine's heart started pumping a mile a minute when she saw Corin's fangs lengthen. Corin heard the thundering of her heart and felt sick to his stomach at what she was going to have to go through. He wished it were under different circumstances, that her change came about.

"Do not fear little one, I am here." Without warning, Corin brushed the hair from her neck and sank his fangs into her. Josephine's body reacted to the pain, her body arched. He held her by the small of her back and drank; he drank until death was literally knocking on her door. When he was sure that her body was ready, Corin used one of his fangs and pierced his wrist. The blood trickled from the open vein and he brought Josephine's mouth to the wound he had inflicted. Holding her lips at the open wound, he held her there. "Drink." Corin said gently. Her body refused, she was weak. There was reluctance. "Drink." Corin commanded. Josephine was confused, scared. Then words shimmered in her mind. *You will be alive for your family. Please, just drink, it will save your life.* Corin felt the swirl of her tongue on his skin, as the first few drops entered her mouth. Power, life, and strength started to course through her weakened body. As she became more alive, she pulled his wrist closer and gripped him harder, she was nursing the wound. Corin let her take his life force into her, and he enjoyed the feel of her mouth on him, how she gripped his body.

"Josephine you must stop, now," Corin said. Josephine refused, she didn't let go. Reluctantly, Corin pulled free from her sensuous mouth. Cradling Josephine's head, he knew what was about to happen. He had no time to warn her before the first bout of pain ripped through her. Josephine screamed, and tears streamed uncontrolled down her face. Her hands went protectively over her stomach. It didn't last long. It was about a minute later when the second round of pain ripped through her frail body, ridding itself of human remnants.

"I can't do this!" She cried out. Instinctively Corin held her protectively while her body convulsed and seized.

"I am here, little one, I am here" Corin said gently, soothingly. The last session of pain came on hard and strong. Purging the last of the human toxins left in her system. It lasted longer than the other attacks and Josephine went into a final seizure, then several bouts of puking up bile. Then, finally, it was over. Corin felt her body go limp in his arms. "It is over." He kissed the top of her head lightly and laid her down to rest. Josephine felt serene, at peace when she finally allowed darkness to embrace her.

Corin had watched her, making sure her body started to heal. He watched as her lacerations closed and the bruises started to fade. When he was satisfied, he walked over to dresser; he went through all the drawers until he found what he was looking for. Pajamas. He grabbed them and walked to the bathroom. Running the water he waited until the temperature was just right; then he went and got Josephine. He took off the shreds of clothing that remained, lifting her body he carried her to the bath that he prepared for her. Taking the showerhead from its cradle, he cascaded the water over her body as the tub filled with water. He put some liquid soap on to the shower puff and lathered her full of the scented soap. He was trying hard not to look at her body but found that he couldn't resist. His eyes slid over her perfectly sized breasts, letting his gaze rest on her erect nipples for a moment. His eyes then moved over her torso that was so perfect, taut, with perfectly toned abs. Her centre was perfectly shaped, a triangle of auburn hair. Her legs were shapely and muscular. . Sculpted perfectly. Her toenails had a deep burgundy on color on them, which made her pale skin stand out. She was perfection. He savored her, admired her beauty. *One day I hope to touch and caress your silken skin. I want to show you how much I have come to love you how much I want you how much I need you.*

Corin washed her gently, being careful not to disturb her. Using the shower puff, he glided over her soap covered body once more then he turned the water back on and pulled the shower head once again from its cradle and rinsed her off. Corin made sure to get every crevice and secret place. The water was turning a shade of pink from all the blood coming off of Josephine's body. Corin's stomach turned realizing that the woman he craved would not have suffered these injuries had he done his job. Looking down at Josephine he saw her blood matted hair flowing around in the water, he closed his eyes as he reached for the bottle of shampoo. Lathering the soap in her hair he turned the water on to rinse her off. Then he added the conditioner and rinsed her hair and the remainder of soap on her and released the water. . Corin picked her up, covered her with the towel, and carried her to her room. He laid her down on the bed, then he dried her. Corin found that his groin was coming to life as he dried Josephine's breasts. The more he touched her the more he wanted her and by the time he reached her centre, he was fighting the urge to take her. Corin turned away for a brief moment to re-focus his attention. He had to get her dressed and fast. When he was done, he placed her under the covers.

Next Corin needed to ensure the room remained dark. The curtains on her windows would do, he just needed to ensure that the room would remain dark through the morning light. He went to the linen closet and pulled out two extra blankets. He placed them over the curtains and ensured that no cracks of light could get in. When he was finished, he lay down beside her and let the regeneration sleep claim him.

chapter 13

Jonah was the first one to get up, after Corin knocked him to the ground. Growling in fury and unsure whether or not, the plan had succeeded. Had they kept Corin distracted long enough so that their rouse would succeed? He walked up to Nawzir who was still on the ground.

"Brother, are you injured?" Nawzir let a groan escape. He placed his palms on the ground and pushed himself up, accepting no help from Jonah. Looking disgruntled, he brushed his clothes free from the dust.

"Corin has escaped; if Josephine lives, then we have failed," Nawzir said as he slammed his fist into the concrete wall of the church.

"It is only one battle. We will get them in the next round, Brother," Jonah said, as he placed his hand on Nawzir's shoulder. "We should never have taken the second female, she complicated our plans. No matter, we know what Corin's weakness is now. He will protect all the humans, not just Josephine. This can work to our advantage," Jonah said, thoughtfully. "Question brother, was it wise to damage Josephine as you did? I was under the impression that we wanted to have Corin suffer at our hands, while we inflict pain, not to mention amusing ourselves," Jonah asked.

"I have played carefully for two years now she was tempting and ripe. So I played a little with our new toy. The bitch deserved everything she got and she deserves more." Nawzir hissed out between clenched teeth.

"What about the other?" Jonah asked.

"The other, she is just a bonus. Would you like a piece of her as well as Josephine, I don't mind sharing," Nawzir said licking his fangs.

"That was not part of the plan, we must watch ourselves, I don't want any distractions, although, the second female is quite the catch. Maybe I will play with the spoils," Jonah shot a wicked look at Nawzir.

Nawzir paced around and Jonah watched him. "What is our next move?" asked Jonah.

"I am not sure. I have to think about it. One thing is definite, Josephine's life was slipping away, I could feel her fading. I am sure Corin had to turn her, in order to save her. We can use that as well, her life as she knew is over. If she manages to survive the change, then she will be stronger than what she was, she'll be able to communicate with Corin; and he will be able to locate her anywhere that we take her. This is also to our advantages." Nawzir rubbed his chin, a small smile curving his mouth.

"There may be another complication. There is a new player in our game. One that I recognize, Donovan O'Hara, I believe his name is. He is part of the group of people that brought Rowen down. I know Corin was the one to destroy Rowen. Josephine and Donovan played their roles, whatever they may have been, either way they contributed to Corin finding Rowen, end of story. For that they shall all pay. Corin, most of all," Jonah said, as he glared into the dawning sky. "We must come up with a new plan."

"Well what do you suggest?" Nawzir said as he started to pace.

"Tomorrow night. Now is our regeneration sleep," Jonah said as he slipped into the basement.

"What did he do to you?" She asked. Donovan was driving home, while Marcia took care of Mallory.

"It's not so much what he did to me but what he did to Josephine. If she recovers from her injuries, we'll have to worry about her mental state of mind. That man is crazy and he used me against Josephine. I honestly don't know how she kept herself from just dying."

"What did he do to her?" Marcia asked, calmly as color drained from her face, her blue eyes were blazing as her anger grew. She looked up at rear-view mirror catching Donovan's eyes. She glowered for moment before pressing on. The only thing that kept her from lashing out was the regret that crept into his amber eyes.

"I...he violated her with a billy stick. I assume he was using it hit her with as well, prior to my arrival... I don't know," she sobbed. Mallory's face was red and tears fell from her eyes. "When he captured me, he knocked me around a little and hurt me as well, not as bad as Josephine but enough. Then when I started retaliating, he broke my jaw." Mallory's voice was getting louder as she explained what else transpired. "At some point Josephine became semi-conscious, that's when he inserted that thing into her, and he played with her as if she were a toy, fondling her breasts. Then to top things off the bastard put his sex in her mouth while she was helpless, and by helpless I mean tied down to a bed with her legs spread eagle and her arms tied to each bedpost. He slapped her first of course to open her mouth then he slid it in and out, while he held her mouth in place, then he thrust in and out until he ejaculated," Mallory spat out, while holding her stomach. "He ejaculated in her mouth and on her face," Mallory continued to say, hate laced every word. "I doubt she even knew what was happening," she managed to say through clenched teeth and fresh tears streaming steadily down her face. She looked away from Marcia, defeated. Ashamed. "I cou-couldn't do-do anything to help her because he had me chained to a pole. All I could do was sit and watch in disgust. Finally, I just ended up keeping my mouth shut so he couldn't use me against her. I didn't want Josephine to be put through that shit again."

"Shh. It's okay, Mallory. This isn't your fault. Don't blame yourself. Josephine wouldn't want you to put yourself through that," Marcia cooed. "Everything will be fine, right now; I need you to concentrate on getting better. You're going to have to be strong," Marcia said soothingly. Her eyes were soft as she spoke the words. Mallory leaned over and hugged her, her body convulsing, as she continued to cry in silence. *That bastard is going to pay.* Marcia thought to herself. Marcia stayed with Mallory until she fell asleep. "Can you pull over at the next stop? I'm hungry, I need something to eat. Try to get a drive thru place, if you can," Marcia said, exhausted.

"Sure, I think all the Tim Horton's around here have drive-thru so no worries," Donovan said, as he looked at Marcia through his rear view mirror. Marcia took solace in his eyes. They warmed her body, taking away the chill from the events that had transpired. Marcia felt the tension ease. Donovan pulled his eyes away, wishing he didn't have to, but he was driving, his attention was required elsewhere. Donovan saw a sign that indicated another five kilometers until the next rest stop. "Marcia, it's another five klicks until we reach a Tim Horton's," Donovan said.

"All right. I'm gonna have a jumbo black with two sugars and no cream. I'll also have a chicken salad sandwich, actually make that two, we'll get one for Mallory in case she wakes up. Also, get an iced tea, please," Marcia finished rattling off her order and realized that she would probably have to repeat it once they get there. She couldn't help but laugh at herself. Donovan glanced back at her.

"You all right back there?" he asked. His voice held some hint of laughter.

"Yeah, I was just thinking that it was silly of me to give you my order when we aren't there yet. Maybe the stress of this whole ordeal has finally got to me," Marcia said her voice more serious.

"Hey, don't knock the 'laughing' part. As a cop, you need to develop that sense of humour, even in the grimmest situations, if you don't you're likely to get overwhelmed. That's actually part of our training. The majority of the time, that's where you'll see sarcasm at its best," Donovan said.

Marcia didn't have a lot to say after Donovan's little speech. She just sat back and looked as if she were thinking about what he had said. Donovan pulled onto the turnoff for Tim Horton's and went through the drive-thru. He gave the woman his order and added an extra coffee. "The voice in the speaker rattled off the price. Donovan pulled around to the window, retrieving his wallet. He gave the woman the money. Donovan got the change.

"Thanks," Donovan said with a smile on his face. He took the tray full of coffees from her, carefully placed it down on the seat, then he reached out to grab the bag of sandwiches. "Thanks again," he said. He rolled up the window and started to head out when Marcia asked him to pull over.

When the car stopped, Marcia got out and made sure that Mallory was sleeping comfortably, and then she closed the back door and hopped in the front. "Okay," Marcia said. "I'm ready." Donovan looked over at her and smiled. It felt good that she was sitting next to him. He looked over at the gas gauge, noticing that the tank was low. Before getting back onto the highway, he stopped for gas. As he filled the car, Marcia inhaled her sandwich; she was just starting her coffee when Donovan entered the car. Donovan looked at Marcia, then at the crumpled sandwich wrap on the floor, then back at Marcia. Shaking his head, he started laughing. The sound of his laughter melted her insides, even though she was angry. "What are you laughing at?" she asked, trying to hide the laughter in her voice.

"Nothing, I just like a woman who can eat and isn't afraid of showing it." Donovan said as his eyes wandered to the crumpled garbage on the floor; once again, his laughter filled the car. Marcia smiled at his comment. As they continued to drive, they heard moans coming from the back seat. Marcia glanced over at her friend to ensure she was okay and that nothing was happening.

"Bad dreams, I guess," Marcia said. There was sadness in her voice.

"I can't say that I blame her. Hopefully she'll get through

this," Donovan said with an apprehensive sigh. Listen, Marcia, I'm so sorry for not coming clean with you about everything," Donovan said earnestly.

"It's okay. I understand why you couldn't tell me. I guess, I was, just hurt that you didn't trust me enough, then again, you haven't known me very long, have you?" Marcia said. Lowering her eyes, she was silent for a moment before she asked the next question. "Do you think Josephine is okay?" Marcia looked up at Donovan with glistening sky blue eyes; she was looking for some reassurance.

"I think, Corin is doing what he can for her," Donovan said reassuringly. Marcia sucked in her breath at the words. Fear replaced the worried look that was only moments ago. "What? What is it?" Donovan asked.

"Do you think Corin changed her into a vampire? What if the smell of her blood was too much for him and he lost it? God, we shouldn't have let him take her! We don't know what he is capable of! Not only that… you know he lied to us, to Josephine, just to get into our little circle of friends. We can't trust him. He betrayed us from the beginning." Marcia continued her ramblings. Her mind was racing with all kinds of ideas.

"I think you are over reacting just a tad, Marcia. Get a grip. If he wanted to kill Josephine he could've killed her a long time ago. I think, and I hate to say this, but I believe he actually cares about her. I don't think he would harm her," Donovan stated, which compelled Marcia to calm herself instantly. In the back seat of the car, Mallory was coming around. She had heard the conversation.

"Corin will do whatever he must to keep Josephine alive. Even, if it means changing her," Mallory said in a ragged breath. Donovan and Marcia both looked back at her, not sure how to respond to this new information.

"What do you know about Corin?" Donovan asked.

"I know that he's a vampire. I also know that Josephine knows," Mallory said, more awake now.

"What!? How does she know?" Marcia asked, taken aback by the statement.

"I don't know all the details, all I know is that she knows, she's the one who told me."

"Well, son of a..." Donovan didn't finish his sentence. "What else does she know?" Donovan asked, trying to get answers from her and determine what, if anything, that Josephine and her knew.

"Look, I can't recall the entire conversation," Mallory said, exhausted. "I'm pretty sure that she knows about Corin; that's the only thing I know for sure." Mallory said, with a little edge to her voice.

Donovan shook his head. *This is not good. How did this get so out of hand? Manny's gonna understand, but the chief is going to hit the fan. Can't think about this right now. There are more important things to do. Like getting to Josephine before Corin can do anything, if there is anything left to do.* Marcia just sat quietly, looking at Donovan, wondering what was going on in his head.

"Donovan, don't worry, we'll think of something to cover up what we know; especially the part about who knows it. Right now there are more important things to worry about, when the time comes to deal with all this stuff, we'll figure out to deal. Now's not the time to cross that bridge. Just make sure you don't say anything to anyone, until we can sort things out, it will work out, you'll see," Marcia said, gently being as comforting as she could be. Donovan looked at her, he didn't need to speak, his eyes said everything, expressing his worries and his gratitude.

They'd be at Josephine's house soon, but it wasn't fast enough, the drive seemed to take forever; there was an awkward silence in the car. Each of them hiding in the depths of their minds and fearing the worst. All of them secretly praying for nothing short of a miracle. Marcia periodically looked back at her friend, who was sipping her iced tea. It dawned on Marcia that Mallory was probably hungry, reaching down on the floor between her feet got the chicken sandwich. She handed the bag to her friend.

"Thanks, I'm starved." She took the bag and pulled out her food.

"Can't drive like this," Donovan said breaking the thick air of tension. We need to be ourselves; at least act like we are in control. Josephine has been through enough, if we all walk into the house like this, she's going to stress out. What she needs from us is support. We can't anticipate nor should we assume the worst. She needs us, and the safety cushion that only we can represent right now. If Corin changed her, in order to save her, then so be it. We don't know anything and we can't assume. We are gonna be at the house any minute and we better get our game faces on. Josephine is going to need our support. Nothing else. No condemnation, no questions. Just support. Josephine needs us, whatever the circumstance, now more than ever. I doubt that Nawzir is finished with Josephine or us.

"There's a second one." Mallory stated.

"What are you talking about?" Donovan asked, playing dumb.

"It was someone different that took me," she said smoothly.

"Jonah." Donovan said, looking at Marcia.

"I think that was his name, when he grabbed me, I tried to fight him, I went to call out for Corin when I was punched, and knocked out," Mallory said. She sat in the back, muddling through all the information she had absorbed. Donovan watched Mallory from the rear view mirror; her facial expression told him that she had pieced things together. As the emotions of confusion, and anger rolled across her face, it became apparent to Donovan that he was going to have to tell her the story. Donovan started to tell his story, all of it. When he finished Mallory had stayed silent. There was nothing to say. She glanced over to Marcia and then back at Donovan. Bowing her head and feeling a little betrayed, even guilty, she remained silent. She had known things that Marcia didn't; she had no reason to feel betrayed. *Everything happens for a reason,* Mallory told herself. That would have to be enough for her. Silence again, except for the occasional sob that escaped Marcia. Mallory stayed hidden the shadows of the tinted windows, fighting to hold back tears, they came anyway; accompanied by waves of emotions, one after the other. Mallory prayed. She was not one for praying but she… *they* needed all the help they could get. *God we need your help. All of us. We've got to survive this ordeal. Josephine's children need her. Give us the strength to get through this, please. Let the good triumph over evil, please, God.*

chapter 14

Nawzir and Jonah wasted no time planning their next move.

"I want to see Josephine and Corin suffer," Jonah said. "We need to come up with a well-orchestrated plan. We cannot have any loose ends. Everyone will die. Getting all the people we saw is going to take some doing; we need a plan that is foolproof." Jonah stated. "Rowen was our brother, he must be avenged," Jonah demanded.

"I have no doubt that Corin changed Josephine to save her life, we should expect that as fact. The amount of damage she sustained and her blood loss were significant. There was no way for her to survive without his aid. Nevertheless, we should expect resistance from her, when we try to take her. She will not be able to defeat us, however she might cause some minimal damage, she is a trained fighter. We also have to consider the others," Nawzir said thoughtfully.

"A challenge then" Jonah said. "I enjoy seeing my victims squirm," he said with a smug smile on his face.

"Getting Corin and Josephine will not be the problem,

keeping them long enough to kill them will be the challenge." Nawzir said firmly.

"What makes you say that?" Jonah asked.

"I believe Josephine will attempt to come to us, thinking herself as someone to be contended with. Her quest for justice in Rick's name will be her downfall. As for Corin, he will come after her, he cares for her, she, is his weakness." Nawzir said.

"What about the others will give us trouble, you think they will come for them?" Jonah asked. "We are going to have to bind Corin and Josephine once we have them," Jonah added.

"I have a few ideas. We will make use of blessed shackles, we should get some holy water, wood and some carving knives. We will have to make our own stakes, fitting that Corin and Josephine will die the same way as Rowen, and with a weapon crafted by our own hands," Nawzir said confidently.

"A question Brother, how will we obtain holy water, it will burn us as it will Corin," Jonah asked.

"Do not worry about how I will get the holy water; what I need you to do is find a shelter, someplace where we can put both Josephine and Corin. We are running short on time, which is very precious. Remember, the place you find Jonah, must keep us sheltered from the sun. Try to find a location that is daunting, I do not want Josephine or Corin to be comfortable, I want them to be out of their element. Josephine will be the easier of the two to intimidate," Nawzir said thoughtfully.

"I have not had the opportunity to take in the sights around here. I have noticed that there are some mountains across the river; there could be some caves around. I will have a good look around," Jonah said."

"This is the plan; I will go and get the holy water and the chains from the church. You find a location that suits our needs. We will meet back here in say an hour or so. We will have to prepare whatever our new location is for our guests," Nawzir said. Jonah acknowledged his brother by nodding his head. Jonah used his preternatural powers and whisked himself away into the mountains. Nawzir did the same, only he went into the city to look for a church.

Nawzir found a suitable church. Before he entered the building he stood back and admired the building, as if he were in envy. He stared at all the stained glass windows, and then he looked upwards toward the crucifix. He stared briefly, only for a moment, before he leapt to the top of the stairs. Nawzir pushed open the wooden door and entered the church. When he was inside, he looked around, moving forward, cautiously. . He had no desire to be in here longer than he had to. He hated being in a church, but he required the water. Scanning the room with his senses he located priest. He was inside one of the confession boxes. Angered, he stalked around until the priest was done, he saw the occupant leave the church. *Lucky human. I cannot afford to draw attention to myself.* Nawzir grumbled to himself. Putting on his most pleasant smile he walked gracefully and predator like to the priest. "Father, I require a favor from you. I need some of your holy water with an additional blessing from you," Nawzir said in a most pleasant demeanor. *The things one must do in order to get things done,* Nawzir kept the façade up, knowing that this was a means to an end." My son, it's a strange favor you ask. Do you mind telling me why? Holy water is sacred and not a toy to be used for some sinful act," the priest said.

Nawzir was losing his patience, although he had anticipated that this would not be an easy task. He had to think quickly. "Well Father, I think I have a demon problem and I am hoping to capture him and render him helpless, I think the holy water and blessed chains will contain him. Will you help me?" Nawzir said as he put his fake pleading face on.

"Young man, surely, you don't expect me to believe this little tale of yours, do you?" the priest asked annoyed yet calm.

Nawzir just looked at the priest. "If you require proof, Father, then so be it. Here is your proof," Nawzir said as his fangs elongated and the predator in him took over. The priest watched in horror as the man before him turned into a demon. Eyes that were human had changed into an eerie yellow colour that were outlined by red. The priest stood and crossed himself for protection as he said a prayer of mercy and protection. Nawzir's evil laugh echoed off the cathedral ceilings. "Now Father, about my request," Nawzir said as he stalked towards him.

With shaking hands, the priest obliged. When he was done, he made the sign of the cross and whispered prayers of forgiveness under his breath. "Don't worry, priest I have eaten already for the night and it is not you that I want," he said. The next thing the priest knew was that Nawzir was gone.

Jonah had searched several caves in the mountains across the lake from the old abandoned church. When he found a cavern that tunneled deep underground he made sure to explore the passages within, ensuring that it was suited for what him and Nawzir intended. Jonah was satisfied that they would have safety from the sun's rays and confident that it would be next to impossible to track, let alone find anyone. Satisfied, Jonah used his preternatural speed and went back to meet Nawzir.

"Did you find what we are looking for?" Nawzir asked as he sensed his brother approaching.

"Yes. I believe you will like it," Jonah replied. "And you? Did you get what we needed?"

"Yes, and I had some fun well," Nawzir said with a laugh.

"We should get going; we have things to do so that our guests will be suitably accommodated when they arrive," Jonah said with anticipation in his voice.

chapter 15

Corin's eyes opened. He looked over at Josephine and she was sleeping like an angel. Sighing, he waited patiently for Josephine to rise, he wanted to help her when she woke. He was not entirely sure if she had comprehended what had taken place last night. His fear right now was that the change would make her crazy, dangerous enough to possibly kill herself. As the sun started to fade from the sky and the night shades covered the world outside. Josephine's eyes fluttered, then, slowly opened. A little disorientated, Josephine slowly began to sit herself up in her bed. She said nothing. Looking around, she noticed that her sight was sharper; she was seeing clearly in complete darkness, total clarity. Realizing that something was different about her she started breathing quicker, her heart was beating so loud it was thundering. Josephine quickly realized that her not only was sight changed, but her hearing was enhanced as well, the sound of her own heartbeat was excruciatingly loud. She lifted her hands over her ears to drown out the noise. She was still looking around in awe when she realized Corin was standing next to the bed. Towering over her.

"What have you done?" she said in a low whisper.

"Josephine, you were dying, I had no choice. I asked you, I let you choose your fate. You chose life." Corin said flatly. He was telling her something, something important, but the noises were so loud, she couldn't concentrate on his words.

"The noise is so loud, I can't make it stop," she whimpered. Her hearing was heightened. It was more defined. She was able to hear the panting of her dogs downstairs, clearly. She heard the beating of Corin's heart and his soft breaths. Feeling overwhelmed, panic started to set in.

"If you concentrate you can turn the volume down. Try it, it might be a little disconcerting at first, however as you become accustomed to your new abilities you will find that the ability to control them will be natural." Josephine obeyed and suddenly found herself feeling less angry and more curious.

"How are you feeling now?" Corin asked. Josephine heard more than just the words; she heard the concern in his voice. She felt it, his emotions pouring into her soul.

"I…I… I'm fine, I think. What happened to me? I feel…I feel…. different, somehow, I feel like I am feeling your emotions. How is that possible?" She asked looking at up at Corin, with bewilderment in her eyes. She was a child of the night asking a parent for help. Although she put on a brave face, Corin knew she was frightened, uncertain of what her life would become.

"Tell me what you remember," Corin said tenderly.

"I remember getting ready to come home from the Island. Mallory and I put the kids in the car then I saw her face. She was white as a ghost. Then, I turned and saw Nawzir, from then on everything is a blur," her voice wavered. "I remember waking up, strapped to a bed." The words were stuck in her throat; she forced them out. She fought to hold back the tears which were starting to form in her eyes. "I...he...I was held in place while he..." She broke off. She couldn't say the words. Corin entered her mind, looking for the answer. When he found what he was looking for, she watched as his eyes changed into darkness with a blue flame that indicated to her that his beast was just beneath the surface. His eyes had a feral look in them, filled with so much hate, she felt consumed as the emotions rolled off him in waves. They were suffocating her. His emotion was a living, breathing entity that he was engulfing her room. Josephine wasn't prepared for his reaction. She wasn't ready for the intense anger that she was suddenly feeling; without warning fear gripped her. She was unsure whether she should continue or not.

"There is no need to go on Josephine, I know what he did." Corin said angrily. "What else do you remember?" he asked, trying to soften his voice, realizing that he was scaring her and this is not what she needed. She needed comfort and he was not giving her comfort he was making her afraid of him, afraid of his wrath. It was Nawzir who should be afraid of Corin's retribution. Corin realized his mistake and knew he had to regain control of his emotions. For Josephine's sake he had to.

"Mallory, I remember Mallory, she was yelling at him, trying to lure him away from me, it was making him angry. It didn't work. I remember being awake and asleep, I didn't know if I was dreaming, couldn't tell what was real, what was fake," she lowered her head in shame. Her breathing was becoming erratic and in quick bursts. "He was on top of me, slapped me, putting himself in my...my...mouth," she said as new tears spilled from her eyes. "I think...oh God; he held my mouth closed, pushing inside me, in and out! In and out!" She cried. "Oh God! What did he do to me? Why?" Anger and disgust coursed through her body, she wanted to hit something, someone. Corin was still in her mind, watching as the memories like a movie before him. Once again, he had found out what his enemy had done. He saw her pain, felt her pain as if it were his own. Corin's anger grew and the air in the room became more turbulent. A storm. Josephine thought her room was going to explode with bolts of lightning.

Nawzir you will live only to regret the humiliation that Josephine suffered. A promise, Corin meant to keep. Sitting down beside Josephine, he held her close while she cried; her whole body was trembling, her breathing coming in short quick breaths, as she continued to cry. Corin realized in that moment that he never felt so helpless. He had no words to comfort her, so he remained quiet.

Josephine remained in Corin's embrace as her crying subsided. He gently brushed his hand through Josephine's hair, pulling a tendril of hair back from her forehead, exposing her glistening emerald green eyes. The smell of her hair was like Lavender and Vanilla. Her sweet fragrance stirred a hunger deep within him. He tried to pull away from her, knowing what he needed to sate his hunger. Josephine refused, she held him tight. Understanding what she needed, Corin found that he could not pull away. Fighting the urgent need rising inside him, he placed her needs first. When Corin looked down at her, he saw her enormous eyes; they were starting to fill with tears. He wiped the oval drops that slid down her cheek, and again the need to comfort and care for her surfaced. Corin found that he was struggling for control despite his best efforts. *Desperate times call for desperate measures.* He caressed Josephine's cheek once. Twice. Then in one fast movement, he moved from her, grabbed her by the chin, and forced her to look directly into his eyes as he began to speak to her with soothing words. A comforting, calming voice.

"Josephine, we have to talk; I need to explain some things to you, but first you must believe me when I tell you that things are going to be okay. You will be able to find peace and draw strength from your ordeal. As it is with all things, you will need time. Time to heal. Time to adjust to your new abilities. Time to learn your weaknesses. Then when you are well, together with the aid of your friends, we will get Nawzir and we will finish this together," Corin said undoubtedly, confidently. "Right now, you need to concentrate on what you have and what you have gained. Focus your energy on getting better, stronger. You are safe and you are alive. More importantly you are here for your children. That is what you need to concentrate on," Corin said encouragingly.

Josephine was a little angry at what Corin said, albeit she understood what he was trying to do. Forcing herself to relax while. Corin adjusted the pillows behind her she sat back., Looking at Corin silently, thoughtfully.

"You're right," she decided. "I have my life and my children. I feel strong, and healthy." The words strong and healthy echoed in her head. *How could I possibly be strong and healthy? That bastard raped me, beat me, and cut me all over. How can I be here, alive? I should be in a hospital bed near death.* Josephine pondered over her thoughts for a moment. Corin watched her intently as she realized the truth. She watched Corin with weary eyes waiting, wanting him to say something. *Vampire. Corin is a vampire, Nawzir, is a vampire. Am I a vampire? How? Who?*

Me. It was me. The words entered her mind. Her green eyes flashed up at Corin.

"I did it. I brought you across." Corin started to pace. "You were dying. There was not enough time to get you to a hospital, and even if I had, you would have died. You simply sustained too much blood loss from your injuries. Once Donovan and Marcia came for you and Mallory, I had to keep both Nawzir and Jonah from getting to you. When you were safely away from them, I was able to get away, I retrieved you form Donovan and came straight to your home. Corin told her the tale of how he came for her and Mallory. *"I waited until just before dawn to help. It was a mistake. One that would cost you your life. I came in, broke the bonds that held you and Mallory, I told her to keep you safe until Donovan and Marcia came for you. They reached the place after dark. I had no choice, I had to hold off Nawzir and Jonah until you and Mallory were free. Unfortunately, I could not fight them both without causing serious injury to myself, a necessary price. I had no time to finish Nawzir and Jonah off; you were running out of time. When I got you home you were dying, I asked if you wanted to live and you said yes. I did what I had to do to ensure that you could live; I bathed you, dried you and put you to bed. I stayed by your side until you woke,"* Corin said, as he continued to pace.

Shocked Josephine sat in silence. She wasn't sure what she was angered by more, that a man whom she'd known for only a few days saw her completely naked while he bathed her or if it was because he had turned her into a vampire. The emotions that played across her face told Corin everything.

Fear followed by anger, then fear again and finally concern. Emotions played across Josephine's face as she struggled to gain control. She was changed. There was no going back. *Deal with it Josephine, you're alive,* she thought to herself and took a deep relaxing breath. Moments later, calmness flowed through her; washing all of her fear, anger, and concern away. Corin was still pacing, like an anxious father. Making a small noise with her throat she got Corin's attention, Josephine patted a spot beside her on the bed that invited Corin to come and sit.

"I have questions," she said, as Corin walked over to her side. He sat down on the place she had patted on the bed.

Corin faced Josephine and their gazes locked. They stayed like that for a few moments, as if they were choosing the correct words to say. "Corin, I want you to know that I'm not upset by what you did, as a matter-of-fact I'm actually kind of grateful. You may have changed my life but I at least I'm alive. I'm just a little um… overwhelmed, I guess; my life has suddenly changed, and not in a small way. I don't quite know how to deal with it. What am I going to do when you leave me? How will I be able to take care of my children? Will I be able to see them, grow with them, or will I miss out in their life because I can't be with them during the day?" Josephine tried to keep from crying but the thought of not being there for her children was too much for her to bear. As hard, as she tried the tears came anyways.

Corin felt her words; they struck painfully, into his entire soul. Corin reached out for Josephine, pulled her close. "Do not worry my little one; you will have your life, with your children, I promise you." He brushed a lock of hair behind her ear. Corin, pushed Josephine away gently, he looked into her emerald green eyes; he kissed her gently on her forehead. He was about to explain things to her when he got distracted by her wide glistening eyes, and her shiny moist lips. Unable to resist; he couldn't stop. He leaned in and kissed her. He tasted her, savoring her as if she was his for all time. He tasted the salt from her tears, and the warmth of her moist mouth. Corin was expecting her resistance, but when she didn't pull away Corin took full advantage. He kissed her hard, devouring her mouth, taking control. He explored the warmth of her, memorizing the shape of her lips and her sweet taste. The longer they stayed joined, the more he deepened his kiss. His fangs threatened to break free, his body instantly hardening. His body wanted more, demanded more. Corin pulled away, he could feel the silent protest come from Josephine.

"I am sorry," he said as he got up from the bed. "I should never have done that. Forgive me."

Josephine looked up at him, her eyes betrayed the hunger she was feeling for him. She was all too aware of him; it bothered her, not understanding why she was feeling this way she was, she retreated into her mind. "I...uh...don't worry about it. Things happen. We just got caught up in the moment," she managed to get out. She lied. There was more going on then she wanted to admit. *What in the hell is wrong with me? I have two kids and my husband just died—I haven't even buried him yet. This is wrong. Relax Josephine. Calm down. One. Two. Three. Four. Breathe. One. Two. Three. Four. Breathe. This is nothing more than vulnerability rearing its ugly face, that's what it is. It's rebound. Vulnerability and rebound. What a kiss though. Stop it Josephine, NO more thinking of kisses of any kind!* Josephine forced the thoughts of kissing him from her head. *Deal with this later.* Forcing herself back down to reality, Josephine focused.

"Corin, I can't think straight right now. I'm confused, more than ever and…" She trailed off. "I need to stay focused; I need to see my children. Where are they? Where is everyone? Mallory? Marcia and Donovan?" Still recuperating from what just happened Corin looked at Josephine, confused, although he seemed to understand. "Corin?" Josephine said his name.

Corin smiled inwardly. His chest a little bigger; *she may want me after all. This is overwhelming for her. All she needs is time.* He knew that this dilemma would end once Nawzir and Jonah were destroyed. Another spark of hope filled his chest.

"Corin," Josephine said his name again getting his focus back to her.

"They were coming home when I left them. They should be here momentarily," Corin said as he came back to the present situation. "Did you plan on telling them? What are you going to tell them about your situation? Mallory knows, that just leaves Marcia and Donovan. I suspect everyone is aware of my secret. As for your children I assume they are with your mother," Corin said. "You should probably call to let her know you are ok," he added as an afterthought.

"You're right. I'll call her now." Josephine got up from her bed, grabbed the portable, and punched in the numbers. "Mom? Sorry it's so late. I'm fine, really. Well I'm glad Marcia filled you in and I'm glad you listened. I was calling to let you know that I'm fine. I wanted to check on the boys. I need another favor from you; I need you to keep them a little longer. I need make this situation go away, and I don't want them being around all this ugliness. Do you mind? Great. I promise I'll be safe. You could say I've got a better handle on things," Josephine looked in Corin's direction. "Have Rick's parents arrived yet, obviously I don't know since I've been tied up. Okay well when they do would you mind? Thanks again! Rick's body is being released at the end of the week, the funeral will be a small one, and it's going to be at night. Can't explain right now, but I will soon, I need to deal with something first. I love you Mom, and please keep my boys safe, they are all I have. See you soon, I promise. Give the boys hugs and kisses for me please. I miss them terribly," Josephine said. "Thanks again, for everything. Bye." Hanging up the phone, she glanced at Corin. "Okay, tell me what changes have taken place with my body. Will I die in the sun? Do crosses burn me? You know; are all the things that the myths and tales say true?"

With a hearty laugh, Corin said, "I will answer all your questions. First off, you already know about me, about vampires. Sunlight can kill us. We need blood to survive, but that does not mean you have to kill to live. We live in the twenty first century; there are other ways to get what is needed. During our regeneration sleep, all our wounds heal. We are immortal, which means, you will never grow old and you will never suffer from any diseases. We do however have our weaknesses, first and foremost is the sun. Ancient vampires, such as myself can withstand the morning light, provided there is overcast; in direct sunlight, I would no doubt die. I can survive because I am a 'Pure Blood' and because of my age. Being a 'Pure Blood' gives me an advantage along with different strengths. Being newly turned, you will not be able to withstand the sunlight. Some of our other weakness that can be fatal if not handled properly is when we bleed, we bleed a lot, if a fatal wound is left un-attended, and we can bleed out especially without being replenished. One of our blessings is our curses, it is our ability to feel things deeply. Whether it pain or hunger. We feel it intensely." Deliberately he decided to leave out the part of having a heightened sexual drive, knowing that he was leaving out important information. . He figured that she would come to realize this, and if the question arose he would answer her.

"Is that all?" Josephine asked skeptically.

"There are a few more things you need to know; first, you and I are linked, there is a blood bond between us now. This became permanent when you drank from me. Second, we can talk telepathically, more intimately than before. I will always know where you are, no matter what the distance, the same goes for you. Third, whatever you feel, I can feel. In other words, when I am being hurt or have been hurt, you will feel my pain and the same will be for you. I have told you what you need to know," Corin said, even if it was only half the truth. "You will learn what is left on your on your own. Nevertheless I am sure you will have questions, when you do, please ask." Corin said.

Josephine sat speechless on her bed. Not quite sure what to do with the information she was just given. She just sat. Corin looked at her, trying to ascertain how she felt without going into her mind. "Are you okay?" he asked with some concern in his voice.

"I'm fine; it's just a lot to take in," she said calmly. "Corin, how will I live?" she asked.

With those simple words Corin started to pace, like a caged tiger. "I was thinking…and this is just a thought. I own property in Ireland; it belonged to an Irish family clan a very long time ago. It was in ruins when I found it. I had it restored. The land is plenty and the Residence is big enough that anyone living there will have privacy. I was thinking if it is acceptable to you, that you and your children could move there, with me."

Josephine's face had turned ashen; she had a blank look on her face. "I have lots of wealth, you would not have to work and your children could go to school or have a home tutor. You would not need anything; I will provide for you."

"What about my friends, my mom?" Josephine asked. "You're asking me to give up everything," Josephine stated.

"You can bring your friends, even your mother, if they want to come. There is more than enough room. They could look after the children during the day. They would also be able to provide protection for us. I will give you anything that you need Josephine. You are not alone in this," Corin said with a much softer almost pleading voice. "Come, stay with me?" he said.

Sure. I'll come to stay with you, what choice have I got. She thought to herself. "I'll have to think about it," she lied. Corin smiled knowing exactly what thoughts had just passed through her mind.

"Sure. Take all the time you need, I know this is a big decision," he said, confidently. Josephine looked at him, confused. "I should probably tell you that unless you guard your thoughts I can hear them," he said with a serious voice. Josephine had heard his words, but she hadn't put one and one together yet. Then, flushed with embarrassment when she understood, she took a pillow and threw it at him.

"Ass!" was all she managed to get out. Changing the subject quickly she asked. "What are we going to about Nawzir and Jonah?"

"First we will wait for your friends to arrive. We will not be mounting a counter attack without them. In the meantime, we should discuss some things about Nawzir. I probably should have told you sooner, but I did not expect that the situation to turn out this way. Since you are now a vampire, you need to know the entire story behind Nawzir and Jonah. I suspect that Donovan has other information for you. For now though, you will hear my side of the story."

Josephine looked at him. Suddenly very aware that she was breathing quicker; her stomach was tightening. She started recalling the conversation that they had when she first found out about Corin, there were things that he had said, which at the time, made no sense to her, because she couldn't quite understand what he as telling her, she chalked things up to delusions, 'a misunderstanding' of the information. Josephine suddenly became aware of her feelings. She was feeling fear. She searched her mind, remembering Corin's earlier words, the ones about guarding her thoughts; she quickly envisioned a huge stonewall; building it up in her mind as it appeared in her vision, it enclosed her feelings and thoughts. *What should I know? What could he possibly have to tell me? Nawzir and Jonah, are murdering, sadistic bastards, who kill for no reason. They rape and torture women, for their own twisted pleasure.* "Go ahead, tell me what you think it is, I need to know," she said.

Corin couldn't read her thoughts. "Nawzir and Jonah are two of three people that I transformed into vampires. It was a long time ago. They were all dying. I saved them by siring, all of them. In essence, they are part of me, my family in a manner of speaking. I showed them the ways of our kind, I taught them all that they needed to know to survive. When it was evident that Nawzir, Rowen and Jonah did not want to live by our rules, it was too late; had I known why they were being stoned and learned of this before I sired them, I never would have turned them. They were killers; realizing the mistake I had made, I vowed, after being approached, by the elders of my people, that I would hunt them down and destroy them. Meanwhile they became even more ruthless, more dangerous. Rogue vampires, which are how my people know them. They hunted and killed without mercy and have been doing so ever since. Corin said.

"Why do they call themselves brothers?" Josephine asked.

"They consider themselves brothers because they were all sired by me. I should have let them die and never brought them over," Corin hissed, as he turned away from her, trying to hide his shame.

"Wait a minute. Who in the hell are Rowen and Jonah?" *Rowen, Rowen. I know that name. From where?* Josephine held her head, her thoughts were in chaos, and there were flashes of Donovan, of a man, ashes. "AHHHHH!" Josephine screamed. She fell to floor still holding her head. Corin turned, sensing her pain. He went to her. Putting his strong arms around her, he lifted her to the bed. "What do these two other men have to with this?" She asked, before Corin could ask what was happening to her.

"Rowen is dead. I killed him two years ago after *someone* tracked him down. I have been after these vampires for some time now. Rowen, made a kill fifty years ago, the case remained unsolved until a highly classified branch of the law, reopened the case, with outside help, they were able to track him down. If it were not for that group, I would not have found him. Anyways, Nawzir and Jonah are after me because in their eyes, I killed their brother. They want me to suffer for what I did. Capturing you was a lure, meant to get my attention," he lied. "When we go up against them next time, I have no doubt that Jonah will be participating. These vampires are dangerous; Josephine, I would also understand if you choose to take your family and leave. I can take you to Ireland until this is over, you will be safe there, I have friends that I can call, they will watch over you," Corin said.

Josephine's stomach tightened, she felt ill. The thought of Corin going up against these vampires alone made her angry, she found herself feeling particularly protective. *I don't understand the feelings I'm having. God help me, please.* "I'll stay and help bring these bastards down Corin. I'll help you destroy them, I refuse to let you fight on your own, especially after all that you have given me," she said adamantly.

Corin's heart melted at those words. He felt pride and it showed in his face. *God, how I want to kiss you, I need to kiss you. I want to make you mine, claim you as my mate. Be patient.* A smile curved Corin's lips. *I will have you Josephine. I know you want me; I felt it in your kiss.*

Josephine just sat and watched Corin. He was thinking something but when she tried to search his mind, she found that he had closed her off. "Have you told me everything?" Josephine asked, as her eyes searched his face for the answer.

"There are some things I left out because it is not my place to tell you. You should speak with Donovan when they come home. That is all I can tell you." He lowered his eyes, guilt swept through him. *I know the whole truth Josephine, I know you lead me to Rowen. Why do you not remember the past? It is as if it has been erased. When the truth is revealed, I hope you can deal with it. You must deal with it. If you are unable to, then, I will be here for you. I will always be here for you.*

Puzzled by the comment, she didn't push. *I know there's more to this I can feel it in my bones.* Getting up to shake off the unwanted thoughts Josephine suddenly heard herself screaming as she saw red, holding her stomach, she was screaming in pain doubled over in pain; both knees on the floor one arm across her stomach as she cried out again, while her other hand held her steady. She looked up at Corin as fear swept took over. The pain was so intense and that wasn't the worst of what was happening. Something strange was happening in her mouth. Running her tongue across her teeth she realized that she was growing fangs; dragging her body over to the mirror, still clenching her stomach, she pulled her body up, placed her hands flat down on her bureau. She opened her mouth. Her knees buckled. Corin was right there to catch her in his arms.

"Corin." she screamed through clenched teeth, "what is happening to me why am I hurting like this?" she cried out. "Why. Don't. I. Have. A. Goddamned. Reflection?!" she tried to say in a calm manner. "I believe you forgot to mention that part."

Corin held her close, as he steadied her over to her bed. He once again placed her gently down and faced her. When their eyes met, he saw a storm of fury welling up. The predator that she became was trying to surface. Her eyes, turned black, she was about to explode. As he caressed her face, he watched as another emotion sparked in the depths of her eyes. Her black eyes, started to turn back to their natural state. The emerald green eyes that held anger just moments before were now burning with hunger.

"I am sorry I didn't tell you. The pain you feel is hunger and yes, your fangs, will lengthen when you are hungry or angered. Strong emotions bring them forth. When you feed, the pain will subside. As for your reflection, I am truly sorry. I have lived without one for such a long time I had forgotten. I am deeply sorry."

"In case you forgot I don't stock blood!" she said.

Corin looked hurt, when Josephine said those words, not because they had hurt him but because she sounded disgusted with her new life. She had hurt him, even though it was unintentional. Lowering her eyes; she grabbed his hand. "I'm sorry, I didn't want to sound like I was disgusted; the words just came out that way, the words just came out wrong," she tried to justify.

"You will have to take from me. Later we will find some blood and stock your fridge." Josephine opened her mouth as if to speak, then she thought the better of it. Looking at Corin directly in his eyes for a moment, her gaze wandered over his perfect face, down to his neck; there she found the vein that pulsated. She swore that she could hear the blood flowing through him, calling to her. Josephine didn't wait for his instruction. Pulling Corin to her, she brought her lips to his neck. Her tongue lapped his neck, for only a moment, and then without warning, she bit down gently puncturing his vein; blood flowed into her mouth. As she swallowed, the pain in her subsided.

Meanwhile it was taking every ounce of strength that Corin had to not throw her down on her bed and make love to her. The feel of her tongue, the movement of her lips, as she suckled, had the most erotic feeling. His body was reacting, the pleasure and sensuality he felt. He wanted her, his body demanded that he take her. His groin hardened and his breaths became quick as she continued to suckle. Finally, he pulled himself away from her. His body was hot and beads of sweat had formed on his brow.

"I am sorry, you have to stop, if you do not, I will not be able to control myself," he said as he turned away from her, not wanting her to see his shame at the lack of his control.

Josephine looked at him. "What just happened?" she asked. I felt funny. *Okay, so I'm lying. I felt good and oh, how I wanted him, I needed him to take me. So, this is what it means to be a vampire. Now I've become a bloodsucking nymphomaniac. Great! Just great!* Josephine forgot to guard her mind. It became evident when Corin let out a laugh.

"No, you are not a nymphomaniac, but you are a more sexual creature. As I said before, sex and bloodlust, when combined is very powerful. Your body was simply reacting to your hunger and when you fed it became more than hunger, it became something that needed to be sated, physically," Corin said.

Great…just freaking great. I can't even deny my feelings. My vampire self won't let me. Now I know what it feels like to be betrayed, by me! I'll be sleeping with tall, dark and handsome before I know it. As if that's not enough, I'll be enjoying it. Great! Allow me to flush the toilet! There goes my mourning period. "I know this will be hard for you Corin, but I need your help to control this. I'm just not ready for this yet," Josephine spread her arms wide, embracing the air around her. "I'm confused. This thing between us, whether it's the sex, bloodlust, a blood bond or just true feelings. I can't deal with this! I don't want this to be a rebound thing and I definitely don't want to hurt you," she sighed. "I need time, to work things out in my head, to be okay with what I decide, *and* more than that, I need to be able to live with the consequences of my decision. Please understand," she said. The honesty in her voice touched Corin.

"I do and I will. We will get through this together and when you are ready we can explore, or not, whatever feeling or issues you have. I am not here to conquer you or make you mine against your will. I will however, concede that I want you, but you have nothing to fear from me," Corin said. He had said the words that she needed to hear. He also knew that he would keep his word. This battle required his strength. For both their sakes.

Josephine smiled at Corin, she had found comfort in his words, and her instincts confirmed that she had nothing to fear from him. She got up from her bed and looked at Corin's neck; she was surprised when she saw no wounds. She walked over to him, touched where she had moments ago bit him and drank from him. There was nothing but smooth skin. He stood there, motionless, not even daring to breathe, for fear of inhaling her scent, which would send him over the edge. Corin let her explore, all the while, his body was burning all over from her soft touch. Corin explained it quietly to her mind and she accepted the explanation without any questions. She pulled her long delicate fingers away from him. In silence, they both walked downstairs. As they reached the bottom, they heard a car pull up. Josephine walked quickly over to the door and opened it.

Donovan, Marcia and Mallory were getting out.

How do I tell my friends I'm a vampire? As her friends approached, she could sense their apprehension.

chapter 16

Jonah brought Nawzir and the supplies to the cave that he had found. They went down deep into the core of the cave. When they reached, the depth that they were satisfied with, they went through a series of mazes. They had found a chamber, which had an underground water source. Not that they needed it. It could however come in handy for their guests. Nawzir and Jonah left and continued searching.

"We need a place that we can mount the chains. I would like to have both Josephine and Corin against a wall with their hands above their heads," he said with some thought. After some time, not too far from the water source, Nawzir found a suitable place. "This chamber will do," Nawzir said. Jonah dropped the bags, and began preparing the chamber with its new décor.

Even someone as old and powerful as Corin would not be able to break his bonds. The priests' prayers and the additional blessing on the Holy Water would give the dipped chains power to weaken him, especially when his skin is burning. Nawzir smiled at his ingenuous.

Jonah had walked over to him and handed him a pair of leather gloves. They each put them on and pulled out a set of chains each. They dipped the chains again as this Holy Water now had an extra blessing and then they proceeded to mount them on the two rock formations, which had protruded from the wall itself. The two of them worked hastily as time was of the essence. They laid down the wood and each pulled out a knife. They each grabbed a pile of stumped wood; they began hacking away at the wood until they started to come into form. As quickly as they started, they finished. Each of them had made several stakes. They placed them where they would be accessible. They also strategically placed them a means of intimidation, not so much for Corin but for his possibly new fledgling.

"Jonah we must do something to get Corin and his new mate out here. The catch is that it has to be only the two of them. Once we dispense with them, we can move on or claim this territory as ours. If their friends insist on playing the game then we of course, shall oblige them," Nawzir sneered.

"Well we could summon him telepathically and challenge him, we could also inform him that if he brings the mortals, they will be dealt with, and their blood will be on his hands," Jonah said thoughtfully. "We could also track them, wait for Corin and Josephine to go out searching for us and capture them," Jonah added.

"Decisions. Decisions." Nawzir said with a wicked smile. "We could also hit Corin where it counts. We can always start to go after humans, leaving a trail of dead bodies to lure him in."

"What about..." Jonah was cut off.

"I am not worried about the police because Corin will

undoubtedly clean up our mess. Yes. I think I like that plan better. What do you think?" Nawzir said as he tapped his finger on his chin thoughtfully.

"I think, I like how your sadistic mind works," Jonah laughed.

"Let us wait until tomorrow then. Tonight, we shall feed, enjoy the night, find us some women, and see what the rest of the night has to offer," Nawzir said finishing the conversation.

Jonah did a once over of the party area, when he was satisfied, sure that all things were in place and ready for their guests' he nodded his head in approval.

Perfect, everything is perfect. Would you not agree Nawzir? Jonah directed his thoughts at Nawzir. Nawzir looked at his brother and readily agreed, the nod of his head showed his approval.

"Shall we go?" Jonah asked.

"Let us go out and hunt. A celebration hunt," Nawzir finally said. "Then we can go and mingle among the humans at one of their night clubs. No one would be the wiser." Nawzir added.

"Agreed." Jonah smiled.

With their preternatural speed, Nawzir and Jonah went to the city where they mingled amongst the humans gaining entrance to one of the establishments; once inside, both went their separate ways, always maintaining contact. Nawzir found a nice dark corner to hide in, scanning the mindless humans until he came across one he liked. Focusing on her mind he located her amongst the stinking drunk, and the high crowd. Stalking up to her as only a predator could, stealthily and concealed in the shadows he manoeuvred around until he found her. There she stood a slender woman with ample curves, the movement of her body, made him hard. Her appearance did nothing for him; it was her mind. She was dark. Very dark. Her mind was beautiful; full of depravity, filled with torture and sadistic rituals. *My type of woman.* He approached her, not waiting for an invitation; he pulled the chair out and sat down. Nawzir called to his brother telepathically.

Come join me, I have someone interesting to introduce to you. I believe you will like her.

chapter 17

Josephine was panicking, as everyone got closer to her. Gripping Corin tighter and tighter, she was losing her nerve; she knew he was behind her, towering over her. *I am here little one.* Corin sensed her fear and her sadness; his heart ached for her.

Calm yourself, little one. Things will be okay. Your friends are stronger than you think. They are more accepting of things that go bump in the night than you know. You will see. Corin gave her arm a gentle squeeze to snap her out of the trance-like state.

"Corin, Josephine." She heard a strong, male voice. It was Donovan. Corin acknowledged with a slight nod of his head. Josephine, still held by her trance, said nothing. Her face was blank, without emotion. "Josephine? Are you all right? Let's get you inside and sit you down. You look like death."

If only you knew how right, you are. Josephine thought to herself. Donovan ushered her inside, pushing past Corin. Snapping out of her trance, she realized what was happening and came back to the here and now as she let herself be guided into the house by Donovan. "I'm fine, Donovan. Thanks for asking," Josephine said, as she sat down and watched her friends all gather into the kitchen. Josephine didn't expect Mallory to get all huffy and puffy about her current situation but she fully expected that Marcia would try to kill Corin. She also didn't expect Donovan to be acting so calm.

Before Josephine could get a word in edge wise, Mallory piped up. "Corin, you fixed her? Is she like you?" Mallory asked.

Corin just stared at her for a moment. He was trying to get a grip on her straight forwardness. "Yes," was all he said, his voice held anger yet he maintained his composure.

"How do you feel, Josephine?" Marcia said. Her voice was a little shaky.

"I...er...uh..." Josephine stumbled over her words.

"Spit it out woman, how does it feel to be a vampire?" Marcia asked openly. Josephine said nothing. The shocked look on her face spoke volumes. She turned to Corin, silently, asking for help.

It is okay, he whispered to her mind.

"I know that Mallory knew. How did you guys know?" Josephine asked, more relaxed. Suddenly she felt accepting of the situation. It wasn't as bad as she thought it would be.

"Donovan, I know that there's some stuff you need to tell me," she said as she made direct eye contact with her piercing emerald green eyes, it was a hard, cool stare that bored into him. Donovan nodded. There was a silent understanding that had passed between them.

"Long story short," Donovan began. "Corin called us to come and get you and Mallory, when the shit hit the fan. When we got there, you were badly beaten with severe lacerations. The cut on your head looked as if it had opened and closed several times. Corin told us to grab you and Mallory and get out while he held back the others," he droned on, as if tired of saying the same thing over and over.

"I already know that much," Josephine said. "You owe me other explanations," Josephine demanded.

"Oh." Donovan said, lowering his eyes, hoping that the crimson color wasn't showing all over his face. "Fine, I guess there really isn't a better time than the present," Donovan started all over again. "The truth is I'm not an ex-cop. I'm still employed. Not only am I still employed but I lead a group of specialists. We investigate and try to solve paranormal cases. They are actually cold case files, which are left aside because the circumstances surrounding the deaths are not...normal if you get my drift. Manny and I have worked cases together before, so have *you and I*. I work in conjunction with the CIA and the RCMP. Two years ago, you assisted us in a case that has been dead for about fifty years. A man was murdered. Details of the case indicated that there was no blood left in the body, and not much left at the scene itself. We re-opened it, and with your assistance, we were hoping to solve it. The victim had his throat ravaged. The autopsy indicated there were two puncture wounds on his throat. It also indicated that there was massive trauma to the body. For some reason you were able to find solid leads. At the time, we couldn't figure out how you were putting things together but you did. In any case, you led us to a character by the name of Rowen. I guess you indirectly led Corin to him." Corin cocked his head sideways. "Let me finish, you'll understand," Donovan said as he looked at Corin, warning him not to say anything. "We found Rowen; rather, we found a pile of ashes and a wooden stake. During the course of Josephine's investigation, we were able to determine that Rowen had two companions. Nawzir and Jonah. We were unable to find them. There was a witness who saw you, Corin," Donovan said. "The witnesses gave us a description but we were unable to find you. We did the only thing we could, we had the witness give a description to a sketch artist," Donovan stopped. Josephine was numb all over again. Mallory, who had only known part of the story now had the entire truth; and remained quiet.

"Is there anything else, or is that it?" Josephine asked as she pushed her anger down.

Donovan dropped his head forward. "Yes, there's a little more," Donovan added. "When Josephine brought you home, I contacted my resources and asked for confirmation on Corin, and any current paperwork. When my colleagues finally got back to me, the paperwork they sent me included a sketch of Corin. It was then, that I realized I was dealing with vamps."

"I don't remember any of this. Or you," Josephine said as she turned to face Corin. "You knew. You knew, this whole time." Josephine said through clenched teeth.

"Josephine, Corin didn't know, he couldn't have. When you first came in on the case, Manny and I sat you down and explained the repercussions of you knowing about these things. We had advised you that 'the powers that be' wanted a safety net, the only thing that we found acceptable, was putting you under hypnosis. You agreed to this and even signed the waiver. After we finished our investigation, you agreed to come in for some tests. We needed to know how you were able to hone in on our perp. As it turns out you have psychic abilities, ones that you even weren't aware of. Therefore, after we concluded the tests and closed the case we had you hypnotized, as per, the agreement upon which you took the job. You have to understand, *this had to be done*. We are a classified agency. We couldn't and *can't* afford to have you slip up. When you approached Manny and asked for help, he knew something was up, he blames himself for what happened to your family. He reached out to me and asked that I get involved. I had to come in undercover to keep information that came out to a minimum," Donovan finished off.

"Is that all of it?" Josephine asked with a bite to her tone.

"I'm truly sorry for deceiving you, Josephine. We feel bad but we had to do our jobs. We've been aware of the existence of vampires for a long time. We don't usually bother with their kind but there has been a rash of killings going on so we had to intervene. I had assumed that's why Corin came, after I had determined he was a good guy. Unfortunately, keeping Marcia out of the loop failed. Anyways that's my story in a nutshell," Donovan said, lowering his eyes because he knew he was guilty of keeping a secret that had put not only Josephine and her friends at risk but it had already taken Rick's life.

Numb from the confession that just spewed out of Donovan's mouth, Josephine just sat there, absorbing the information. The blood started rushing to her face, the tears that had started to moisten her eyes fell, and still, she said nothing. Josephine's stomach started to tighten; her anger was so intense she thought she was going to explode. She was positive that there was steam rising from the top of head.

Calm down my sweet. What is done is done. There are more important things to worry about. Josephine slammed down a wall in her mind, hoping to keep Corin out. Corin pushed past her blockade and stayed as a shadow, hidden in the corner of mind. Josephine did not want to hear reason right now. She pushed Corin's words from her brain.

"I will not calm down. My life has been at risk for at least the last two years and I didn't know." She said out loud. *Maybe I did know. The dreams that have plagued me endlessly started two years ago. Did the hypnotism block my abilities? I knew someone close to me was going to die, it happened. I knew. My sub conscious knew and was trying to warn me and I didn't listen.* Josephine thought to herself. She knew Corin could hear her but he said nothing. *I killed Rick, I got him killed.* The words echoed in Corin's mind.

No, little one, you did not. Your husband died at Nawzir's hand not yours. Corin's words whispered in her mind.

Corin's last words made Josephine feel uneasy. She squirmed in her seat, trying to hide her uneasiness from her friends. Feeling the eyes of all her friends on her uneasiness grew. Feeling sadness and confusion, the emotions played across her face. Then anger and finally guilt, she had come full circle. Then the overwhelming emotions of everyone in the room combined with the loudness of her friends beating hearts were beating at her mind, they were hurting her head. Unable to control the sounds, she was losing control. She needed help.

Lower the volume. Corin instructed her, the words shimmered in her mind. Focusing she concentrated on lowering the volume. Relief surged through her when she heard only her thoughts.

"I am not crazy, a little on edge, but not crazy." Josephine said as she shrugged her shoulders and smiled. Her friends stopped whatever it was that they were doing, which just happened to be sitting at the table with odd thoughts going through their minds, they stared at her in silence, with confused looks on their faces. "New house rule," Josephine said. "I'm not going to hold grudges, or get even with everyone who has kept me in the dark," she said as she glared at Donovan. "I'm going to accept that I am no longer human, that there are deranged vampires hunting me for something that I don't remember doing, I'm also going to accept the fact that I'm very confused and I have a variety of very messed up emotions that I need to get a handle on," she eyed Corin. "I'm going to sit back, absorb all of this new information, and then I will come up with a plan to save my ass and the asses of my family and friends. We're going to work together like good little girls and boys to accomplish this one simple task." Does anyone have a problem with that? It was a rhetorical question, but she had to ask.

Mallory and Marcia said nothing. They sat silent for a moment, absorbing all the events that had transpired. When Marcia could not hold her tongue anymore, she decided to try and make light of the circumstances to ease the tension.

"So, Josephine, who's vampire ass our we kicking first? And...Er... where are we going to get food for you because I still want to eat with my BFF, I just am not really into your new diet," Marcia said with a very cocky smile on her face. "You're not going to make us bring you people are you, so you know, you can feed? Are you?" Marcia asked with a horrified look on her face.

"I think you have read too many vampire novels and watched too many movies," Mallory said out loud, as she erupted into a heartfelt laugh. Josephine looked over at Mallory, Marcia and then Donovan; and she burst out laughing so hard in fact, that she had tears in her eyes.

"I'm not going to eat you or turn you into a slave," Josephine said with a devilish grin. "Maybe just a drink or two," she added. Josephine winked at her friend as another bought of laughter filled the room. "Corin has explained what I need to do and where I can go for my new diet," Josephine stated. "My life has changed significantly; I'm going to need all the help you guys can give me," Josephine stated. "Right now, though, my main concern other than Alex and Charlie is to find the bad vamps and end this, once and for all. Once that is over, then I will have to focus on my life, "Josephine said as she looked at Mallory, Marcia and Donovan.

Josephine was being a trooper, she was putting her anger and fears on the back burner, she was determined to deal with the problem at hand. Josephine looked over at Corin, "So, what's the plan Stan??" she asked as candidly as she could.

Corin looked at her with his brows furrowed. "I am four millennia old, and you call me Stan. Will wonders never cease? I have never been addressed like that in my entire lifetime." Corin said with indignation.

"Can we skip the lectures?" Josephine said with a tired, smug smile.

"Back to the matter at hand; Nawzir and Jonah have been ruthless and relentless. We know that they are here to avenge their brother Rowen. Josephine and I are the targets; Nawzir has made that quite clear that he intends to watch me suffer. According to Nawzir, by capturing Josephine he will torture her in unspeakable ways while I am forced to watch her torment," Corin stated. He turned to Josephine, "since you are new to this life; you are not as strong as you would like to be. You will do as I say," Corin said gently, it was a command, and everyone recognized it as such. Josephine ground her teeth.

"I will do no such thing, I have my own mind and my own will, and for the record, I may not be working but I'm still a trained P.I, with my own set of skills. I didn't know who or w*hat* I was up against. Now I do and lest you forget, I am not some docile woman from the sixteen hundreds, don't you dare start treating me like one. My family and friends are at stake here, I will most certainly not sit on the goddamn sidelines while two psycho vampires try to destroy me and everyone I love, you arrogant, self-absorbed, obnoxious man." Josephine announced back adamantly.

"This is no time for dominance or arguments. We have other things to worry about," Donovan said, apparently deciding to be the voice reason. "Corin what is your suggestion, let's figure out a plan," Donovan said.

"I know that Nawzir will not be foolish enough to try and come for us. I also know he will also choose another playground for us, which will be well-hidden. They will also allow me to locate them. I believe, if they can, they are hoping to lure Josephine as well. They will undoubtedly plan for you to try and follow but they assume that you won't be able to track them, hence the new location."

"So, in other words, they have a trap waiting," Mallory said.

"Yes. I believe that Josephine and I should be the ones to settle this matter. I can tolerate more than Nawzir and Jonah are aware of and I am older, which means I have different strengths. Nawzir and Jonah are not purebloods and will not does not because I am a pureblood. That is I am born a vampire. I turned Nawzir, possess what I do. This does not negate them though as a threat. Even with all my power and strength, I still have weaknesses," he said as he stared into Josephine's eyes. "I believe the best course of action is for us to track Nawzir and Jonah and face them. This battle will be to the death," Corin said.

"Why?" Josephine asked horrified.

"The only way to destroy a vampire is to kill a vampire."

"That should be easy enough," Donovan said. "A stake through the heart, right?"

"No, not really. A vampire can regenerate by going into regeneration sleep for a long period of time, they can also regenerate if another of their kind is close, and all we require is the blood of a vampire to be spread or dropped onto deep cuts or wounds that could cause significant blood loss. For fatal wounds we require the life force…the essence of another vampire to force regeneration. If this life force is not available we can go into the ground and sleep, in our way of regeneration sleep and heal, this process takes a long time and leaves us quite vulnerable. To 'officially' destroy a vampire you must make the heart explode within the body and then you must incinerate the body itself. If this cannot be done because of circumstances then a stake through the heart as well as the incineration of the body will destroy a vampire. In either case, you must see that the body be burned," Corin stated. He was uneasy; he had just told everyone how to kill him.

As if on cue, Donovan spoke, "Thank you for telling us, for trusting us enough with your vulnerabilities. You don't have to worry about us Corin."

"I believe to win, we must play their game, but no one said we couldn't modify the rules," Corin said with a smile.

"The problem that I see, is that I will not be able to take both Nawzir and Jonah alone, not to dismiss you Josephine, but you are new and not at full strength, it is not enough to take on Jonah or Nawzir, it would only serve to get you killed. That I cannot allow. We will need your help, it will be how and when you strike, that will be the difference, of our success or failure," Corin stated.

"Can't you see what they're planning, you know that mind thingy," Marcia suggested.

All eyes went to Marcia, and then focused back on Corin. "No, unfortunately, I cannot. He has blocked his mind and I can't break through his barriers." Corin said bluntly.

Donovan decided that he would jump into the conversation. "I have an idea, why don't Corin and I go to track Nawzir and Jonah, and then Josephine can do the 'mind thing' with *you*. She can track us, Mallory and Marcia will be back up for her. I don't think they will expect that. I think they are counting on luring you and Josephine to them. I may not be immortal but I have dealt with this type of thing before and I'm well versed in defending myself. I can probably be more of an asset to you then Josephine. Sorry but it's true," Donovan said, throwing Josephine a wink.

"What? No way." Marcia said.

"Like hell. This is my fight and I will not put anyone's life at risk! I don't need another death on my hands," Josephine declared, her eyes turning black.

Mallory watched as the argument unraveled. She decided that if everyone else is putting in their two cents, then there was nothing to stop her from doing the same.

"Uh, excuse me I think we are all jumping the gun. I think we should sit and talk rationally." Everyone turned and looked at Mallory. "Josephine, this is not up to you. If Marcia and I decide to help, then that's what we're going to do, period. You can't stop us. Second, our plan should be thought out. We need to think of all the consequences here, there is a lot at stake. We should be thinking of all scenarios, not just the obvious. As previously mentioned there are serious stakes involved here, not just our lives but also the lives of Josephine's children. We're all adults let's start acting it," Mallory said glowering at everyone in the room, including Josephine.

"Okay! Okay! Point made. We're all adults. Let's think this through," Donovan said agreeing with Mallory. Corin watched impatiently as the 'battle royale' continued.

"I am justice right now for my people and I have a job to do. I cannot afford to worry about the safety of humans and a newly made immortal," Corin said matter of factly. "I have to go in swift and hard. I have been hunting these rogue vampires that have haunted my race for two hundred years, this ends here," Corin stated. "This situation is new and dangerous, if I should fall in battle then you and the human race will never be safe; and Josephine will not see the light of tomorrow or her children again," Corin pointed out.

"First of all Corin, you underestimate us. Second, no one asked for your protection, you assume too much. Third, Donovan has dealt with situations like this before; his experience is an asset and not a liability, the fact that he's human gives you an edge. He can work during the day, whereas you can't. As for me, as I've mentioned already I'm a trained P.I with skills, thanks. I have always been able to hold my own ground in any situation. And again, now that I have all the facts, I'm not just a helpless 'newly turned immortal' as you put it," Josephine snapped. "As for Mallory, she has proven herself as a survivor; she's gone up against Nawzir and is still alive. Marcia has cunning and knowledge," Josephine said as she got up out of her chair and shoved at Corin's broad chest. "How dare you think you are the knight in shining armor here. Everyone here knows what you are, what we are," she said as she encompassed everyone in the room. "Everyone one of us can help so get over your old-world philosophy crap and join us in reality," Josephine added for good measure to make her point.

Everyone, including Corin, looked at Josephine with expressions of shock on their faces. Corin grabbed her hands. "I am truly sorry, I meant no offence. It is just that I have dealt with these filth and their treachery for centuries without the aid of anyone. I am not used to relying on others, especially when there is so much more on the line. If something were to happen to any of them….you…" he trailed off. "I would not be able deal with the outcome of that. If you were you to blame yourself, or hold me responsible for something happening to any of your family, I would not be able to live with that," Corin admitted as he lowered his gaze, ashamed. He let Josephine's hands drop.

"It's very considerate of you to take Josephine's feelings into consideration, but in the grand scheme of things, we're all going to do what is right. After all, Josephine is now what you are, so her well-being is our concern, and right now, we have to figure out how to stop Nawzir," Mallory said.

"What we need, is vulnerabilities. What are their weaknesses?" Marcia said.

"Besides what I already told you, greed, ego, and power," Corin said flatly.

"Forgive my bluntness, but what makes you different from them?" Mallory asked.

"I am pure blood, born a vampire when I came into the world. They were mortals, they were criminals; I did not know this about them when I saved them. I do not relish the idea of torturing victims. I do not feed as they do. When I take blood, I do not inflict pain or fear, I compel the person, take what I need, and leave the person with no memory of the incident. I also do not feed regularly on humans; I use blood from blood banks. I try to blend in among the humans and work along with them. They do not. They enjoy the kill, they relish the fear they invoke and they enjoy torturing their victim," Corin stated. "Make no mistake, I am not the same as them; they are vile, and with each kill they make, it makes them more unlike me. Eventually their soul will die and they will become pure evil. Then they will truly become 'The undead'. I am not a hunter; however since I created these monsters they have become my burden. There are others, like me, they hunt as I do; to preserve our kind, keep our presence hidden," Corin admitted as he shifted his gaze over to Josephine.

Reading her thoughts, *do not worry little one, you will not become like them. You are not like them. You are goodness and light. Do not be worried.* Corin broke his connection.

"This battle must be fought with cunning and we must fight hard. I believe that Donovan's plan will work," Corin said. "I must thank you all for your persistence in showing me that fighting alone was never an option." Everyone sat around the table discussing plans and who would be doing what.

Little one, there are things you must know. What I have to say will not be easy for you to hear and may be difficult to understand.

Since we have shared blood, I have made my claim on you as my mate, normally this would have been consummated, however under the circumstances, this cannot happen until you are ready. Nevertheless all vampires will know that you are to be my mate for eternity. I did not want to this to happen like this but it was the only way to save your life. The reason I am telling you this is because the bond that binds us allows us to feel and share our emotions and any physical pain. Most times this is a pleasurable experience but in this situation, it will undoubtedly cause pain, for both of us. The only time you will not be able to sense me is if I am unconscious or I am dead. Should this happen you will know immediately. I needed you to know this because it will be most difficult.

Josephine was a little angry at the news of her being the new mate to a vampire for life. She had not even had a say in the matter. Well that wasn't entirely true, she just didn't know what she was doing. That should count for something right? In hindsight, though she understood and accepted the situation. Things had happened that were unforeseeable.

Corin, I can admit that I'm having unwarranted feelings when it comes to you, and I can also admit that I don't quite understand them and they may be worth exploring. You have to understand that I can't possibly love anyone let alone be a mate for eternity. My husband just died; I have children. I simply can't commit myself. I understand what you did and why, .but this is too much right now for me. Maybe you should have let me go. Josephine projected her thoughts to Corin

I could not let you die. There was a connection between you and me, before the blood exchange. I felt your sorrow and your pain before I even came here. You have been part of me since I first saw you two years ago. I myself do not understand how this came to be, I just know that it is. I have come to love you over time. I saved you because I had to, not because of your family or friends or because of some debt. I saved you because everything in me demanded that I had to. I do not expect you to understand, but know this my life is yours and I will do everything I can to ensure your happiness. I know that you believe my words. Merge with me and you will have a better understanding. When you are ready seek out my mind, you will know the truth. Corin answered on their mental path.

Corin, I need time. I'm sorry; I just can't do this now. I need time. I need to adjust to this life as I am now. Please understand. Josephine answered him back sending waves of gratitude for his understanding.

I do little one. Take your time. Corin answered with a smile and an embrace. Both Josephine and Corin were brought back into the reality of things when Donovan spoke their names. "Corin? Josephine? What do you think?" Josephine looked in Donovan's direction and then glanced at Mallory and Marcia as if she were thinking things over. She opened her mouth to answer, but Corin cut her off. Corin had looked into the minds of Donovan, Mallory and Marcia; he knew where the conversation had gone so he answered.

"I think that will be fine. And I think I can say that this plan sounds safest for all involved."

What did you agree to Corin? Josephine asked

My little one we are going with the original plan that Donovan and myself will seek out Nawzir and Jonah if we run into any problems I will call to you for assistance. Corin responded.

Are you sure? Josephine asked.

I am. Don't worry everything will be fine. Corin left her with thoughts of warmth and safety.

Josephine brought herself back to the original conversation and said nothing although everyone was waiting for her input.

"Are you going to say anything?" Mallory asked.

"No. Donovan is right. If anything goes awry Corin can call to me. I will just leave it at that," Josephine said. Josephine was feeling tired and she missed her boys. She wanted to find a hole and crawl into it. One minute she was a living being, enjoying some time with her children and the next she was a rape victim, almost murdered and now she was a vampire. A freaking vampire! To top things off, she's a vampire that's having lustful thoughts of another man. *God what have I done to deserve this? This is punishment. I'm being punished.* Mallory and Marcia could see that their friend was in need and in great distress.

"What can we do Josephine? How can we help?" Marcia asked as she massaged Josephine's shoulders.

"Nothing. I just need to think. I need to be alone for a while. I need some air." Josephine got up from her chair and walked toward the door. "I'll be back. I just need some time." She left the room before anyone could protest.

"We can't just let her go walking in the dead of night. They could be out there waiting for her," Mallory stated furiously.

"Relax, I can sense Josephine, we are bound. I will know if she is in trouble," Corin said confidently. "However, if you want I can shield myself from her and follow her."

"No, let her be. She needs time to adjust. Let her walk it off," Marcia said and she turned instantly towards Donovan and gave him a warning look. Donovan understood and reluctantly kept his comments to himself.

chapter 18

awzir introduced his new young woman friend to Jonah. *You will like this one. I sense a very dark side to her. I think she will do nicely to help entertain our guests.*

Well if you insist brother. I have been thinking. Our plan needs some adjustments. Let us conclude our business here and tend to matters that are more important.

Nawzir took his female companion's hand and he bent his head and kissed it gently. "Would you like to join us, my sweet?" Nawzir asked.

"Sure, what do you have in mind?" She answered with a provocative smile.

"Come, let us leave this place." Nawzir gave a little push with his mind to compel her to listen. They all rose from their seats and left table. They walked to the exit with no hassles and left. Keeping their eyes open Nawzir and Jonah looked for an isolated alley, using their senses, scanning the area for any threats. "What is your name?" Nawzir asked.

"Scarlet. What's yours?" she asked.

"I am called Nawzir and this is my brother Jonah. I sense that you are alone, do you have any family here?" he asked.

"I have no family. I grew up in foster homes. Then I went to the streets. Nothing big really, I answer to no one but myself. I do what I want when I want. I do what I need to survive," she said belligerently as if defending herself.

Nawzir smiled at her, then at Jonah. Jonah smiled back, licking his fangs under his closed lips. *She will be a great addition to our little family, brother.* Nawzir projected at his brother.

We do not need complications. Jonah said. The trio turned onto a street, they continued to walk for a short distance. Nawzir stopped when he found what he was looking for. They turned into the alleyway, Scarlet's warning bells were going off choosing to ignore them, she continued. The alley was dark and deserted, even if it had it been occupied it wouldn't have stopped Nawzir. He was burning to taste his new acquisition. He was reading her thoughts and the darkness in her aroused him, it called to him. Her fear was also contributing to his excitement. Nawzir could feel his groin was tightening with anticipation. The thought of tasting her made his fangs ache to protrude. He needed her feeble struggles against the strength of his strong arms. He would relish the fight. It would only add to his satisfaction. In the end, the result would be a futile fight for her life, and ultimately her surrender.

Nawzir led her into the deepest section of the alley, hearing her heart jump; was making him feral. She attempted to pull away. Smiling wickedly in the dark, Nawzir licked his fangs. He put both hands on her shoulders and pushed her in. When he was satisfied that all of them were hidden Nawzir pushed her back against the brick wall. He raised both her hands above her head and held them there with one hand, as he explored her body with his free hand. He turned her head and licked the place where her pulse was most strong. He nuzzled his head nicely in her neck, nipping and licking. While his free hand ripped her blouse, which earned him a scream. Jonah moved in on the other side of her. He let his hand drop and he reached between her thighs. This earned and another terrified scream. Jonah didn't hold back, his fangs lengthened, showing them to Scarlet, who now knew that she would not survive this encounter. She tried to fight, but with her hands above head she had nothing to fight with. Her legs were pressed against the wall with Jonah's hand shoving up inside her, yet she still tried to kick with her stilettos. Everything was happening to fast. Then she felt the first pang of pain as Jonah sank his fangs into one side of her neck.

Nawzir was fixated on her breasts; hurting her, as he man handled her, twisting and pinching her hard. Her vision was getting blurred and it was getting harder to focus as the blood left her body. Hard as a rock and hungry, Nawzir wanted blood, seeing the fear in eyes and knowing that this woman was a person who got off on violence he couldn't wait to sink his fangs into her. He slowly licked her cheek and then again on her throat where the vein life flowed. He was in a lustful and feral mood; the color of his eyes had changed. Nawzir looked at her and he forced the eye contact with her so he could feel her terror. It worked, she let out one agonizing scream and then he sank his fangs into her neck. Already feeling the effects of being drained Scarlet's frantic fight for life had slowed, she was dying. Nawzir and Jonah thrived on this elixir. They kept sucking on her, savoring the taste of death. With blood soaked smiles on their faces they fed on her like frenzied sharks, her body became limp as her essence was depleted. . Her neck was ravaged and torn. Her body bruised and defiled. Licking their lips Jonah and Nawzir let the lifeless body drop as if it were nothing more than a piece of garbage.

"What should we do with her?" Jonah asked.

"Nothing." Let Corin find her, he can deal with the refuse. You know, she was delicious; perhaps we should have kept her. One day I will have to find someone that is my equal, so that I can keep her," Jonah said thoughtfully as he licked the last bit of blood from his lips.

"All in time. All in good time, Jonah," Nawzir said. "Tomorrow is our immediate concern and if it is to be ours, we need rest. Corin is old and powerful, we need to be at our best. Nevertheless, he does have a weakness. Josephine. She is a fledgling; her strength is not a threat to us and the humans are merely a distraction," Nawzir said with a shrug. Vengeance is ours; our brother will be avenged. You said you wanted to change something, what?" Nawzir asked.

"Josephine. We should get her; we should not let them come to us. I don't think they would expect us to come for her again," Jonah said. "Corin is experienced and knows our ways. Throwing him off would be an advantage," Jonah added. Looking at Nawzir, he waited for the response.

"You are correct, that move will not be anticipated," Nawzir stated, rubbing his chin. "Do not get caught brother," was all he said before disappeared.

chapter 19

Strolling leisurely down the street, Josephine enjoyed the night air. The warm breeze was having a rather soothing effect on her frayed nerves. The words, *psychic abilities* and *vampire* rolled around repeatedly in her head and each time she heard the words she became more agitated. "What was it Corin had said?" Josephine muttered out loud. *He said that he picked up on my sadness, my pain, did I draw him here? I can't be responsible for someone else's death. I won't be.* She tried to recall that conversation. Josephine grabbed her head as her emotions started to overwhelm her. She refused to lose control she pushed through all the painful memories and upsetting conversations. *I'm losing it,* she thought to herself, as she examined her sanity and her feelings especially the ones that pertained to Corin and her. Sighing, she knew she was doomed. *Own up to it girl, you have a comfort zone with him and you feel safe. You know it bothers you that he is leaving...are you going to lie to yourself or be truthful? Your old life, as you knew it is gone. What are you going to do?* She shook her head to clear her thoughts and focus on the night air.

Running her fingers through her hair, she gazed up at the night sky, looking for an answer. Josephine knew that when she looked into his eyes she saw compassion. She saw his love for her every time she looked into his eyes. It was as if he saw her and only her. His hunger and desire were evident; unfortunately, it was pulling her closer to the edge of insanity. *Who am I? My husband has died; here I'm actually becoming involved with someone else. Worse yet; I may love someone else. What will his parents think? What will my mom think? What will my friends think?* The voices in Josephine's head started talking, voicing their opinion. *"Are you so vain that you worry about what other people think? You're better than that."* The voices shouted at her. Josephine clasped her head, to make the voices stop. *They're right, those annoying voices, I have to ask myself; who I am? Has Josephine died? Am I no longer who I was? Have my children lost both their parents?*

You are a vampire, little one. The words shimmered in her mind, followed by thoughts of a strong embrace, comforting her.

Corin? Stop it right now, I appreciate your help, but I need my time. She needed her space. Her thinking time. Alone. She needed to sort through her confused feelings, *her* reeling mind. Josephine walk down the sidewalk and passed shops and bakeries; she finally stopped in front of a showcase window to see the display when she realized that no reflection stared back at her. She pinched her nose as she remembered that yesterday she was a human, that died and today… well she was not what she was, she had been reborn as something else, a vampire. Her first instinct was to smash the window, watch it shatter into small bits when she realized how much she wanted to destroy something, anything, she dropped her head.

What would destroying things get me? Nothing, that's what, no sense in getting angry, what's done is done. Now all I have to figure out is how to live. Again. Josephine found that she had wondered quite far, deciding that venturing out further might not be a good idea; she just turned around and started heading home.

Walking home her mind delved a little deeper into what she wanted and what her body really wanted; unfortunately, the two items were entirely different things. She wanted to take her time and not rush into anything, but her traitorous body wanted the exact opposite. Josephine's body shuddered at the thought. She shook her head, *betrayed by one's own body, humph.* Josephine didn't blame herself for her covets, she managed to justify her lust by blaming the desolate longing, she saw when she looked into the sapphire, depths of Corin's eyes. She had no doubts that when she did give into her wants and desires, Corin would undoubtedly quench her hidden longing. Josephine knew that Corin was dangerous to her; feeling as if she was spiraling out of control, her brain told her that she should run from him, but her survival instincts told a different story. With a heavy sigh, Josephine hung her head. The inner conflict would go on. Somehow, she would deal. She had to. For now all she could do was hold out as long as she could. The new emotions, the new instincts and emotions that were involved were raw, overwhelming. They continuously fed her desires, needs and wants. Heightening her to the point where she would inevitably lose control. In that new realization her brick wall a crumbled; the battle wasn't about fighting for what was right and what was socially acceptable, the battle *should have always been about doing what was right for her, to be alive and whole once again. I'm tired of this fight. Things are different now. I should accept what I have been given. Embrace this new life.*

Josephine's hunger was increasing, to the point where she felt her fangs lengthen. Forcing her hunger down; she fought the pangs of pain she refused to suck blood from someone. Forcing herself to focus, she centered her thoughts, bringing her inner battle back to the front of her mind. Muttering a curse when she realized that she wouldn't mind feeding from Corin. Damn him, everything came back to Corin. Corin had called her his mate. *Could I really be his? Can I get past my guilt? It's threatening to consume me?* Guilt, was now invading her thoughts, it coursed through her. She felt guilty at how she *wanted* Corin. Guilty that she *could* want him. *I have to try. My life is no longer the same and it never will be.*

Well at least you are coming to terms with things, my little one. I will give you the space you need; we are bound, we are mates. There has been a blood exchange and there is nothing that can be done. Nothing that I will do can change the outcome. Know this little one, my feelings for you are real; I will care for you always and forever. You will never ant or never need anything. I will provide and care for you. I am willing to give you the space you need, I have an eternity to wait to be with you. Be well, little one. Come home to me soon. Josephine rolled her eyes at him and hoped he could see it or feel it; however, he received it.

After what seemed like an endless battle, Josephine decided that things weren't all that bad; she was alive in a manner of speaking, she had her children. *Learning to be with Corin, wasn't going to be so bad, she could do worse.* She smiled to herself. *Under the circumstances, not many people would fault her for choosing to have a life with him.* A smile curved her lips once again. With Corin's help, patience, and support she would...*they* would get through this. Now she had questions.

How will we live? I can understand the connection, between us Corin, but how will I survive? I need my children; I have to be part of their lives.

You worry for nothing, little one. I have a home big enough to bring all your friends and family. I will provide for you all, should you choose that root.

Yeah, okay. What are you, some millionaire vampire? Josephine heard him laugh. She smiled.

Actually, yes, I am. I am known as Lord Corin O'Leary although titles mean very little since the nineteen hundreds in Ireland. You already know that I own a large amount of property there. I have enough money that your friends and family would not have to work. Over the centuries, I have acquired much and learned to use my old-world brain. Josephine had to laugh hard. 'Wow' was the only word that came to her mind. Talk about taking someone by surprise. She heard Corin's laughter as he touched her mind. *I told you that earlier, there is no need to worry. What is mine is yours. Albeit that our situation is unique, your happiness is important to me. I know what your family means to you. Since we have to be in regeneration sleep during the day, I thought that your family would be able to watch over the boys until you wake. It will take some time, and adjusting no doubt. Nevertheless, I do believe that we can all adapt.* Corin felt her smile and his heart melted, in that moment he realized that he did need her in his life, just as much as she needed him.

While Corin retreated to the shadows of her mind,

Josephine continued with her leisurely stroll. Now she took the time to really embrace the night paying attention to the stars, allowing herself to hear and take in the new sounds. She soon realized that she was looking at the world through new eyes. Finally, she was enjoying and taking her new life by the horns. Marveling at her improved vision, she was seeing with total clarity in the dark. Old landscapes and buildings were now alive with life. Her hearing was also improved, she could hear the bum that sat on the corner of the street muttering, she could feel the love emanating from the couple that walked on the other side of the street. She could also sense the malice of the drug dealer that hid in the shadows of the alley.

Corin what else, can I do?

You can do many things my little one. You are young, it will take time to master the art of shape shifting but in time this to will become second nature. You can also control the elements as you get older.

What? You mean I can change into animals and control the weather. Or do you mean fire and water?

Yes. You can and will be able to shape shift, along with the ability to control fire and water you can command the skies. There are many wonders that your new life has to offer. "Wow! That sounds so cool," Josephine said with a smile, Corin could feel her happiness, it brought him comfort. Josephine stopped to get her bearings, when she knew where she was she headed for the park. Going to the park, she figured that she could sit on swing and just relax, if only for a few moments before heading home. Paying no particular attention, she stared up into the night sky fantasizing while swinging lazily back and forth. Imagining what it would be like to change into a bird or some other creature. She hadn't noticed the man that was stalking her, watching her. Waiting for the moment when she would be vulnerable. Leaving the park and the comfort of her swing Josephine was oblivious to the danger that was following her; walking into secluded poorly lit area; she kept going to reach the path beyond. Then before she knew what was happening to her, she found herself on the ground looking up into a stranger's face. It was twisted with a scent evil permeating from him. Josephine was on the ground with her arms trapped beneath his legs. The man was tearing at her clothes. When she started struggling to break free from underneath him; that is when she felt it, the ice-cold blade against her throat.

"Give me a reason to use this, bitch, I don't care either way," the man growled. With his free hand, he undid his jeans. He was breathing heavily and the stench of his alcoholic breath was engulfing Josephine. The smell was so strong, with her heightened senses; she could smell the stink ten times more. The fetid smell of booze and drugs made her stomach lurch. The smell was literally making her gag. Taking his knife from her throat, he split her bra in half. This is what she was waiting for, this moment. Taking advantage of the situation, she struggled to bring her arms from her sides where the man had pinned them down. She managed to get at least one hand free. When he realized what had happened, he quickly added more pressure on her other hand with his leg, then he fought to grab her free arm, once he had her, he pinned it above her head. With both her hands secure, he reached down and started undoing her jeans. She tried once again to take advantage of the situation and struggled to gain her freedom. This time, the man pressed the blade into her throat and as her delicate skin broke, the smell of fresh, warm, blood floated into her nostrils, it was her blood. Something feral took over, she felt it, but instead of embracing it, she squashed the feeling, uncertain of her new abilities and strength.

Corin! I need you! Hurry, please!

Corin stood up suddenly. Before anyone could ask, he was gone. His blood was boiling at the sound of her distress. He opened his mind and reached out to her. He saw through her eyes for a brief moment, his fangs exploded in his mouth. Josephine felt Corin and the rage that was consuming him.

"You don't have long to live," Josephine threatened. "If I were you, I would get up and go while you still can," she said confidently. The man was no longer struggling with her jeans. Now he was working to get her panties off. Josephine might have been unsure of herself but she wouldn't give up the fight. She bucked under the man throwing his balance off. Angered, that he was having a difficult time with her constant moving and trying to keep the knife at her throat, he lashed out her, in the hopes that he would scare her enough into submission. Josephine got her arm free and slashed at his face drawing blood. Enraged he backhanded her with the hilt of the knife. Josephine said nothing and she kept squirming.

"You stupid bitch, struggle all you want, I will make sure to make it last longer!" The man slobbered out as he continued to curse. Josephine continued to fight. He was just about to pull her panties down when he felt a hand grab him by his neck. His grip on the knife tightened as he raised his hand and turned to face the person who had dared interrupt him, he slashed at his attacker. One of slashes caught Corin's wrist. Wild, and untamed, the beast within Corin surfaced as he threw the man against a tree and stalked slowly over to him.

"Come and try that with me," he growled baring his fangs. The man swung at Corin endlessly, each time missing his target. Corin slapped the man's hand down knocking the knife to the ground; he stepped in closer so that the man could see the demon that he had brought to life. The man stood face to face with Corin, staring into eyes that were black and soulless yet they looked as though they were on fire. The man started to scream; Corin quickly grabbed the man by his neck and snapped it without thinking twice.

Corin walked back over to Josephine who was doing up her jeans. Her hands were trembling. Grabbing her throat to stop the bleeding she realized that her wound was already starting to heal. She watched as Corin pricked his finger and smeared the blood on her wound. Instantly, the stinging was gone. She felt her throat once again and found that the wound was completely gone. Corin put his arm across her shoulder and they walked over to the partially concealed bench by the bushes. He sat her down and examined her more thoroughly.

"Are you all right, Josephine?" Corin asked as he removed the tendrils of hair from her face. Josephine could hear the concern in his voice and she took solace in that as she placed her head against his muscular chest. His voice was like velvet and it soothed her, helped to calm her. She lifted her head to him, looked into his eyes, and saw only tenderness and love. Corin wanted to take the pain away; at that moment, he wanted only to shield her from further harm. Josephine snuggled her head into his broad, muscular shoulder and allowed his arms of steel to hold her close.

"I'm okay," Josephine answered, she wasn't sure if she believed what she said, but what else could she do. These last few nights had been a living nightmare and all she could do was get stronger, not weaker.

"Why did you not fight back? You could have killed him yourself or at least defended yourself against his attack." Corin's voice was calm, not condescending. Although it was a question, there was still a gentle reprimand in there and Josephine recognized that. After all she sat not a few hours ago arguing the point that she could stand her ground. So much for that grand idea.

"I don't know. I think I was shocked, I was afraid of my new abilities," she managed a nervous laugh. She answered honestly.

"Well, my little one, you have the strength of ten men. You could have fought him off easily. When things have settled down, I will be sure to teach you our ways. Until then, if you ever need me, all you have to do is call me. I am but a whisper away," Corin said, smiling gallantly.

"You killed that man without a second thought. Do you think because you….we are stronger that we have that right?" Josephine asked the question without reprimand or judgment.

"No, my love, he attacked you and would have hurt you had you tried to fight. That is not acceptable, it could not be allowed. I am a vampire, and you are my eternal mate. It is my right to protect you," Corin said matter of factly. "No one shall hurt you or your family. If they try, then I will deal with them as I see fit. The man was not right. His aura reeked of evil and wrongdoing. It is better that I dealt with him than let him live to attack someone else." Corin answered her with complete honesty and Josephine accepted that. To Corin, his answer was logical and justified.

Corin pulled her close and if possible held her even

tighter, cradling her head to his shoulder. He brushed her cheek slightly and sparks of electricity from his touch came in waves that shook them both. Josephine felt the electricity and she slowly allowed it to embrace her. Without conscious thought, Josephine suddenly reached up to Corin's face and traced her finger along his jaw line. She raised her head, cupping his face in her hands, and then she brought her mouth to his. She kissed him softly, erotically. Then she forced herself to pull away and that left her feeling a little bereft, "I forgot to thank you for saving my life. Thank you." She nuzzled her head once again. Josephine found herself considering how hard it was for her to pull away from him. His kiss was powerful, alluring even. Tender. If she let it, it would consume her body and soul.

Unable to control his hunger or his beast any longer; he pulled away from her so that he could peer into her enormous emerald green eyes. He stared at her for a moment, taking in her beauty. She looked ethereal, with her pale face and her huge eyes. Her lips were full and held secrets that he longed to possess. Her hair was wild and silken. Corin reached for her; he ran his fingers through her auburn hair and then his hand fisted into her hair. Pulling her close he closed his mouth over hers. He forced her lips to part with his probing tongue and then he devoured her mouth. Corin tasted her sweetness and feasted. Josephine didn't fight the intrusion; she allowed it, her kiss matching his as aggressively.

Their tongues entwined and danced. His mouth took control and finally dominated hers, she didn't resist. Her need was building, matching his, as though their minds were becoming one. Josephine stopped momentarily; to look into his sapphire flame eyes; she found desire and passion, only for her. Corin impatiently pulled her back and continued his fiery kisses.

Corin let his gaze drop to her breast that was already partially uncovered, his gaze lingered for only a moment before he pushed the remains of the confining material out of the way. Her body voluntarily reacted to his touch. Josephine's body arched, exposing her breasts and inviting his touch. Her nipples hardened and formed tiny pinkish peaks as his thumb and index finger played; she let out a small groan. Her hands were all over him, before she could stop herself. She found his erection and she explored him, all of him, over his clothing. Josephine was undoing his pants so that she could release him but he stopped her and took control. Corin wanted to touch her, explore her. He continued to entice her by continuing to play with her nipples, then, when he was satisfied, he dropped his head and tenderly suckled on each breast. He let his other hand fall and started working her pants, while he let his mouth continue to devour her breasts, making sure to pay attention to each one. His hands successfully undid her pants and removed them. Josephine let out a gasp when she realized that she was completely nude.

"People can see us," she said quietly so she wouldn't draw attention to them.

"You worry for nothing love. I have shielded us from everyone's vision."

Josephine's head lolled back exposing her slender neck, her supple breasts and taut nipples, her body calling to him, beckoning him. Corin peered down at her, his sultry siren. Corin answered her invitation; removing his clothes, his erection burst free. He didn't try to hide his hunger from Josephine. He just simply continued with what he was doing.

He cupped her breast and then started sucking and nipping her nipple while his free hand made a trail of fire down her midsection. He found her entrance. He probed her determining if she was ready for him, slipping two fingers in gently at first, then moving at a quicker pace, maintaining his gentleness. He was relentless and domineering, allowing for nothing but Josephine's pleasure. Savoring every moment. Joining his mind with Josephine, he felt her as she climaxed, she let out a low groan and raked her long nails down his back and drew blood. Corin maneuvered his body so that he was kneeling between her thighs on the ground and Josephine was on her back on the bench. He leaned up over her torso and licked a straight line to her belly, smothering her body with kisses as if she were a goddess. She clawed at his back and moved her hands over his chest; she took her time committing every inch of him to memory.

His shoulders were broad and his body was rippled with muscles. He was so strong and he wielded so much power but when he touched her, he was gentle as if he were handling a baby. Josephine tried to sit up but Corin gently pushed her back down so he could have full access to her curvy luscious body. Josephine pushed back, sitting up; she was determined to taste him. She triumphed and she pulled Corin up. .

Josephine covered his body with her sweet, hot kisses. She gave him endless kisses as she touched and explored him; every crevice had been touched and committed to her memory. She touched his flat nipples with her tongue and flicked them until they became hard. She suckled each one and circled them. Then with her tongue, she moved slowly down his torso until she could feel that she was driving him over the edge. He was arching his body to meet her mouth. Josephine kept lowering herself; when she reached her intended target, her mouth slid around his length and tasted him. As her tongue tasted the tip of him she wrapped her hand around the base of him and stroked him. Gently nibbling; a low growl escaped him.

Woman you are going to drive me crazy. Can you not feel how much I want you? How much I need you?

I can. She laughed teasingly. *Can you feel me and the fire that you started within me?* Directing her thoughts at Corin.

Corin lifted her and pressed his body against hers so that she could feel his hardness. He wanted to show her that she was not the only one. He showed her how his body needed hers. As he towered over her, planting kisses on her sweet mouth, he gently lowered her down on the dew soaked grass; manoeuvring himself so that he was on top of her. Corin was like a wild animal trapped in a cage, when Josephine looked up into his eyes. There was wildness about him; he became feral as his hunger for her took control of him. He placed her hands above her and he put his head of his shaft down at her the junction between her legs. Josephine reveled in his power, enjoying the lack of control that he was trying to hide. Corin let his shaft explore her sweet, wet, entrance. Entering her slowly, Corin wanted to feel her muscles surround him, and pull him in. Josephine's body welcomed him, she was on fire; his mouth took hers as he forced his way in. His hands cupped her breasts his thumb and fingers rolled her taut nipples. Her body arched as he thrust into her warm sheath. He grabbed her bottom as she pulled his great taut ass into her. Sensation overwhelmed her. His mouth continued to suckle on her breasts, and he kept going until she had another orgasm. She climaxed and as she did, there was a sensation of relaxation and her body shuddered as she saw white stars; Corin bit down on the swell of her breast, drinking his fill.

"Corin." Josephine cried out.

Corin couldn't stop until he spilled his seed in his intended mate. As Josephine writhed underneath him and rode his shaft, Corin's climax came and he raised his head to the skies and roared his contentment until his body emptied into his Josephine. Corin let out a sated groan as the feeling of ecstasy took over. As the waves of sweet torment washed over Josephine and Corin, both lay on the grass and Josephine was still under Corin, resting her head on her arms.

Corin gently moved Josephine to his side; cradled her beside him as they both lay in the cool grass, still shielded from passer-bys. They rested. "My little one we should leave this place and go to the comfort of your home," Corin said in a smooth, sated voice. He had never in all his centuries felt so complete. His physical hungers, as well as his bloodlust were quenched. He turned to Josephine and smiled at her, his sapphire eyes gleaming against the light of the moon. He brushed the back of his hand against her cheek. "I love you, my angel of darkness," Corin was not asking for anything in return he was just stating the truth. Josephine sensed that and she hugged him close as if to say thank you.

Corin kept the shield up so that he and Josephine could dress. When they were dressed, he wanted to show her how to take to the air. He thought of an image. Corin -sent the image of a falcon to her then he coached her until she was able to shape shift on her own. Both of them took to the air

I love this. I feel so...free. I feel as if a weight has been lifted from me. Thank you, Corin. Thank you for giving this to me. Josephine was laughing and enjoying her new freedom.

Laughter was emanating from her as she swooped in low and used her powerful wings to pull up and soar to the sky.

I knew you would enjoy this, Corin laughed. He watched her, as she enjoyed herself. Being able to see her happy and not weighed down by the burdens that she had or the upcoming battle that she would have to face was something that only he could give her and he relished the thought. Tonight, was theirs and they would enjoy it. . Flying high overhead, Josephine enjoyed the view, breathing in new scents; they differed when she was in the form of a bird. Like a child she noticed all the differences and reacted with such a childlike excitement. Corin took pride in that. He watched as she had reveled in the power of her enormous wings. Before long, she realized that they had been flying for a couple of hours, exploring her new powers. She was starting to feel tired.

Corin, I'd like to home. Can you take me home now?

Follow me. Corin swooped in beside her, guiding Josephine to her home. They touched the ground about half a block away from her house and returned to their true forms. Corin reached for her hand and entangled his fingers with hers. He felt her reluctance at first but then he felt her welcome his touch. Corin knew that things would take time and he even entertained the idea that tonight was possibly a rebound situation. The idea saddened him. Almost instantaneously, Josephine felt his pain, an ache that felt like a knife through his heart.

Josephine thought about talking to his mind so that she could understand what was happening. Not sure how to handle the situation but needing to understand, wanting to clarify things, she stopped walking.

"Corin, please don't think of tonight as a rebound

situation. It wasn't. I'm not sure how or why but since we first met I have been drawn to you, like a moth to flame. It's weird, not normal. I've been at odds with my feelings, constantly in conflict; I have this thing…"she trailed off. "My mind tells me I shouldn't be feeling this way." Josephine paused. "You have to know that if I didn't want you then you would never have had me." Facing Corin and looking directly into his now flame blue eyes, she cradled his face. Standing on her tiptoes, she leaned into him and kissed him. Passionately, tenderly. Lovingly.

Her touch sent fire through his veins and he could once again feel the beast trying to surface to take what was his, to have her. He fought for control but each touch that she gave him and each taste of her tongue made him crave her. He not only wanted her, he *needed* her. Josephine was also fighting her own demon, something she had not anticipated. As she pressed her body against him, she could feel his erection fighting to burst free from his pants. Their heartbeats quickened, her body was on fire, she was wet and ready for him; her body was becoming a pliant, willing participant. Corin quickly planted the image of mist into her mind. Josephine followed Corin's lead and she followed. They slipped into the house unnoticed and went up to her room where they took their true forms. Corin ripped the clothes from her body as she frivolously clawed away at his. Josephine took control this time; she forced Corin towards her bed. There she dropped to her knees and traced a line on his inner thigh with her tongue until she found his erection. Her breath was hot as her breath grazed tip of him.

Corin released a low growl. *Woman you are going to kill me as surely as you are going to be my savior.* Corin's laugh whispered to her and pushed her to tormenting him even more. Josephine was pleased with herself as she felt Corin harden. Sliding her tongue up and down his shaft, she found the vein that brought him pleasure. Her silken, auburn hair grazed his body causing his body to shudder. Her touch was fuel to his fire, which was quickly growing out of control. Corin fisted his hand in hair, his body moving of its own accord and finding its own rhythm to keep in sync with the movements of her sweet mouth as she devoured him. She licked him and tasted him. She suckled him to the point where his knees buckled. Corin pulled Josephine away from him with the intention of putting her beneath him so that he could invade her. Instead, once again and to his surprise, Josephine pushed him backwards as she impaled herself on his erection, moving slowly, up and down. Quickening her pace bringing him to the point where he was going to explode. His growl was low and hungry. It was a warning. He wanted her and he wanted to possess her in a way that no man could or ever would. Josephine rode him hard and fast; bracing herself against his legs as she leaned back, inviting him to play with her breasts that were already stiff. He sat up slightly and thumbed her nipples. He cupped one, and then used his mouth on the other. She let out a moan as she continued to ride him. She could feel her fangs slipping out of their sheaths. Groaning once more she leaned forward so that her breasts were in Corin's' face.

Bending her head she ran her tongue over Corin's shoulder and with no warning she bit down deep. Josephine drank. While her mouth moved erotically and suckled Corin, she felt her body ripple with waves of sheer ecstasy. The white stars appeared swamping her mind, as waves of pleasure made her body shudder and contract around Corin's shaft. Corin's body was hard and pulsating deep within her. The intensity of what she felt invaded his soul; now it was his turn. The intensity of Josephine's first sexual feeling combined with his need was overwhelming; the erotic sensation of her mouth moving against him drove him mad with desire. The feel Josephine's muscles as they clamped around him, encouraging his seed to flow into her was too much for him. Corin ran his tongue over her neck and found her vein; he could smell her blood flowing. Without warning he bit down deep into her vein, as he tasted her sweet elixir his seed spilled into her and he thrust into her. In and out, in and out, faster and faster until all that remained was the sound of their two beating hearts.

Reluctantly Josephine removed herself from Corin. She turned onto her side, pulling Corin with her, nestling him comfortably against her bottom. Corin held her close. Feeling the imminence of regeneration sleep, Josephine succumbed. Corin knew that Josephine's windows were barricaded properly, yet he quickly looked over at the windows ensuring they were secure. Confident no sun would penetrate the barriers, he closed his eyes, welcoming the regeneration sleep.

chapter 20

Corin woke from his slumber before Josephine; he enjoyed watching as Josephine's body drew in the breath of life. Josephine's eyes fluttered opened, she found Corin watching her. She didn't say a word, she just lay there for a moment, savoring the peace and tranquility that she felt. Moving herself over, she snuggled close to Corin. Embracing her in his strong arms, Josephine sighed. Finally, she felt safe. She reached out to Corin's mind even though he was there right beside her, she found that she enjoyed that intimacy, and she was thrilled to death that she could now have private conversations without anyone being the wiser. She felt Corin stir in her mind; there in the shadows of her mind he was there smiling.

"We'd better get out of bed, if we don't the troops will coming looking for us," Josephine said, smiling her sweet smile. Corin smiled, loving the way her luscious lips looked, they were moist and full; he couldn't help but reach for her so that he could claim her mouth. She obliged him at first but as her body heat rose she forced him away, knowing where things would inevitably lead if they continued. "No, we can't, we have to get ready," she said as she shoved the blankets off and stood up, realizing that she was completely naked. Trying to hide her embarrassment, she left her face neutral but it was too late; a slight reddish color appeared on her cheeks. Reaching quickly for the nearest blanket, she wrapped herself in it. Josephine looked at Corin who was lying there on her bed as naked as she was, he was not even hiding his erection. It pleased her knowing that he wanted her, that he desired her. Corin smiled. He liked the idea that she was looking at him and that he pleased her.

"You should wipe that smirk off your face, it's unbecoming of you," she said while she pulled on some sweats. Josephine stopped dead in her tracks, her eyes wide.

"What is troubling you, Josephine?" Corin asked concerned.

"Nothing, really. I just…I'm hearing voices. I'm hearing Mallory, Marcia and Donovan. This happened last night but it was different, I guess I'm not used to hearing everyone."

Corin laughed. "Not to worry. That is normal. Everything happened so fast, I mean when I brought you over, our lengthy conversation, then your friends arriving home. I did not have the chance to explain the changes that would take place and how fast you would become accustomed to them. I am sorry for not telling you everything at the beginning. I simply figured that we would have plenty of time to go over all your questions." He smiled, knowing that he had reassured her and put her at ease.

"Corin we've got to go downstairs and assure everyone that I'm all right. I can feel the insecurity and tension emanating from them. I would also like to call my mother. I need to speak to Charlie and hear his voice. I miss them terribly," Josephine said as she lowered her face, trying to hide her pain. "I'm going to take a shower and freshen up. I'll meet you downstairs, if you need or want to freshen up you can use the bathroom in the basement." Without looking at Corin, she grabbed some clothes and hastily walked to the bathroom. Corin could hear the water running as he gathered his clothes and dressed.

I want to be with you, little one. Can I join you in your shower?

No, I need this time alone. Sorry, your touch drives me crazy with want and need. I need to settle my nerves. Maybe we both need take a cold shower and calm our hormones. Josephine caught the echo of Corin's laugh, making her smile. Corin reluctantly went downstairs, the man and the beast within him both protesting.

Do you feel what you do me, my little one? Corin's mind was silent but she felt him, there were waves of love and assurance filling her mind. Josephine smiled.

Thank you, Corin, for your understanding. Finishing her shower Josephine threw on some black dress pants, which hugged her bottom nicely along with a red spaghetti strap tank top, which hugged her breasts and made her even more alluring. Josephine braided her long hair, and made her way downstairs. Everyone had been lounging around, waiting for her. Donovan and Marcia were huddled close on the sofa watching a movie of some sort, Mallory was in the kitchen, drinking a coffee, and thinking about God knows what.

"Well it's about time you woke up," Mallory said teasingly. Marcia and Donovan popped up their heads to peek at her, getting up quietly they sauntered over to the kitchen.

"We didn't even hear you come in. You had us all worried.

One minute, we were sitting around talking with Corin then poof! He's gone. Not a word. Don't you think we've had enough surprises for one life time? Keep us in the loop, please, so we don't die of heart attacks," Marcia said half jokingly.

"I'm sorry. I ran into trouble last night and I called for him. It won't happen again, I promise," Josephine said.

"Trouble? What trouble?" Mallory asked, shaking her head.

"Nothing. Really, it was nothing. I sorta tried to deal with it on my own but it was a no-go, so I called Corin. Telepathically," Josephine added for clarification.

"No fair! How are we supposed to compete with that?" Marcia said pouting.

"Well, hopefully after tonight, we won't have to communicate like that. As a matter of fact, I really hope that I don't ever have to rely on people to come and save my ass any more since that seems to be the trend these days," Josephine said flatly. Corin walked in just as the conversation finished. He bowed his head in acknowledgment to everyone.

"Did I miss anything important?" he asked as he stood and faced everyone in the room.

"No. Not really. We were discussing my needing to call on people for help because I can't manage to take care of myself," Josephine said with some humor in her voice.

Everyone needs help at some point in his or her life. I am sure you will not be making a habit of it. Although... I do not mind coming to the rescue, if you plan on thanking me in that special way of yours, all the time. Corin laughed silently. Josephine heard the taunting in his laugh. No one else was the wiser. However, everyone in the room understood that there was a private conversation going on, that they were not privy to. No one said anything, but Josephine felt the tension, it was as if a blanket was floating gently down, suffocating the room.

"Coffee? Anyone?" Josephine said, trying to keep the awkwardness to a minimum.

The shake of heads answered Josephine questions. Marcia and helped themselves to some coke while Mallory finished her coffee. Josephine poured a cup for herself, as soon as she brought it to her mouth her stomach rebelled. *Force of habit, I guess I'm passing on that cup,* she thought to herself as she gritted her teeth.

Don't fret, little one. Have some water or juice; it will help with the discomfort. You should feed though you will need your strength tonight, as will I. How would you like to proceed?

Not sure yet. Leave it with me, at the risk of sounding mean; I apologize for my next comment. We can't talk like this in front of the gang like this. Can't you feel the tension?

Yes, little one, I can feel the tension. You must forgive me, this way of communication is more intimate and personal. It is more natural for us. I will try to keep the feelings of your friends in mind.

"I think I'm going to call mom and see how the boys are," she said, picking up the portable she walked into the living room. Corin waited until Josephine was out of the room. Clearing his throat to get everyone's attention he wanted to discuss the plan of action for the night.

"I think Donovan and I should head out. I'm pretty sure it will be easy enough to follow his tracks. What do you think Donovan?" Corin asked.

"I'm game. The faster this is over with the faster we can all try to return to our normal lives. If...pause. We can go back at all. Just let me get my stuff," Donovan stated.

Corin, Mallory and Marcia watched as Donovan grabbed his bag and checked it over to make sure he had everything he needed. Marcia was on the nervous side; Donovan could see it in her eyes, even though she had put on a brave face. He kept his eyes lowered as he loaded his gun, cocking it so the chamber was loaded. He wanted it ready to fire should the need arise.

"I'm ready." Donovan said, as he looked up at the woman he was starting to fall for. Donovan avoided touching Marcia, he was already in trouble with her and he knew it. He simply looked her way and nodded his head. .

"Mallory, will you let Josephine know that we have left. Be sure to tell her that I will call for her should we need assistance," Corin said in a polite voice. Mallory nodded her head in compliance.

"I still don't like this; we are stronger together. Do you even know where you are going?" There was a subtle reprimand, but not an argument. Corin respected that and appreciated her concern.

"This is a dangerous route to take, I agree, yet the only way to ensure that neither your or Josephine are no longer in danger is to dispatch justice to Nawzir and Jonah, the battle must be brought to them, not the other way around. This is the only way. My enemies are fools and they will allow me to find them, of this I am sure. I noticed that there were some mountains across the river. My guess is that they have taken refuge there. It is just a matter of finding them," Corin said, with a confidence in his voice, which even Mallory could not doubt.

"I'll let her know," Mallory said reluctantly.

"Don't worry; I have every intention of coming back.

We have unsettled business you and I," Donovan glanced longingly at her once more and then walked out the door. Marcia didn't even have time to say bye. He was already out the door trailing Corin. Marcia was about to close the door when she saw Donovan turned and looked at her; she waved him off and closed the door. She didn't wait and linger there because she knew she wouldn't be able to let him go. Josephine walked back to the kitchen where her friends were. She looked around the room with a puzzled look. Her eyes were flickering with emotion as she looked at Mallory.

"Where's Corin and Donovan?" She asked. Josephine knew the answer, her insides started to tighten.

"They left. Corin said they were going by the church where they found us. He said that there were some mountains across the river and that's where he expected to find Nawzir and Jonah," Mallory answered.

"I've gotta sit down," she said, placing her hand on the table for support. Both Mallory and Marcia came over to help steady her, cautiously.

"What's wrong? Tell us what to do," Marcia pleaded, her anxiety betraying her.

"Nothing. There's nothing that anyone can do. I refuse to go through this again! More death," she cried, as she covered her face with her hands. "Now, Corin and Donovan are out there risking their lives for me. I should be the one out there. Not them. And certainly not you guys!" Josephine said, as she slammed her fist down onto the table, breaking the corner off. Mallory and Marcia both jumped back in surprise to sound of the cracking wood.

"Listen to me," Mallory said, as she grabbed and shook Josephine with her shaking hands. As if the act of doing this was going to make Josephine come to her senses. "You. Are. Not. Responsible. For. Ricks. Death. You have to stop blaming yourself, and just for the record, why in the hell *are* you blaming yourself?" Mallory asked.

"I've been having a dream, more like a nightmare, for the last two years. My guess is it has to do with the physic ability that I have. In any case, the dream was about and has always been about death. I dreamt that I was going to lose someone close to me, and well… Rick's dead. How can I not blame myself? I knew about it. My sub conscious warned me and I did nothing about it." Josephine explained.

"That still doesn't explain how you were supposed to know," Marcia interjected.

"Did you see Rick's face; because I'm pretty sure if you did, you would've said something?" Mallory asked.

"No, I didn't see any face at all, all I knew is that the feeling that I had when I woke up each time was painful… I was hurting, emotionally," Josephine said, looking up at her friends.

"Well, if you saw no faces, how could you possibly know that it is was Rick? It could have been anyone. There is more than one male in your life that you are close to, you know. There is no way you could have known," Mallory said.

"Not to sound like a bitch, but I think you should worry about Corin and Donovan right now. You're going to have to get past the notion that you are responsible for Rick's death, I'm sorry. We… meaning all of us, need your strength right now, mentally as well as physically. This distraction of yours, is something we really can't afford, I'm sorry honey," Marcia apologized.

After that little speech, Josephine nodded her head

in agreement. She had to focus on the situation at hand; she knew, without a doubt, that what Marcia and Mallory had said was true. With all the strength she could muster, Josephine made the decision immediately, from this point forward she refused to allow self-doubt and pity consume her. Along with Josephine's new bravado, came the realization that she was getting hungry. She reached out with her mind until she found Corin.

I need food. What should I do?

I'm sorry darling, but you will have to hunt among the people or you can go to the nearest blood bank.

People? Won't I kill them?

No. Just take what you need. You have the ability to compel them and you can wipe the memory. Your saliva will close the bite and by sunrise tomorrow, the wound will be completely gone. You can ask your friends if you are comfortable, enough and you do not have to feed from the neck.

If I need you, will you be able to help me?

Yes. Just touch my mind. Josephine looked at Mallory and Marcia. Instantly they knew something was up.

"You need to feed don't you?" Marcia asked.

"Yes. Corin says I can go to a blood bank. In which I would have to steal or I can take from a person." Josephine looked as if she were going to be sick.

"So what you are you going to do? Kill a person for blood? I think you'd be happier stealing." Marcia said.

"No, I don't have to kill. Corin says I can compel a person and then wipe their memory. He also said that I can heal the bite with my saliva and the bite mark itself will be gone by morning."

"Really?" Mallory said.

"He said I should ask one of you, but only if I feel comfortable. He really didn't say much else," Josephine said.

You are so brave little one. I have to keep reminding myself of all that has happened. You lost your husband; your life has been threatened, more than one occasion. Most recently, you have become a vampiress. Now, here you are telling your most trusted friends that you have to feed. You are incredible. You accepted me for what I am, easily, before your change and even after we had lain together, you accepted me and accepted the changes that have become part of you. I am truly humbled by you and the fact that we are bound to each other eternally. Your strength and courage is a true miracle. I am in awe of your strength.

Josephine smiled at him and Corin felt her. *I have a lot to be thankful for. You've saved my life more than once. You've ensured that I will be there for my children. You've given me strength, which I could only dream of, Corin. I have many reasons to be thankful. As for our making love, well, I have never been so bold in my life and considering what could have happened if you hadn't come for me, well, I'm not sure even that I can explain. I guess I needed comfort; I needed to feel sexy, wanted. Maybe I needed to know on some level, that it wasn't my doing, or my fault, that I was attacked. It doesn't actually matter now anyway. When we made love, it was magical. I felt wanted, loved and desired. I'll remember it that way, without all the horrible things that happened prior.* Suddenly, Josephine felt as if Corin were there, embracing her in the safety of his strong arms. She felt love and acceptance.

"Josephine, snap out of it. Stop talking to him, and don't bother to deny it. Your face reddens when he's talking to you and you smile, a lot. I don't even think you know you are doing it," Mallory said, teasingly. "You've got to eat. What are you going to do? Mallory asked."

"Not really sure yet. Obviously, I'm not going to ask you ladies, to supply my food," Josephine laughed. "I will go out and either rob a blood clinic or find a person. You women, however, should probably grab something as well; I can hear your stomachs growling. What were you thinking of doing?" Josephine asked, casually.

"I guess we'll order out. I'm famished, what about you Mallory? We can go pick it up; we haven't... I haven't been out all day. I need the fresh air," Marcia said.

"I'll go too. We'll give you your privacy, for whatever you choose to do," Mallory added.

"Okay then! We'll meet back here. If Corin calls for me, I have my cell; I'll call you immediately, make sure that yours is turned on," Josephine said.

"You go ahead, Josephine; we still have to order our food. We'll lock up before we go," Mallory said.

Josephine grabbed her stuff and went outside.

You do not need your car keys, you know. You can travel by air; it is much quicker and easier. Corin slipped into Josephine's mind.

Won't people see?

No. You will appear as a blur. You will be moving too fast for the human eye to see.

How, exactly do I accomplish this? You helped me shape shift last time, remember?

Easy think about where you want to go. Envision the place; imagine yourself there, and then just go. You can shape shift but I think you are not ready for that just yet, it takes much skill and practice.

Ha! I can do anything that I put my mind to. Don't underestimate me, Corin.

You are not yet able to hold the form you take, you must concentrate on the image and hold your form at the same time, it is difficult, trust me little one. We will practice this when the danger has been neutralized.

You're an arrogant man. Josephine laughed. Corin heard her laughter and it warmed him. He enjoyed listening to her, and even more than that, he enjoyed annoying her with his old-world arrogance. Corin decided to remain as a shadow in her mind, ensuring that she was safe. He wanted to feel and see all that came her way. This way he would know immediately if she were to run into trouble. Although he felt uncomfortable with what he was doing, it was a necessary precaution, there was too much at stake and too much going on. Remaining as a shadow, without her knowledge was the only way. *I am sorry my little one. I will do what I must to take care of you.*

Josephine focused on where she wanted to be, just as Corin had said, and just like that, she was where she wanted to be; in the blink of an eye, she was there. It felt like a vortex of wind picking her up and taking her to where she wanted to be. *That was cool!* She thought to herself. *I could definitely get used to that.* Smiling outwardly and proud of her first success, Josephine proceeded to walk among the crowd of people that filled the downtown area. Opening her mind and embracing her new unique gift, she scanned the area, to her amazement she almost immediately honed in a lone male, walking on the opposite side of the street. She used her newly acquired ability and made herself appear on the same side at the opposite end. She walked in his direction making sure to come from the opposite way. Then she intentionally banged into him, head on. Pretending to be stunned, she apologized. She helped the stranger up and then started a conversation. With her soothing voice, she commanded that his mind become blank, then she convinced him that he had nothing to fear from her. With a last command, she took them out of view from the other passers-by. Without reservation, he followed her into an isolated alleyway. Josephine made sure to hide behind a dumpster and then, as she felt her fangs lengthen she leaned in to his neck, where she found his pulse. She bit down gently, careful not inflict a lot of damage and she drank. She took was needed to sate her thirst and then she licked his wound. With the pin pricks sealed off, she helped the man to the ground, placing him carefully. Josephine then wiped the memory from him, astonished that she managed her second feat she gave herself a mental pat on the back for a job well done. Then she stood in the shadows, waiting for the man to get up, and with her mind, she directed him to walk out of the alleyway. Once he was back in the safety of the street, she released him from her thrall. Josephine walked out from the shadows of the alley and watched as the man kept walking as if nothing had happened. Proud of herself she touched Corin's mind and explained what had happened.

Meanwhile Corin was fighting down his urge to kill the man that Josephine had fed from. The thought of his mate taking from another male brought out his jealousy out in full force. He tried to keep calm, knowing that Josephine would sense his emotions if he didn't.

Go home little one. Rest. When I need you, I will call.

Instead of using her preternatural speed, she decided that she would walk and enjoy the night. She had kept her mind opened and continuously scanned the area for any danger. She did not feel like running into any more problems.

I've had enough problems for one lifetime and then some. She felt Corin laugh. *What am I going to do with you?*

Anything you want little one. I am open to anything you wish to try on me. I am actually looking forward to your experiments. With that, Josephine sent the most erotic image her mind could conjure up. She felt Corin's breath stop and then slam out of him as he forced himself to breathe. Josephine laughed at herself for her little indulgence.

You know, you should be mindful of others. Two can play the game you know and I have had centuries to practice. Josephine felt her face flush as Corin sent back the most intense, erotic images, her mind had ever seen; she could even feel his hands splayed over her body, touching her in secret places that she didn't know existed. Her body, had an apparent mind of its own, started to react as if he were right there with her.

Stop that! Don't you have work to do? Corin laughed, but he did as she requested. Just before he let Josephine think that the connection was broken, he smiled that smug smile that males always seem to do and retreated into the shadows of her mind where he could continue to watch out for her.

Yes, little one, I have work to do but I can still be in your mind. I believe the word I am looking for is multitasking. Corin laughed once more and continued with job at hand. Josephine felt him retreat from her mind. She was just about to sing when the attack came.

Although her senses were open and she continuously scanned the area she was in, she was unable to detect her adversary. He was already taking hold of her, whisking her from the ground. Struggling with him relentlessly she managed to loosen his grip, she assessed her situation and her adversary; she could feel the power radiating from him. She knew she was no match for him, but she would stop fighting either way. She reached out for Corin's mind, once more on her mental path to him hoping that this vampire couldn't pick up what she was doing.

Corin someone has me. I couldn't feel his presence, I don't recognize him, but my gut tells me it's Jonah. He's too strong for me and I'm not on the ground anymore, what do I do?

Corin had known something as terribly wrong when he felt Josephine's struggle. He already knew that it was Jonah, since he had remained as a shadow in her mind. *This could be to our advantage little one. He will take you to where he wants us to go. Donovan and I will track you. Be strong. Trust in me, little one.*

"Jonah has Josephine," Corin announced angrily to Donovan. "He took her from the street and she is airborne, I instructed her to let him take her, this will be our way to tracking her," he added.

What about Mallory and Marcia, they'll worry when I don't return. Josephine interrupted.

I will have Donovan contact them. I will be able to keep track of you. Corin broke the link between them, as he pulled into a vacant spot in the woods. "Call the others and tell them to start heading out to where we are. Tell them where we pulled off and to keep the vehicle hidden," Corin instructed exiting the car. Donovan was already on the phone explaining what happened. Hanging up the phone, Donovan got out of the car. Corin looked around and inhaled the air. With a grim look Corin turned to Donovan, "I can smell death on the air, we are in the right place," Corin said, with a low menacing voice. Donovan didn't ask any questions, he knew better than to question how Corin knew. Although this wasn't Donovan's first battle with a vampire, he was still on the nervous side, Corin sensed it. He could hear Donovan's heart beat pick up and the quickness of his breath.

"Do not fear for Josephine; our enemies have not considered how strong she is. I am sure they believe her to be weak and of no use to us. They will fail," Corin said confidently. His confidence and conviction helped to ease the tension of the situation.

Both of them started the long hike to their destination, and just as Corin predicted the clues that were leading them to Josephine were dead on. Any other person on this mission would have been in shock, yet Donovan's constant exposure to death was constant, he had seen death up close this was easy to deal with. What was disturbing to him is that never, in all his time as a cop did he witness such useless, cold-hearted murders.

"Holy. Shit. What a massacre. What an incredible waste of life," Donovan said as he lowered his eyes and shook his head. Corin stared at the bodies, silently saying a prayer for the dead. He knew what Nawzir and Jonah were capable of; this was no surprise to him. Now, not only did they have to find the new lair, but also they had to make sure that no one would find the bodies, they had to eliminate them.

Corin and Donovan quickly gathered the bodies and put them into one place. Donovan was unsure of the reason behind this, but he kept his silence, watching, as if he were taking notes. Feeling frustrated by the amount of time they were wasting, Donovan thought about saying something then thought the better of it. Corin's face remained expressionless, although inside rage built with each body that was added to the growing pile. Corin was relieved that Donovan stayed silent and out of his way.

"We have to destroy the bodies so that no attention will be brought to my people. I will burn the bodies so that they will not be discovered," Corin said. Puzzled by the remark, Donovan just nodded his head, then it sunk in what had happened.

"You know, I sure would like that ability to read minds," he said with a bit of bite to his voice. "Do you need any help with this?" Donovan asked, as he swung his arms in the air encompassing the area of dead bodies.

Corin heard the hint of anger in the man's voice but could not argue about the matter. "This is what has to be done. I feel bad about the families who will never know what happened with their loved ones. However I cannot take the chance on people finding out about vampires, surely, you can understand this. If the former reason is not good enough then perhaps this one is, you must know that you would be putting Josephine at risk. Is that what you want?" Corin asked. Donovan was about to answer, but Corin interrupted. "There are people out there that don't accept vampires and would never tolerate our existence. I cannot and will not take that chance. I am sorry but I must do what I must do." Corin said, as he gathered his strength and called upon his demon. With a simple wave of his hand, a blazing fire appeared; the bodies started to burn and the stench of death was now forever etched in Donovan's nose. Corin immediately erected a veil so that none passing by would be able to see the billowing smoke clouds or the raging fire to call for help. Once the remains were just ashes, the veil would lift automatically.

"Wow, everything I have read and studied is true," Donovan whispered. Donovan looked at Corin, for the first time realizing and understanding the power that Corin wielded.

"We must get to the caves. Josephine is coming: I can sense her strongly now. Jonah is no doubt moving quickly to ensure that she is secure in the trap before we can get there. Mallory and Marcia are on their way, right?" Corin asked.

"Yeah, they are, but how will they find us?" Donovan asked.

"I am not sure, I can read thoughts and compel people and even implant thoughts but I can't communicate telepathically to humans, unless of course they have psychic abilities. The only thing I can think of is to compel them to come to the caves, but they will have to get into closer proximity, and even if they manage to get closer, I cannot guarantee that my ability to compel them to work. It would require a lot of power. "Corin stated.

"Well you've got power Corin, so what are you worried about. Didn't you say you were older and more powerful than them?" Donovan asked.

"Yes I did, and yes I am, but I have not fed and incinerating the bodies used a lot of power."

"So what you need to do is feed and then you can do the compelling thing or whatever it is you do? So feed what's the problem?" Donovan wished he could take back his words as soon as he heard them. With a shuffle of his foot, and his hand through his hair, he thought about the situation. "Will it hurt? The biting part? Will I know what is happening and most importantly will you kill me in the process?" Donovan looked at Corin; his eyes were that Sapphire blue with the subtle flame burning in them.

"No. I will not kill you, and if you choose, I can erase your memory. It may sting at first but nothing more," Corin stated, honestly.

"Do it. Do it now and do it quickly and *don't* erase my memory," Donovan said.

Reluctantly Corin put Donovan into a trance and then took his wrist and sank his fangs into him. He drank until he was sated. He released Donovan from his thrall. Donovan looked puzzled and remembered some of what happened and the remainder was blur. He didn't bother asking.

"Thank you," Corin said as he bowed his head to Donovan. "You should know that I can now sense you and track you," Corin said.

"Now you'll be able to do the compulsion thing, right?" Donovan asked wearily.

"Call Marcia and tell her to call us when they are in the woods," Corin said.

"We'll just have to pray that your little trick will work," Donovan said. Praying silently; for Corin to be as powerful as he claimed to be. Corin grabbed Donovan without warning and the next thing Donovan knew was that he was in a vortex of wind moving swiftly through the air.

chapter 21

Jonah touched ground; Josephine was clinging tightly to him as opposed to struggling to get free, although periodically she kept up the charade, fighting him at select moments. Josephine made sure to get in some good shots; she was using her new abilities. *At least my martial arts training is going to be tested, it actually has an impact on people...okay, not people, vampires.* Jonah, who was expecting some resistance, he wasn't prepared to have to deal with someone who could fight and actually make use of her power. Jonah had to admit he was surprised, when her punch struck him and he flew back. Corin had made it clear that she needed to be captured, she knew what she was up against; this was a test of her control, her sense of self-preservation just refused to go down without a fight.

Do not become over confident, little one. These pitiful excuses for vampires may not be ancients however they have power and strengths that I would rather you not be exposed to. Please tread carefully when you provoke their demons. Donovan and I will be there shortly. Do what you can to avoid losing your freedom. There was no reprimand in his voice only caution. Josephine would do what she could, to ensure that she was not rendered helpless so easily this time. This time was personal for her.

Jonah grabbed her by the throat he wasn't releasing the pressure and yet he wasn't putting any more on. Either way this left Josephine with only one choice; although she hated to fight dirty she would do what she had to do if it helped prevent her from losing her freedom, she kneed him in the balls and when he released her, she gave him a tiger paw move, which threw him once again away from her. Giving her the time she needed to run. Josephine knew she couldn't beat him, however she could always run, stall for time. She took off into the forest, and tried to take the form of the falcon that her and Corin had taken but the panic must have prevented the shift, because the next thing she knew was the steel of a hard fist which had slammed into her face, knocking her off balance. She fell backwards and hit the ground hard, landing on her ass, shaking off the force off the hit she looked up into those cold black eyes and saw Jonah. Reaching back with her hand, she grabbed some dirt and grass, flinging it into his face; she picked her butt off the ground turned around and ran at full speed. Scanning the area, she kept going until she ended up in front of Nawzir; who appeared out of nowhere. This time she faced him taking a fighters stance. Fists up protecting herself she was ready for him. She wasn't ready for Jonah who attacked from the back. Nawzir smiled and shimmered away.

I'm sorry Corin. I'm done, better to be captured then be killed, she whispered the words. Jonah dragged her through the rough ground, branches, rocks, twigs. Whatever was on the ground scratched her body, her face, and her arms. Once they reached the cave, Jonah let her walk; pushing her forward through the long passageways leading down further into the depths of the cave, once there he released her and threw to floor. Josephine landed at the feet of Nawzir.

"Any other day, I would have accepted you, groveling, at my feet for your pathetic life, but somehow I don't think that I would get the same feeling of pleasure and ecstasy as I would by watching you die."

Jonah grabbed Josephine by handfuls of hair and lifted her from the ground, she bit back her scream of pain, determined not to give them the satisfaction. As Josephine, rose and met her attackers face to face, the site Nawzir made her sick to her stomach. The memories of what he did to her overwhelmed her. When she saw the smug smile curve Nawzir's lips, she knew her mistake; immediately she envisioned a solid stonewall in her mind and slammed it down to keep Nawzir and his lackeys' out. Nawzir tried to probe her mind again when he didn't succeed, he shrugged his shoulders. He had already taken what he wanted. He had seen the images that plagued her mind.

"That, my dear, was all my pleasure," Nawzir said, as he bowed, as if he was accepting applause from a crowd. Josephine was disgusted with this vile creature. With emotions running high, and her not thinking clearly, out came the words that she wished she never said.

"At least Rowen got his just rewards." Josephine said. Nawzir stood in front of her face, towering over her. Without warning his fist slammed into the side of her jaw; there was so much power, behind the strike, that she flew into the wall of the cave. Josephine spit out blood and it hurt her immensely to move but she managed to regain her posture, facing him defiantly, she stood there her eyes flickering from black to green, with blood coming now from her now broken jaw.

That is not taking precautions, my dear. I said avoid to losing your freedom, I did not say to get captured and get the life beaten out of you. Corin was trying to be serious; there was reprimand in his voice, although he knew that what he said sounded like he was teasing. Corin was trying to remain calm even though his anger was rising from the depths within him. He was frustrated that he was not there, but carrying a grown man slowed him down somewhat, unable to do anything, he continued on his way. Corin decided that there was only one thing to do; at once, he summoned his strength from the depths within him, directing his power at the cave where Josephine was. Suddenly the ground in the cave started to shake; lighting danced across the sky, thunder rumbled and cracked, as if the gods were threatening to destroy the world. The thunder was so loud that it echoed even within the depths of the cave; it was so intense that Josephine had to hold her hands to her ears. Nawzir laughed, taking comfort in the fact that he had struck a nerve. It also confirmed his suspicions that Corin was monitoring Josephine.

Regaining her balance Josephine felt long cold fingers wrap around her wrist. With her long nails she scratched and kicked and she even threw punches as Nawzir dragged her deeper in to the caves. She didn't stop fighting; punching him square in the mouth it was her that drew blood this time and she raked some scratches across his face. Nawzir was relentless; finally, he managed to get her where he wanted her. Pinning her up against the wall with his grotesque body pressed into hers. He was relishing the feeling of disgust that Josephine harbored for him. His breathing was hot on her, as he continued to rub his shaft against her. Josephine squirmed to avoid his touch. Nawzir simply held her tighter. Jonah was right there beside him when Nawzir raised Josephine's hands above her head so that Jonah could place the shackles on her, then Jonah bent down and shackled her ankles, leaving her exposed and vulnerable. When the metal blessed with holy water touched her silky, soft, skin she screamed in pain, as her skin melted and her flesh seared.

The smell of burning flesh permeated the air it surrounded Josephine, in that moment she cursed her newly heightened senses. She fought the pain; refusing to scream further which would give her tormentors satisfaction. Knowing that whatever stresses she faced Corin could also feel, through their mind connection. She needed to focus on her wall, keeping her mind blocked. Corin felt her trying to form a barrier around her mind, and although she was strong, determined even she would not be able to keep them out because of the psychic link that existed. Even if he was thousands and thousands of miles away, nothing would be able to break that, even her. However, he let her think that she succeeded, if this was going to help her, then he could accept that.

Corin felt her pain as the chains seared her skin. He also felt her revulsion when Nawzir touched her and pressed his body into her, muttering an oath in his native language, he continued, determined to get there as fast as he could. They weren't far. *Nawzir and Jonah will suffer for this.* Donovan could feel Corin's anger; it was rolling off him in waves. They plummeted down toward the earth where Josephine was. Once they touched the ground, Donovan grabbed Corin.

"Listen, buddy, I know you're mad as hell and you want those bastards to suffer but you need to focus. Block her out or whatever it is you do. You're of no use to us or Josephine if you die." Donovan hated being the voice of reason but this situation called for focus, not anger. Corin glared at Donovan, his eyes black as an abyss, with blue fire in the depths; he was a merciless killer, waiting for the chance to exact his revenge. Turning away from Donovan; knowing what Donovan had said was true. He calmed his beast.

"You are right. I must remain focused." *Josephine I am sorry to do this but I have to block you out of my mind, your pain and fear are a distraction. I need my full attention to go after Nawzir. Forgive me little one.* Josephine was shocked when she heard Corin. She didn't even bother trying to figure out how or why.

Corin do what you have to do. It's a trap, Corin, you should just leave me here, protect my family.

I will do no such thing. You will live. You must live.

There's something on these shackles, they are burning my skin, and I suspect they want to do the same to you. Josephine summoned all the strength that she had left and she erected a wall, using every ounce of concentration to keep him from her mind.

The abuse continued, beatings that as a human she would never survive, hearing her own screams she silently found herself wishing for death, as the torture continued. Nawzir lashed out verbally at Josephine and blamed her for involvement in Rowen's death; with every condemnation, he slashed her body with his long, sharp, vile nails. Blood trickled from the open gashes, the smell of her blood was enveloping Nawzir and Jonah. Jonah and Nawzir were becoming more restless, pacing like the hungry predators that they were. Nawzir stalked up to Josephine and started groping her, touching her breasts, touching her most private places, Josephine squirmed but she was unable to move away. Jonah stood in the background. Watching, getting harder by the minute. The sight of Josephine struggling was turning him on. Jonah found himself wanting Josephine, and he wanted to *play*. He was getting restless and angry that Nawzir was having all the fun.

Josephine's stomach turned over at his touch. She wanted to crawl away from him and wash herself, rid herself of his filthy touch. When Josephine didn't whimper or cry out Nawzir withdrew a blade and ran it down her torso. In a fit of rage Jonah came at Josephine wanting to have some fun of his own, Nawzir went to stop Jonah. It backfired plunging the knife into her body. *Great now I am losing more blood, maybe tonight is my night to die,* she thought to herself as pain ripped through her battered body. Her clothes torn from Nawzir's ravaging hands. Left her exposed as her blood started to pool. Jonah was hard and aching, he wanted to taste Josephine. He pushed his way through Nawzir, to get to her.

""Nawzir" Jonah said through gritted teeth. "We need to keep our toy in decent shape, she is no use to us dead," he said flatly. Jonah took this opportunity to get Nawzir away from Josephine. "Let me look at her and fix the grave injuries at the very least," he said. Stepping in closer to better inspect her wounds, noting that some of her lacerations were shallow, and others were deep. Unfortunately, she was losing blood fast; Jonah slashed his wrist and covered the more severe wounds on Josephine. He didn't want her dead before he had his fill.

Jonah checked her over once again pretending to be looking at the wounds, all the while he was looking at her body, admiring what he was going to take. He was already rock hard for her, after all, just because she killed his brother, didn't mean she wasn't a good fuck. Jonah kept a watchful on Nawzir he didn't want to be seen as paying too much attention to the 'bitch'.

Without warning Jonah struck, he bit down hard as he sunk his fangs deep into her throat. Josephine felt the piercing pain of his canines as he sunk them even deeper. He drank his fill; when she thought he was finished he turned her around, so that her faced was pressed solidly into the wall, at the same time, her battered, bruised, bleeding, fragile body, was pressed into the coldness and roughness of the wall. Pulling what remained of her clothes from her body. Jonah took her from behind, pumping ferociously into her, smashing her already bruised and broken body into the cold rock, ripping her delicate skin as he pounded into her repeatedly. He was trying to hurt her, perhaps even tear her insides. Josephine stayed quiet, only a tear trickled from her eye; she swallowed down the groan of pain. Her silence enraged Jonah, when he wasn't satisfied he withdrew, turning Josephine around so that could savor the look of fear. Instead, Josephine stared at him dead in the eyes she showed no emotion. Jonah forced her mouth open and as his tongue invaded her, despite the horror of her present situation, Josephine took advantage of the opportunity that presented itself; she bit down, hard, drawing blood. Her fangs, piercing his lip and tongue; jumping back, he ripped both his tongue and lip. He muttered an oath in his native language and then he struck her so hard, her face turned sideways and then snapped back and hit the wall. Nawzir lunged for Jonah, not liking that he took Josephine. This was his prize, his to take first.

Corin hated the separation between Josephine and him.

Not being able to touch her mind at will was driving him insane. Although he had wanted to cut himself off from her he was not was expecting that she would try to block him. Despite the situation, he found a smile forming as his heart and mind filled with pride. Corin could not stay out of her mind he needed to know what was going on, he needed to know if she was okay. Using his great strength, he broke through her barrier. When Corin touched her mind he wasn't prepared for mind shattering emotions; forcing his way through he merged his mind with hers; pain, grief, disgust, humiliation, they overwhelmed him. Corin felt her essence, it was weak, and she was dying.

Corin searched her memories, witnessing, reliving what had happened to her. A cry of such pain and anguish came from Corin, startling Donovan. Corin's anger was living and breathing; his demon came forth, demanding revenge. Trying to regain control was impossible, he couldn't. The beast within him was out, instead of fighting for control over his demon he embraced it, drawing on its strength. No one who touched Josephine would live. Roaring his anger to the heavens, Corin called to her, the beast alive and ready.

Josephine, listen to me. Hear me and hear my words. You must shut your heart and lungs down. You must do this to survive. Hear my words, I am here, in the cave, I just have to find your location. The others are on their way. You are no longer alone.

I can't shut down my heart. I don't know how, Josephine sobbed. Corin's heart wrenched at her pain. He managed to control the demon that had surfaced. Josephine's distressed voice brought Corin back giving him back the ability to take control. Corin was angry. Angry that he could not stop what was happening. With the demon forced back down, he focused on helping Josephine. The demon in him would rise again, when the time was right. At this moment, his focus was Josephine.

Josephine I am going to command you to sleep the regeneration sleep of vampires. It must be done; I do this because you, yourself cannot shut your heart and lungs down.

Please Corin, do what you must. I'm tired, I'm scared. I'm weak and in no condition to help you.

You are a fledgling and you do not know our ways. Your brain is thinking in human terms. Rest easy. I want you to sleep Josephine. Sleep and do not wake until I call to you. Corin gave a strong push to Josephine's mind allowing her to fall into the regeneration sleep. Corin reached out with his mind once more and scanned the surrounding area, when he found who he was looking for he planted the compulsion. Mallory and Marcia knew where they had to come.

Donovan looked at Corin, and what he saw was something that scared him more than the fireball incident. Corin had contained the demon; yet it was not far beneath the surface. His eyes were now black onyx, and in the depths of his eyes, he saw the flicker of flame. Corin truly, looked soulless, merciless, but there was a calmness to him. The calm before the storm. Donovan's cell phone rang, he answered, and hung up just as quickly.

"They are here, are they not?" Corin asked.

"Yes, they found the car," Donovan said. Then he just watched as Corin allowed the beast within him to surface. "How did you know?" Donovan asked.

"I have already called them to us," Corin said. Both Marcia and Mallory were heading towards them and they were running at a proper pace. They would get to this location shortly. Corin would continue to send a map outlining where they were. Donovan was confident that all who opposed them were going to die. Corin's fangs elongated and his demeanor changed, he let his anger take hold. He was an ancient warrior and nothing would stop him. This was going to end tonight, even if it killed him.

"We must walk through this passage, she is deep in the bowels of the cave. I will go in first; I will take out whom I can. You will follow and guard my back," Corin barked out between clenched teeth.

"No. That is what they're expecting. It's a trap, like Josephine probably told you, it's meant for you," Donovan refused. "Let me go first, I doubt they are anticipating an attack from a human. I have been doing this for many years; I've killed vampires before, for the crimes that they have committed against humanity," Donovan almost regretted his words. He went on, "I'm an experienced hunter given the fact that I'm a human," Donovan added.

Corin was shocked at the confession but understood. "I will allow you to go first, but I am going to shield you. No one will see you; I would recommend that you rescue Josephine from her restraints rather than engage in a battle. The shackles that she wears are burning her skin. I must also warn you that she will appear dead. She is not, she is merely sleeping, 'the regeneration sleep' of vampires. I had to shut down her heart and lungs in order to stop her blood loss and prevent her from further suffering. She is wounded. Badly. You must get her released and to safety. You must also know that once she is released the others will know you are there, I cannot stop that," Corin said.

"I understand," Donovan said as he grabbed his weapons. "I'm ready," Donovan said. Corin nodded his head in agreement and focused his energy at Donovan.

"You may enter when ready." Donovan entered the cavern slowly, cautiously; even though he was shielded from everyone, he was still unsure and wary. Corin found that he was thankful that fate had intervened and allowed him to take Donovan's blood, this would allow him, if the need arose to see through Donovan's eyes and to take necessary action. Once Donovan got through the passage, Corin entered the cave himself, following the path that Donovan laid out. Corin continued to monitor all of Donovan's moves, through his mind. At one point, he stopped to monitor the progress of Marcia and Mallory. When he was satisfied, he returned to Donovan. Corin knew he that he had to use every advantage to get the upper hand. He also knew that Nawzir and Jonah were going to pay dearly. They would not survive.

Donovan's eyes went over the area carefully as he continued to walk cautiously through the vampire nest. When he spotted Josephine his stomach rebelled, his anger took a firm hold of him at the sight of her battered, nude body. It forced him forward. Now he could appreciate what Corin must have been seeing and feeling, he realized that he wanted Corin's demon to surface and wreak as much damage as possible. *These bastards deserve to die.* Josephine was not badly wounded, she was severely wounded, *how in the hell is she going to survive this?* Donovan was realistic, but he had no idea if even a vampire could recuperate from these wounds. The male vamps seemed enraged at the fact that she was sleeping. Nothing seemed to wake her. The torture they were *trying* to inflict was now useless.

"This was not part of the plan Nawzir, you said she was young and not knowledgeable in our ways," Jonah hissed.

"She does not know how to shut herself down. It had to be Corin, I knew he was near; he must be closer than I expected. He has to be. That is how she shut herself down. Corin put her to sleep." Nawzir looked as though he were scanning the area. "He has masked himself, I am unable to sense him, can you Jonah?" Nawzir asked.

"No I cannot. Can he shield himself from us?" Jonah already knew the answer but wanted confirmation.

"Apparently he can. He should not be able to shield from us. We have a blood connection, he is more powerful then I had anticipated. Try and find his mental pathway," Nawzir suggested. "We should be able to link with him," Nawzir added.

Jonah tried to pick up on the pathway that they all once used. He found nothing. Puzzled and frustrated he turned to Nawzir. "I cannot link with him," Nawzir tried with the same results. "He is blocking us," he said finally. "I have found a barrier. He has put up a mental barrier that is preventing us from penetrating his mind. He is here. Prepare yourself and stay focused. Leave the girl. We will deal with her later," Nawzir said, excitement evident in his voice. Donovan saw his opportunity and took it, while Jonah and Nawzir busied themselves elsewhere.

Donovan reached Josephine. When he got to her, he almost cried out at the sight of her. She was pale, fragile looking. He was afraid to undo the chains because it seemed that the chains were the only things holding her up. Donovan put down his bag and pulled out tools to pick locks. These were easy enough locks to pick, doing it though and trying to get out unseen, is another ballgame all together. While he worked at undoing the shackles, Corin was making his way in. When Josephine was loose, her body all but fell on top of him, he slumped Josephine over his shoulder, watching ever vigilantly, so he would know the exact moment that her captors were aware of what was going on. Donovan started making his way to the entrance of this room, to his amazement; the others were so focused on trying to locate Corin that they didn't notice what had happened, right away. Donovan kept his gaze focused and in front of him hoping to make it through without being noticed.

No such luck. The attack came from behind him. They were shielded by Corin but Josephine's blood inadvertently gave their position away. Corin did warn him of this. Josephine's body fell to the ground with a loud thump. Instantly Corin released the shield, so that he could put a barrier around Josephine, with her secured in the barrier nothing could touch her. Donovan, however, was now visible to the vampires. While he was under the shield, he managed to get his wooden stake and a knife so that he could defend himself. He also had his gun with a round already in the chamber. He knew it wouldn't kill the vamp but it would slow him down. Donovan turned to face enemy number one. Jonah's fist struck him hard, hard enough to send him flying into the cold, stonewall of the cave. Donovan didn't have a chance; he succumbed to the darkness that embraced him, the last thing he saw, was Corin bursting into the chamber. Donovan lost consciousness.

Jonah was rushing Corin, when Mallory and Marcia entered the chamber; Corin recognized their scents, released them from his compulsion, and continued to battle. Corin struck hard and fast, knocking Jonah unconscious. With the demon fueling his power and demanding retribution for Josephine, her slain husband, the torture she endured, at the hands of Nawzir, the torture that Mallory had endured. Corin roared so loud; it threatened to bring the cave crashing down around them.

Mallory and Marcia were kneeling down beside Donovan. Marcia had Donovan's head cradled in her lap. She was praying, barely audible but Mallory heard her. Mallory tried to comfort Marcia but she needed to have her attention focused on Donovan. He had received a bad cut from having been thrown so hard. Mallory took inventory on Donovan, ensuring he had suffered no other serious wounds. When she was satisfied, she attended to the cut on his head. He was losing blood fast so she applied pressure to the wound until the bleeding stopped. Mallory pulled out some gauze and tape and did a makeshift dressing to keep the wound covered and cleaned. She knew he would have to go to a hospital as soon as possible. When she finished, she looked up at Marcia and told her, in a soothing voice, to keep him still and, if the bleeding starts again, that she should apply pressure. Marcia looked at Mallory with her tear-stained face, fresh tears falling.

"Will he be okay?" It was a mere whisper but Mallory understood.

"He'll be fine. He'll probably have a concussion but I think that's all. As soon as we get Josephine, we are outta here. You just have to hang on. Keep talking to him that will help. I'm going to help Corin and Josephine. I'll be back." Marcia didn't even have a chance to protest. Mallory was already up and sprinting towards Corin.

Corin was already engaged in battle with Nawzir. The ground was shifting and Mallory was fighting for balance, she managed to keep her footing and made her way to Josephine. She tried to grab her, to pull out of harm's way but when she tried to grab hold of her, she hit something. Mallory looked around and saw nothing, puzzled she reached for Josephine again and still she came up against some sort of barrier, Mallory gave up after something clicked in her brain. Looking around on the floor, she spotted Donovan's pack she got up and ran to it. Mallory opened the bag, reaching inside she found a weapon to finish off Jonah. She reached in and pulled out a gun and a stake. Mallory was so focused on grabbing weapons that she had no warning. Marcia called out to her but the noise from Corin and Nawzir was deafening, and she didn't hear Marcia calling to her.

Jonah picked Mallory up by her long hair, flinging her as if she was no more than a piece of garbage. Mallory was shocked but her adrenaline kicked in and she was in a flight-or-fight mode. She chose to fight. Jonah was in front of her, in a flash. She didn't see him move and yet, he was there. He grabbed Mallory by her throat and picked her up off her feet. She was just a rag doll to him; he was shaking her viciously, violently.

"I will enjoy tasting you as I finish you off," he sneered.

Jonah bared his fangs; Mallory fought with every ounce of strength she had but it was hopeless. Jonah was already savoring the kill. He brought his mouth and foul breath down to her neck; he sunk his fangs in deep. Mallory screamed as the pain started to overwhelm her. She continued to fight him as best she could but he was draining her to fast, she was feeling weak. With a last ditch effort she managed to get the gun she had stashed in her pants, it was too late though she didn't have enough energy to pull the trigger. The gun fell from her hand as her body began to succumb to the darkness.

Marcia sat there in horror, frozen with fear, as her friend slowly slipped away. Suddenly, a strange compulsion came over her. Out of nowhere she let go of Donovan, she didn't fight the compulsion. Marcia carefully laid Donovan down; she walked up behind Jonah, careful to not to be caught. Jonah didn't even hear her coming, he was too busy drinking. Silently, Marcia picked up the gun, which had fallen from Mallory's hand. Holding the gun in front of her, she took aim. When she visualized where Jonah's heart would be, she fired once. Twice, three times. Jonah turned, a look of shock on his face, replaced the hatred and lust that was there while he was feeding on Mallory. Jonah dropped Mallory. She crumpled to the ground. Jonah stalked towards Marcia; once again, she fired unloading the remaining rounds into Jonah's chest until she watched him fall. When she was sure that he couldn't move she ran over to her friend, felt for a pulse; she found one but she was at a loss. She couldn't do anything for her. Mallory needed blood. She looked around for Corin; panic was taking hold of her. Corin felt her fear; he knew that he had to finish this fast.

Corin's distraction is all that Nawzir needed; he attacked. Nawzir lunged at Corin, his arm straight, driving into Corin's chest, trying to get hold of his heart. Corin pushed him off with his great strength but he knew that he had been dealt a severe wound. Gathering his remaining strength, he grabbed Nawzir by his neck, pushing him back against the cave wall, holding him there with one hand, he drove his free hand into

Nawzir's chest, penetrating the bone. He grabbed Nawzir's heart and squeezed until he felt the heart burst. He pulled his hand from Nawzir's chest cavity holding the remains of the shattered organ. Corin threw the vile organ to the floor. With a wave of his hand and caused the heart to go up in flames. With a final burst of energy, he sent a call out to his brethren, the elders of his kind.

I am in great need. My mate and her human friends have been injured in a battle against two rogue vampires. Without your aid three of us will die. Two humans are alive, one is gravely injured.

We can do no other than to help you. We have linked our minds with yours. Fear not ancient one we are coming. Corin looked to Marcia and compelled her to come to him.

"There are others coming to render their aid. Do not fear them. They will help us all. I will remain sleeping, like that of a mortal should you need me." Marcia sat there among all the bodies, the dead vampires, her friends. She was unscathed but felt tremendous guilt. Going back to Donovan, she checked him for a pulse. She found one. Marcia crawled back to Mallory to check if there was still a pulse. Relief flooded her when she found one. It was weak but it was there. Slumping against the wall Marcia cried and waited.

Jonah was coming around; his brother was dead, and no one that was a threat to him was conscious or aware. His wounds were grave, yet he managed to find the ability to turn into mist with the little strength he had left; he fled to the inner most bowels of the earth. Opening a hole in the ground, he crawled in. He covered the hole and went into the regeneration sleep of their kind.

It had seemed like an eternity before the other vampires

came. When they arrived, Marcia was relieved. She rushed to Corin, and pushed at him.

"Corin, Corin, wake up please. I don't know who these people are," she pleaded. Corin was so weak he could barely open his eyes. Scanning the others that were there, he opened his eyes and reassured Marcia.

"They are here to help. They will take Mallory, you and Donovan to the hospital, you must allow it. Josephine and I will remain here; there is much damage to be repaired, much work to be done." Corin said weakly. Marcia didn't have a choice but to accept what Corin said. Marcia nodded her head. Corin closed his eyes.

A tall, elegant looking man came to Marcia, while two other exceptionally elegant vampires went over to Corin and Josephine. "I am Wolfgang the others are called Chase and Midori, they will remain here. I will take you and your friends to the hospital; do you need me to mask the experience for you?"

"No, that's quite all right," Marcia, said shaking her head. "I've witnessed all this death and horror I should have no problem witnessing whatever it is you're going to do," Marcia tried to put forth a courageous smile; she hoped that she had been portrayed herself that way. Wolfgang gathered up Donovan and Marcia picked up Mallory, and they left the cave. Before Marcia knew it, they were at the hospital. They landed outside so they wouldn't provoke any questions. Marcia quickly went over to the desk and explained the situation, leaving out the vampire parts; the nurse quickly admitted the patients.

While Donovan and Mallory were wheeled on gurneys to the trauma rooms, Marcia approached Wolfgang.

"I have to go back and aid Corin and his beloved. I will return to ensure that all attending your friends have their memories wiped and replaced with some other memory. We cannot allow the extent of the injuries to instigate any questions," Wolfgang stated. "Your friend, the female, was bitten and drained; the medical technology will not be able to explain such a loss. I will return tomorrow evening to let you know what the status of Corin and his mate is," Wolfgang supplied.

Marcia looked pale and exhausted. She nodded her head to acknowledge what he said, as her brain tried to assimilate the information that was being thrown at her. "Thank you for your help," was all she managed to say. Wolfgang bowed his head to acknowledge her and then he walked to the doors. He went outside before shape shifting and taking to the air.

chapter 22

Midori, we need to assess how bad the damage is and who is worse off, Chase said. Looking at both of them Midori was appalled to see how badly the woman had been beaten. If the woman lived through this ordeal, she would be surprised.

"I will attend the female," Midori said making her way over. Lowering herself to the ground to start assessing Josephine's wounds, Midori was shocked when her hand came into contact with a barrier. "You must get Corin to release the barrier Chase," Midori said softly. Chase observed Corin and knew instantly that he was in a mortal sleep; he called out to Corin on the mental path that they had always used.

Corin, you must release the barrier around your mate. Midori cannot penetrate it. Corin heard the request and complied. Chase looked over to at his mate for verification that Corin had heard the request. When Midori tried to touch Josephine, she was successful. Midori gently turned Josephine over. Enraged by the damage that had been inflicted a gasp escaped her, instinctively Chase turned to look at her.

"It is all right Chase; I was just not prepared to see this kind of damage. Justice must be brought to all those who did this," Midori hissed out between her elongated fangs.

"Nawzir and Jonah, they will get what is rightfully deserved, Corin will see to it. They wanted retribution for the loss of Rowen. However, it puzzles me, why humans are involved; there is much to be explained about what has transpired this night nevertheless our priority right now is to see to Corin and his chosen one. The wound Corin has is severe yet is not fatal, I must ensure his heart is in proper condition, I have provided my blood to the wound in his heart however I must ensure that there is no damage. He will also require blood."

"Go, my love, and hurry. I require your assistance with this one," Midori said calmly. Midori watched as Chase combined his life force to Corin's and forced the rejuvenation process. The cave filled with a current of power, she watched as the rejuvenation process increased steadily. Corin's wounds were healing nicely. Corin would need blood so would Chase. They would all need to sleep the sleep of their kind, the regeneration sleep.

While Chase healed Corin, Midori made a cut on her wrist, so that could use her blood to begin the healing process on Josephine's more shallow wounds. It was only the beginning, in a very long process. When she was finished healing the small wounds on Josephine, Midori, took some blood from the wound and smeared across her wound so that her wound to close. Josephine had several deeper wounds, these, she was unable to heal without assistance. She had no choice; she had to wait for Chase. Chase disconnected from Corin's life force; the easy part was over.

"Corin requires blood. Now the hard part comes," he said. Midori just looked at him. She knew that this would drain him. They were both counting on Wolfgang's return. Cutting his wrist open, he forced his wrist to Corin's mouth and allowed Corin to drink.

"Drink my old friend, my blood is your blood, we are family." Corin latched on gratefully and when he was done he bite his finger and allowed his blood to heal the wound on Chase. It was the least that Corin could do.

Corin opened his eyes and with the aid of his friends, he stood up and looked around him. He found Nawzir's torn body. Then he spotted Josephine, a low growl escaped him. Angered. His job was not done, he must destroy the bodies; he looked at Chase, without words, Chase already knew what had to be done. Corin and Chase gathered the body, Corin raised his hand to command fire, but he could not.

"Allow me, Corin," Chase offered. Chase lifted his hands and called upon the fire, the three vampires watched as the inferno claimed the body of their enemy. Corin looked around once more, a frown formed.

"What is it Corin?" Chase asked.

"Where is the body of Jonah? I used the human female Marcia to stop him from killing the other, Mallory. Where is his body? I saw him fall. Marcia used all the bullets on him."

"Perhaps she didn't. In any case, he is gone. It is possible, that he shut himself down to regain some strength and then left," Chase stated. "It is of no consequence, we will hunt him another day. Right now, you have to help heal your mate. She is badly wounded I am not sure she will survive this ordeal," Chase said, gently.

"She must, she has children. She has ties here in this

human society. She must survive. I *need* her," Corin said unashamed of his confession.

"We will do what we can, but she will need the regeneration sleep and a tremendous amount of blood. She will have to sleep many risings and will have to be fed continuously until she heals," Chase explained. "Midori has tended the shallow wounds but she has grave injuries that were intended for torture and to make her bleed out. Midori and I will merge with her life force; you must connect to her mind and keep her grounded so that she does not choose to move on. We will use all our energy to force her body to rejuvenate more quickly, it may cause Josephine some discomfort; it is a necessary measure. The healing of your mate will require that we all work together Corin, I know you are weak from your ordeal but you must remain strong for her sake," Chase said.

"There will be four of us," Wolfgang announced, as he entered the cave. "It is good to see you, my friend, although I must admit you have looked better," Wolfgang stated, with a smile.

"It is good to see you too, Wolfgang," Corin said agreeably, as he walked over where Josephine was lying. His heart ached, and his stomach tightened, when he saw what had been done to her perfect, lithe body.

"She has endured much," Corin stated to no one in particular, as he shook his head in disbelief. "This is the second time that Nawzir and Jonah have had her and this is the worst by far. They have done the most heinous of things to her; undoubtedly, this event will leave emotional scars. I am not sure if she will be able to deal with this once she is healed physically. The last time she was their captive, she was unconscious, due to her injuries, she was not fully aware of the sadistic things he did to her," Corin said coldly. "I will get retribution for her; I will not stop until I have killed the last of those three vile monsters," Corin added, with a deep calmness. There was no mistaking his statement. It was a clear promise of revenge. The three vampires could see the red haze of anger and the demon lurking below the surface. They stood silent while Corin gathered Josephine in his arms and cradled her like a baby and reiterated his promise to her.

"Enough, Corin, we must heal her; it will take time and dawn is approaching," Chase commanded gently. Corin reluctantly, placed Josephine on her back, her head rested in his lap. As Corin merged his mind with hers, he commanded her to awake so that the others connect to her life force. Josephine's eyes fluttered open and then closed. She was in a mortal state of sleep, Corin was a strong presence in her mind, while the others forced all their energies and life force into Josephine, pushing her body to rejuvenate, forcing wounds to close. The healing and closing of Josephine's wounds took several hours. Each of the vampires had to take a turn leaving her so they could feed. Sated and with extra blood they returned, forced Josephine to feed. Corin had remained linked with Josephine's mind, constantly muttering words of warmth to keep her grounded, so she would not slip away. When the feeding and the major healing of Josephine's body was completed, Corin disconnected from her mind; cradling her head.

"She will live, Corin but she must sleep in our way, in order for the healing process to have a full effect. Since we have no coffins available; all of us must sleep in the soil," Chase pointed out. Corin heard the command in his voice.

"We will stay with you until your mate is healed fully," Midori added gently.

"And you, Wolfgang, what will you do?" Corin asked.

"I would like to check on the humans; I need to check on the one called Mallory. She has lost a lot of blood. I also have to ensure that the memories, of this event have been adjusted in the minds of those who attended the injured," Wolfgang said.

"Well, we wait to see what comes of that," Chase added, Wolfgang bowed courteously and took his leave. Corin picked up his fragile, looking Josephine as gently as he could, afraid that he would break her. He walked deeper into the caverns until they entered a chamber that had some small ground-fed springs. With his last bit of energy, Corin waved his hand, opening a large hole in earth for the two of them. He placed Josephine down carefully, and then placed himself at her side. He kissed her forehead gently. "I love you Josephine," he said, then closed the earth around them.

Chase and Midori followed Corin and set barriers, so that no one could enter. Chase opened the ground with a wave of his hand, Midori and he then floated to their resting place.

<hr />

Marcia waited anxiously for the doctors to return with news on Mallory and Donovan. Her hands were twisting restlessly. Wolfgang had landed outside and entered the hospital searching for Marcia. He saw her and glided silently over to them, like a predator on the hunt. He put his hands on Marcia's shoulders and she nearly jumped out of her skin.

"What the hell? How did you? I didn't see you come in," she finally managed to spit out.

"I guess you were not paying attention," Wolfgang said with a smile that without doubt. "Have you heard about your friend? I am curious about Mallory, she lost a lot of blood," he admitted.

"Mallory did lose a lot of blood but the doctor said they will give her a transfusion. The doctor came out once to advise us of what he was going to do, however he hasn't returned with any updates," Marcia said with a hint of aggravation in her voice. "There is no news about Mallory or Donovan," Marcia said as tears formed in her eyes. She turned trying to hide from him. Wolfgang grabbed Marcia, gently, by her shoulders forcing her to face him; staring into her eyes, he forced Marcia to fall into the depths of his mysterious stare, she tried to fight him but it was futile. Marcia reluctantly fell captive to his curious stare.

"You will sleep deeply, you will awake only when I call for you," his voice was gentle, soothing, but there was a command in there and Marcia's subconscious had heard it. Unable to resist she closed her eyes and fell asleep. Wolfgang caught her limp body and placed her down gently on the chairs in the waiting room, her body claimed three chairs. It wasn't too long after Marcia fell asleep that the doctor arrived with some news. Wolfgang called to Marcia.

Wake up Marcia, I command it. Marcia came out of her sleep and did a quick glance around to get her bearings. When she realized what had transpired, she walked up to Wolfgang and shoved him as hard as she could.

"Don't you ever do that to me again." she hissed. Realizing where she was and who was present, she forced herself to calm down. Marcia saw the doctor that had attended to both Mallory and Donovan; she pushed away from Wolfgang and rushed over to the doctor, with Wolfgang trailing behind her.

"Where are they? How are they? Can we see them?" Marcia asked. The questions came right after one another, leaving no opportunity for the doctor to answer.

"Slow down. I'm Doctor Reid," he began. "Donovan has a concussion and has lost some blood from the wound on his head, nothing to be concerned over. He'll be fine, I'll be keeping him over night, just for observation; he can go home in the morning. As for Mallory she has suffered severe blood loss, we're giving her transfusions now to bring up her blood level. I had x-rays done; I found nothing other than…" Dr. Reid was searching for the right words. "Well, to be honest, it looks as though she had been attacked by an animal; we found two puncture holes on her neck and some bruising. Was she in the woods or something?" he asked inquisitively.

"Uh…yes," Marcia started to say but she was cut off.

"She was in the woods and we heard some wolves or coyotes. We were separated for a short time, which is when we believed she was attacked. When we found her, she was lying face down," Wolfgang interjected.

"In the woods, face down, separated, wolves. I see, I understand," Dr. Reid reiterated what was said. "In any case she'll be fine. She is unconscious right now but that is from the blood loss. We are going to keep her overnight as well; we will see how things are tomorrow. We'll let you know. You can stay the night if you want to, we'll arrange a room, or you can leave, the choice is yours," he said with a smile and somewhat confused look on his face.

"Thank you. I'll let you know what I want to do," Marcia said.

"There's no need for that, just see the nurse at the desk," Dr. Reid waited a moment before turning on his heel and walking away. Marcia turned her attention to Wolfgang.

"How's Josephine and Corin?" Marcia asked looking directly into Wolfgang's eyes.

"Josephine has been healed but she needs to sleep for several risings. Corin is also well but requires rest," he explained, there was not any hint of concern.

"Where are they?" Marcia asked, as she nervously rubbed her hands together.

"They are at the cave, and will remain there, where no one can get them." Wolfgang said.

"I guess, then, that I'll stay here and wait for Donovan and Mallory," Marcia said, unsure what to do with herself.

"I will wait with you until I have to leave. I will return tomorrow," Wolfgang said as he sat himself down in a chair. He waited for Marcia to go and tell the nurse her plans. Marcia was at the desk talking with nurse. Wolfgang listened to everything that was said with his acute hearing. When she came back, Marcia told Wolfgang that the room was being prepared. She also took the opportunity to ask the nurse if she could go and see Donovan and Mallory and she managed to get the room numbers.

"I'm going to go see my friends," Marcia announced.

"I will accompany you, I would like to see Mallory and ensure that she is alright. I would also like to verify for myself that Donovan is well," Wolfgang explained. Marcia's eyebrow shot up and she found herself becoming very protective about Mallory and her well-being.

"Why are you so concerned with Mallory?" she asked calmly, with a protective voice.

Wolfgang took a moment to read Marcia's thoughts before answering; he was able to confirm what he already knew. Marcia was uneasy with the idea of vampires existing. She was worried that Wolfgang might pose some threat to Mallory.

"I am concerned only for her well-being. Rest assured that I am not the same as Jonah or Nawzir. I have lived long and I have never killed, unless it was necessary," Wolfgang assured.

Marcia paused long and looked as if she were sizing him up and trying to decide if he was worthy or un-worthy. She motioned with her hand for him to follow her.

"I take it, that I am worthy of your trust," Wolfgang teased. A smile formed on his face. Marcia stopped dead in her tracks and glared defiantly over her shoulder at him.

"I don't think you want to take that path," she snapped back and continued walking. Wolfgang smiled wickedly, knowing that he angered her.

※※

It had been three days going and going onto three nights. The sun was starting to set. Slowly, the first breath of air entered Corin's lungs. As he inhaled and exhaled his first breath, Corin's eyes opened. He woke early to ensure that when Josephine woke she would not be covered in soil. With a thought, Corin removed the soil from the top of them, he thought about letting her wake on her own, but quickly decided against it, he needed to know that she had survived; he called to her.

Josephine, little one, wake up for me. Josephine's heart started to beat; air filled her lungs, her eyes fluttered beneath closed lids. The sensation was amazing; she opened her eyes. She looked up and found Corin looming over her. He lowered a hand to her and she reached for him. He pulled her gently from the ground and closed the earth so that it looked as if it had been undisturbed.

"How do you feel little one?" Corin asked hopefully.

"I...I....I'm not sure. What happened? Why are we still at the cave?" Josephine asked, confused. Corin was about to answer when Chase, Midori, and Wolfgang suddenly appeared. Josephine gasped, clenching Corin's hand, hard.

Corin sensed her fear right away; instinctively he tried to calm her. Her heart was racing.

Little one, it is ok. They are my friends; they came to aid us.

"Allow me to introduce them, this is Chase and Midori, they are mated. Over there," Corin gestured with his hand, "this is Wolfgang.

"It's a pleasure to meet you," Josephine said as she extended her hand. "What happened here, Corin? Where are Mallory and Donovan? Where is Marcia?" Josephine asked concerned.

Calm yourself little one. They are well.

"We have much to discuss about the recent events. I feel it is best to leave before we discuss things, further. I will tell you everything when we are settled and in a more appropriate setting," Corin added. Corin turned to his loyal friends. "Will you do me and Josephine the honor of being our guests this evening?"

"We would be honored, but do you not want to be alone to discuss the present situation?" Chase asked.

"You have come to my aid; I can see no reason to send you home when you have become part of the situation. Please join me and Josephine," Corin offered.

"We shall join you for a short visit, and then we will take our leave and return to Ireland, where I hope you will be joining us," Chase insisted gently. Corin grabbed Josephine and pulled her close. *We will travel our way.* Josephine had no time to protest. Corin scooped her up in his arms and held her close, as he used his preternatural speed and took them to her home. They materialized inside her house.

Marcia nearly jumped out of her skin; she wasn't expecting to see Josephine and Corin. When she came back to her senses, she jumped up out of the chair and ran to her friend, hugging her tightly.

"I am so glad you are ok!" Marcia exclaimed.

"I'm so glad to see that you're okay Marcia. Is Mallory and Donovan okay? Where are they?" Josephine asked.

"I'm all right, so are Mallory and Donovan. Come in and see for yourself." Josephine walked through the kitchen into the living room, there she found Donovan lying on one couch and Mallory on the other. She quickly walked up to Mallory and gave her a tight hug.

"You're okay! I'm so sorry you went through this," Josephine said, her voice cracked. Reluctantly she released Mallory from her death grip hug. She walked over to Donovan, and touched his head where the bandage was and her eyes filled with tears as she hugged him. Josephine released him, glancing around the room she looked at all of her friends, tears welling in her green eyes, threatening to spill.

"I'm so sorry that all of you had to risk your life for me. How can I, ever thank you? How can I ever repay you for ensuring that I lived? Wolfgang. Chase and Midori, you saved my life without even knowing who I was, how can I ever repay you? I owe you my life." Josephine stated humbly. It was a statement; it was honest and heartfelt.

"You owe us nothing Josephine; just make sure that you and your family remain safe. You are our sister kin now. You are family; we can do no other than to bring you into our protection. You are Corin's chosen one. Thus, you are of us," Chase explained in his old-worldly fashion. Josephine was humbled by their allegiance to Corin. She was a little uncertain about 'chosen one' but she hid her feelings well. Not allowing her uneasiness show; she showed no anger, only happiness. She did however file 'chosen one' away in her brain for later analysis.

"We have to take our leave of you for now but we hope to see you and yours in Ireland." Mallory looked up when Wolfgang made his announcement; remaining silent, as she glanced over at Wolfgang.

"Wolfgang, I would like to thank you for help; I'm sure that, if it wasn't for you, we'd probably all be dead. Thank you," Mallory said. Wolfgang bowed his head in acknowledgement. Donovan, feeling somewhat shallow since everyone else had spoken out, added his two cents.

"Thanks, Wolfgang, we really do appreciate everything you did for us. Midori and Chase we can't thank you enough for keeping Josephine and Corin with us," Donovan said with sincerity. "I've never worried about myself in all my years as a cop, but the other day when I saw Josephine looking the way she did my duty never became more clear. I'm not one for words but I have to say that, if you people had not shown up... what you did, many good lives would have been wasted.

My thanks for your help and, should you ever be in need of my services, please don't hesitate to ask," Donovan said. Everyone heard the truth in his words, and the respect that he was giving.

Chase once again acknowledged everyone's thanks and hospitality. "We really must take our leave; we have matters to attend to. We hope to see you soon. Corin, should you need us again, please call for us, we will answer." Without waiting to hear any protests, all the vampires shape-shifted into mist and took their leave.

"Corin we've got to talk," Josephine suddenly said. "Actually we all have to talk. I want to know what happened," she made it a demand. Corin took the floor and everyone settled back into sitting positions.

"I have destroyed Nawzir. Jonah lives. He gave Donovan his wound and nearly drained Mallory of her blood, he has escaped." Corin said.

"I thought I killed him," Marcia said frantically.

"Vampires do not die from bullets, broken necks or wounds of any type. To kill a vampire one has to make the heart burst, then the destroyed organ must be set it on fire, incinerated. You can however render a vampire useless in any number of ways. The problem is if a vampire can get to their coffin or can bury himself in the earth, he or she can rejuvenate. When you shot Jonah, Marcia, you merely slowed him down. Josephine and I were too incapacitated. Our friends' only focus was to heal us first. The only way that Jonah could have survived was by shutting his system down, when he woke he must have realized that no one was paying attention and used the opportunity to slip away," Corin said, sighing heavily. "Not that this matters. He is younger and alone. I will hunt for him once again, when everything here is settled here."

"Settled?" Donovan said.

"I have a castle in Ireland. It is very spacious and privacy will not be an issue. I have asked Josephine if she would like to move her and her family, which includes all of you, to come and stay in my home. I have acquired a vast amount of wealth over my long existence. There would be no need for anyone to work, should you choose not to. Keeping in mind of course that Josephine is now like me, and like me she has weaknesses, she cannot tolerate sun and will have to sleep during daylight hours. Alex and Charlie will require daytime supervision. My hopes were that everyone one of you would agree to join me so that her children would have familiar people around them during the day. Please, all of you think about it. It is very important to me that Josephine is happy. There will obviously be some adjustments to make but we can make them as we go. Right now protecting Josephine and her children is paramount," Corin stated.

"Josephine and I must eat; will you please excuse us? We will return shortly." Josephine was furious. She wanted to protest to everything Corin said. *Wait, little one, we have much to discuss. We will do this between ourselves. All your questions and fears will be addressed.*

I need clothes Corin, in case you haven't noticed I'm wearing a long shirt and only a long shirt. And for the record you should have discussed what you were planning on announcing tonight.

I will take you upstairs and then you can change, trust me little one.

I can go on my own. I am not a child.

We should leave together. I am sorry that I did not mention my plans, it was wrong. We need to look as if we are on the same page. Trust me little one.

"We will see you soon," Corin said, as he gently pulled Josephine to him and shimmered out of the room.

chapter 23

Corin brought Josephine back to the caves; not the same one where she was captive, this was a different one; one of the other surrounding caves. He flew in and so deep that she was expecting to see the lava flow any minute.

"I'm hot, Corin," she whispered, barely audible, but he heard.

Imagine what is to feel cool. Your body will regulate itself. He whispered back to her mind.

I can do that? Josephine asked and she smiled inwardly. Following the instructions she was had been given she felt her body starting to cool off, she smiled. Corin felt her smile and it comforted him. Talking to Corin's mind took some getting used to. It was more intimate and she found that she enjoyed this way of communicating. Being able to have *their* own private conversations in front of people, no one to overhear, and it was cool. Still a shadow in her mind Corin smiled, knowing that Josephine was beginning to come to terms with her life. She was starting to accept her powers and gifts.

Corin found the spot he was looking for Corin. Gently

he lowered Josephine to the ground. They were in a chamber with a ground-fed spring, Josephine walked over to it, lowering herself she dragged her hand through the water, it was hot but not scalding hot. She looked up at Corin and smiled. "I didn't bring my bathing suit," she said teasingly. Corin smiled, of course, there were other springs that were closer to the surface of the cave; nevertheless, he wanted to be down deep where no one would be able to find them.

"That is fine by me," Corin said, winking at her. He walked over to where the spring was, extended his hand down to Josephine, and helped her up. "I do not think that will be a problem," Corin said in a husky voice. Corin held Josephine's hand as they walked deeper into the passageway, he was looking for something. He spotted a piece of wood, both of them walked over to it; Corin bent down and grabbed it. Josephine watched curiously. She wasn't sure what Corin was up to, and she didn't ask. She played along. Walking back to the chamber with the ground-fed spring, Corin walked over to the wall and then with just a thought he lit the wood, now they had a torch.

"Nice," Josephine said smiling. Corin found a crook in the wall and placed the torch there, allowing an orangey glow to fill the chamber. Corin held Josephine's hand once again and pulled her over to where the glistening, hot, water was. Without asking, he proceeded to undo the buttons on her cotton shirt, which was perfectly fitted to her sensuous, curvy, body. A little shy she took a step back. Corin grabbed her wrists gently and pulled her back.

Do not be shy little one; you have the most exquisite, perfectly shaped body. You are beautiful. I want to revel in the silky softness of your skin. I want to make love to you, endless and forever.

Josephine's face reddened, she felt her skin flush, she didn't try to hide it. Josephine knew that she enjoyed his touch, her body was already becoming wet and pliant— she was burning for him. Her body shuddered as Corin continued to undress her, slowly. Teasingly. Her nipples hardened as they fought to break through the confining material. Undoing the last button on her shirt, he pushed it gently back, the shirt slid from her body, exposing her flat stomach and her perfectly sized breasts. Undoing her bra, the straps loosened, allowing them to fall to the sides; he helped them along until her bra was completely off. With her bra on the ground and her taut nipples exposed, inviting him to take his prize; Corin lowered himself on to his knees. He pulled Josephine into him, so that his face was resting in between the swell of her two breasts. Corin kissed each nipple and each breast, while his hands were busy working away at the button on her jeans. Her blood was starting to boil, threatening to catch fire, with his next touch. Corin stayed in her mind feeling her emotions, feeling her passion and his body took on a life of its own as it started to react to her responsiveness. Josephine felt him harden as he stood up to embrace her. Corin gently pushed her away from him so that he could admire his sultry siren. Josephine had never had anyone stare at her like this. Slightly embarrassed, she wasn't sure what to do. The desire in his eyes, spoke to her, and made her blood heat more; she was on fire and getting more aroused.

With her body wet and slick, ready for him she swayed her hips provocatively as she walked up to him, letting her hands fall to his pants, she began to undo them; first the button followed by his zipper. Corin's excitement heightened she could hear when his breathing quickened; a low, hungry growl escaped him. His muscles became taut as she ran her hand over his body. Josephine felt his heat through his shirt; she carefully, teasingly, started undoing his buttons with her mouth. As she did, she could feel him struggling for control. When she finally and successfully undid his shirt, she bushed the material to the sides and gently kissed his hardened nipples, running her tongue seductively over his solid chest.

Corin couldn't take anymore he grabbed Josephine by her hair, pulled her into him, and forced her mouth open, engaging in a long, seductive, passionate kiss. He released Josephine, reluctantly.

"You are driving me wild woman," he said out, as if in a sexual frenzy. Josephine looked up into his sapphire blue eyes and smiled at him with mischief in her eyes.

Corin being unable to control his overwhelming desire to be buried deep within her pulled her close once again. He lifted her into his arms and lowered the two of them into the glistening water. Corin's hands were moving everywhere, touching, feeling, caressing all her secret places. Josephine's body squirmed underneath his; Corin felt her burning skin, saw the feral hunger in her eyes, he bent his head, dominating her mouth. Josephine accepted his probing tongue. Cradling her face in his hands as his mouth possessed and captivated hers. He let his hands fall once again to her breasts, playing with her pink, peaked nipples. Then he slid his hand further down, caressing her stomach, drawing lazy circles around her belly button. Josephine's body tensed as he brought his hand down to her slick, wet entrance, probing gently, with two fingers, and then switched to playing with her sensitive nub. When he switched back again and filled Josephine with two fingers, she rode him, her body pleading for release. She wanted to feel him inside her.

With Josephine digging her nails into his back, Corin decided that he needed to feel her warm sheath; he took his hand and guided his shaft into her. Corin slid the tip of him in first, teasing her. *Corin, I need you, now!* She screamed to his mind. Corin pushed the full length of him into her, impaling her. Josephine moaned. He went slowly at first, then without warning Josephine started to take control, she lifted herself up and then came down on him, as she did her head lolled back, exposing her supple breasts to him, her nipples taut and just ripe for tasting, Corin brought his mouth to those perfect nipples, suckling each of them, biting at each, gently. Josephine kept gliding up and down, up and down, spearing herself each time as she took all of him inside her. On the last thrust, Josephine bent her head down and when her fangs elongated, she bit down. Her lips and her tongue moving over his vein, his life force, was the most erotic feeling. Corin was in heaven. Josephine was riding him faster and harder, lapping and sucking his sweet nectar when she climaxed. The white lights were exploding in her mind as she soared. Corin was on the brink of his orgasm, and as his seed spilled into her, he bit down, deep, into the swell of her breast. The erotic movement of his lips against her skin sent Josephine spiraling and into another climax, now both of them were soaring, together, higher and higher until they were so exhausted that they floated gently back down. With sweat on her brow, Josephine reluctantly pulled away from Corin, bringing her legs down and finally resting her head against his very beautiful, masculine chest. Corin held her close and rested his head on top of her wet, long hair.

Thank you Corin," Josephine said, exhausted.

Corin was a shadow in her mind; he knew that even though she was tired, there was much to discuss, their situation, everyone involved. The funeral she had to prepare for, just everything.

"Tell me, little one, why are you so sad this night?" Corin looked at Josephine.

"I'm…There's a lot that has happened, Corin. It is overwhelming for me."

"Tell me. Let us discuss what troubles you; your pain is breaking my heart," he said.

"Well, for starters, moving me and the children is one thing, moving my friends' is another, not to mention the fact that everyone almost died because of something that I helped you accomplish two years ago. Hell, I died!" Josephine lowered her eyes. "That's not what I meant, what I meant to say was that I was close enough to dying that you had to convert me to save my life. I can see it now; '*Hi mom, Corin here saved my life by turning me into a vampire and since I was human and I had human children he has offered to take me to Ireland, along with my friends and family in order to keep me from further harm and to shield the boys from my transformation until they are of age; so are you in or not?*'" Josephine finished off with a sigh. "Not only that, but I'm still wondering how it is that I can feel the passion and desire for you. How can this be when I loved my husband? I don't understand my feelings. I loved my husband with all my heart yet when we made love, it just wasn't an intense as this. I never felt such passion and intensity as I feel when I'm with you. I'm very confused and to be honest, it bothers me," Josephine added. There was no anger, no regrets. Just truth. Confusion.

"Well, little one, which problem shall I address first," Corin asked tenderly. "I will start with the last because that is the easiest. The reason you feel your emotions so deeply, passionately and intense is because you are a vampiress now. The heightened senses that come with being a vampire translates into every aspect of your life. Vampires are very sexual creatures by nature; it is natural for your feelings to be intensified. There is no shame and you should feel none. It is part of who you are now. As you grow older, your powers, feelings and sensations…you name it… will all increase. There is more that you should know, but for now, we will deal with your questions. I, *we* have plenty of time to discuss other things. Our gifts are a blessing, as well they are our curse. That is what I can tell you about being a vampire and the intensity of your feelings. Second, the reason I want you to come to Ireland is so that I can be with you as you experience the changes, so that I can help you and answer your questions. As for asking your friends and family, I was thinking of you, the sadness you would feel, should you decide to accept my offer. I would not be able to bear your sadness. Should you choose to stay here in the city, I will remain; I will miss my homeland, which is the reason I suggested we go to Ireland. I have been gone for so long. You need to understand me completely, in this matter; I will remain by your side, no matter what you choose," Corin said with conviction, although he was tender and gentle. He didn't make her feel guilty. "Josephine, I believe that your friends will choose to be with you. I have offered them a very attractive incentive. You need, *we* need someone to help us with your children. They must be brought up properly and have a proper education. Whether you are here or in

Ireland, you cannot accomplish this feat on your own, you are a vampire. You have limits. We need their help or that of a stranger. I am sure you would rather have your friends and family, and I believe your children will prefer the people they love and recognize rather than a stranger. I am also confident that your family and friends will choose to help you. On the other hand, if they choose to abandon you, I can always compel them," Corin said seriously, donning a wicked, smile. "Worry not little one, I already know they have accepted my offer, I have already seen it in their minds, more precisely in Donovan's mind, I will explain that, at another time. It is also my belief that they have accepted my offer, because they all need to escape this place, to rid themselves of the recent events, which have transpired. Perhaps the thought of losing you and your children..." Corin was cut off before he could finish.

"Don't even...You will not. Don't even joke about it Corin." Josephine snapped as she pushed at his solid wall of a chest. "By the way, I prefer to think that the thought of losing me and my children was the persuasive factor, you big lug," Josephine said haughtily. Corin laughed.

"Of course it is, little one. Now, to address the last issue... the matter of me, converting, you, into a vampire. I had no choice. My feelings for you have been growing, do not forget I have been connected to you for two years, and for two years I have been with you, experiencing your pain. Your joy. Then when I realized who you were, I was helpless. You are and have been my world. No matter how long it takes you to adjust and come to terms with your new life, I will wait. I was not willing to stand by and watch you die. *I could not stand by and watch you die.* Do not blame me for that, little one. I have come to respect and appreciate your family, even if you should choose not to be with me, I have taken them into my keeping, they will be for all time, as long as I live, be under my protection," Corin explained. "I apologize for not being able to court you properly; however I do not apologize for bringing you over. The bottom line was, and is, your survival. I did and will continue to do what must be done in order to ensure your safety and your life. I will follow you and remain by your side, no matter what you choose." Corin said.

In that one moment, Josephine realized the scope of his feelings and it brought tears to her eyes. Turning she walked away from him. Corin watched as her body swayed in the water. His eyes followed the beads of water as they sluiced down her glistening body; her hair was flowing in around her in the water.

Josephine felt his gaze burning her skin; abruptly she turned and walked backwards, allowing him to view her breasts as they hovered in the water. Corin's gaze lingered for a moment, before he sought her eyes. His gaze rested there locking with her emerald green eyes, he was truly humbled by her sensuality and beauty. Staring at her in awe, his eyes wondered finding her perfectly sculpted lips. Then he followed her neckline down, until his eyes came back to her exquisite breasts that were crying out for his touch. Unable to control himself, he moved with a burst of speed; Josephine didn't even see him coming. She felt his hands cup her breasts, as his hair fell to the side of his face, gently caressing her, brushing against her already erect nipples. Josephine pressed her body into his, feeling the hard length of him and her eyes widened. "You can't possibly..."she stopped suddenly as he pushed her flush against the flat smooth rock. He kissed her once before ushering her to turn so that her bottom was against him. He took hold of her wrists, situating them above her head. Holding her wrists gently in place with one hand, he explored her body, touching her with his other hand. When he found her entrance, he inserted two fingers, testing her readiness for him. He probed her gently confirming what he already knew.

"I want you, Josephine, right now, but I want, *I need* to explore your body," Corin turned Josephine and lifted her so that her triangle of springy curls was vulnerable to his mouth. He tasted her, first licking, then an occasional nip. "Open wider for me, little one," he said between her thighs," then his tongue entered her wet, hot channel. His tongue pushed in and out, each time taking her sweet juices into him. Josephine was grabbing his hair by the fistfuls, her hips thrusting upwards, her back arching, to give him better access.

"Corin, please, now, I want you now!" Josephine pleaded with him, her breath coming in short, rapid breaths. She moaned, calling his name repeatedly as if he were a god. Her body shuddered as wave after wave of pleasure coursed through her body. One orgasm. Two. Three. "Corin! I can't! I need to feel you inside me, please take me!" Corin pulled her back down and turned her around so that her bottom was once again nuzzled to his shaft, rubbing her body against his, tempting him, inviting him to enter her. Slowly, Corin inserted himself into her hot sheath, pushing her fragile body in the rock and holding her arms above her head, he teased her, going in a little and then pulling out. Josephine screamed as she came again, and finally when Corin could no longer control himself, he thrust into her, hard and fast. He was relentless and rough as he took her. He pushed into her faster and harder until they were both out of control. It had felt as if the heavens were coming down around them. Going deeper and deeper until Josephine was pushing against him, he felt her moving up and down matching his tenacity, until both of them were on the brink of ecstasy. Once again, he brought them to orgasm; he exploded, his seed spilling into her. Her muscles tightening and contracting as she came, then slowly, they both came down. As Corin reluctantly pulled out of Josephine, she turned and faced him once again. Corin embraced her, holding her close.

"Corin, I'll come with you. I would come with you even if my mother and my friends wouldn't. I'm not stupid; I know there is a real danger to me and my children, as long as Jonah lives. My children are all that matter to me, with you at least I know they are safe," Josephine said, exhausted. Corin pulled her closer and hugged her tighter.

"I love you Josephine. I will protect you and yours with my last breath."

I know Corin, I know you do. Now we just have to deal with my mother and a funeral. Josephine used the intimate way of talking, mainly because she was too tired to open her mouth and form the words.

She will come, little one do not worry, I will not even have to compel her.

Give it up already! Josephine smiled and snuggled into Corin's large frame.

❄❄❄

When Josephine woke, she was dry and fully dressed. Corin was there laying beside her, on his side, his forearm on the ground, holding his beautiful upper body up. With his free hand, he was moving the wild, long, tendrils of auburn hair that had taken up residence across her angelic face.

"We should go to your mothers first for two reasons; to let her and your children know that you are alive and well, and second to advise of her your decision," Corin said.

. "I agree," Josephine said. Once again Josephine demonstrated her strength and her acceptance of her situation; she was accepting him into her life. His heart warmed as it filled with a new sense of belonging, *belonging to her*. Corin could do no other than to pick her up, holding her close, protectively. This motion was all he could do; he had no words for her.

"We have to go," was all the warning she got before he used his preternatural speed, and took to the air.

"What's the rush? Shouldn't we go back home so the others know all is well. We told them we would be back shortly," Josephine said, keeping her head against his chest.

"Little one, you fell asleep. We have been gone for one night and day. While you slept, I used the opportunity to go back to the house, I let everyone know that you were resting, and that all is well. They officially gave me their answer about Ireland. As I told you, they are willing to come. What remains now is telling your mother, and seeing and holding *your* children," Corin explained.

"Oh, I see." Josephine said out loud.

"What?" Corin said, frowning.

"Never mind, let's just get to my mother's. I want to see Charlie and Alex," Corin took the directions from her mind; in a few short moments Corin and Josephine landed at the foot of her mother's drive way. Josephine brushed out her clothes and smoothed out her windblown, hair. They walked casually up to the doorway, and rang the bell. Rachel opened the door and gasped at the sight of her daughter and Corin. Rachel looked over Josephine's shoulder and found that her driveway was vacant of a car. Confused she looked back at Josephine, not asking any questions.

Rachel cleared her throat, and then invited them in. Josephine walked upstairs immediately, to see her children, both Corin and Rachel followed. Alex was sound asleep; he looked like an angel. Charlie was still up, fidgeting around and trying to find a comfortable position, noticing his mother, he jumped out of bed and ran to her. Josephine lowered herself onto her knees, opening her arms wide, to embrace her son. Holding onto Charlie for what must have seemed like an eternity she finally pulled him close and whispered in his ear.

"I love you, baby, mommy missed you so much." Josephine said as tears flowed from her eyes.

"I love you, mommy," Charlie replied. Reluctantly, Josephine released her son and brought him back to his bed. She tucked him under the covers and kissed him gently on the forehead.

"Go to sleep, baby," she said as she stood above him, looking down at him, cherishing him, and thanking God that she had survived these horrible ordeals. They walked out of the room; pulling the door shut after them, leaving it slightly opened. "Mom, we have to discuss something very important." Josephine was first down the stairs. She walked to the living room, Corin and Rachel followed.

Once they were seated, Josephine recapped the entire story, leaving out no details. She told her mother about all of the events that took place, leading up to why Rick died, what prompted her to dig around and investigate Rick's death, everything. When she came to the vampire part she kept her mother as calm as possible, but she reiterated every gory detail, including how she almost died, twice. Nothing was left out, her mother had a decision to make. More than that she wanted her mother to know whole truth, whether it was painful, distasteful, or horrible, Rachel needed to know. Josephine continued to hold her mothers' hands as she informed Rachel about Ireland and her decision to move there. When Josephine was finally finished, Rachel was visibly distressed.

Rachel stood up and paced, she asked her questions, and surprisingly, she demanded no proof. Corin had graciously offered the services of his lawyers and his real estate people, so that she could be reassured about her property. At the end of this trying conversation, Josephine told her to take her time; that there was no rush for her decision. Rachel put her hand to stop her daughter from speaking.

"Listen honey, I'm not sure I believe all the things you've said, I'm not even sure if I want to believe them, but I do know one thing, I'm not letting my only daughter go off to Ireland with my two grandchildren, never to hear from her again. You're all I have, I'll come with you, on one condition; you and your new friend don't try to push me into understanding and accepting everything that you've said. I don't believe in vampires, in time maybe I will, on my own terms. I can accept your abilities, only because of things that you did when you were younger, you have always had an intuition, a sense of things, which were beyond my comprehension," Rachel admitted. Rachel went to say something more, but she was interrupted.

"Hold on just a minute. You knew about my psychic abilities? Why didn't you say anything?" Josephine asked. She looked as if she had been punched in the stomach. The pain was evident on her face.

"You never asked. Besides, how was I supposed to answer you or explain something that I knew nothing about? I couldn't have answered you, even if I wanted to. I just accepted things as they were, that's why eventually, I know that I'll accept the idea that vampires exist, but I'll do it in my own time. I need time to deal with any loose ends that maybe lurking around. Your secret is safe with me, Corin, you don't have to worry about that," Rachel said. Corin acknowledged by bowing his head, not questioning the 'gut feeling', he suddenly had.

"Rachel, please take the time that you need. We will not leave here until all issues have been dealt with," Corin assured.

"I expect that I'll have all my loose ends cleared up in a few days, Corin can you leave me numbers to get in touch with your people?" Rachel asked. Corin pulled out a little gold box that held business cards; he pulled out two cards, and handed them to her.

"Corin we should go, we've still got things to settle," Josephine turned to her mom and gave her a big hug. "I love you," she whispered into her ear. Josephine pulled away from her mother, "Can the boys stay with you tonight? Tomorrow is the funeral…" Josephine choked on her words. "I'll get them tomorrow," she said.

"Sure honey. If you want I can bring them to the funeral home, have you made the arrangements, you can't be out during the day if vampire folklore is true," Rachel replied.

"With everything that has gone on, I hope that Mallory or Marcia made the changes," Josephine said worriedly.

"They have," Corin replied.

"I'll see you tomorrow, then," Rachel said. They all walked to the door and Rachel let them out. She watched as Corin and Josephine walked hand in hand staring up at the sky when they got out of her view she closed the door. Rachel locked up and then walked over to the phone; she punched in some numbers and tapped her right foot impatiently until she heard someone answer. "I'm out!" was all she said. She hung up the phone.

Corin swept Josephine up and took her home with his preternatural speed. They walked in the house like two normal people. Marcia, Mallory and Donovan were all watching television, Dracula 2000 happened to playing. Corin saw the actors and a smile curved his face. "Hi guys! Please say that the funeral arrangements have been changed to accommodate my new life style," Josephine said pleadingly.

"It's been taken care of hunny bunny," Mallory assured.

"Are you ready for this Josephine?" Marcia asked concerned.

"Is anyone ever ready to bury someone they love, to say that final farewell, to watch her children say goodbye or goodnight to their Daddy, not understanding that they will never see or play again with him," Josephine asked as tears formed in her eyes. Once again, her mind reeled with confused emotions. "No, I'm not ready," she sobbed, as she crumpled to her knees, hands covering her face, her body convulsing from powerful sobs escaping from her. Corin's heart ached for her, he knelt down beside, holding her he raised her off the floor and brought her to her friends. Mallory and Marcia took hold of Josephine and held her close as she grieved. Both Corin and Donovan left the room, giving the women their space.

Dawn approached and Josephine felt the pull of the regeneration sleep, falling asleep on the couch watching TV Corin retrieved Josephine, and brought her up to her room where both f them would be adequately protected from the harmful rays of the sun. Corin placed her in her bed and covered her, and then he placed himself beside her.

"I am so sorry my little one, I will help you anyway I can," he vowed. It was just before dusk when Corin woke; he changed into mist, allowing him to get out undetected so he could feed. He fed well, so that he could feed Josephine. Returning quickly he changed into the appropriate clothing for the sad event, which he would be attending. He finished dressing just as Josephine woke. She was hungry, so much so that he could feel her hunger pains. Before she could speak, Corin slashed his wrist so that she could feed. He offered his wrist to Josephine; confused she took hold of him and fed. She didn't ask why he used his wrist and not the crook of his neck; she had just assumed that it was for decency, rather than doing something much more intimate.

"Thank you, Corin, for your understanding," Josephine said with gratitude. She quickly gathered some clothes and got into the shower. With her stomach in knots and her emotions all over the place, Josephine stood under the spraying water and cried, she let the water absorb her tears. When she had a better grip of her emotional state, she turned off the water, dried herself and got ready. *This is it, how am I going to get through this night?* She thought to herself, as she looked into the mirror.

With the strength. With the love and support of your friends, little one. The words echoed in her mind, bringing her comfort but not complete solace. The night moved forward, at record speeds, Josephine finally found herself at the funeral home; she was the first one to approach Rick. She noted how well the cosmeticians had worked on Rick, other than him sleeping in a coffin, he looked normal, absolutely and without a doubt as handsome as the day she met him. Tears welled in her eyes threatening to overflow should anyone disturb her concentration. His hands were together and a fake wedding band replaced the original. He looked so peaceful. Josephine placed her hand on his, he felt warm against her skin, but then again she was dead in a manner of speaking. As her friends and family gathered around they could see her lips moving but heard no words, Corin did. "I love you Rick and I always will, and I will see you every time, I look into our children's smiling faces. I hope you can forgive me for my irrational behavior these past days; things have changed greatly in my life, losing you, having to raise our two children and mostly because I'm no longer human, that's really not a good reason, but it's the only thing that makes sense to me. I have to believe in my heart that you understand and that you would want me to do whatever I believe is right. He'll protect me; he'll protect our children, from the evil that took you away from me…us. I have to believe Rick, that you understand or I can't do this and I can't forgive myself. Therefore, I'm going to say good-bye to our life, because I have to. I have also died in a manner of speaking, I have been reborn into a world of darkness, and I have embraced that life. Yet I will carry you with me forever. I will endure and I will protect our children, I will ensure that the monsters that did this to us are dealt with. One down, one to go. I love you Rick and hope that wherever you are that you'll watch over us." As Josephine bent over to kiss his forehead, Rachel arrived with Charlie and Alex. With tears still fresh in her eyes, she turned quickly and wiped them away, putting on a strong front for her children.

"Charlie, look at Daddy. Doesn't he look nice?" Josephine asked, shakily. Charlie nodded in agreement. "Honey, you have to say goodnight now to daddy, remember I told you he's going sleep in heaven, so he can watch over us? Well now is the time that we have to say goodnight." Josephine picked Charlie up, so that he could see his daddy properly, so he could say goodnight, one last time.

"Goodnight daddy, I love you." Charlie leaned forward so that he could kiss his father. Alex didn't understand, yet he understood that something was wrong; he demonstrated his uneasiness by letting out a few low cooing noises. Marcia quickly grabbed Alex, and moved away. Josephine listened for a few more moments while Charlie talked to his Daddy, finally ending his one-sided conversation with "I love you, goodnight, I see you soon." Not being able to control emotions any longer Josephine put Charlie down, pulling him away and putting some needed distance between her and Rick.

Corin said nothing; he put his hands on her shoulders, sending her waves of reassuring feelings. Lending her his strength, so she could get through this night. The funeral proceeded; she talked with Rick's parents and accepted condolences with grace and strength. When the burial ritual was completed and she had thrown down a single white rose, she looked over at her friends tear stained faces and without words pleaded for their help. Rachel took the boys, while

Marcia and Mallory gathered Josephine and her things. They stood by her, lending their strength to her, while she thanked everyone for coming. Josephine looked up into the sky before leaving, as if saying a final goodbye, and overhead with her new vampire sight, she saw a lone eagle, flying with grace, donning its power. Watching the skies as if was defending its territory. Josephine smiled to herself, lowering her head. If reincarnation was real, then that eagle with all its grace and power represented Rick. She took solace in that one comforting thought. Tomorrow would be a new day, and with every new day comes a new beginning.